grounded

The Seven
book 1

heather ordover

other books by
Heather Ordover
What Would Madame Defarge Knit?
What (else) Would Madame Defarge Knit?
wwmdfk.com

—————————

If you have questions or comments about this book, or need information about licensing, custom editions,
special sales, or academic/corporate purchases, please contact
Crafting-a-Life Books: books@crafting-a-life.com or 325 W. Bridge Street, #253, New Hope, PA 18938.

For Crafting-a-Life Books
Editor: Katie Givens Kime about.me/kgkime
Cover Art: Mike Young IamMikeYoung.com

The book Casey is reading in Chapter 46
is *Cryptonomicon* by Neal Stephenson
© 1999 by Avon books • ISBN-13: 978-0380973460
a wonderful book you should read, no matter what Izzy thinks.

Printed in the United States of America

For Andrew.
Always.

grounded

The Seven
book 1

CRAFTING-A-LIFE BOOKS
Tucson, Arizona

Heat

1 Introductions

THIS ALL STARTED BECAUSE I lit my boyfriend on fire.

That, and a few other things.

2 TRAFFIC

IT WAS HOT OUT.

Again.

Unseasonably hot, which sounds weird when you consider I live in the desert. But really, you shouldn't be able to fry eggs on your dashboard in June, and I'm pretty sure you could have on mine. Some kid at the U of A did it, anyway. Or at least, that's what they said in the paper.

"Hey, cut it out." I reached out and stopped Lindy's hand from pounding my car again. "Beating the air conditioning isn't going to help."

"It can't hurt."

I pulled back. "True." But instead of taking a whack at my car again, she lifted the handle on the backrest of her seat and flopped back, flat.

"Cooler down there?" I asked, wiping a sweat-drenched strand of hair off my forehead and tucking it behind my ear.

"Ha," she said, wrinkling her nose and blowing a raspberry at me.

"Charming," I said.

I turned back to the road. We'd moved maybe two feet in the last twenty minutes and my poor car was not happy. Something bad must have happened to get the traffic on Oracle Road to stop dead like this. It was three lanes wide in each direction and sort of a highway. But right now, all of the northbound lanes were still. Dead still. You could see the heat rippling upwards off of the hoods of the cars. Mine especially.

Yes, I'm well aware that driving a black car in the desert is stupid. Sue me.

The radio echoed in the heat, " . . . *bringing you the top hits of the 90s and dragging you in to the new millennia . . .* "

Lindy groaned, "Oh, make it stop. It's hot . . . " I turned the stereo off.

From the nether reaches of the seat Lindy dug up a map, circa before I was born, and rolled her head to the side so she could fan her neck. "*Hace calor.*"

"I know," I sighed. "I'm sorry."

"Not your fault."

"No one's fault," I said, squinting and rubbing the space between my eyebrows with the heel of my hand. "It's just that some guy backed his eighteen-wheeler into a power pole and it's hanging over the entire road—it flattened some big thing. They've almost got it under control."

Lindy was silent for a while, which is not her natural state, so I looked over. She had scooted as far away from me as her seatbelt would allow and narrowed her eyes. "I hate it when you do that . . . that . . . "

"What?"

"That *knowing* thing."

"Riiight. From now on I'll try to be stupider for you."

"You know what I mean. Just, just cut it out, wouldja?"

"Okay," I shrugged, then fiddled with the air conditioning controls in the futile hope that not having the cold up all the way at max might give the engine a chance of fulfilling at least a little of my request.

"You know," Lindy said, after raising her seatback and looking ahead of us, "you'd think drivers in Tucson would know about cactus."

I followed her gaze to the huge Suburban a little ways up that was trying to cut across the center divider filled with trees and succulents—the kind that fight back when provoked.

6

"You might think that," I said, nodding, "but you'd be wrong." We watched the driver get out with her cell phone, examining the remnants of her front tire.

I listened to my air conditioning strain and tick.

"Embarrassing that it's a woman."

"Yes," I agreed.

"You know what?" Lindy asked.

"Windows?" I answered.

Lin nodded and we rolled ours down, while I lowered the fan's whine.

My car is so old that we actually had to use handles to lower the windows. I'm sure there are some kids in America who've have never had to do that, and I feel bad for them. They're missing out, is all. So Lindy was working away on her window when she sprang back, nearly taking my temple and part of my jaw with her, "*Aaaah*!"

A motorcycle, cutting through traffic—because he could—whizzed right by her mirror, almost clipping it. The noise alone was enough to make us both jump. I leaned over Lin and yelled out the window after him, "Idiot! You'll *kill* yourself driving like that!" I pulled my head back in. "Jerk," I muttered.

Lindy brushed herself off. "Thank you for defending my honor like that, Rosie."

"Anytime."

"Don't know that he heard you though."

"Did he need to?" I put on my best *Law and Order* lawyer voice. "Isn't the full force of my rage going out into the universe enough? I mean, really. How much punishment can one mortal take?" Lindy managed to hold it together for about three seconds before she snorted. She has a very snorty laugh that always makes me laugh, too.

When we finally paid attention to the rest of the world, there was a space in front of my car.

"We're moving!" Lindy clapped her hands like a toddler, which just made me laugh more.

As our lane crept forward, we could listen to the radios on in the other cars pathetic enough to have their windows down, too. Lindy sneered at one that was playing, "Lady Marmalade."

"Don't you hate that song? I hate that song. I hate that movie."

"I know."

"I mean, the video's bad enough."

"I know."

"Did you see it?"

"Not yet."

"I mean, did you *see* what they put Pink in?"

"I know. It offends your 1938 values."

"It does."

"I know."

This is one of the ways Lindy and I bonded, lo those many, many years ago in pre-school. My dad loves showing me old movies, but Lindy wants to *be* in old movies. She'd have made a super screen siren back about sixty years B.L.B.— that's Before Lindy's Birth, which is how she measures time—and I definitely prefer movies from then. We're a good team. We've been a good team for years.

We were about to crest the hill coming up Oracle from River Road when the top of the power pole hanging over the three lanes of traffic came into view. I could feel Lindy staring pointedly at the side of my head, but I didn't feel like giving her the satisfaction. Instead I heard her give in and sigh, and I'm pretty sure she said, "hate you, Weej," under her breath.

I'll live.

As we got closer, we could see more and the scene was pretty grim. Our lane of traffic, to the far left, was the only one moving. I guess they had to start getting some of us out of there to ease the backup. I was willing to bet that they'd secured the affected power lines, but the sharply angled pole had crushed the back of an RV in the lane closest to the curb and some kind of damage had been done in the middle lane too. There were two ambulances and more than that many fire trucks. I tried not to spend my time looking—my Dad calls it "R.P.S." Residual Pinhead Slowing—but I did notice a motorcycle down on the ground as we crept by.

"Is that . . . ?"

"Don't know . . . . Can't quite . . . " Lindy's head was far out of the window, so I knew could rely on her for a full report later. Which I was pretty certain she'd offer at the least convenient moment.

3 SET UP

"I can't believe you didn't see it!" Lindy was standing with her jaw open—not her most attractive pose.

"I was driving, hello? I get paid the big bucks to keep my eyes on the road."

"Ha. Ha," Lindy said. "With all the drama out there, I can't believe you didn't try to get a better look."

I shrugged and kept prepping the table for dinner. Lindy sighed then put her hands on her hips. "Wait. Do you know how often I eat with you?"

I stopped and raised an eyebrow at her.

"I mean," Lindy said, "like—do you guys ever *not* eat together?" Her normal state of confusion was officially surpassed.

"Um . . . "

"I know, Friday night is *actually* a religion thing, but you all eat together so often that it's like every night—"

"It's just how we roll, Lindy," my Mom said, sweeping into the room with a tray of ice water for us to put out when we were done setting the silverware. She winked at me on her way out.

Lindy smiled at me. "See? I mean, I couldn't even pay my mom to say something like that."

"That might not be a bad thing, Lin," I said.

"I heard that," called Mom from the kitchen.

I grinned at Lindy. She was standing there, counting place settings. "There's an extra?"

"The boyfriend."

"Tim's back?"

"No, dork. Chloe's."

"Oh. Ew?"

"Ew," I agreed.

"Chloe's here tonight?"

"Yeah, you know. It's some post-college-free-food-at-mom's thing."

"What is it about you and Chloe and guys?"

"Not everyone can have a perfect boyfriend, Lin."

"I do have a perfect one, don't I?"

"Yes, you do." I refolded a napkin.

"And he's handsome and charming, isn't he?"

"He is." I adjusted the knives.

"And he's—"

"—Probably really sick of hearing you talk about him that way." Dad snuck up on Lindy, making her jump.

"Oh! Hey Mister T," she giggled. "I didn't hear you. And you don't think I'd ever let Drew hear me say those things, do you? I don't want to scare him off."

"Wise girl," Dad said.

"I've read *The Rules*."

"I take it back," Dad said, heading to the kitchen to talk with Mom while I walked over to Lindy.

"So, I think I broke up with Tim," I whispered.

"You *what?!*"

"*Keep your voice down!*" I hissed.

"You what?" she yell-whispered.

I shrugged. "Rob and I have been talking. Tim wasn't calling—for like, a month. So . . . " I straightened up. "So fine. Done. Finished."

"Oh Mah Gaw. I can't believe you dropped Lousy-Boyfriend-Tim. How?"

"I called?"

"Did he sound all *I'm-in-Paris without you* guilty, or just guilty?"

"He didn't sound anything. I got his voice mail."

Lindy stared.

"What?" I stared back.

"That is the skankiest move."

"Not."

"Is."

"Not!" I protested. "He hasn't picked up when I've called *for a month*. What did he expect?"

"Why are we still whispering?"

"I still haven't told Mom."

"Seriously?"

"I didn't want to make a big deal of it. I'm hoping the 'rents will forget I ever went out with him."

"Um. Rosie. You went out with him for most of a year."

"Not that long."

"Yes that long."

"Off and on. Not all the time."

"But enough."

"Everyone makes mistakes." I turned and went down the hall.

"You're not everyone." She followed me to my room.

"What's that supposed to mean?"

"Well, geez, Rosie. You're, like, the golden girl, you know? I mean, you can do no wrong. You have good grades. You're getting a scholarship internship thingy—"

"In the *running* for the scholarship. I'm actually *doing* the internship."

"Whatever. You're in with the competitive hospital thing. Your parents never get irked. They talk to you like you're human. You're, you know . . . special."

"Seriously? You make me sound like a poster child."

"Well," she said with a smile, "you kind of are."

"Hushup. Help me pick out something to wear tonight."

"Only if I get to wear your new flats."

"You drive a hard bargain, Brewster."

"Deal?"

"Deal."

4 Service

Dinner was as expected, though Chloe's boyfriend was late. No tragedy. Lindy, however, kept everyone riveted to their seats—or maybe had put them to sleep sitting up—by reenacting our adventure of the day.

"You should have seen it Missus T, the RV was just flat. Flattened. Pancaked."

"I have the image," Mom nodded.

"And there must have been, what, Rosie, seventy?"

"At least." I tried to sound like I wasn't paying attention.

"At least seventy fire trucks."

"Hyperbolize much, Lin?"

"Shh. I'm on a roll."

I shrugged and let her keep going. I had enough to do to keep eating while my head was killing me. Every so often I get these short-circuiting headaches. Mom's taken me to the doctor, but they only say I need to relax. I'm guessing they've never been on a very competitive swim team heading into senior year of high school in a brand-spanking-new millennium, in an internship at the med school, and working for an athletic scholarship that might lead to a free ride into the same med school—and all that while dragging along a seriously lousy boyfriend. They gave me pills to help me relax, but I don't take them. They make me feel foggy.

"Ari-the-Boyfriend's here," I said before I could stop.

Conversation at the table froze and when I looked up I noticed that everyone was staring at me.

"What?" I protested. "He is."

Which is when the doorbell rang.

"Don't call him that, Rose," Chloe sighed at me.

"What? He's Ari. He's your boyfriend."

Dad gave me a look as he went to the door. We listened to each other chew until we heard Dad say, "Ari, we wondered if you were going to make it . . . "

"OhMahGaw, Missus T. Rosie's on fire today."

Mom hadn't taken her eyes from me yet. "Really?" she asked Lindy as Dad walked Ari in. Chloe started a plate for him with the food closest to her.

"Oh yeah. She knew all about the power pole before we got there and then there was this motorcycle—"

"Lindy, no one wants to hear about the motorcycle."

"What about the motorcycle?" Chloe asked while mad-dogging me. I wanted to stick out my tongue back at her but I was supposed to be more mature now that I'm going to be a senior. Whatever.

"Well." Lindy slapped the edge of the table lightly, launching into a new epic. "Ol' Weej here—"

"Weej?" This time mom's eyes were on Lindy.

"Yeah, well, that's what my boyfriend Drew—you know Drew—anyway, that's what he calls Rosie when she's like this. You know. Weej, like Ouija boards?" I watched mom process this. She and Chloe did not seem amused, though Ari the Boyfriend barked. Seriously. Even though she drives me nuts and I'd never say it to her face, Chloe could do better than Ari.

"Anyway, so there we were, on Oracle, going north up that hill, from River, you know? And we're being, like, good responsible drivers and only laughing at the stupid people who tried to drive across the divider."

"The one with all that cactus?" Chloe asked, a smile playing at the corner of her mouth.

Lindy pointed one finger at her nose and the other at Chloe then kept talking. "So it's hot and the AC isn't really up to speed, if you know what I mean —Missus T you might want to invest in a repair for Rosie—"

"I'll keep that in mind—" Mom was absolutely icicles.

"So we're rolling down the windows when this motorcycle comes whizzing by just seriously like millimeters from my arm. I could, you know, *feel* the wind from the bike."

"Wow," the boyfriend said.

"I know," Lindy agreed. "It was really scary. But Rosie, you know, she was right there and she yelled at him."

"Effective," Chloe managed.

I wished I could throw cutlery without Mom seeing.

"No, it was great," Lindy said, defending me. "She was all, 'You Moron! You're gonna die driving like that!' and you know . . . " Lindy turned sober, very Screech-in-Principal-Belding's office, while I got more annoyed. Like, Russell Crowe wanting to go all Gladiator on her. But Lindy kept on. "You know, he really was totally reckless, and *we* would never drive like that, and—"

"Lindy, come on." I nudged her.

"She's blushing," the Boyfriend said, pointing at me with his fork. Chloe was trying to snatch Mom's attention from Lindy. Meanwhile, I felt the muscles in my neck and shoulders bunching up, my teeth grinding. The surge of pain that hit between my eyes was worse than I'd ever felt.

Lindy was still at it, so I broke in as I reached for my water glass, "Lind, I really don't think my Mom needs a public service—" when we all stopped dead, because my water glass exploded all over the table.

"What the hell?" Lindy jumped backwards, nearly falling over her chair.

"Nice one, Rose," Chloe glared at me.

"Chloe," Mom said seriously, calmly. "Go get the bathroom trash can?" Chloe hesitated, but there is really no way to say "no" to Mom.

Mom next speared me with her eyes. "Are you bleeding?" she asked at pretty much the same time as Dad asked, "Are you okay?"

Everyone was looking at me and my hand, still frozen in the shape of my nonexistent glass. Crushed crystals lay in a perfect circle over the dark stain of water spreading out over the tablecloth.

"What?" I was too loud. "It was an accident!" The fog lifted and I was more in control of my voice. "But, yeah, I'm fine. I'll . . . go get another glass." As I got to the kitchen cabinets I could hear that Lindy had covered the silence by droning on.

"Sit down and put your head between your knees," Chloe whispered as she passed with her tools.

I glared at her—while gripping the counter until the dizziness wore off.

I washed carefully, letting the water trickle off my fingertips in case there were shards stuck to my hand. There weren't. Teetering, I walked back in with a new water glass, the dustpan, and a rag. With the rag, I guided the glass shards into the trashcan that Chloe, who was now whispering to Mom, had put next to my chair.

I tuned in to Lindy's monologue. " . . . Well, but that isn't the weird part, you know? The weird stuff is that when we finally got to the front of the traffic jam I saw the motorcycle guy."

This surprised me. "You didn't tell me that, Lin."

"I started to," she defended. "Well, I mean I saw his *bike*," she said conspiratorially. "He was with an EMT I think . . . " She faltered. "Actually all I could see was the EMT's back." Then she recovered. "But Rose was right; he totally wiped out! He was so lucky there was already an accident with an ambulance there."

I sat silent, slowly rolling the remaining splinters of glass into different shapes with the rag before guiding them off the table's edge and into the can. Tiny rainbows, each shard full of all the colors ever seen.

Mom cleared her throat. I glanced up to see her eyes on me for a second before she returned to Lindy, who had moved onto a story about Drew's new summer job as a lifeguard at the Y. I couldn't tell what Chloe was trying to say, whispering in Mom's ear at the same time, but she seemed ticked.

I sighed and returned to the chicken. I assume it was chicken. It tasted like chicken, but I hear rattlesnake does too, so what do I know? All I was going to let myself think about now was the party tonight and the guy who might be there.

Not my Lousy Ex-Boyfriend.

And definitely not water glasses.

5 PREP

IF LINDY BRUSHED HER hair any more, it was going to turn to spun gold. That's all there was to it.

We were in my room getting dressed for the party that night. Lindy watched me in the mirror as I fiddled with buttons on a shirt I was going to wear over my tank.

"Really?" Lindy indicated the shirt.

"What?"

"That?"

"I *like* this shirt."

Lindy had better fashion sense than I did, but she also had a Visa card her dad paid for. And yet she wanted to wear my shoes. She's a mystery, and as she gave up on my wardrobe choices, she sighed, "So, you're not going to backslide, right? L.B.T. is still Lousy-*EX*-boyfriend-Tim?"

"Yep. I'm done. It's easier that he's in Europe with his family."

"He called yet?"

"Nope."

"Not once?"

"Nope. He's been there a month, Lin. As far as I'm concerned, he broke up with me."

"Jerk."

"Yep. He is, indeed."

She turned, hairbrush in hand, contemplating, "Did he think he broke up with you before he left, or something?"

"Probably. He may have just forgotten to tell me." I wasn't going to go into why he might have wanted to break up.

"Sounds like him," Lindy sighed. "Rose, why in the world did you ever go out with him? I mean, he's okay-looking, but . . . " She put the brush down and turned to perfecting her lips in my mirror. "Why did you stay with him? No one likes him."

"Inertia?" I started digging in my closet for my shoes.

"Ooh. You and your SAT study sessions."

"Oh yeah, because you never made it past third grade reading and math."

"Fifth. I stopped at fifth grade math," she said, defensively. "And I read. Some."

"Whatever. Cosmo."

"Seriously, Rosie." She sat on the edge of my bed. "Drew's all worried about your self-esteem and stuff, and I have a hard time defending you."

"Then don't. Not everyone treats Oprah like a religion the way Drew does."

"No, I mean it, Rosie. What was going on in your head that told you to go out with him?"

I'd located my shoes but not Lindy's flats. "He asked."

She looked at me critically. "Beyond that?"

I thought for a minute. "I was bored? It meant I didn't have to be a third wheel all the time?"

"Yeah, but no one liked him. *You* didn't particularly like him."

"He was okay. In the beginning."

She shrugged and looked at her nails. "Delusional much?"

"Not much."

She went back to looking at herself in the mirror. "Lousy-EX-Boyfriend-Tim," she murmured. "He sounds like a car now. LexBT."

I chuckled, emerging triumphant. "Found them!" I held up the shoes and Lindy took them from me, trying them on.

"Rob gonna be there?" she asked.

I paused—not for long, but for long enough. "I really haven't given it any thought."

"Liar."

"I guess." I leaned back on my closet door frame. "I mean, I've known him forever."

"I know. Complete boy-next-door action." She sat down on the floor across from me.

"Yeah, but he called last week when I was out."

"You didn't tell me that. Did you call him back?"

"No."

"Why not?" She smacked my foot.

"I . . . this will sound so lame."

"It won't be a first," Lindy said without mirth.

"Funny." I got up and went over to the mirror, pulling my brown hair up off of my neck, wishing I'd been using *Sun-In*. "I guess I just wanted to figure out what to do about Tim."

"Doesn't Rob still think you're going out with Tim?"

"We, um . . . we'd talked at a practice about how I'd been thinking about breaking up."

"And were you ever going to tell me this?"

"*Seig heil.*"

"Well, whether Rob knew it or not, leaving a breakup message on voice mail isn't your best move ever. Even if it was for Tim."

I let my hair down again and whined. "He hasn't called. He hasn't written."

"You think he knows how to write?"

I stopped laughing when we heard the knock followed by Chloe's voice, muffled through the door. "Can I come in?"

If she couldn't hear how annoyed I was by her presence, then she needed surgery. "What?"

Chloe slipped in, closing the door behind her. "Sorry if I'm ruining your play time—"

"—What do you want, Clo?"

She didn't dawdle. "You need to cut that stuff out, Rose."

"What are you talking about, Chloe?"

"And Lindy," she turned, "you're no help with your story and all that Weej garbage."

"Moi?" Lindy placed a hand on her throat. "Don't bring me into your co-dependent-excuse-for-sibling-rivalry."

Chloe ignored Lin, turning back to aim at me. "I mean, everyone's used to you knowing things, Rose. Fine. Whatever. But that dinner stuff. Especially in front of Mom. It really upsets her."

"What *dinner* stuff are you talking about, Chloe? Mom usually likes it when we eat."

She glared. "Your glass?"

"Are you kidding me? Or what, like Perfect You hasn't ever broken a glass?"

I could see the vein in her temple throb and felt rather than saw Lindy's jaw gradually descend, "Rose. Please, don't be an idiot—"

"—I don't need a lecture—especially from you, Chloe." I turned to my mirror, my back to her. "Can we drop this? I'd like to go have a nice time at the party tonight without having to obsess about you bossing me."

For a second there, I thought she was really going to light into me in front of Lindy, whose head had been bobbing back and forth like she was watching the U.S. Open.

"Fine." Chloe turned and left. "It's your funeral," I heard her mutter as she slammed my door behind her.

"Whatever," I said, picking up a different pair of earrings. Lindy was looking at me like I'd sprouted antlers.

"What?"

Lindy had to clear her throat twice. "What did she mean, Rosie?"

"Who listens? Hand me the hairbrush, wouldja?"

Lindy hesitated, then handed it to me while I attacked the knots in my hair, brushing away the feeling that I should pay more attention to my sister.

Fire

6 Party

LINDY AND I ARRIVED at the party and found that half of the people there were swimming. It was just as well that we didn't know in advance and so didn't bring suits. I don't do night swimming. As a kid, an older cousin showed me the movie *Jaws* when I was too young, but Dad thinks that's a ridiculous excuse. He thinks I'm intelligent enough to know that sharks don't come out of drains in swimming pools at night. I've informed him that we learned in physics that just because you haven't seen something happen doesn't mean it *can't* happen —I get all sciencey on him like that sometimes. I love the way the pool light looks at night, though—even if it does attract demons of the deep.

And Lindy thinks I'm smart.

Whatever.

Right now, though, she was annoying me.

"How can you not remember?" I asked.

"I forgot. It happens."

"How can you forget?"

"Because the words sound the same, okay? I can't remember if he said there *are* or there *aren't* try-outs. It sounds the same when someone is a fast-talker."

"That's true," Lindy's boyfriend Drew added. She was leaning back on

29

him on a chaise. We were on the top level of these tiered patios going around the pool, which also had two levels—the top was a steamy Jacuzzi spilling into the cooler pool water. They'd done it all in natural rock so it looked like you were in some enchanted grotto somewhere or something.

"Don't go defending her, Drew. You wouldn't be that laid back if she was misunderstanding something about your Sims."

Lindy turned her face to look up at Drew, channeling her inner Myrna Loy, "She has a point, darling. You know that you—" Then Lindy sat up suddenly and leaned toward me, whispering conspiratorially, "—Rose. Quick. Do this." She rubbed a finger across her front teeth.

I had no idea what she was on about, but I follow instructions pretty well. So there I was, rubbing away when I heard this voice behind me.

"Hi, Rose," spoke the god.

"Rob?" I mouthed at Lindy.

I prayed I was the only one who could see Lindy nod. My face flushed as I stood and turned awkwardly. While I'd known Rob since kindergarten at least, I'd had an unrequited crush on him pretty much that whole time—tall, gorgeous, smart, a water polo player—nice too. And he was always a good friend. Just. But towards the end of junior year he started talking to me more after practice. Sometimes he'd let me know if there was a party or something going on. And sometimes he'd ask me about Tim.

"Rob!" I wanted to grab my squeal back as it left my mouth. Too happy. Too happy. Take a breath. Count to three. "I mean . . . hey . . . hi . . . I didn't know you'd be here . . . " I tossed my hair over my shoulder with my hand and looked down. Total idiot.

"Whoah there, Tex," Rob laughed. I'd nearly spilled his Coke with the hair flip.

"Sorry," I winced.

He shoved my shoulder gently with his. "No worries."

I melted.

Just a little.

Okay, a lot.

"Hey Lindy. Drew." Rob raised his can at them.

"I thought," I had to steady myself and tried again, "I thought you were at Rocky Point?" *But I hoped you were back,* I thought to myself.

Something flickered across his face before he smiled and said, "I was. We had to come back for try-outs." I mad-dogged Lindy.

"Try-outs," she said. "Definitely."

"Just varsity?" I asked Rob.

"JV and varsity. Everyone. We're supposed to be there Monday at six."

"Wow. That's hard-core for summer."

Rob nodded.

"But, you know," I could feel my heart skipping beats, "I guess it's good, you know, that it's not tomorrow at least, because I probably won't sleep enough tonight and I'd be all slow and . . . I should . . . I'm going to shut up now."

Rob laughed and toasted me with his can, "That's why I like you, Rose, you're—"

And right about then everything shifted to slow motion.

First I heard a murmur behind me. I'm lame enough that Rob smiling at me had thrown me off balance a little, so when I turned towards the voices I was unstable to begin with, and then I had to go and gasp in an entirely dramatic way. If I hadn't been freaked out I would have laughed at myself.

Lousy-Ex-Boyfriend-Tim was standing at the entrance to the pool deck, all tensed jaw and grasping fists, and looking angrier than I'd ever seen him. His normally thick brow was even more furrowed than usual. Thinking hurt him. It's a fact. You could watch his face like ticker tape, and right now the news on the wire was coming in fast and it wasn't good.

My mind, on the other hand, had left the building. Tim was *In Europe.*

He was *Not Calling Me*. He was *Far Away. On a Trip. With His Family*. And tonight, I was supposed to be Talking To Rob.

"What the hell are you doing, Rosie?"

"I can escort him out, Rose," Rob whispered down to me.

I shook my head.

"I'm at a party, Tim." I said, moving forward a step, "talking to friends. I didn't know you were invited, what with you being *out of the county* and all and, you know, *not writing or calling*."

"I got your message."

"I left the message this afternoon, Tim. Even you can do that math. You can't fly back from Europe in three hours."

He looked confused, "No, I mean we got back early and I got your message. Your sister said you were here."

"You talked to my sister?"

"I called your house."

I was gonna kill Chloe.

I could feel myself getting angry in that lame I've-been-caught-doing-something-innocent-but-it-makes-me-look-guilty-anyway way. "What do you want, Tim? I told you we were done."

"You told my voice mail," he corrected. "I thought we should talk in person." A buzz started around me in the crowd.

"We have nothing to talk about, Tim. Your radio silence made it pretty clear that you weren't going out with *me*. Now I've confirmed it for you. Stay or go, but I'm here with my friends." I turned back to Lindy, Drew, and Rob, who moved closer and started to whisper something else to me when Tim yelled, "Don't you *dare* turn your back on me, Rose Tyschler."

I froze.

"I can take him," Rob murmured, but I shook my head again.

"Or what, Tim?" I turned back to him, trying hard to keep my voice down. "Or what?"

"You want to do this in public?" He sounded genuinely surprised.

"Do what? I broke up with you, Tim. It's over." I hated this. Everyone at the party had stopped talking. My eyes strained in the candlelight.

"You . . . you want everyone to know what a freak you are?"

My stomach hurt. I felt my brain grasping, "What are you talking about, Tim?"

"Rose," Lindy said quietly as she reached for my hand. "Let it go. You need to breathe."

But I only sort of heard her.

"Hey?" Tim called to everyone at the party, "You wanna hear a great story about Rosie?"

"Don't." I didn't have to work hard to sound menacing.

"So, back on her birthday this year, she—" and then he screamed.

I was a little surprised about the scream.

I was surprised until I saw that he was on fire.

He started to whack his backside, then dropped to the ground and rolled, just like they taught us in kindergarten. Then Drew jumped up and dumped the remnants of an ice chest on Tim's lower half, putting out the last of the fire.

When Tim recovered what was left of his small share of dignity he yelled over at me, "You bitch!"

"That's it." Rob strode across the deck, took Tim by the shoulder and helped him towards the stairs. Drew held the gate open.

"Yeah, Tim," I couldn't help sneering, "Yeah, I'm the bitch. 'Cuz I lit you on fire from *all the way over here.*"

My legs folded under me as soon as the words were out, but Lindy was fast with a chair, making it look like I'd finished and was sitting down on purpose.

"You're a freak!" Tim yelled, fully ignoring Rob's presence. He kept yelling at me as my hero dragged him out, but we couldn't hear the words any more. He was just noise. After the glow from his headlights faded, Rob came back and sat down with us. Everyone had started to breathe again and the inevitable murmur began anew.

"Uh," I began, still fighting waves of nausea, "Sorry about that . . . I guess we're definitely not dating any more." Pathetically, I tried to laugh. "Drew, Rob, thanks."

Drew nodded and put his hands up as though refusing to sign another autograph, "No, no, my dear, don't thank me. It was purely selfish," then he dropped the magnanimous act. "I didn't want to get stuck driving him to the hospital."

I pointed a finger at him. "Ha. Ha."

"You're shaking." Rob took my pointing hand. "It's okay, Rose. Take a deep breath."

He sort of petted my hand, trying to stop the shaking. Even though I was tall—nearly as tall as Rob—his hands were bigger than mine and I felt strangely settled having him touch me this time. I took more breaths and was doing everything I could do not to think about Tim catching on fire. Everyone was still looking at me. And there was that buzz, or maybe it was a ringing in my ears.

My head hurt.

7 GOODBYES

As we were leaving, Rob offered me a ride home, but I declined. I ached too much to enjoy the trip.

"I'll call you tomorrow?" he asked, making the statement a question.

"I'd like that," I nodded, hoping I didn't look as wiped as I felt. "A lot."

"Good then." He started to go, then turned around really quick and kissed my forehead. It almost made my head stop hurting.

My forehead. How cute is that?

"He's an idiot, Rose," Rob called to me, walking backwards to his car, "and idiots do things like backing into *luminarias*." He waved and turned around.

Lindy swiped her shoulder into mine. "Nice work, lady."

She couldn't see me shrug in the dark. An hour earlier and I would have been over the moon about something goofy like a forehead kiss. Now I was tired and relieved that Drew was taking Lindy home. I wasn't up for listening to Lindy's rehash of the evening. I didn't want her to see how worried I really was.

Worried that Tim was right.

The house wasn't dark when I got home — a bad sign. It wasn't all that late, but usually Mom and Dad read in bed for a while before giving in, so the front room lights are usually out. This time the lights were on, and before I even touched my key to the lock, I gasped like I'd been kicked in the chest. My whole world crumbled before I could open the door.

8 ROOFTOPS

TRYING TO BE QUIET while entering the house was a waste of effort. Dad was leaning against the back corner of the foyer. Just waiting.

"Hey Dad." I tried to sound chill, hoping he couldn't tell how dizzy I was. "What's up?"

"Are you drunk, Rose?"

"Of course not!"

Dad studied me. I had, at best, a 50/50 chance of falling over right there, or at least having him notice me shaking. "Mom's on the roof," he said finally, and turned blankly, walking down the hall to his bedroom.

This was bad news, and news I was not prepared to hear. The roof was the place for Serious Talks. My mind spiraled through paranoid fantasies first of boarding schools, then of juvie, as I headed down the hall, around a corner, into the straw-bale addition to the house, past Mom's floor loom and basket of washed wool, and out the Dutch door to the backyard. I turned left and plodded up the side steps to the roof ramada, holding onto the railing the whole way up.

It was sad that Mom always had the serious talks up here, weighing this place down with memories. Still, of all the things my parents added on to our house, this was my favorite. Our house is . . . let me put it this way: it looks like Victor Frankenstein designed it. The original part is adobe, dating back before any of us were born, so by Southwest standards, it's ancient. The add-ons are a mish-mash of rammed earth, straw bale, faux adobe, and red brick. "A pastiche," my mother calls it. Funky is what my friends say. I call it home.

I reached the top of the stairs and saw Mom already sitting under the loosely latticed Ocotillo roof, hugging her knees and looking out at the lights of the city. There is nothing as clear as the desert night. Clean air, lots of stars, diamond city lights.

"Rose?" She didn't turn.

"Yep." I hesitated, then moved up to sit on a woven chaise next to her and criss-crossed my legs.

"Well, you really stuck your foot in it this time." Her tone was more gentle than her words, but it didn't help.

"What?" I couldn't breathe.

"Tim's mother called me."

"Oh."

"'Oh' is right." She was angry. Why was she angry? "Rose, what were you thinking?"

"Me? What was *I* thinking?"

"Yes, you."

"Wait a minute," I said, narrowing my eyes. "What did Tim's mother tell you?"

Mom flattened me with one of her looks. "That you were, I hate even saying this, *making out* with some guy—some college guy—in front of everyone, and Tim caught you. Then you two argued and you threw a lantern at him as he left, and his clothes caught on fire."

I spoke slowly, like she was three. "Does that, even for a second, sound like me?"

"I want an answer, Rose."

"Mom. Hello? You always say you can read me like cheap fiction. If I were going out with a college guy wouldn't you know?"

"Probably . . . " She unwound a little.

"And have I ever made out with anyone in public?"

"I'm not sure I know the answer to that any more."

I squinted at her and rubbed my temples.

"I'm not sure what's happening with you, Rose, but I called your Aunt Mina all the same."

"Aunt Mina?"

"Yes, she's . . . very good in these situations."

"In situations where . . . " I was having a hard time catching on, "situations where your daughter is falsely accused of mashing on some unnamed college guy?"

Mom ignored me and continued, "We talked for a long while, and she and I agree that a change of pace would be helpful."

"Change of pace?"

"Yes. You'll go out for a visit."

"To Brooklyn?"

"Yes."

I almost thought *eh, I like my cousin. New York can be fun*, but something in her voice made me stare her down.

Mom pointedly looked away. "And there's more to it than that."

"What?" My brain started to whirr, "Mom? Mom . . . when do I go?"

She paused and gave off the unmistakable feeling that she was revving up to rip off a Bandaid, "Tomorrow morning."

"Tomorrow. No. See, that's not possible, Mom. *Tomorrow*? I've got swim try-outs for the varsity slots on Monday. If I leave tomorrow, I'm not going to be back in time for them. I'm not blowing my scholarship for a weekend trip. That's nuts! Who'd fly to Brooklyn just to turn around and . . . "

The crickets were mighty loud.

"Mom?"

She reached out to take my hand, but I pulled away. When she finally spoke, her voice was pinched in her throat. "I know. And I know this is going to be hard. But you have to trust me, Hannah Rose. You have to trust us that this is the right thing to do. We wouldn't be sending you if it weren't important. We just . . . we want you to be safe. We want everyone to be safe."

"Mom, how long am I there for?"

She swallowed audibly, "just the summer . . . We—"

"Are you kidding me?" That pain in my forehead was pushing out like it wanted to grab mom and shake her. "You're sending me off for the rest of the summer before my Senior Year of high school? My final year? My senior-class-of-2002-coast-to-the-finish-line? I'm going to miss swim team—they'll make the teams while I'm gone. Do you realize what this will do to my chances to get me to college and med school? You're making me miss the start of the internship."

"Yes." She'd been nodding along with my rant, but spoke simply, sadly. "Daddy is going to make some phone calls for you, delaying your start date so you won't lose the internship. You can call Coach yourself. He'll understand. He needs you as much as you need the team, Rosie. It's . . . you'll understand soon. You'll understand when you get to Brooklyn."

"And if I don't go?" I snapped.

"You have to go." The words slapped me, though her voice was gentle. "We all agree that it's just not . . . safe here for you any more. You'll be better off— you'll be safer—"

"Safer from what? What are you talking about? You're not making any sense!" I squinted the pain back into my skull.

"Please try to stay calm, Rose. It's . . . " she looked apologetic, but I didn't care. "There are things you need to learn—things Dad and I can't teach you—that will keep you . . . that can keep everyone . . . Oh hell's bells, Rosie. You have to trust me. Aunt Mina will explain things more clearly when you get there. I know it's a lot to ask—"

"Damn right it is, Mo—" and I was cut short as the chaise beneath me snapped a leg, throwing me off to the side. I had to jump up or fall over. "Damnit!"

"Rose?" She was reaching out to me, "I told you to stay calm."

"Why are you so concerned about keeping me calm? Have you lost your mind?"

"Rose, sit." It was a command, but not mean. More like exhausted.

Rather than sitting on a different chair, I leaned against the edge of the retaining wall, breathing hard. I could tell from the look on her face that whatever was going on was difficult for her, too. But I really didn't give.

"Look back at your day, Rose. The motorcycle, the glasses, Tim—"

That set me off, "I don't care what he says, I did *not* throw a *lumenaria* at him! You know I can't throw!"

"I know."

"I was, like, twenty feet away from him!"

"I know."

"So, what? You still think I lit him on fire?"

"I know you did. Mina does too."

I looked at her carefully. "You've lost your mind."

"And you're still going to Brooklyn. Your aunt will—"

"I'm not going."

"Yes. You are. I know you don't believe me, but this is killing us. If there were any other way . . . but there isn't. Your bags are packed. Anything we forgot, we'll ship. The sooner you go, the sooner you'll be able to come back. Your father's taking you to the airport first thing in the morning."

She got up and walked to the top of the stairs as my stomach churned. Staring at the moon, she sounded tired, "Hannah Rose, if it was okay for you to be around your friends, then you wouldn't have to go. But you . . . it's not good for you to be here right now. We have to protect you, but we want to try to protect everyone else, too. There really isn't any time to waste."

I couldn't come up with anything to say back to that other than "Why?" I felt the tears on my face. "I don't understand. Why can't I stay? I want to stay."

Mom kept looking up at the night. "I'm so sorry," she whispered. And she turned and went down the stairs.

9 Packing

AFTER THAT, I REMEMBER moving slowly.

Climbing off the roof and walking back to my room, I moved numbly. Images of the day flickered through my head, shoving out all the thoughts of Brooklyn and my mom's words. After washing up, I stood for a long while, looking in the mirror in our cavernous tiled bathroom. My green eyes stared vacantly back.

Freak, I thought. *Total freak. No, everyone thinks that, right. Everyone says when you're in high school . . . but that doesn't mean I could have . . .*

I threw cold water over my face and hair, stung myself thoroughly with Sea Breeze, and brushed my teeth. The normalcy of these actions calmed me a bit. When my long hair is damp, it needs to be braided before bed or I wind up looking like Hermione Granger wrestling a shrub—with the flora winning. In the mirror, I watched my fingers tremble as they braided. Even the freckles across my nose looked scared. I finished, then flipped the braid over my back, squared my shoulders and looked at myself critically.

Unsafe, I thought. *You are unsafe.*

Rob's better off with you in Brooklyn.

The lights were off in my room and I left them that way, curtains open. I leaned on the pile of pillows covering the back edge of my bed for a long time,

43

not looking at anything but hearing things in my mind—stone buildings, green parks, enormous skyscrapers, tunnels, hot days, ice cream, lakes, cabins, forests. This time I paid attention.

Sometimes, it's like I hear images. It's not a movie, not like I close my eyes and "see" pictures on the dark insides of my eyelids, but that I get a very clear understanding of a place in my mind. I can walk around any house in perfect darkness without ever bumping into anything—something I can't do when it's light—but in darkness, I know where I am. So it's more like I know the words to describe places and events—I hear them. It's the words. Like making brain pictures when you read a good book.

Yeah, it's weird.

And I had some very clear pictures of Brooklyn coming in.

My eyes drifted around my room in the night's blue light. My bags were next to the door, already packed. I shivered and leaned over to my desk to launch the music program on my birthday iBook, then walked to the window while sad tunes wrapped around me. My room looked out in the moonlight on a little garden Mom and I'd created. Mostly it was medicinal plants, local herbs. Mom believed that one of the reasons we were all so healthy was because of her tea expertise. I swear, the woman could brew tea out of anything: bark, bugs, burnt offerings. It was all good. It didn't always smell good, but she found a way to make it all tasty.

She wouldn't be making me tea this summer.

I stood at the window for a long time. The moon was fully up now, and the yard was blue. A gorgeous, desert, moonlit blue. I could hear coyotes not far away. They must have found something to eat, because they sure were making a racket. My music was barely audible above them, but my stomach unclenched, my breathing slowed. I wished I could climb in bed and sleep without leaving the window.

I noticed my foot was asleep, making me wonder how long I'd been standing. I turned back to my room, slowly checking on everything in the gloom, trying to decide what to do next. I limped over in the dim light and dug out my current knitting project, a few other sizes of needles, my journal, my favorite pen and my Discman case with CDs, and stuffed my life as I had known it into my backpack. I'd add my computer in the morning.

Finally, I turned down the music a bit more and climbed into bed, leaving the curtains open. I pulled up the cool sheets and fell asleep almost immediately to the glow of the moon and the soft notes. I dreamt of airplanes, blue skies, fluffy clouds, the steel skyline of New York—and I didn't think twice about it.

10 Airports

With the weak pre-dawn light filtering through the huge windows, I sat next to my Dad in the tiny Tucson *International* Airport. I know. *Insert Joke Here* is how we all thought of it.

People were watching us while we sat there. However, instead of lighting them all on fire like the 'rents expected, this time I was knitting the most amazing pair of fingerless mittens on a set of five double-pointed needles. The work kept me awake, at least. No matter what you think about the needle arts in general, this kind of Extreme Knitting just looks cool. It's kind of like manipulating a flexible ninja throwing star or something, with all the needle points shooting off the sides. I smiled at my adoring fans. I chose to believe they watched because the mittens were gorgeous and I was stupendously good at knitting, not because I was a level five rogue geek with a thousand experience points in an archaic art form.

Adding to the geek thing, I listened to the soundtrack from *Fiddler on the Roof* on my Discman, trying to tune out the hole in my stomach. I'd been in one of my rare silent moods and Dad sat next to me, reading the paper, also silent. I still couldn't figure out what he thought about all of this, but he sure acted like he thought it was a good idea.

He finally nudged me. "What are you listening to?" he said.

"*Fiddler,*" I said.

"Really?" He lifted the earpiece off my ear.

Is this the little girl I carried . . .

Yeah, I know. Cheesy and cliché, but it's a great soundtrack and it fit my mood.

He almost smiled at me. "I'm always surprised you like that show so much. It seems so . . . old . . . "

"No one beats my man Zero, Dad."

He chuckled, "You're such an anachronism," and gently let go of the earpiece.

I don't remember growing older, When did they?

My dad and I spent most of my childhood watching videos—and when we were lucky, borrowed laserdiscs—of movies that he'd watched with *his* dad. It was fun for me, like getting to learn the history of the world, even if history was always black and white. None of it was boring, and I got to have some great conversations with Dad afterwards. Like, who knew that *Casablanca* was being written as they filmed it or that Bogart's part was supposed to be played by Ronald Reagan? Or that no one *including* Raymond Chandler knew who killed the chauffeur in *The Big Sleep*? This is what you get from watching hours of American Movie Classics with your old man. I think we bought or taped off HBO, AMC, and TMC every classic film ever made.

But none of that was going to stop me from going to Brooklyn.

When did she grow to be a beauty . . .

I leaned over and put my head on Dad's shoulder, using it to slide the earpiece behind my ear. "I know, Dad, but that's why you love me, right?"

He swallowed. "You know, Hannah Rose, we wouldn't be doing this if we didn't know it was the best thing for you." He leaned his head onto mine.

Wasn't it yesterday when they . . . were . . . small?

"Of course. I understand. You think I'm a dangerous fire-starter. It's definitely best to send me as far away from you as you can."

"Sarcasm isn't your most attractive trait, Rose."

"Not sarcasm," I lifted my head and looked him in the eye, "honesty." He flinched microscopically. "But you know, Dad, there's one thing you didn't consider."

"What's that?"

"Maybe I can light you on fire all the way from Brooklyn. I might be a super villain."

"Rosie, don't. It's not funny."

"It is to me."

"Really?"

"No, it's not."

"No. It's not," he agreed.

"Well, what am I supposed to think?" My words tumbled out. "I mean, you're shipping me off. No one's even coming with me."

"We could only afford one last-minute ticket."

"I know, but if I'm such a threat, should I even be on a plane?"

"You'll be able to stay calm on the plane. Mina assured us—"

"You're kidding. I'm like, America's Most Wanted one minute with you people, and the next minute you try to put me in a tin can with tons of innocent people for hours and think we'll all be safe?."

"Well, that's why she wanted you to have this before you got on the flight." He handed me a small yellow pill and a bottle of water.

"You're joking."

"I'm not. Drink up."

"And if I don't?"

"You'll be in the tin can, too, Hannah Rose."

He had a point.

I gulped. But I glared.

"I know it doesn't feel like it," he apologized, "but we love you so much. There really are reasons we have to do this." I heard him swallow hard. "Look, HR, you're angry, and I don't blame you, but in a few hours you'll understand everything."

"Then why make me wait a few hours? Tell me now." I was exasperated. "Why can't you guys just explain things?"

Dad ran his hand through his greying hair, "Oh brother. I think I'm the last person you'd want explaining this to you."

"Oh, Dad." I corrected him, "You know better than that. *Chloe* is the last person I'd want doing it."

Dad couldn't help laughing a little. "That's probably true."

"Does she even know I'm going?"

"She knows." Dad hesitated. "It's . . . hard for her to watch you go to New York."

I snorted, "Yeah, right! Like 'don't let the plane door smack your butt on your way out of town.'"

Instead of laughing, which I expected, Dad looked sad. "Someday . . . someday you and Chloe will get along."

"Yeah, well, my breath isn't held." I put my head back on his shoulder. "I hate this, Dad."

"I know you do, HR. I do too. But it'll be good. And you'll like getting to spend time with Jennifer and you like New York, so, there's a bright side. Maybe you can go to the museums? Maybe even make an appointment at that textile museum you always wanted to get to? We never had time to do that before."

A mechanical voice clicked onto the speaker. "Flight 111 to Phoenix, connecting to New York, LaGuardia, now boarding at gate 10."

"That's you."

"Yep."

"Now, you remember what to do?"

"Yes, Dad. When I land, I call Aunt Mina's cell phone number *before* I head down to baggage claim."

"Excellent."

"As long as I can find a working pay phone in LaGuardia."

"Um . . . right. You have change for the phone?"

"Yeah, I know." I recited, "Find a pay phone at the airport. Roaming charges are insane. Only use the cellphone in an emergency. And . . . I think Mom must have snuck about four hundred dollars in quarters in my backpack—it weighs a ton. Where've you been hiding so much change?"

Dad chuckled, then looked serious, "I'm going to miss you, Hannah Rose."

"I'm going to miss you too." My voice cracked, "This really sucks, Daddy."

He swallowed hard, "Only until you land. It'll get good after that."

"Right . . . "

"Call when you get in?"

"I will."

"And try not to be angry."

I looked at him.

"Okay, try not to be *too* angry."

"I might be able to do that." I kissed his cheek and he held my face like he was giving me an eye exam. Then he turned me around towards the line of people boarding the plane. I dragged a sleeve across my eyes, and handed my ticket to the flight attendant, turned at the doorway and waved one last time. Dad gave me a half-wave with a super-sad smile on his face that I couldn't look at for more than half a second before I had to head down the ramp.

It echoed.

My flight to Phoenix was nothing much—one of those "up—down" deals. Then I switched onto the larger plane for the longer flight to New York. I found my seat with no trouble and pulled my Discman, my book, and my knitting out of my backpack before stashing it in the overhead space. Along with my knitting came a ball of sky blue, lace-weight yarn with a tag attached, "Handspun love from home," with "Mom" swooped across the bottom. I used my sleeve on my eyes again and stuffed the ball back for later use.

After adjusting into my window seat, I dove into my book. Drew had given me a few graphic novels he liked a week or so earlier. His copies—I had to send them back. I was already nearing the end of this freaky, faux-pocalypse comic called *Watchmen* when we landed in Phoenix, and I couldn't wait to finish it on the next flight.

On my New York flight, they had just taken off the seatbelt light as I reached the final page and started to exchange it for my music and knitting, when I noticed the guy sitting next to me. It was pretty obvious that he'd been reading the book with me, and now he was looking at it longingly. I was a little surprised because, first, I'd only just noticed him (that's how good the book was), and second, he was really hot. I hesitated, smiled, and pulled it back out of the seat pocket and handed it to him.

"Really?" he asked.

"Well, not to keep," I smiled again, feeling my face flush.

"I don't usually read comic books."

"That's okay," I smiled, "you can call it a graphic novel if it makes you feel better."

He laughed. "Well that makes sense. I've never seen a comic like that."

"Yeah, *Watchmen* isn't your run-of-the-mill Superman comic."

"And you . . . " he looked at me instead of the book in his hand, "You like comics like this?"

I hesitated, unsure, "Well, sure. But, I mean this is the first one I've really ever read cover to cover. Well, this and *Sandman*."

He shook his head, "I haven't heard of that."

"If you like this you'd like that. Very mythic, very epic."

"I usually don't go for the epic things."

"Well, it's not like *The Odyssey*."

"Oh. Well, then maybe I would like it."

This guy was cute but I wasn't that into him any more. At least Rob knew how to read.

He didn't seem to notice, though. He thanked me for the loaner and flipped back to the start. I wondered with a book like that if reading the end first would spoil the beginning. I figured not.

Sometimes knowing the end means you pay more attention to how you get there.

I turned my mind to my knitting and music choices. Lindy, whose father was a bit of a Tech Guy, had worked with her dad and made me a set of mix tapes before my last trip to New York a few years ago. At my request, he recently transferred them to CD for my new Discman. My timing couldn't have been better. The one I had in was *Flying Tunes*. There were also CDs of *Subway Songs* and the charming *Music to Get Mugged By*. Some of the flying CD was hilarious, like she had included "Leavin' on a Jet Plane," which I swear is moldy by now it's so old. Some were odd, like "Airplane," by the Indigo Girls—the one about Emily hating to fly because she's convinced she's gonna crash. I thought Lindy had perhaps not really thought that choice through so carefully, though I liked The Roches doing backup. But overall the music was good, and the knitting was complex stranded work on those amazing mittens, and pretty soon, I was more-or-less asleep.

I entered one of those mental states where you know you're dreaming, but you're not about to wake yourself up because Something Very Interesting Is

About To Happen. Or at least you think something is about to happen. In my dream, *I'm sitting in my seat on the plane but my hot-if-not-bright seatmate isn't there. The cityscape is wide open below us. I feel a tap on my shoulder and drop my knitting. The cute guy is back. He looks serious, and motions for me to follow him, so I unclip my seat belt, untangle myself from the yarn, and slide out. He leads me through first class and towards the forward galley, bathrooms, and cockpit. He reaches for one of the roller carts from the galley, but stops, then motions me forward again. With a finger on his lips he slowly puts his hand out onto the cabin door and pushes it open*—when I woke up with a start. I was sweating, and cold, my heart racing. The guy next to me was gone—with the book—and for a second I thought I was still in the dream or that we'd landed and I'd been left behind on the plane. Then I heard the engines and felt air flow into my lungs again. It took me a minute to get my heart under control. The dream was *so* vivid and things were so *not right* in it.

I looked out the window—the real window—and realized we were getting very close to New York. In the distance I could see the elongated iconic buildings—the Empire State, the World Trade Center towers, the Chrysler building. I love that building—the design of the roof on that thing is wild. It looks like it belongs in *Watchmen* more than in real New York.

My B-seat hottie came back, looking sheepish for having taken the comic to the bathroom with him, I guess. I'm sure I was looking a little sheepish myself, having dreamt about him. He held the book up, asking if he should relinquish it. I waved him back to it. I didn't want to risk starting a conversation while my head was in the dream.

I tried to look busy with the window and my knitting. Just like my real flight, the dream trip led ultimately to Brooklyn. Even though I never got there in my dream, I knew where I was going, which wasn't anything like my current real life. I hadn't known any of this was coming and that tied my stomach in knots. It's not like I live in a state of pérmà-vu—where I'm déjà-vu-ing all the time—but if

I'm going to be honest with myself, I have to admit that I often have a pretty good idea of what's about to happen. It's usually big stuff I know about, like Christmas presents, not normal stuff, like what's for dinner. Not unless I really concentrate. Right now, though, even if I tried to concentrate it felt a lot more like those chalk paintings in *Mary Poppins* after the rain. Blurry images and shapes. Nothing definite—like anything could happen and the possibilities were changing and shifting all the time.

My knowing things drove my Dad nuts. He didn't like it very much. Don't even get me started on Chloe's reactions. I guess it got annoying for them because I always knew when they were going to surprise me, always knew what I'd get for my birthday. We finally arrived at a truce—I would act all *whoop-dee-do,* and they wouldn't ask me if I was "really" surprised. It had worked pretty well for the last few years.

But that seemed light years away. Now I was unsafe, they said. *Everyone* was unsafe around me. I wished the mittens on my needles were an afghan I could pull tight around me.

I looked out as we buzzed New York City—I loved that view. Maybe this wouldn't be the worst summer of my life. Maybe the city would make up for my friends and starting my internship and swim team. Maybe I could wrangle a scholarship to a school in New York—college with Jenn was an old dream of ours, so maybe I'd get myself a little closer to that.

Heck, maybe pigs would fly. What did I know, right?

Earth

11 Doors

AT THE TOP OF the brown-gray stone steps, my aunt held open the huge, brick-red wooden door for me. I hesitated and looked at her.

"Go on in, Rose."

"This isn't your house, Aunt Mina." This place was all rough-hewn stone and stained glass and huge. Their place was smaller, just a floor in a brownstone on another street.

Mina shrugged and smiled, "You haven't visited in a while."

That was true, but no one told me they'd gotten rich. I walked past the front door into this little room where piles of shoes were jumbled in baskets and some mail was on the floor.

"It's fine, Rose." Mina bent to pick up the envelopes, her dark, bobbed hair hiding her eyes momentarily, "You can take your shoes off if you want. It's not a rule, but most people like to. It's quieter on the wood floors."

I nodded and slipped my flip-flops—Official Footwear of Tucson—into a large, woven basket. I heard Mina shuffle her shoes off behind me as we passed through another heavy wooden doorway, this one with a huge, leaded, clear glass window, and entered a darkish hallway, punctuated with blotches of blue and green from the stained glass half-moon window over the outer door.

While my eyes adjusted, I cautiously put my bag down in the entryway between the heavy oak stairs and an antique umbrella-holder-chair-mirror thing. It looked as though it might walk off, like one of the furniture people in *Beauty and the Beast*. It was big, but way more delicate than the chunkier antiques I was used to in Arizona. Lots of scrollwork, fiddly bits, and little metal coat hooks that looked like animal paws. I loved it.

Letting go of my bag was a relief. The flight had been easy, LaGuardia a nightmare. In the airport, Mina had laughed when she—finally—found me. "I know, they should hang a giant banner that says, 'Welcome to New York!' with a picture of a hand holding up its middle finger."

The cab ride from the airport wasn't much help in calming my nerves either. Mina apologized that my Uncle Bill had the van, but didn't seem to mind the seven or eight times that our cab driver aimed us at railings, pilings, support beams, pedestrians, and once at a police car. I have never been happier to emerge from a mode of transportation in one piece—and that included being in the car when Lindy drove. But here, in this gorgeous, old stone house, I started to breathe at last and look around.

The room to the left lurked behind enormous, wooden, sliding doors that were partway open. Embedded in the doors and over the doorway were panels of clear and frosted glass. Misty light sifted through them, dim, cool and dreamy. It reminded me of the doors of the rich girls' houses in Sam Spade or Marlowe movies—breakable, beautiful, and beaucoup bucks.

I whistled, "You live *here*?"

The furniture looked like something out of British movies—all dark wood and rich colors, gold and red velvet, actual color on the walls. No thick white adobe windowsills with avocado seeds perched recklessly in jars of water. These windows were framed by long, dark wooden columns with embedded shutters that matched. Scrollwork, marble tops, orchids, lion's foot chair legs, and converted porcelain lamps filled the room. I turned to Mina and she pointed down the hall towards the back of the house where there were more doors.

"You live here too, for now. Go on. Go in," Aunt Mina said cheerfully. "Look around."

Mina told me at the airport that we had to wait "to have our talk" until we got inside, here. But all of the other questions fighting to reach the front of my brain drifted away as soon as I crossed that threshold. I didn't climb the heavy wooden stairs that hugged the wall on the right, a thick burgundy-patterned carpet running up them, inviting. Instead I slunk past a phone table nestled in a shallow alcove under the stairs and headed to the back of the house, as Mina had instructed.

I felt alien here. Like I didn't want to take up too much space.

As I passed the phone, I noticed a smallish door. I pointed and asked over my shoulder, "Harry Potter?"

"Basement," Mina smiled. "No orphan wizards. Sorry."

I pointed into the next small room, "*Godfather*?"

Mina laughed. The open door had revealed a marble-countered, black and white, hexagonal-tiled bathroom. Aside from the lack of blood on the floor it looked like a scene from Coppola's opus—one of my Dad's favorites.

To my left, across from the bathroom, another door opened to a formal dining room. "You eat there?" I asked.

Mina nodded.

"There are . . . how many people live here?" The table was big, sturdy, long and well-loved—like those chunky antiques in Tucson.

"Enough," Mina smiled.

I walked to the end of the hall, pushed open a half-closed door, and blinked in the bright and sunny kitchen. I turned to Mina. "Aunt Mina, you understand that if my mother were here, she would either publicly fall on her knees and thank God for this kitchen or have a contract put out on you so she could have it."

"Or both," Mina laughed.

There was a large central island with a sink, second stovetop, and facing counter with stools for three. Butcher block slabs were firmly nestled into the sparkling counter tops on the island and on the regular counter too. There was a huge restaurant-size stove/oven monster with a griddle, six burners, and a warming oven. A deep multiple-basin sink faced the windows at the back end of the room.

I couldn't fathom how long—in feet or meters—this house had to be front to back. It didn't seem possible in a city like Brooklyn. Long and lived-in. And it smelled good.

There was a large pot of something heavenly softly simmering on a back burner. I breathed in deeply and sighed.

"Jewish penicillin," my aunt smiled, coming in behind me, "It'll be good for you to have some soup after being in that airplane air this whole time. It's a wonder anyone survives."

"It wasn't that bad," I said automatically, and gazed around the rest of the room. The windows looking onto a backyard deck and a green garden below were tall, the top half leaded and etched. At the base of these bay windows was a richly padded window seat that had arrived straight from *Pride and Prejudice*.

It was heaven.

What I whispered: "I'm going to live here?"

What I thought: *I'm in a different century.*

My aunt chuckled, "And you haven't even seen your room yet."

Mina gently pulled my sleeve and I followed her to the stairs. We started up, passing the second floor. "Our room." She pointed at the large bedroom at the back of the house as we climbed on, passing other rooms, continuing up to the third floor. She nodded her head at a door in the middle of the landing. "Toilet, shower." She pointed at the stairs up to another floor. "My studio's up there." Then, ignoring the closed door to our left at the front end of the house, she pushed open the door on the right, revealing a back bedroom that looked down on the garden. It, too, had a bay window, though of a normal height, and a window seat. There were two beds. The one closest to the door had my bags on it. I started to ask her about how they got there when she interrupted.

"This is your bed. You'll share the room with Jennifer. Towels are there, and this is yours," she pointed at the wooden armoire.

"You're serious?"

"Well, there aren't any closets in these rooms. Taxes used to be calculated by number of rooms—and closets counted as rooms. So."

"So I have a wardrobe."

"So you have a wardrobe," she agreed.

"I can deal with that."

"Good." Mina hesitated, like she was about to say something different, then said, "Well, I'm sure you'd like some time to put your things away and relax a bit. Come downstairs when you're ready and we'll have a late lunch."

"I ate on the plane."

"That's not eating," Mina looked disappointed, "that's sustenance. Here, we eat."

I smiled. "Okay. I'll be down in a sec."

"Don't rush." I heard that hesitation in her voice again, ". . . Okay. I'll see you downstairs."

I nodded and turned back to the room as Mina closed the door. What I wanted to do as soon as I was alone was jump up and down on the bed like a kid. It looked so big and fluffy and it was mine. I almost forgot everything I'd sacrificed for a summer of puffed up mattress space and an armoire.

Almost.

But not quite.

12 DRAWERS

I TOOK MY TIME putting my things in drawers and hanging them in the wardrobe. Normally, I'm not this meticulous, but the place kind of demanded attention. I wanted to talk to Jenn and ask her all the things I didn't want to ask Aunt Mina. I looked at her side of the room—neat as a pin—and saw that she had books open on her desk. Mina didn't say anything about her taking summer classes. Maybe that's where my cousin was right now. I glanced at the open page as I put jeans on a hanger. Looked like Shakespeare to me. As I put my journal and pens away in the small desk at the head of my bed, I saw that Jenn had left me a note. *So glad you're here, Rosie! Can't wait to catch up!* Some people use exclamation points when they write. Jenn uses them when she talks. I wasn't surprised to see them on her note.

Jenn and I had always gotten along. She was only a couple of months older and I know sometimes that leads to fighting, but it couldn't have been better between us. Being 3,000 miles or so apart, we didn't see each other all that often, but when we did get to spend time together, it was like we'd seen each other just the day before. Some of this might have been because we spent all of our summers and holidays together when we were little—less of late.

See, my generation of our family is all mixed up. Some are Jewish, some are converts, some never converted but decided to raise the kids Jewish, some are

65

flat-out confused. So December was always especially interesting. My Mom and her sister both celebrate Christmas the same way that some people celebrate Thanksgiving—an excuse to decorate the house, fill the air with heavenly smells, and make a ton of really good food. I remember being surprised—when I was old enough to get it—that it was a religious holiday season at all. It always seemed like family time for us and nothing more.

When everyone got together during winter break it was generally a gift-giving-food-eating orgy. And fun. Always fun. If Hanukkah happened to fall during the break, then there was extra excitement. Candles, prayers, dreidels, latkes, and of course, arguments over whether it was kosher to use a Cuisinart to shred the potatoes or whether latkes needed to be made entirely by hand—(I am firmly pro-mechanical device, but anti-unnecessary-technology. I haven't yet figured out how that one works with making latkes, but I'm sure it'll come to me).

Anyway, that's the long version of explaining that we all got along. So, it was nice to see Mina and it was going to be great to spend time with Jenn. I certainly got along with her better than I did with my real sister. But this didn't mean I'd taken Mom off my "list"—she needed to suffer a little more from the pain of my cold shoulder.

I finished setting up my desk right around the time the hungry stomach shakes caught up with me. Maybe Aunt Mina was right—too much lousy plane food. Or not enough. I went to the bathroom to wash airport grime off as best as I could, then headed downstairs to see what Aunt Mina had concocted. Half-way down, I remembered and went back to the bedroom to grab my knitting, then trotted breathlessly down the stairs, sliding my hand along the waxy-smooth banister rails all the way.

My aunt was making sandwiches to go with the soup, and smiled as I walked in. "Find everything okay?"

"Yep . . . at least, I think I did. Hey, is Jenn in summer school?"

She watched the bread as she carefully cut the sandwiches in diagonal halves, her bobbed hair sifting down the side of her face, hiding her eyes from me. "No. Why?"

"Dunno," I shrugged and put my knitting bag next to me on the counter. "She had some pretty hefty books open on her desk. It looked like she was studying."

"Ah. Well, no, she's not in *official* summer school, but we have a kind of summer program here for some kids."

I nodded lamely, the way polite people do when they don't know how much they're supposed to understand in a conversation but don't want to ask anything yet. I'm a pro.

She handed me my sandwich and a mug of soup, and started to sip her own, leaning back on the counter. I set my sandwich at one of the stools and sat so I could face her as I ate, waiting for her to enlighten me, as promised. I thought I'd been terrifically patient so far.

She passed me a glass of water and I mumbled a "thank you." Then my mouth froze—I stopped mid-chew. She had made my favorite sandwich: tuna, Miracle Whip, sweet pickle relish, lettuce, a thin layer of yellow mustard on one slice of bread and—the secret and belovéd trashy *coup de grace*—a few crunchy potato chips hidden inside. My eyes must've been bugging.

"You made my favorite?" I said covering my mouth. I think it sounded more like *yaw maw ma fahwit.*

Mina smiled sweetly at me. "Is something wrong?" she asked, all innocence, but there was laughter behind her eyes.

"Did Mom tell you?"

She shook her head and laughed lightly, but didn't answer directly, "I imagine you have a few questions about why you're here. Right. No need to glare. I know. Your mother told me you were a little angry about this."

I swallowed my bite of heaven, "That, Aunt Mina, is an understatement."

"I hope you find a way to enjoy your summer."

"It's not like that. I love you and Jenn and Uncle Bill. It's just—"

"Well let's start with what your mom *did* tell you?"

My shoulders drooped, "That I had to come here to be safe."

I listened to Mina finish a bite.

"That's *all* she told you?" Mina sounded surprised after she swallowed. Then she sighed, and hopped up onto the counter behind her like my mom does. Boy, every once in a while you could really tell they were sisters.

She looked up at the ceiling fan for a long minute. Long enough that I glanced up too while I was chewing. I didn't see anything worth looking at, though I was impressed at the size of the fan blades. Our ceiling fans at home are smaller and—to be honest—older and probably cheaper than the, oh, I'd say Cessna-sized propellers that cycled above our heads.

Okay, that's an exaggeration. But you get the idea.

When she spoke, Mina's voice was different. There was no lightness behind it now. "Well, I'm sorry your mother didn't tell you more, but I know she gets a little . . . over-wrought about these things. Before I explain, you should know that your mom knows all this. And your dad does, too," she hesitated. "So does your uncle and so do all the kids who are staying here. So it's fine to talk to them about it . . . but no one else. No one outside. Got it, kiddo?"

I nodded and shuddered, not liking the sound of this.

"All your parents said was that you would be safe here, eh?"

"Yeah. I mean, they all said it was safer for me and for . . . everyone . . . for me to be here."

"Do you have any idea *why* that might be?"

"Because my mom thinks that I broke my water glass."

Mina looked at me, waiting. I looked back and didn't blink. Finally she sighed, "Rosie. You're smarter than that."

I shrugged and took another bite. "How about you tell me, then."

She talked to me like I was two. "Isn't there anything, Rose, in the past few days that stands out as a little . . . odd to you?"

"No."

"Rose," she was waiting for me, but I didn't feel like playing. "Rosie, you're not going to shock me . . . or make me laugh."

I sighed. It wasn't like I could run anywhere. I was a bug in a jar. "You mean stuff like Mom thinks I lit my ex-boyfriend on fire from across the roof."

"And *did* you light your ex-boyfriend on fire from across the roof?"

"No!" Mina looked at me, making me feel like I was made out of spun sugar. Nothing but fluff. I caved, "Maybe?"

With patience in her voice, "Well, if it's 'maybe' then your parents were right to send you here."

I looked up at her, "Why? You can stop me from blow-torching people? You run a home for abandoned freaks?"

"You're not a freak, Rosie. Or abandoned. You're gifted."

"Riiiight. Can I have the return slip?"

"Yes." She didn't miss a beat. "But you'll regret it. You're . . . you're going to find out all sorts of wonderful things about what you can do while you're here."

"Aunt Mina, no offense, but you sound like a Disney character."

Mina smiled a stomach-settling smile. "I probably do sound a little phony. I haven't given this talk to—well, to family in a very long time. However, it's important. I want you to be prepared when the troops return."

"Troops?" And there went my stomach again.

"Your parents really didn't tell you *any*thing?"

"They told me you'd tell me."

"Well, that was . . . convenient of them." Aunt Mina drummed her fingers on the counter top then lasered in on me. "When did you first realize you knew things other kids didn't."

I stared at her with my best blank stare. "I have no idea what you're talking about."

"Rosie, you may as well get used to it now. You can't lie here. It won't work."

"I'm not lying."

"The sooner you master everything you came here to learn the sooner you get back to your internship and friends. So. Again. When did you first realize you knew things other people didn't."

The bug feeling returned. "About second grade, I guess."

Mina's eyebrows lifted. "Hm. Early. And when did you first notice things around you behaving . . . oddly sometimes?"

"Odd like..?"

She clarified slowly, "Odd like moving, or disappearing, then showing up again?"

I felt the color rise in my cheeks, "Oh . . . um . . . not much after that, I guess."

Mina looked like she was trying not to laugh, "And didn't you think that was a bit . . . odd?"

"I guess," I squirmed, "but I was little and I never did stuff like that on purpose and . . . and I guess . . . I got used to seeing it happen? Maybe?"

Mina nodded microscopically. "Well, now you'll have a chance to get used to controlling it better."

"*That's* what I'm here for?"

Mina nodded. "We have a kind of summer camp here. There are three other kids, all learning to control and refine their gifts. And another friend of mine joins in from time to time to keep her skills up and help me with training."

"So, Jenn, and . . . ?"

"Oh, no. Jenn's just along for the ride. She doesn't really have a gift for most of these abilities. She can block and read cards, things anyone could do, but that's about it. She's very tolerant and understanding about what Bill and I are doing, though."

"So, what *are* you doing, exactly? You hold class?"

"That, my dear, is a conversation for later. Your eyes are drooping. I think you need a nap."

I yawned. Which was funny because I hadn't felt all that sleepy before. "Yeah, a nap does sound good." I picked up my knitting and started to walk towards the stairs when Mina called after me.

"The light up there is wonderful for reading, especially on the window seat. Have a nap and come down when you're rested. We'll all have dinner together."

" 'Kay." Then I turned back, remembering, "Aunt Mina?"

She looked up.

"Am I . . . I don't want to . . . I *can't* hurt you or Jenn or Uncle Bill, can I?"

Mina smiled a sad smile, "This place—this house—may be the only place where you can't hurt anyone . . . at least not until you learn more." She winked. "We're all pretty strong here, and good at deflecting trouble. And the house itself is protected. So, don't worry about us. Just concentrate on learning as much as you can. As fast as you can." She added.

I nodded and turned away again.

"Oh, and Rosie? House rules. Aside from the obvious clean-up-after-yourself and bring-your-laundry-down-to-the-basement sorts of things—don't swear in the house."

"Aunt Mina . . . "

"No, it's important. I mean that both ways—don't call on God—or gods for that matter—" Mina smiled at herself, "—to take your side in *anything*. But also don't use curse words. Especially not in the house. It fights against some of the protections we've put in place . . . but . . . you know what? That's probably too much information, too. For now, go upstairs and rest for a bit."

Up in the room, I grabbed my backpack and a book about Brooklyn from Jenn's shelf and climbed onto the window seat cushion — not as soft as it looked. I needed to do something to help ease the ache of missing Lindy. And Rob. I put my knitting on the other side of the long bench, then I took the book, my journal, and pen and put them next to me, arranging my legs and leaning back onto the window frame. I was sure this looked more charming and graceful than it felt—it always seemed so attractive in those old movies—Empire waists, ringlets, sighing heroines palming a delicate book of verse from the safety of the window seat. However, in the real world, the frame pressed into my back at an odd angle and the seat cushion wasn't cushiony enough. But the view of the many backyards was kind of amazing and made the discomfort worth it. To the left I could see a patch of tree-lined street poking through the backyard trees. To the right, all the brownstone buildings had little rectangular gardens, each separated by fences of various natures. Some families had clearly put a lot of time and effort into their yards, placing flagstones, statuary, fountains, furniture, even gazeboes back there. But my aunt's backyard put them all to shame.

I felt my eyelids drooping, but I couldn't stop staring. Mina and Bill's yard was—there was no other word for it—magical. Even in the daylight. Looking down I could see unlit twinkle lights nestled into tree branches and climbing vines dripping with long clusters of purple flowers crawling off the wooden deck. Varieties of blossoms that we didn't get in Arizona surrounded the brick patio that housed a long wooden table and chairs. Sturdy, but beautiful. There were lanterns hanging there too. I wondered what the place looked like at night. It looked like a lot of work to light all the lanterns.

All the green, however, made me remember my bug spray. I'm crazy allergic to mosquito bites and anytime I'm around humidity I have to slather myself with bug juice to keep myself itch-free. The bites don't itch on my skin. They itch *in* my skin. Nothing helps. Nothing. Thinking of humidity made me think about the heat. It was hot outside, and humid. But it was comfortable in our room . . . a room at the top of the stairs . . . at the top of the house . . . where heat rises . . . and sits, and makes me miserable. The house was so old, I was sure it didn't have central air. So I looked from my vantage and, sure enough, could see no vents.

There was plenty I had to learn.

I rubbed the sides of my head and picked up the book—good for disengagement.

It didn't work, but I was getting used to the strangeness of the seat and the pages looked pretty. Then, they didn't look at all. And then I was asleep with no hint in my mind that the entire trajectory of my life had taken a sharp turn, separating me from everything I'd ever known.

13 SHIELDS

A COMMOTION WOKE ME, but I couldn't process the noises I was hearing. I winced. Opening my eyes in the fading light, I was surprised to be slumped at an uncomfortable angle, with my cheek against the middle pane of the back window. A blob of drool rolled down the glass. I quickly wiped at it with my shirt, which didn't help at all. I sat up, rubbing my eyes with the heels of both hands.

About then, everything came zipping back to me.

I was in Brooklyn. I was also psychic, according to my aunt, I was dangerous, according to my nuclear family, and something was happening downstairs.

I knew that last bit because it was noisy, not because I could see through the floor or anything.

I wobbled to the shoebox—I mean bathroom—in the hall, splashed water on my face, ran my fingers through my tangled hair and found it sticking to my neck. I went back to the bedroom to grab a banana clip from my bag, twisting up my hair to free my neck from its oppression as I headed downstairs.

I heard distinct voices long before I reached the bottom of the staircase. I definitely recognized my cousin Jennifer's voice. She was laughing, which was pretty normal. There was a male voice and two other female voices, one of them accented and melodic. And I could hear my Aunt every so often.

I found it ironic that they were talking about freak shows.

"I don't get why they can't do it anymore."

"Justin, that's horrible," my aunt said, but I could tell she was trying not to laugh.

"It's not horrible." His voice mocked, "We all have *gifts*."

"You *belong* in a freak show."

"Jealous?"

"Yeah, right."

" '*Ello . . . we* were there. It's not as tho' it was freak-*less* . . . " said the accented voice.

"We weren't in a *show*, though, right?"

"There's a movie about freaks coming out in August—*Bubble Boy*, with some phat guy in it," from the male voice.

"Show off . . . "

"I'm just sayin' . . . "

"What*ever* . . . "

"Shhhh!"

As I passed the hall phone they all stopped talking. If everyone in the next room had taken a breath at the same moment and were waiting to exhale on cue, it couldn't have sounded weirder. I stopped dead. Hours must have passed while I stood like an ice sculpture, unsure of what to do. It crossed my mind that I could go back upstairs and wait for Jenn, but that was stupid. They knew I was there, so I walked in.

My aunt was back up on the counter, smiling at the group of kids. They were all looking, waiting. My aunt raised an eyebrow, "Good nap, kiddo?"

It took me a sec to realize she was speaking to me. I nodded, then she cleared her throat and said, "Rose. I need to introduce you around. You know Jennifer." There was a momentary pause, then sweet-faced Jenn said, "Oh duh!"

and made a bee line to give me a hug. "I so would not have recognized you. Look at your hair!" She looked around my back, prodding at the clip on my head, "Man, it's gotta be down to your butt now!"

A little shorter than me, but not by much, Jenn held me out to look at me from the front like a discriminating artist. She started to say something, then shook her head and hugged me again.

I hugged her back and said softly, so only she could hear me, "I'm glad you're here." Jenn pulled back again and looked at me more pointedly. She looked softer than the last time I saw her. With her peaches-and-cream face, the opposite of my freckled one, we made a funny-looking team. I still have no idea where her coloring came from, but it wasn't a bottle. Both her mom and her dad, Bill, had dark hair like me, though I had more red in mine than they did. Jenn's hair was both blonde and straight. Super straight, kind of like Lindy's. It's good there was so much to like about them, because that hair could have been a friendship deal-breaker on someone else.

Finally, she smiled again and squeezed my shoulder.

Mina broke in, indicating, "And this is Jasmine."

"It's lovely to meet you." The accented voice drifted over smiling to shake my hand. She was lovely. Ethereal. Unreal.

"Jasmine doesn't live here," Mina continued, "but she does study with us. She's the friend I told you about who helps me with training when she can."

"But not as much as I'd like to," Jasmine smiled.

"Hey, Jasmine," I couldn't do better than a whisper. She was more—I don't know—more solid than the rest. She didn't look that much older, but that could have been because her skin was that smooth cafe latte color that never seems to age.

"Sometimes when I'm over to help, I bring my son, Tyrik. I'll make sure you meet him soon."

"Is he a . . ."

"No, he's like me," Jenn smiled. "Riding shotgun. Jazz is the real deal."

"Jazz?"

Jasmine smiled at me, "The children call me Jazz." Hearing her call them "children" didn't sound like an insult. It sounded like a compliment—like it was the best thing you could be. "But the adults still call me Jasmine."

She didn't look like a Jazz to me. She was graceful and lithe, the way I'd imagined an elf in *Lord of the Rings*. I wanted to be her.

"Hi there! I'm Izzy and that's Justin," bleated a tiny, smiling blue-haired girl, bouncing on the arm of the couch and pointing at the head of the thin, African-American boy next to her. He smacked at her hand. Gently. Playing.

"Isobel, please don't break the couch," my aunt sighed. Izzy tried to stop, though her spiky blue hair, pointing in every direction, looked like it might be the source of her energy. A bouncing blue nuclear plant. Next to her, Justin rolled his eyes and flipped a delicate hand my way once in greeting. "Hey." He sounded bored.

"Hi . . . " I smiled and my face froze in that position. Justin wouldn't stop squinting at me. I squirmed until he spoke again. "So welcome to Brooklyn . . . Weej!" He doubled over in laughter.

Jenn looked at Izzy, "What'd he say?" Izzy shrugged. Jasmine turned to the windows, her hand over her mouth, while my aunt growled Justin's name.

I looked at my aunt, "You *told* them?"

She shook her head. "I said nothing. If Justin pulled a memory from you, then you've just had your first lesson."

"Great teaching method," I grumbled.

"Don't look like that," Mina said gently. "It *is* why you're here."

"Yeah," my temples started to pulse so I reached up to rub them. "Right. You're supposed to teach me a lesson."

"Not like that—" Mina started when Justin interrupted.

"Um, Mina," he said, sounding like the smart kid in class that everyone hated — the one who asked questions to show that he already knew the answers. "Why *is* she here, again?" He looked straight at her, challenging—like an equal, not a student. She stared him down and eventually he looked away, sucking his teeth.

"Hey, Rose . . . why don't I help you unpack."

I started to tell Jenn that I'd already unpacked, but even coming from my sweet cousin, it was obviously not a request.

"That's a great idea." Mina sounded happier than she appeared. She was still scowling at Justin.

Jenn took my hand gently. "Come on. I want to hear about your trip and . . . whoa . . . when was the last time you were here? So much has happened . . . "

I let Jenn pull me along, but kept my eyes on the people in that room as long as I could. Izzy's face was almost a blank now, like she was looking inside rather than at me. Jasmine had turned back, smiling, and waved lightly at me. Mina appeared to be having a silent conversation with Justin, and it didn't look like a happy one.

Good.

But if I thought today would be my worst day with Justin, I was so wrong.

14 Ps and Qs

JENN AND I SAT upstairs and talked, catching up on the last couple of years—school, boys, music, movies, books. The nutshell: she liked school; she didn't have a boyfriend; she was saving for an iPod thing; they don't have cable but they rent movies; she's read anything and everything written before 1950 due to a competition she had with a friend at school during freshman year. Her favorite book was *Phantom of the Opera*, with *Pride and Prejudice* running a close second. She filled me in a little—not a lot—on this summer camp thing my aunt and uncle were doing. She was very blasé about it, but I kept thinking it must be weird living in a house of psychics when you weren't one of them. She made excuses for Justin, but said Izzy and Jasmine were wonderful, though Jasmine's Wall Street job kept her busy most of the time. Izzy and Justin, however, were good friends and messing with that wasn't a good idea.

"I wasn't going to mess with anything," I defended myself.

"Oh, I know you wouldn't do anything on purpose, but Justin," she picked up a pillow from the foot of her bed and hugged it, "Justin's had a harder time adjusting. Izzy's what grounds him."

"What does that mean?"

"She keeps him . . . here. It's hard for them, doing this kind of work. It's easy to get lost in the psychic stuff and . . . stay there. Izzy gives him a place to come back to. Most people who deal with this craziness need a ground. Otherwise they don't last long."

"Like what? You mean they die?"

"N-no, I mean it's hard work."

"It's hard work reading people's minds?" It was hard not to sound sarcastic.

"No, it's hard work protecting yourself."

I put my knitting down in my lap. "Jenn. What am I doing here?"

"You're . . . you're going to learn stuff."

"Stuff."

"Well, this all kind of runs in our family."

"But not you?"

Jenn shrugged. "I got the blonde hair instead?" It came out as a question.

I laughed. "Interesting choice. Be psychic or be blonde." Jenn laughed too. "And you're okay with it . . . with not being . . . "

"I'm happy to be normal," Jenn smiled. "But, you know, normal's tricky too."

"Right. But normal folks don't have to protect themselves."

"Well, sure they do. It's always a good idea to know how to protect yourself."

"So this is all psychic *tae kwan do*?"

"Sort of," Jenn looked at the floor. "Okay, so look. Imagine you can see the future, and people know that."

"Imagine?"

"Right, well, okay, then. Doesn't that cause trouble for you?"

"No . . . I . . . "

"Honestly, Rose. Do your friends at home *really* understand?"

I had to start facing this, didn't I? "No. No, they don't really understand."

"And it's scary to know sometimes."

"Yes."

"And sometimes what you see is pretty awful."

I felt tears building up behind my brain, "Yes."

"Okay, now imagine all of that, but imagine that you can read minds too, or talk to dead people, or know when people are going to die and how it will happen as soon as you meet them, or that every time you meet someone new you know all their darkest secrets."

"Oh."

"Right? So that's why sometimes we—they—*you* might need someone who gets you. Or maybe you're lucky enough to find someone who understands but who also has a grounding effect on you. Like a lightning rod. They help you find a better place to put the hard stuff."

"Will I need . . . "

"Dunno, Rosie," she shrugged, "I'm not part of the psychic posse. It's possible."

"And really? You don't mind? Not being psychic. In the middle of all of this?"

"Smoke crack much?" Jenn laughed. "I really, truly like being normal. Not to be harsh, but have you ever met a happy psychic?"

"I don't think I've ever met a psychic. I mean, before today."

"Hm." Jenn said, looking out the window. "I'll just say 'I don't envy you' and let it go at that. One of mom's big goals is to make sure that y'all can be happy."

"So this isn't Hogwarts."

"It so isn't Hogwarts. And you're not Harry Potter."

"Bummer."

"I know, right?"

"I was looking forward to the Chocolate Frogs."

Jenn laughed, then got serious. "It's going to be okay, Rosie. But mom's worried that you're fighting yourself. You know, that you're so unhappy that—"

"She told you?"

"About this—"

"I'm not fighting myself."

"You are. *She* thinks you are. You're . . . you're still back in Tucson. It's all you're thinking about."

"So? So I got here today! I miss my friends. Is that bad?"

Jenn sighed. "It's not that. It's . . . the way you almost came back upstairs instead of meeting everyone. The way you reacted when Justin pulled the memory."

"Well, how was I supposed to react?"

"Ask how he did it? Ask to be shown, so you can do it to?"

"Dude, it's my first day!"

"I know, I'm just sayin.'"

I took a breath to respond but changed topics. Jenn and I hadn't ever had a conversation this serious and it was bugging me.

"Hey, I keep forgetting to ask, did you live in this place when I was here before?"

Jenn seemed happy enough for the change, "Oh, no. That move was a while ago. Dad got lucky and the theater did really well."

"That old theater in the city you guys were always working on?"

"That one."

"Sold it?"

"Naw. That show *Bash!* with all the drums and trash can lids and stuff."

"No idea."

"Well, anyway. The show did really well. This is the house that *Bash!* built."

"Cool."

"I know, right? So we were able to move to this place right before everyone started showing up for boot camp."

"How long ago was that?"

"Oh, a few years. I like this block much better, too. Better stores, closer bagels—the important stuff."

I had so many more questions I needed to ask Jenn. But eventually, we were drawn downstairs for dinner by the most amazing smells. Food awaited us in a warm oven, though we were the only ones eating together.

When I emerged from the bathroom that night, Jenn was in bed reading with her little nightlight aimed over her shoulder. She smiled and waved her fingertips at me, but went back to reading. I climbed on my bed and sat there for a minute. I was tired. God knows I hadn't slept much the night before—and the nap hadn't really helped either—but I felt restless. I leaned over on my desk and got my journal and pen.

Dear Lindy,

Well, here I am in Brooklyn. My aunt's place is different from the one I came to when I was a kid, so I have new digs to learn. It's awesome though. Huge. Looks like a movie set. You would love it, but you'd be bummed Cary Grant didn't live here with you.

The flight was fine, though Drew's Watchmen was nearly hijacked by a cute-but-dumb guy. Don't worry. I was brave and got it back. Don't tell Drew. He'll get ticked that I risked his Precious at all.

I miss you.

This really sucks and I hate being here.

Come rescue me?

I left the letter in my journal.

That night, I slept like the dead.

15 Pitching

IN THE MORNING, I rolled over to see Jenn's bed already made. I noticed that I couldn't hear anyone on our floor. I found clothes, grabbed my towel, and took a quick shower. I pinned up my dripping hair and got dressed, trying to find myself in the foggy mirror. I felt tiny trickles of water break away down my back every so often under my shirt. It felt good.

As I reached the last bit of staircase, I knew—without seeing—where everyone was on the main floor. Jenn was in the front room, Mina and Justin were in the back. Izzy was at the bottom of the stairs holding the phone.

"Good timing," Izzy smiled, holding her hand over the receiver. "It's Tucson."

My first reaction was to feel sick. Second, I shook my head. "I'm not here," I whispered to Izzy.

"Yes, you are," she fake-whispered back to me. "I already said you were coming down."

I swallowed and took the phone. Izzy walked to the other room where Jenn was, giving me space.

"Hello?" I had to clear my throat to get it out.

"Rosie? OhMawGaw! Where are you?" Lindy was breathless, "I tried to call your cell thing yesterday and I left messages but you didn't call back. I called your house yesterday and Chloe told me you were gone. What the hell? Why did you go? Did you make it? Are you okay? How were the planes? Was it all weird flying alone?"

"Breathe much?"

"Ha. Seriously. I didn't get up at, like OhMyGodO'Clock to get a dose of your lovely sarcasm. C'mon Rosie, how is it? How's your aunt's place? Why all the mystery? Whatsup?"

"Um. Things are good. The phone is in the front hall."

"Okaaaayyy. Oh, *I* get it. You can't talk."

"Yes."

"Okay. Well. Blink once for yes and—wait, that won't work. Cough once for yes and twice for no."

Cough.

"Right. Good. Okay. So you made it to Brooklyn."

Cough.

"Was the flight okay?"

Cough.

"Chloe wouldn't tell me why you were gone."

I didn't know how to answer that. I guessed. *Cough.*

"Wait," Lindy mused, "That means yes . . . yes, Chloe wouldn't tell me?

Cough.

"Okaaayyy. Can you tell me? I mean when everyone's not around? Rosie? You there?"

Cough.

"Oh good. I thought I'd lost you."

Cough cough.

"So, how about I write you? Then you can write me back since people are listening. I mean, people are listening, right?"

Cough.

"Well, that bites. But I'll write you a really fabulous letter, maybe even with a calligraphy pen. You'll write back, right?"

Cough.

"You probably could have said the answer to that one."

"Yes, Lin. I'll write you."

"Good. And, um. Rosie . . . are you okay?"

"Yeah. Fine. Why?"

Lindy paused and I knew she was trying to figure out how to ask. "Nothing. No reason. I'll get the letter in the mail today."

"Okay," I said. Then quietly, "I miss you, Lin."

"Me too. I have a million questions, but I'll put them in the letter."

"Okay."

"Okay, well . . . later."

"Bye."

Dazed, I walked into the kitchen.

"Morning, sunshine!" Mina greeted me at the kitchen door.

"Hi." You wouldn't think it would be jarring moving from Loud Lindy to Perky Polly in the kitchen, but it was. Mina was too chatty and I wasn't into it.

"Breakfast is in the oven, or if you prefer, cereals are in that cupboard."

I peeked in the oven—pancakes and bacon. What's not to love?

"Turkey bacon," she said.

"Huh?"

Mina smiled, "Bill's turkey bacon—"

"Uncle Bill is here? Where?" I looked around.

"He's up at summer stock. He'll be back. Awhile ago, he got obsessed with this bacon. He found a farmer up in Massachusetts who cures it himself. Bill's got a freezer down in his study, and I'm rather certain that if there's ever an emergency, we could live for at least six months on his bacon supply. He's excited that you're new blood—everyone else is getting a little sick of it."

"No, I like it. That's cool," I smiled, making myself a plate and taking it around to the side of the island with the bar stools.

"How did you sleep?" Mina was wiping down every counter surface she could reach. Picking up the countertop appliances as she went. Nervous energy?

"Okay."

"The bed okay?"

"Yeah, it's great." I could tell that Justin was sitting off to my left somewhere, but I wasn't exactly sure where. And I didn't want to look.

"Did you have a nice talk with Jenn?"

"Yeah. Sure. Look, Aunt Mina—"

"I know," she cut me off. "I should have anticipated something like that. Justin's a tease and took advantage of your newcomer status."

Now that she was talking openly about Justin, I turned to look. I could see him through the huge bay window. He was reading on the back deck, drinking a glass of juice with his feet up on the railing.

"So," Mina continued, "we're going to start over again this morning. We'll teach you to block and shield first. That way, you won't be vulnerable to anymore attacks . . . from Justin, or . . . "

"Or?"

Mina turned to open the fridge, "We have three different juices. Do you want orange, apple, or cranberry?"

"Cranberry. Or what? What other kinds of 'attacks' on me are you expecting, Aunt Mina?"

Jenn walked in. "Hey Sleepy McSleepster." She walked to her mom and grabbed the orange juice right before the refrigerator door closed. "You were dead this morning."

"Time change," Mina said.

"Probably," I agreed. The bacon was really good. I could see why Uncle Bill was obsessed. I picked up another piece. I was still bothered by what Mina had almost said. I wanted to think it through, but she and Jenn kept interrupting my flow.

"I think I only had a time change problem that first time we went to England, right, Mom?"

"Oh! Yes, I'd forgotten. Oh, she was sick for a week, Rosie. It was awful."

"I hope that doesn't happen to you."

I watched them work off each other, moving around the kitchen like dancers. It took all my focus to follow how they kept me distracted, which drove me nuts.

Jenn must have noticed, because she asked, "You done eating? I wanted to show you this book I'm reading before we start." Without time to take a breath, she'd swept me up and walked me—grabbing for my last piece of bacon—into the front parlor, while Mina nodded at me with a smile and swiped my plate and silverware.

Izzy was lying on one of the couches, writing something in a little journal. Jenn's open book was sitting on the other couch, face down. Moving it, she sat and patted the seat next to her. As I sat, she leaned over, conspiratorially, "Try not to get on Justin today."

"Wha—?"

"He's just . . . he's sensitive is all. He doesn't want his status usurped. He's used to being the baby—"

"I don't want to be the baby!"

"I know, but when Mom told—"

"Okay, everyone," Mina entered the room followed by Justin. "Rosie needs to learn the basics before we do anything else, and Justin, since you're our best blocker—and as a way to show your support for our newest camper—would you like to fill her in?" Mina looked pointedly at Justin. Her question was a not-well-disguised command. He sat down, spine straight, looking very prim, and spoke like a kindergarten teacher.

"First, do no harm."

"I thought that was for doctors," I interrupted. So sue me. He already drove me nuts.

As though on cue, the phone rang. "Oh for the love of Bob," Mina muttered. "Keep going, you guys. I'll be right back."

Justin dropped the proper behavior act like a hot rock. "We have to live by that rule, too, girl." He turned his head dismissively, "*You* can't be too careful."

I started to say something, but Jenn rested her hand on mine and everything looked cool and blue and calm. *Mentholyptus* on the brain.

"Okay," I said from inside my ice-blue, watery landscape, "Sorry. Do no harm. Check."

"This isn't a game."

"I didn't say it was," the blue was fading fast.

"But you don't think you should follow the same rules as us—or be here at all, do you?" It felt like he was poking my chest with each word—picking a fight.

"No," I tried to find a way to say this that wouldn't make everyone else angry at me. "No, it's not that—"

"Cuz, girlfriend, you are broadcasting your feelings all over this room like you're freakin' Cokie Roberts on NPR." Okay, that impressed me. "Don't try to deny. We *all* know what you're thinking—"

"What Justin is trying to say," Izzy broke in as Mina re-entered and the blue calm resettled itself on my brain, "in that special way we all know and love," she glared at him, "is that you need to learn how to block. It's different when you're around muggles—"

"You're kidding, right?"

Izzy shrugged, shaking her head slightly, making her hair dance, "It's easier to talk about them like that. Especially in public. Anyway, when you're around muggles, you don't always have to worry so much about keeping yourself blocked from them. I mean, you'll learn to be able to tell when you have to worry and pull your shields up strong. But for now, you need to know that you're in a room full of people who can . . . well . . . tell what you're thinking."

"Oh my God," I whispered to myself as this sank in my thick skull.

Justin *tsked* at me.

"And you have to watch what you say," Aunt Mina added, sternly.

"What'd I say?" I looked at Jenn.

She leaned over and whispered in my ear, "You said 'oh my G—.'"

So I whispered back, though why I bothered is beyond me, since everyone already knew what I was thinking. "I can't say that?"

Jenn shook her head, "We can't curse at all."

"That's a curse?"

"In here it is," Izzy nodded.

"We don't make the rules," Jenn added. I looked at Mina. It occurred to me that she might not have made these rules either.

"Bill and the kids and I have worked hard," Mina began, "to make this house a . . . oh, what would you call it? A demilitarized zone? A safe house? You all are protected and able to learn here, but we also have to be sure that we don't do anything—accidentally or on purpose—that might weaken those barriers. We all have to watch what we say and do in here."

"It's not hard, Rose," Izzy smiled. "And if you mess up, there are lots of ways to clean it up and re-protect the house."

I nodded as if I understood, while inwardly trying to scream in my head at everyone to stay the heck out of my thoughts. Instead, I sighed from my teal-tinged outlook. "Okay," I said. "I guess I need to learn this blocking thing in a hurry. What do I do first?" I asked, looking to Justin as instructed.

Jenn squeezed my hand and smiled at me.

Justin sat up tall again. "First, you need to focus."

"On what?"

"On what I'm *telling you*. On keeping people out of your brain, girl!"

Izzy put her hand on Justin's arm as Mina shot him a momentary glance that could have melted rock. "Before you can learn to block, Rose, you need to recognize when someone's trying to get in. That way you'll know what to protect against." I could almost hear her add, *like Justin, for example*. But she didn't. Not out loud, anyway.

"Okay," I said, "I think I get that."

"It's not hard," Jenn whispered to me. "Even I can do it."

"Watch." Justin commanded. "Learn." And before anyone could say anything else, Justin closed his eyes and sank into the seat. Really *sank* into it. My eyes started watering watching him.

"Rose!" My dad was yelling for me from over my shoulder.

There was a wall over my shoulder.

But he was right here! I heard him . . .

"Rose!" Now it was Mom, over my other shoulder. My neck hurt like the girl from *Jaws*—yanked side to side, but the yanking gave me a glimmer. "Stop it," I warned.

"Stop what?" Chloe said.

"Don't." The blue was long gone and the pain in my temples was sharp.

"Rose! What is your *problem*?" Chloe's voice yelled at me from somewhere in front of me, right above Justin.

"*You*—" I felt myself rise off of the couch, an angry wave with a wicked undertow—all aimed at Justin.

Justin flew up and back, torquing like a diver off a platform, while Izzy ducked and rolled off the couch, clearing out of the way. Jenn, in the corner of my eye, reached out, leaning forward—diving forward.

Mina, already on her feet, too late to protect Justin, put out her arm, finger pointing over him. On his way over, his foot hit a side table that held a lovely china lamp. It looked like one from my childhood dollhouse—two globes of painted china, one on top of the other. It teetered and started to fall.

"No!" Mina commanded with voice and outstretched arm.

I watched the lamp on the table hang at a completely unnatural angle, with Jenn, Izzy, and Mina all reaching out towards the empty space formerly occupied by Justin and the lamp. As I stood there, I saw the lamp slowly right itself back to standing. It didn't even wobble as it reached vertical.

"Shit, girl! What the hell? You don't need to try and kill me!" Justin pulled himself with difficulty up the back of the sofa until he was standing.

"Justin!" Izzy looked flat-out scared. Jenn had her hand over her mouth and Mina's look could have killed a weaker student. Even I was ready to man the door against the psychic karma police.

Justin turned as pale as he could get, unnervingly, unhealthily light. His hands were shaking as they covered his eyes, "Oh crap. Dang! Sorry!" If he'd had a tail, it would have been between his legs. "I'm sorry, Mina. My bad. Holy—I'll do the clean up. I'll do it all myself."

"Yes," Mina was ice. "I imagine you will." She left the room.

"She wasn't trying to kill you, crackhead," Izzy said softly, shoving into Justin as he sat down. "She was scared."

"Yeah, too loud, Justin." Jenn said.

"And no fair using her sister." Izzy poked him. "You know they don't get along."

"Oh yeah, dog-pile on the Black man after he's been *thrown across the room* by the skinny, scary white girl. That's real special, you two. Real tight."

Mina returned and handed Justin a glass of water, which he nearly downed in a single gulp.

"But Rosie," Izzy looked straight at me, laser blue eyes behind ice blue bangs, "You *threw* him."

"No," I whispered. I felt sick, just like I did after Tim caught fire. I needed to sit but my legs wouldn't bend.

"You pushed."

I shook my head, "No, it was you guys . . ."

"What did you see, Rose?" Mina asked, still across the room from me, hand on Justin's shoulder.

"Jenn moved. And you and Izzy. Everyone was pointing at Justin. I was just—"

"You were just throwing me over the back of the couch." Justin's voice shook.

Jenn sounded sad, "Rosie, we only moved after you shoved . . ."

I shook my head, closing my eyes, trying to see it all again. "No . . . I didn't . . ."

"How often have you done that, Rosie?" Jenn helped me down and sat next to me. My mouth was dry. Why didn't I get a water too?

"Never?" I sounded raspy.

"Well," Mina tried to sound calm but didn't. She was looking at Jenn, not at me. Mina cleared her throat to try again, "Well, Rosie, I guess your mother wasn't hysterical this time. You understand now why you're here?"

"She's here to kill me?" Justin asked from inside the water glass.

"Naw," Izzy smiled at him, "that's a bonus."

"I told you, Mina," Justin started, "I told you she—"

"So I think today we've learned," Mina cut in, trying to recover the situation, "that blocking is one of the best things we can practice. The best offense is a strong defense."

"And you should have been blocking better, too, instead of trying to be all that." Izzy poked him again.

"I was blocking fine," Justin said, "if I'd been dealing *with a normal freak!*" His eyes sparked.

Izzy elbowed into him, but he wasn't paying attention. He was staring me down, and as he did it, I felt like one of those old card catalogues. He was flipping through my life.

"She's as normal as *you*, Jus," Izzy laughed. Then she looked up at him. "Just? Justin?" She shook him. "Justin, are you okay?"

Justin's head snapped suddenly over to look at Mina. "Why *is* she here?"

"I'm sorry?" Mina looked confused.

"I'm serious. Speak up. Why is she here? What did she do? She didn't just tell one-too-many peoples' fortunes, did she?"

"I didn't *do* anything," I said.

Mina ignored me, "Why, Justin? Why are you—"

His eyes went dead then shot back. "You let a *pyrokinetic* into the house? Are you kidding me?"

"Calm down," Mina soothed, "She's not a—"

"Oh my God, Mina." No one flinched this time when he said it. "You thought she was controlling it. Look again. *Starter.*" He pointed at me, "She started it."

"No, she—"

"Does Bill know? Does Casey?"

"Justin—"

"No, Mina. You let in a rogue adept who can toss me like an apple core and *start fires*? I think it's time for me to go home."

"Justin," Izzy was quietly tugging at his hand, "Justin, you can't go . . . yet . . . "

The room was blurry, but I could tell that everyone in the room was looking at me now. Except Justin. He was looking at the floor, leaning over his knees and breathing heavily.

"And that is why," Mina began crisply though her face had gone pale, "we need to help teach her control, Justin." She looked at me, "Rose, you'll learn to rein in and master your gifts while you're here, but while you're doing that it is rather important that you try to keep calm."

"And you'll learn to block really fast. I know you will." Jennifer Green: Supportive Girl—a new superhero.

"It'll keep people out of your head," Izzy agreed.

"People? Other people can get inside my head? Like . . . like him?"

Mina was moving into soothing mode, "No, not like Justin, or Izzy, or Jasmine. But it's a big city, Rosie, and there are many people here whose minds are . . . chaotic. They fling thoughts, energy, fear, all sorts of things, randomly."

"Um, then wasn't this the dumbest place my parents could have sent me?"

"This *house* is the safest place you can be. Out there . . . well . . . when you're ready we'll all go out together and . . . and we'll see how it goes. But only when you're ready."

"And they can't get into my head if I'm blocking? I'll be safe if I learn to block?"

Mina hesitated. "For receivers like us, it can—"

"It can hurt," Izzy broke in, apologizing.

"Hurt?" I asked. Izzy pointed to her head and my whole world sifted into order, like the end of a game of Solitaire. "Blocking stops the pain?" I heard desperation in my voice I didn't know I felt.

Everyone was quiet.

Finally, Izzy stepped up, "Look, Rose. If you're trying to block and someone gets in, that's bad. But if you can control fire, then you're . . . Okay, look. So let's say something gets past your shields. It makes your head hurt. It weakens your shields *and* it makes you angry that your head is hurting."

"And then I light someone on fire." Then I clarified, in case anyone cared, "Accidentally."

"That . . . that appears to be a possibility, yes," Mina confirmed. "Or you can at least use fire that's nearby." She looked at Justin and said pointedly, "We aren't sure yet if you can create fire."

Justin moaned. I ignored him.

"So. Okay, so I'm a receiver?"

The room seemed to rustle. "A receiver, a sender," Mina said, "and some other things, it seems."

"Mom?" Jenn said in a loud whisper, "She really needs to learn to block."

"Right."

"Not with me. I'm out."

"Exactly with you, Justin. You two have a connection now—" but before Mina could say anything more, Justin was already up and in the doorway.

He turned. "Mina, I've never said this before, and please don't take it the wrong way, but forcing me to work with *her* after *that* is completely whack. I'm gone." And then he fled upstairs leaving nothing but silence in his wake.

16 BLOCKING

AFTER THE PROPER MOURNING period for Justin's dramatic exit upstairs, Mina spoke. "I need to apologize. I thought that giving Justin the spotlight and letting him take the lead would help him feel less threatened. I'm sorry."

Izzy spoke up in the quiet after the storm. "I'll work with you, Rose."

"Thank you, Izzy," Mina sounded relieved. But something passed to her from Izzy: *you'd better watch my back.*

"Rosie," Mina began, "I think we should start by having you try to talk in Izzy's head, the way Justin did to you."

"But without the throwing," I said.

"Yes," Mina smiled, "Let's try without that for a start. After she can hear you, then she can block you and you can watch how she does it."

"Are you sure you're okay about this, Izzy?"

"Yeah. I don't think you'll try to kill me, if that's what you mean." She tilted her head and looked at me with a funny smile, almost like she was looking at me out of one eye. "I don't think there's much of a risk now."

"Whenever you're ready," Mina said in her teacher voice, "focus your intention on Izzy—on her hearing you."

I took a deep breath and tried to do what I'd seen Justin do, settle into the seat in a way that looked wrong.

"And please don't light me on fire," I heard Izzy whisper. I opened one eye and saw her grinning at me. Jenn giggled.

"Don't try so hard," Mina said softly, "Breathe into it."

I breathed into it and thought, *Hi Izzy . . .*

"Yow!"

My eyes flipped open to see Izzy shaking her head like a dog getting a bug out of her ear.

"Whoa! Tone it down, wouldja? You'll split my head!"

"You heard me?"

"Loud and clear. But mostly loud."

"Wow, sorry . . . I didn't try to yell. I only thought your name at you."

"Well . . . think softer. Okay?"

"Softer, right." I closed my eyes again and thought a whisper at Izzy, *You there?*

And as if the whole day hadn't already been weird enough, I heard back in my own head, *That's better. I can hear you, now. But normal volume.*

Tears forced their way into my eyes. Someone was talking in my brain. This went way beyond knowing what I was getting for my birthday.

I'd crossed a line, and I wasn't ever going to be able to forget that I can talk to people without using my voice. *Now I'm gonna block you,* Izzy was saying, *okay? Just count back from five and then keep talking. I won't be able to hear you after you say 'one'.*

Got it. I thought, *Five . . . four . . . three . . . two . . . one . . . Okay, I guess I'm supposed to keep talking . . .*

Izzy hadn't moved a muscle, hadn't twitched, hadn't done anything obvious, and yet I could see a deep blue light fading in around her. It was faint and followed the contours of her body, but it was definitely there—definitely shimmery and definitely blue. *Izzy?* I wasn't sure what to do. *Izzy, can you hear me?*

She can't hear you. Can you see her blocking?

Aunt Mina? It was like a psychic chat room. *I can see that she's all shimmery blue.*

That's what it looks like if you can see auras, which evidently you can. Look again. What else do you see?

I tried to take my eyes out of the mix, like you do when you look at those funny pictures that seem a mess of color and shapes until you de-focus your eyes and suddenly see the Statue of Liberty or something. So, I watched Izzy without "looking." She didn't move. She was barely breathing, but she was calm. So, so calm. Then I started to feel things from her—not like I was feeling them myself, but as if I felt the shadow of something solid. The light was coming from inside her, and her calm was connected to the ground—that must have been the sinking into the chair thing I'd seen before—and the blue whatever-it-was turned out to be very gentle and sort of still.

Now see what you can do, I heard Mina say. So I settled myself again, and tried to tap into the blue that Izzy was cocooned inside. I knew some of hers was coming up from the ground and some looked like it came from within Iz. I watched her more closely and saw that the light seemed to be moving and shimmering around her but always from her center, from the middle of her chest. I focused there on myself and tried to pull up from below and bring out through my middle. And I felt something.

You hear or read about guys like yogis doing things like this in, what, Tibet? Not some blue-haired high school kid sitting in a refurbished Victorian parlor in Brooklyn. It was too much.

And I lost it. The blue disappeared. I couldn't hear Mina.

"Sorry!"

Jenn practically pounced on me. "Are you serious? That was your first time. Are you nuts? Mom, she *is* another Casey!"

Something flickered over Mina's face, but all she said was, "I'm impressed. With all of you."

"Thank you, Izzy," I said. "Thank you for . . . " How do you say *thank you for risking your life to help me start to learn this craziness?*

Izzy shrugged and flashed a million dollar smile at me.

"Rose, that's just a starting point." Mina said, "What you saw and felt you now have to practice on your own. All the time. You understand? This must become automatic for you."

I nodded.

"And Izzy," Mina continued, "I think Justin's trying to clean up from his language. The trouncing he received took it out of him, though. I think he's going to need some help."

Izzy nodded and Jenn got up with her. "I'll help too," Jenn said and they walked out together.

That was convenient.

When they were safely gone, Mina turned to me, "So."

"Yep."

"Well. It's a start. I'm sorry this isn't . . . easier isn't the right word, but . . . "

"That's okay, I'm ready. Let's keep going. What else can you teach me?" Now that I'd gotten the whole blocking thing I wanted more. And I knew the sooner I got it all down, the sooner I could get home and back to Lindy. And Rob.

Mina smiled, but it wasn't a happy smile. "Look, kiddo, watching you now with Justin and Izzy I realize we've . . . we've got more work to do than I thought. I know, I know. But, Rose. You were able to throw Justin like a rag doll. This is *not* something the rest of us can do. I'm going to call Bill and we'll have to do some research, but I want you to promise me that for the next few days you will do whatever you have to in order to remain calm. Do you understand?"

"I think so." I kept my eyes on the floor so Mina couldn't see them starting to glisten.

"This is very serious, Rose. You get angry or frustrated and . . . things happen. You don't seem to have any pattern to your impulses. You've controlled physical things like glass and furniture, but you can also affect *people*, and you even seem to have some control over elements like fire." I wrapped my arms around me. "Your mother says you see the future with accuracy but you don't try to call it to you. You can see some auras—but so far only when you're trying, and you can hear and speak to others using only your mind and you do it without much effort."

"Is that *bad*?" It was like having a teacher tell you all the things you did wrong—over the last four years of school. With charts and graphs.

"No! Not bad. But . . . but I have no idea what else you can do. This is an extraordinary mix already. The more you focus and practice, the more modalities will open up to you, and the stronger you'll become. But all of that will be for naught unless you *learn control*. So: for you, for now, keep calm and avoid frustrating situations. We'll keep working on control with you."

"Sounds like going to the gym."

"It is, a little bit."

"I hate going to the gym."

"Rosie," I heard Mina sigh. "Don't start fighting it now. You didn't fight coming here."

"Yes, I did."

"No. You didn't," she corrected with a Mom Look that stopped me.

"I didn't," I agreed slowly. "Why didn't I? What was I thinking . . ."

"I don't know, Rosie. What *were* you thinking? How did you feel when your mother told you that you were coming here."

"Confused at first, I guess. And . . . and I *was* ticked, but then . . . then . . . I guess I must have just, you know, calmed myself down?" It was a question.

"Well," Mina said. "I think that's a good thing. Don't you?"

"Yeah, I guess."

"So keep doing that here. Keep yourself calm and we'll keep working with you on control."

"Right. So . . . what then? I should sit upstairs and knit until you clear me?" I asked.

She exhaled, "If that keeps you calm, yes. Knitting drives me crazy, so it isn't the first thing that comes to my mind, but if it helps you . . . " She winked and said, "go on up." She got up herself and hugged my shoulders softly. "I'll see you at lunch and we'll all work on a new house calendar for cooking and clean-up duties then."

"Aunt Mina?"

"Yes?"

I paused then changed my mind. "Should I . . . should I call you Aunt Mina around the others?"

She looked at me for a moment, "Either is fine, kiddo. Even Jenn calls me Mina sometimes when everyone's around."

"Okay, and . . . you said something about the . . . some stuff that happened at home . . . I get that you understand what happened here, but did Mom tell you about . . . she never let on that she even saw . . . any of that stuff . . . until I had to leave."

Mina looked at me steadily and quietly, then leaned back against the chair arm behind her, closing her eyes. I felt her. She was there in my mind, flipping through my memories like recipe cards. I watched my life skip past in odd jumps and scenes. They all seemed unrelated, until I saw that they were all moments when I'd warned Mom or Dad that someone was coming, that something was about to happen, or when I knew what was inside a present before I opened it. Then I saw myself sitting at dinner, but this time, instead of looking at Lindy, I was watching my glass shudder within my hand, resting on the dinner table. For a moment, it shimmered a sort of silver color, then it shattered, shards hovering momentarily in the air until they fell in a perfect circle where the vessel had been, instead of scattering like shrapnel. The image blurred, rippled, and was replaced by me getting angry at Tim. I could see a spark of ignition in the air next to him, then a tendril of flame reach out to him from the lantern on the nearest table when he caught fire, creating the blaze. I saw me breaking the leg of the chair on the roof. Then Mina let go, and I returned to her lovely—safe—parlor. I have never in my life been happier to see a room. I collapsed back into a chair. The chair was real and I was relieved.

"What. Was. That?"

"It's a useful trick for teaching. You're not shielding right now, and psychic memories generally glow brighter than the normal ones. It's relatively easy to find them. Then . . . I just let you see at the same time. With you, *that* part is easy."

"Ah . . . well . . . if that's *all* it is . . . "

Her eyes were sad, even though she was smiling, "You understand what I showed you?" She moved over to the sofa next to my chair.

"I understand that you all think I can break everything in your house and toast y'all like the Stay-Puft Marshmallow Man." I tried to laugh, but saying the words aloud made my stomach weak.

"Yes. Well, actually we're fairly certain you *can* do all that. The coincidences are too close and we try never to discount a coincidence."

"Did my parents think they were coincidences?"

Mina thought for a moment, "Your parents love you very much and thought too many things were happening around you, aside from your normal precognition, and of course," she said as though she were explaining the results of my driving test, "there's a propensity for this in our family. We all knew we couldn't risk leaving you on your own any longer."

"Jenn mentioned it was a family thing."

Mina nodded, "It goes back generations. This was the safest place for you."

"And safer for everyone else in Tucson if I'm here."

"Well, there was that too." We sat there in silence for a few minutes while I considered this. "It's a lot to grasp in one day. Are you okay?" She touched her hand to my knee. I looked over at her, and without a second thought, I relaxed and invited her into my mind. I didn't block her or try to shield. It was easier for me to have her *see* how I felt; feel my feelings. And she did. It didn't take long.

"All right," she nodded, "I understand. Forget all of this. Take some time to relax and talk to Jenn. And make sure you take time to call your parents, write friends, and rest. You, Izzy, and Justin all have phone cards in the drawer under the downstairs phone. You don't need permission to phone home, because you can't do this work if you're exhausted and frightened and feeling abandoned."

I stood up as she did, hugged her, and turned to go upstairs, swallowing the lump in my throat.

"And Rose?" I looked back at Mina and her Very Serious Face. "Keep your knitting with you."

I nodded and headed up, passing Jenn who was on her way down. She hesitated when she saw me, then cheerfully announced, "Everything is fine on that floor! I'll be right back up. I have to ask my mom something quick," and hurried past. I was too dizzy to care.

I had spent my entire life as "Just Rosie." I was a good swimmer—good enough to have a great shot at a scholarship—and I was good enough at science to know I wanted to be a doctor, but aside from that, I was nothing special. Those weird things—me knowing things—that just . . . *was*. It wasn't *me*. I held on tight to the polished handrail and continued up the stairs.

Now I wasn't even sure what it meant to be me.

17 WISHING

JENN RETURNED TO OUR room to find me curled up on the bed like a potato bug. "I'm sorry about Justin. He's a little . . . sensitive."

"That's one way to put it," I muttered. "What's his problem?"

"Oh, I don't know," Jenn sighed. "He's used to being the new one—the baby, like I said, and you know, kinda special, and now you're here—"

"He called me a firestarter."

"He exaggerates."

"Really?"

Jenn shrugged.

"Seriously, Jenn. What is it? Why is he so ticked at me?"

Jen grabbed something small off her desk and fiddled with it. "It's nothing. It's just . . . "

"It's just that I could kill you all in your sleep?"

"No, it's not that. We don't think you would—"

"You don't *think* I would. But I *could* right? I *could* do it."

Jenn looked at me and her eyes were honest. "What you *can* do, Rosie, isn't the issue. It's what you need to *learn* to do that's important to Mom. Right now I think she's still trying to figure all of that out. The house has been pretty same ol' same ol' for awhile."

"Yeah, well—it's not like I asked for this."

"I know. None of you did. It . . . you're just going to have to roll with it."

"Feels more like being rolled *over* with it."

"You're not looking at all the positives."

"Seriously?"

"Hasn't it occurred to you that you all—especially you—have some influence over what happens? I mean *really* have influence?"

"We can make stuff happen?"

"Throwing Justin counts, don't you think?"

I shrugged. I wasn't feeling like Professor Positive about any of this.

"Well, I mean, so far, your stuff has been all accidental. But," she came over and sat next to me, "now you can start working on controlling things more."

"Don't I cause more trouble when I do that?"

"You haven't really worked much on the control part. You've been more living in the 'reacting' mode."

"True."

"Look, sit here and close your eyes. Breathe normally and let your heart beat slow down. Your brain stop racing."

"Easier said than done," I muttered, but I took deep breaths to make my cousin happy.

"I know," she said, and waited for my breathing to slow. "Now picture a world where what you want just . . . happens. Where everything is the way you want it to be."

"You mean," I said in a dreamy, zen voice, "Will Smith realizes he loves me, and only me, and we run off to Bermuda together?"

"You too, huh?"

I opened one eye and looked at Jenn. She was grinning so hard that it got me laughing.

"Okay, well, maybe not that." She lost the grin. "But for a second there, you were close. When everything feels crazy, it's good to get yourself to that place. A safe, calm, place where you're in control. Then see what you want—really see it, so the universe can see it too."

"And then I sit here and wait for the . . . universe?"

"No. Now we go set the table for lunch. And after lunch you should call your mom."

After lunch, Jenn took out a map of Park Slope, Brooklyn. She and Izzy talked—and bounced—me through all the things to do and see in the neighborhood. Things I wouldn't be allowed to see until Mina thought I could control myself.

"So wait, guys. I'm going to be stuck in a house with no Cable for days until I get cleared. What do you do to not go crazy?"

"We have movies. And we can rent new ones for you."

"And we all have jobs," Izzy added.

"You do?"

"Yep." Izzy really was a nuclear ball of blue. If her body wasn't in motion, her hands were—playing with an object, twisting a rubber band, folding a piece of paper. "Once we knew we'd gotten enough control, we decided we should put it to the test for real. Do something useful—"

"And lucrative," I added.

"True, that too," she laughed. "But, you know, it gets us out of the house for a few hours a day."

"I read a lot," Jenn added.

"We all do."

"Like research reading?" I asked, "Like about this stuff?"

"Some," Izzy nodded. "Mostly I read for fun. The library's really close by, so sometimes I pick a shelf and cruise through the whole thing."

"Because you can?"

"Because I can," she agreed.

"We go to the park," Jenn said.

"And the movie place down the street," Izzy added.

"And sometimes the city."

"By yourselves?"

"Usually," Izzy said.

"But, Rosie," Jenn added, "they've been practicing for a long time, now. You're starting. Give yourself time to get used to it."

"Was it hard for you?" I asked Izzy.

"In the beginning or in the beginning *here*?" Izzy asked.

"Both?"

She looked at me thoughtfully and stopped fidgeting. "It's never easy, Rosie. It just isn't. I know there are people out there who would give their right eye to be able to do what any of us can do, but they're wrong. It's—"

"It's time for you to call your mom," Jenn interrupted, looking at her watch. "She'll want to hear your voice."

"Right," I nodded, letting Jenn drag me away from a conversation I didn't want to hear. "Show me the phone cards?"

That night in bed, I tried over and over to turn myself that telltale, glowing blue color. Just at the point I thought I'd started to feel something, it would all disappear again. I have no idea how long I stared at the ceiling, trying again and again, but it was long enough for everything to become hot and blurry. If I managed to block at all, I sure couldn't tell. What I did know was that I was lucky Jenn was a hard sleeper. She didn't wake up once.

18 CENTERING

MINA WAS SPEAKING SERIOUSLY to the group of us the next morning before the workers had to start their shifts, but it was impossible to concentrate on her words. It was hot and humid outside, and even the cool house couldn't keep me from melting. With my back facing the window, I found the sun coating my shoulder blades with sweat and dripping misery. The heat, humidity, and news that I was a human blowtorch had completely wiped the shiny newness off everything. I kept trying to figure out how much I could learn and how fast I could do it so I could get back home. It was impossible to stop thinking about Rob and the last time I saw him. Then I thought about the party. Then I felt sick.

"I know this is a review for most of you, but we'll be working on fundamentals like this for a while until we catch Rosie up. So, now that she knows about blocking, the next concepts are grounding and centering. These are the most important things you need to learn," I heard Mina say. "Rosie, after your experiences so far, do you have a guess as to why this would be so important?"

Just because she's your aunt doesn't mean she can't play evil teacher tricks to keep you focused. "Umm . . . I don't know, Aunt Mina. Maybe because . . . " I was too hot to even pretend to come up with a joke. "Because I have no idea."

"I know it's hot today, but you need to focus. You want to go, Izzy?"

Izzy had slowed her bouncing, which must have been what drew Mina's attention. "It's important because what happens to us—the things that are happening to you, Rosie, are," she shrugged, "for normal people it would be pretty scary. The more we can do to keep ourselves here in the real world, the better off we are."

"You know, not to be annoying," I said, ignoring Justin's *tsk* at me as I spoke, "but it's kind of unnerving having you all talk about how what you're trying to teach me is dangerous."

"Well . . . but it is." Izzy looked straight at me, fidgets stilled. "Dangerous. It's all dangerous. Someone who can do what we do, if they aren't ethical . . . if they aren't really ready for what it feels like to be able to see things, and manipulate space or time or thoughts . . . if they lie to someone about what a relative who passed on has said . . . " she started to falter, as though she'd spooked herself. "Well, it's just dangerous."

Mina continued, "Which is why this matters. Grounding is the thing that will keep you here. Centering is the thing that will keep you sane. It is *not* something you can ignore . . . Justin!"

Justin jumped, then smiled sheepishly at Mina and stopped incrementally moving one of the flowers in the vase behind Izzy's head with his finger—a finger that was a few yards away from the blooms.

"I know it sounds dire, Rosie," Mina continued, "but that's because people get hurt all the time, playing with fire, so to speak," she nodded at me. "So for you, learning control isn't only a good idea, it's an imperative."

"All right, everyone." Mina's tone changed as she sat up straighter. "Sit comfortably. Feet on the ground. Hands somewhere they can relax. Soft hands, no tension, Jennifer. And for you three who've done this before, please practice speed and grace when making this connection—especially because you'll need to be helping Rose from time to time to pull her back down as she flies through this crash course." Lovely word choice. They all looked at me, waiting to see me fling Justin again, no doubt.

Mina waited for everyone to refocus. "Good. Next . . . visualize a line, a wire, a cable coming off your spine and going down . . . down . . . down to the core . . . the center of the earth." Her voice grew slower, mesmerizing. "Drop way, way down and connect that cable. Connect it to the center.

"Now, focus on your body again . . . . Picture a vessel that holds everything bad . . . or sad . . . or lousy that you've been carrying around with you. Now," Mina took a slow breath, "remember that a vessel can be emptied . . . Picture how it's full of all the garbage you have to deal with every day . . . the things that annoy you . . . the things to get rid of." *Breathe* . . . "Now, push all of the garbage out, down through that cable . . . . Leave it in the center of the earth where it can be burnt off. Picture a plunger . . . or a vacuum . . . or Brillo and bleach . . . something that gets every corner of the inside of your spirit clean. Clorox it all away. Make it pure.

"Once you've cleaned out all the detritus," *Breathe* . . . "check your connection . . . . Be sure you're hooked in to that warm . . . clean . . . energizing center of the earth . . . . When you're sure you're still locked in, center yourself by starting to draw energy up the cable and into your spine . . . then out to your fingertips . . . then down to your toes . . . then up into your head." *Breathe* . . . "Let the warmth surround and protect you . . . Enjoy the electricity . . . Steady your breathing and relax into it."

I sat there, first thinking Mina was out of her ever-loving mind, but then something surprised me. I didn't "see" things like she said, but the words were definitely doing something to me. Somewhere inside, something fluttered, then shifted, then clicked. I felt all of the stress and frustration and homesickness drain out of my head, neck, and shoulders. I felt lighter and more—well, honestly, I felt spacey and a little dizzy. Then, following her words, I moved from cleaning to drawing, and felt the most extraordinary surge of, not really heat so much as . . . electricity. She was right; it was like touching your tongue to a nearly-dead 9-volt battery. Not a shock. More like a buzz—a hum. And this hum was traveling all through me, starting at my spine and spinning, buzzing, up into my forehead.

Then I knew I needed to be alone. Really alone. Not Near Any People alone.

I peeked out of an eye to see if Mina was looking. Of course, she was staring straight at me. She nodded at me, but I saw her glance over at Jenn, who seemed fine keeping her eyes closed. As quietly as I could, I slunk upstairs, went into the bathroom and closed the door behind me. I splashed cool water on my face.

Funny thing about bathrooms in New York—they're often built next to air shafts. In the West, people have bathrooms as big as—well, as big as New York City apartments according to Jenn. Here, they are little things with dingy windows that open onto brick ventilation shafts.

They aren't always pretty, but they are great places to be alone and think. I stared into the mirror, examining myself. I didn't look any different—well, I dripped a little, but that was to be expected after splashing myself. I didn't glow. I didn't look all spooky. But there was no question; I had been spooked.

What had gotten to me while I was downstairs was a face. Remember, I don't *see* things, I just . . . know things: I know words or facts or events or places or ideas. But suddenly there was this face. A kind, open, generous face. A guy's face. A cute face with floppy hair and glasses. A face I haven't ever seen before. A real, 3-D, I-could-reach-out-and-touch-it kind of face. And this particular face really did unnerve me.

Why?

Because it was kissing me—and I was kissing back.

19 OUTSIDE

"I HAD A THOUGHT." Breakfast was done. Lunch was done, too. Everyone else had left for their jobs. I'd gone back to my room to try to read and now Mina, in a paint-stained skirt, had emerged from her upstairs studio and was standing in my doorway. She craned her neck to try to see the cover of my book. "What are you reading?"

"Some book Justin gave me."

"Who by?" She asked, failing the blasé test.

"Stephen King?"

Mina moaned, "Which one?"

"Um. *Firestarter*?"

"For the love of Frank," she sighed, plucking the book from my hands and heading towards the stairs. "Out! You need a break and so do I."

I didn't need to be asked twice. I grabbed my knitting bag, shoved my wallet in, and didn't even ask where we were going until we were outside.

"Library," Mina said. "We need a walk, and a break, and to get you some decent books and movies or something. You don't need to be reading books like Justin's."

"Isn't it accurate?" I asked, half-serious.

"Ah, well," she said carefully, "there are certainly more accurate books out

119

there. Might not be as exciting, but more accurate, definitely."

"So I'm putting down an interesting book for a boring one?"

"Right now accuracy is a bit more important."

"But I'm already bored. At least I wasn't falling asleep on that one."

"When you know enough to be able to separate the real from the fictional in a book like that is when you can pick that one up again. For now, on this topic, stick to the factual."

"But all those books on Jenn's desk look super dull."

"They are *older*. That's all."

"It's not older that bugs me. I like old books. I love old movies. It's *boring* that bugs me."

"Well," we turned the corner onto Prospect Park West, "boring is sometimes part of it. It's not like this is new technology we're dealing with. It's old stuff. Very old. And those writers weren't trying to write the next blockbuster for our world—though they might have been trying to write the next blockbuster for theirs," she mused. "Anyway, for us the hard part is teasing out the superstition from the useful information. It's not always easy in the old books."

"What kinds of superstition?" I asked carefully.

Mina glanced over at me. "Are you blocking?"

I smiled at her and batted my eyelashes.

"Good work, kiddo. Keep it up."

"Superstition?" I repeated.

"Right. Well," she put her hands in her skirt pockets. "As you can imagine, people like us have survived interesting challenges throughout history. Sometimes we're important—worshipped even—like the Oracle at Delphi."

"That's cool."

"Yes. Yes, it is. Then there are the times we're burned for being witches."

"Not so cool."

"No."

"And that's why we don't talk about it?"

"Yes."

"So what about all those psychics on the street? The fortune tellers with neon signs in their windows?"

"Oh, well. Some of them are legitimate. They can do what you do, somewhat. With some kind of trigger—holding a person's hands, asking questions until they get a vision, using Tarot cards—they can generally see some aspect of a person's future. Some, of course, are dime-store charlatans."

"So, wait, *lots* of people can do what I do?"

"Well," she hesitated, "we're still figuring out what you can do. What you can see."

"I couldn't see you. When I thought about coming here on the plane I didn't see your new place or Justin and Izzy. I didn't see any of this beyond 'Empire State building equals New York' or something."

Mina smiled and started walking again, "Good. That means we've been doing our job." She looked at me out of the corner of her eye and laughed. "It's hard for you, isn't it? You've had a lifetime of seeing the future by accident, then we come along and stop you. It's the protections on the house," she said in response to my look. "You can't get past the walls we built. Which actually makes me quite relieved. We cross here."

We waited for the lights on a couple of big and very busy streets then headed up the steps into the library.

"We should get you a library card first," Mina said, so we got in line in the cavernous lobby.

While waiting patiently for the people in front of us to finish their business, I looked at my aunt. "You know, Mina, this is an excellent test of my ability to stay calm."

"How's that working for you?" She smiled.

"Not too bad right now," I smiled back.

"The real test will be when we get to the front."

It would be easy to stereotype the woman at the desk as a Brooklynite, but it wouldn't really give her the credit she deserves. If you've ever seen the movie *Beetlejuice* you might remember a scene with a dead woman who was smoking—with smoke coming from her tracheotomy tube, too. Yeah, that was our librarian.

"Wat canIdo fowah yoo?" She asked. I was glad Mina was there to translate.

"I would like to get my niece a library card."

"And ahr you willin' to sign a fowm indicatin' that you ahr, indeed, respawnsible fowah any chawges incurred by said niece?"

"Um. Yes." I could see Mina's brain systematically parsing the librarian's words.

"Very good. Siyne this fowhm heah . . . and heah . . . and put herh name heah . . . Now you, miss, you siyne heah." She scanned one thing, typed another, and handed me a brand new Brooklyn Public Library Card.

"Go wit Gawd, deah." She winked at me as we turned and walked to the escalator.

"I don't know that I'll ever get used to this place, Aunt Mina," I whispered once we were at a safe distance.

"At least it's not boring. Our floor," Mina nudged me once I was off the escalator. "We have to go into the religion section to find anything for us."

"Seriously?"

"Well, it's kind of esoteric stuff. No one really knows where to put it. If there were still a 'natural sciences' category . . . here we go."

We were facing a shelf that contained various books on psychic topics—telepathy, tarot, theosophy, parapsychology, Swedenborg, spiritism, automatic writing, precognition, spoon bending, phrenology, auras, astral projection, transference, healing, angels, demons, dreams, and palmistry. I'm sure there were more.

"My head hurts."

Mina froze, "*Hurts* hurts or just commenting on being overwhelmed?"

"Sorry," I smiled, "just overwhelmed."

Mina relaxed, "I don't blame you." She pulled out a book. "You might like this one." She handed me *A Complete Idiot's Guide to Being Psychic*. I laughed and she smiled. "No really. It's not a bad book and could be a good overview for you. There's a lot of simple terminology you probably don't know, so this will give you much of what you need to get up to speed with the others."

"You're serious."

"I am."

"Allllrighty then." I cradled the book and scanned the shelves more. "Jenn can do Tarot, right?"

"Yes, she's pretty good at it for someone who doesn't really fall into the psychic category."

"But she said she can block and ground and stuff like that."

"Well, anyone can do those things. Actually, anyone can do any of this if they're willing to put the time into training. Bill's come a long way."

"Really? Uncle Bill?"

Mina smiled while scanning a shelf, "Oh yes, he's gotten very good at knowing some very odd things. But that's the real pleasure in all of this—you never know what will pop up next. Ah. Here's another you might like." She handed me *The Secrets of the Tarot: Origins, History, and Symbolism*. "If I recall correctly, the author is a knitter too. Enough for now. Let's go get you some movies."

Even though the TV was in Justin's room, she didn't have to ask me twice.

Mina and I walked part of the way home through the park, where she led us by a kid's playground full of little tykes who looked like they were less learning-to-walk and more learning-to-lean-forward-but-catch-themselves-before-falling-down.

"So, you've done very well today, Rosie." Mina indicated a bench to sit on.

"Thanks Aunt Mina. But it wasn't much of a challenge."

"I wasn't sure—" Mina paused and helped a little boy up from the sand in front of her, handing him back to his Mom. "I wasn't sure," she restarted, "how you would react to the traffic or the lines or . . . any of this. Brooklyn is calmer than Manhattan, but they're both more chaotic than Tucson."

"Well, that's true."

"I could tell you were trying to block and when we were in line you were grounding. That was great, and I was really proud of you."

"I hear a 'but' in there."

"Yes. Well. Your mom and dad and I talked last night and . . . we've agreed that you might need to stay here a little longer." I heard her sigh, "Breathe, Rosie."

I did everything I could to keep grounded and tried to stay all blue and calm, but I could feel the throbbing start at my temples. I rubbed the sides of my head with my fists.

"How. Longer?" I managed while pushing my hands into my skull. I had known this was coming. I'd known it was a possibility. Not because I'm psychic but because everything seemed to be going wrong this summer. I held onto the sides of my head harder until I felt the vise around it lift.

"Should we go, Rosie?" I could tell Mina realized this might have been mad stupid on her part, bringing me to a kiddie park, thinking that would keep me tame.

"No." I struggled to calm my racing heart, block everything that ticked me off, and shove it all down into the earth until I was nothing but cool, blue ice inside. "No. I can do this."

We sat there for what felt like forever, my insides waging a war against themselves for control over my body and brain and wherever else this psychic garbage lived. Finally I felt like I could talk without gritting my teeth.

"What did I do wrong?"

"Wrong?"

"Why aren't you letting me go home?"

"You didn't do anything wrong. It's that . . . this is looking more complicated than we thought."

"How could it be *more* complicated?"

"Initially, Bill and I figured it would be . . . well, normally it's just learning to ground, block, practice that for awhile. Then, if other talents show themselves, it's a matter of learning to channel that energy or control the flow of information. You've seen Izzy and Justin. They're experts at grounding and blocking, and their gifts don't throw them. They . . . they just roll with it. When they learn a new bit, they practice it systematically and add it to their menu."

"And that's not what's happening with me?"

"No." Mina leaned back and looked up at the sky. "No, Rosie, you're more interesting than that."

"I hate that word."

"Which one?" Mina rolled her head, chin still aimed at the blue above, so she could look at me.

"Interesting." I dug into my bag and pulled out my knitting.

"Why?"

"It's what you say instead of 'deadly' or 'pretty' or something. 'How was your date?' *oh . . . she was . . . interesting . . .* 'so was swimming with the great whites dangerous?' *oh . . . you know . . . it was . . . interesting.* See?"

"Hmm," Mina thought. "No. I can see why you'd think that, but you really are more interesting than that. It's not a cop out."

I shifted to sit with a foot under me so I could turn and face Mina on the bench, holding tight to my yarn. "Interesting, how?"

"Interesting like a 5,000 piece puzzle when you're used to 500." She sat up straighter and looked directly at me, too. "You're a puzzle. I mean, Rose, you have to know that while Jasmine and I combined are better at all of this stuff than the rest of the kids are, there will come a point when all of you will surpass what we're able to teach you. I don't talk about this with them, but with you . . . well, even as a kid, you always wanted the big picture. You wanted to know when we were going to a movie, which one, which theater, would there be popcorn or candy—you needed the map. And I know it will help keep you calm and focused if you see the map right now—or as much of a map as I can give you. So. The truth is we don't know what we can teach you that you can't already do—we know you can't *control*. Jasmine and I have already seen a great deal from you— many things that surprised us—and we all agree that for you, our primary goal right now is containment. Refining your gifts is secondary. It's the other way around for everyone else. They don't need containment yet. They might not ever need it. They only really need to learn what's happening to them and how to manipulate it all so they can live mostly-normal lives—and also add to their gifts *if* that helps them."

"I don't need to learn to use it?"

"You already use it without even realizing it. Right now *you* need to keep from accidentally hurting people with it—that's the containment. And we also worry—" she stopped and bit her lip.

"You worry that . . . ?" Mina sighed while I waited. Finally I said, "You may as well tell me, Aunt Mina. Chances are I'll figure it out anyway."

Mina rubbed her face with both hands before she looked at me, "Rosie, people like you and Izzy and Justin and Jasmine are bright lights. You . . . you shine brighter than most people. *You* even more than the others. And . . . there are things in this world that are drawn to that brightness. Things that sometimes aren't so wonderful."

"That's the protection stuff that Izzy was talking about?"

"Partly, yes."

"But I can block now! I hardly have to try at all."

Mina nodded, "Yes, that's true. But we have to get you to see the blocking as more than that now. Now it has to be a shield, you have to start using it as a constant shield. But you also haven't had anyone really try to shove in to see why you're so bright."

"It sounds like . . . are you saying, Aunt Mina, that there are actually evil people out there? I don't mean evil like 'Hitler evil' but like, just people who are . . . evil. Normal people, but really bad?"

"Oh, very few are what you mean when you say 'evil,' but there are definitely people who will push through your barriers simply because they're there, or they're curious, or want to know why you're so shiny. Anyone pushing through your defenses—"

"That would tick me off. Then I'd get angry. And that—"

"It would happen too fast for you. Too fast to protect against."

"Why haven't I . . . before?"

"What?"

"I mean, I've been angry before. Why hadn't I torched any of my friends before? Or thrown them? Or . . . " I shivered.

"Well, some of it is you coming into your own at this age. Some of it is just dumb luck."

"Seriously?"

"I know it sounds ridiculous, but adolescence is such a complex time developmentally. The brain is doing all sorts of things and hormones are doing others and they all interact in odd and generally unpredictable ways."

"So this is just another growing pain?"

"For you? Yes."

"So the unpredictable is part of why I need to stay."

"We have to be sure. We'll need to test you . . . "

I turned back and watched the kids. I really did need to stay. The children got blurry the more I realized how trapped I was. "How long am I stuck here, Aunt Mina? I mean, no offense," I swiped at my face. "I . . . I had plans this year. I had . . . things I needed to do. For the . . . the other parts of my future."

"You need to do this, too, Rosie," Mina said softly.

"Right. Or I'm going to torch all my friends. And teachers. And coaches . . . " We sat in silence for a long while, listening to birds, traffic, and the irony of laughing children when I felt so miserable. "How long, Mina?"

"No one can see if you can't," she said finally. "But," she stood and offered me a hand, trying to sound chipper, "today you've had a very successful day. Very successful."

"Yippee," I sighed.

We walked home in silence.

That afternoon I sat on the downstairs window seat and opened a letter from Lindy. It was three double-sided pages of calligraphy-penned questions, with space underneath each to write my answers. I didn't bother picking up a pencil. I couldn't pretend to answer one of them.

20 Knitting

I TRIED VERY HARD to stay calm and focused and keep the headaches away. The trip to the library and a talk with Mina helped some, and getting honest answers helped more. But I still couldn't shake the vision of that kiss. It haunted me for longer than it should have; one of those dreams that won't let go, with feelings that hover for a long time. Having a lingering lip-lock with some strange guy on your mind was distracting, and it was more awkward that the guy definitely was *not* Rob.

After talking to Izzy one night, I was able to figure out that the absolute worst headaches showed up right before I did something destructive, and I didn't always have a ton of time to react. Regular headaches were slower to build and were still warnings, but they weren't dire. Of course, being stuck inside the house didn't give me many opportunities to test this or risk blowtorching something, though Justin could have helped me there.

All this is a way to say that my first stretch of time in Brooklyn was spent mostly in our room or Justin's 2nd floor room—designated Home of the Television—Just Staying Calm. I'd thumbed through some of the books on psychic-ness Jenn had given me, taken notes on parts of the library books I'd gotten with Mina, read an ancient and crumbling Agatha Christie mystery that was lying around downstairs, listened to a lot of music on my Discman while knitting, and generally spent most of my time bored. And Mina was wrong—the psychic books were almost 100% snoozers. I kept practicing the grounding thing and the centering thing, but that quickly lost its sparkle, too.

When my eyes cracked open in the morning I saw that Jenn's bed was empty, again. I guess she'd become an early riser since the last time I visited because she sure wasn't like this before.

What with all the hubbub I'd been causing, and the way Justin acted around me in general, I wasn't really all that interested in showing up for breakfast. Also, I knew Justin had to go to work this morning and I didn't want to get in the way. Instead, I popped a CD into my Discman and tried to chill—relax and let my mind sink into my knitting. The aroma of a home-cooked breakfast was good, but I didn't see that as reason enough to leave the bed.

I felt more than saw movement at the doorway, and slid my headphones off as I looked up.

"Hey stranger," Jenn smiled at me. "I wondered if you were awake. Mail call," she said, tossing a letter at me. From Mom. Not Rob.

"Hi. Thanks. Just knitting."

"Oh," she said, and stood there.

I didn't exactly feel like making things easy for anyone right then. I went back to my knitting.

"So," Jenn was sounding casual—too casual. "Justin's left for work."

"Yeah?"

"Yeah, then he's going out with Bill today."

"Uncle Bill's back?"

"Yeah, he's in the city."

A knot I hadn't noticed started to untangle in my stomach. "Really?"

"Yep. He wanted Justin to meet him at the theater."

"Right."

"Anyway." Jenn sat on the edge of my bed. "Do you think you can teach

Izzy and me how to knit?"

Like so many things in this house, I hadn't seen that one coming.

"You're serious?"

"Yeah." Jenn looked worried, "shouldn't I be?"

"No, that's . . . that's fine. That's great." I pulled my project bag closer to me. "Yes, of course I can teach you to knit."

"Super!"

"Uh . . . " I scrounged around the bottom of my bag, "I'm going to need some supplies."

"Easy. Get ready and meet me downstairs in fifteen." And she was gone.

One of the things I loved about my cousin: you always knew what she was thinking. She didn't have it in her to be sneaky. Knitting it was.

I dug around for clothes and went to take a quick shower.

Mina was mixing something on the stove that had no scent at all. Without looking up, she said, "Hello girls. It's a little early for lunch duty."

"Yeah, we know," Jenn said, looking into the pot. Then leaning her head towards her mother but looking at me, smiling, she said, "Um, you know, Mom, how knitting and all is a really good *calming* thing? For people who aren't you, I mean?" Mina snorted softly. Jenn continued, "So, I'm thinking maybe, you know, since things have been *calm*, that now's a good time for Izzy and me to take Rosie down to The Knitting Garden."

"What's that?" I looked at Izzy.

"A knitting store nearby. Walkable."

Mina had turned and was looking at the three of us, one at a time.

"Okay, Aunt Mina?" I asked hopefully. I hadn't broken anything and I'd been practicing like she asked. I couldn't think of a reason why she'd say no.

She looked at me, not unkindly, "I think . . . " for a second I thought she was about to say *I think it's too soon,* but instead she said, "I think it would be good practice for you and maybe easier if you knew you were going someplace inherently calming to you. Are you two confident you can pull her back if you need to?"

Jenn and Izzy nodded. "I think she's been doing really well," Izzy bounced.

"Well, we were definitely fine at the library. If you're comfortable with it, I think it would be okay."

"Really?" I tried not to squeal.

"Unless, you know," Izzy tried to look all serious at me, "unless you don't *want* to leave the house."

"Ha."

"We'll be back soon, Moms. Okay?" Jenn pulled me towards the door.

My aunt rolled her eyes. "I *do* wish you wouldn't call me that."

We walked out into what could only be called a steam bath as we headed down Carroll and across 7ᵗʰ Avenue. It was a horror. My clothes stuck to me immediately.

"Jenn?" I asked.

"Yeah?"

"Do I look like the guy from *Raiders of the Lost Ark?*"

"Do you look like Harrison Ford?" Jenn displayed her "confused" face.

"You definitely don't look like him. And you're too tall to be Marion," Izzy said.

"No," I said. "The face-melting guy?"

"No, why?"

"You're kidding, right? You don't feel this humidity? My face looks incredulous, yeah? Like a dictionary definition?"

She shrugged. "It sucks, I guess."

"You *guess*?"

"Well, yeah," Izzy said, "I mean . . . what's the humidity in Arizona? Like two percent?"

"Something like that," I sighed. We passed no one on our walk who looked nearly as miserable as me. "Are people here made of sponge, or Teflon, or what?"

"You know, Rosie, even if the humidity was like ten percent you'd feel it, right?"

"That's true," I said, resigned. "How much do you think it is here now?"

"Dunno . . . probably around sixty or seventy."

"*Seventy percent?* Dang! May as well go swimming."

The girls took me and my whining on a walking tour of Park Slope on our way to the knitting store. We turned from Carroll Street south onto 5th Avenue. I looked at the storefronts we were walking past. Some had clearly seen better days; some looked new and trés chi-chi.

"How long did it take you, Izzy?" I asked.

"What?"

"How long did it take you to not mind the humidity when you moved here?"

Jenn and Izzy laughed. "Oh, Rosie. I'm from South Dakota. I think we invented humidity."

"Seriously?"

"Yep."

"So it's just me."

"Yep."

"Terrific."

The walk was beautiful, I had to admit, despite the heat. I was used to early and mid-summer being a time of browns, not greens. In the desert we got our monsoons in late July and August, so June and early July resembled shoe leather stretching across the horizon, but by the beginning of August, if all went well with the rains, we would have green mountains, and the desert would get its second bloom. I know most people think that the desert is only dirt or sand, but the Sonoran Desert, where I live—liv*ed*—wasn't like that. It was full of plants and animals. We had a mesquite tree in our backyard that was at least as tall as some of the trees here. And, yeah, I was kinda proud of that.

"Okay, then, Izzy. How long did it take you to get used to walking everywhere rather than driving?" I asked.

"I moved here before I could drive."

"We don't have our licenses." Jenn added.

"You *what*?"

"Don't need one," Jenn said.

"Just a hassle," Izzy added. "Casey's the only one of us who has a license."

"Well, he needs it," Jenn added.

"True. Comes in handy," Izzy said.

"Who's Ca—" I started to ask.

"Excuse me, Miss?" I felt a tap on my shoulder. I turned around to see an older man, smiling at me in the oddest way. "I'm sorry to bother you ladies but . . . you looked so familiar, I had to stop you."

"Oh, um . . . " was about all I could manage.

"I'm sorry," he got flustered, "this is so out of character for me. I can't believe—where are my manners. I'm William." He proceeded to very politely shake all of our hands as we introduced ourselves.

"I'm sorry," Jenn said with a funny little smile. "What did you say your name was?"

"It's William. William Smith. But all of my friends call me Bill."

I heard Jenn hold back a laugh while Izzy said, meaningfully, "It is *so* nice to meet you, Bill. We've got to be going, though."

"Oh. Right. All right. Lovely meeting you . . . you do look so familiar . . . " he stood there in the middle of the sidewalk with this lopsided smile on his face while Jenn and Izzy pulled me in the direction of the knitting store.

"What was that?" I whispered.

"That was you focusing on Will Smith falling in love with you the other day," Jenn finally let herself laugh.

"Wow. The universe is paying way too much attention to me."

"Truer words were never spoken," Izzy laughed.

"No doubt," Jenn nodded.

"Too bad I didn't clarify that."

"We'll fix it later," Jenn said.

"Here we are." Jenn turned into a storefront with a bright, lime-green metal shutter and doorframe. A little bell rang on the door as I followed Jenn into a pleasantly lit room and whistled softly, "Zowee." We had entered the Land of Wool. With a little friction, it could have been a yurt. Yarn hung in skeins from the walls and high ceiling, more in the shelves that were everywhere, under the front window, in the hallway leading to the back, next to the couch, in wine racks up against the back of the couch. Everywhere. I swear I saw some turquoise skeins stuffed behind a chair and a stray gray lurking under the couch, ready to nuzzle up, cooing, to an unsuspecting knitter.

In a chair, dead center against the back wall, a woman sat knitting. In school we'd read *A Tale of Two Cities,* but this was no old fashioned Madame Defarge. Part of her face was obscured by flaming orange hair. She was dressed head to toe in black, and I thought I could make out black nail polish on her flying fingers. She was using some of the yarn from the wall, apparently making something cabled. I couldn't remember ever seeing anyone knit so fast or with so much precision—and I taught knitting back home. No question. I was in the presence of a master.

She glanced up neutrally, her face launching a broad smile when she recognized Jenn. "Well hello, stranger! It's been awhile!" For a Goth, she had a heckuva Brooklyn accent.

"Yeah, I know," Jenn apologized. "I'm still working on the baby booties."

"You gotta switch over to knitting, Miss. You're destined for the needles, not the hook."

"Yeah, yeah. I know. Today maybe."

The proprietress looked surprised, but only said, "Good." Then the Goth Knitter nodded at Izzy, "Isobel."

"Hey," Iz looked up from the cashmere she'd started fondling.

The woman moved her eyes to me and her face froze. She indicated me with a needle point, "And who is this?"

Jenn didn't seem to notice anything wrong. "Duh, sorry. *This* is my cousin, Rose." Jenn brought me forward. "She's here from Arizona. Rose, *this* is Delphi of the Knitting Garden."

"Hi," I half-waved. My stomach fluttered.

"So?" She looked like she had decided to smile, finally, not like she was happy to meet me. "You knit?"

"Not only does Rose knit," Jenn cut in, "she *teaches* it at home. She's going to teach Izzy and me."

Delphi looked at Jenn for a long beat. "Excellent. Glad to hear you're finally giving in to the inevitable, Miss Jennifer Green." She glanced at Izzy, then turned her gaze to me. "And how long are you here for, Hannah Rose?" It wasn't clear from the look on her face whether she wanted to know how long I was staying, or how soon I was leaving.

I looked at Jenn, who looked back at me and shrugged. "You know, that's a *great* question. We don't really know. She's out here to go to school with me. So, for a while I guess."

"You knocked up? Never mind." Delphi looked back at Jenn, "In *school* school or in *your* school?"

Jenn shrugged as she walked away, examining the yarn. "Both?" It came out as a question.

"So? Nu?" she asked, turning to me. "What's on the needles, new girl?"

"Um . . . I just finished a pair of faux Fair Isle fingerless mittens right now. I'm on the finger bind-offs. Starting a lace shawl." While I spoke, Delphi was tying some red yarn onto Izzy's wrist. Izzy couldn't have cared less.

"*Faux* Isle? Sewn cast-off?" She looked at me sideways as she tied.

"Yes, I'm using more than two colors in a round. I'm casting off with a darning needle."

"Show?" She wasn't unkind, standing with her hand out.

I pulled them out of my bag.

She took them carefully, not touching me, held them, examined them, examined me again, returned to the mittens. It looked like she made a decision and slowly smiled. "So? You wanna work here?"

I laughed, surprised, and Jenn said, "She's kinda busy right now, Delphi. "

"Too busy to teach? You could maybe teach how to make the mittens? This is your pattern, no?"

"It is my pattern. Yes."

"You see?" She said to no one in particular. "This one with the talent, you should teach. So, if you don't work in the shop, you should at least tell me what you *want* to teach and when. I'll calendarize you."

"Um . . . " I stalled. "I need to talk to my aunt? Can I get back to you on that?"

"Yes, sure. I'll be here. However, what do you need to buy today?"

"I wasn't really thinking of anything in particular for me," I said, "but we need to get supplies for Jenn and Izzy so I can teach them."

Delphi looked up at Izzy, then Jenn. Izzy smiled over her shoulder, moving onto some gorgeous, heathered blue handspun. Jenn stood next to me smiling, then breathed like she'd just come up for air, "What size needles do we need, Rosie? And which kind?"

Delphi indicated the wall of knitting tools and excused herself as another customer came in. I pulled a couple of Bamboo US 7s off the wall and helped Iz and Jenn pick some yarn that would work well with the needles. The Knitting Garden was considerably cooler and drier than outside, and the polished concrete floors and slick walls made for a comfortably chilly environment. So while they bought their yarn and needles, I poked around happily and found some gorgeous yarn from a local spinner and dyer. The greens and blues and purples were punctuated with little splashes of red and yellow in ways I would never have imagined combining.

Their work done, Iz and Jenn sat down on one of the comfy sofas, talking quietly while I got my yarn. Delphi nodded approval of my choice but kept sneaking looks at me, making me more than a little self-conscious. Regardless, she tallied my bill. When I went to dig the money out of my bag, my lace shawl project fell on the counter. Delphi pulled away from it and I could have sworn she hissed. She was a sphinx, again, by the time I'd shoved the work back into my bag and had a chance to look at her face.

After an uncomfortable silence, she took my money from where I'd put it on the counter and motioned me back to Jenn and Izzy.

I sat down between Jenn and Iz, and showed them how to cast on. Izzy was a fast learner, Jenn slower, but solid. Maybe it's a psychic thing—maybe they were reading how to do it from my mind. Maybe I was making up stuff to explain them being smart, fast learners. Who knows? Within a half-hour, I'd taught them to cast on, knit a few rows, then knit a row and purl a row. Izzy's knitting was amazingly regular for a first-timer. Jenn kept laughing and tinking when necessary. She loved that "tink" is "knit" spelled backwards and I think she made mistakes just so she could sing, "tink, tink, tinkiddy tinkiddy tink tink."

When we stood to leave, Delphi was standing in front of us. She reassessed me, then motioned to Jenn, who followed her down the back hall of the store. I couldn't tell if I was supposed to follow Jenn or stay with Izzy. On a guess I followed. Delphi was rummaging in a box on a shelf on the wall.

"Jennifer, my dear, you'll need one, too," she turned and tied a small red strand of yarn onto Jenn's wrist. She noticed me standing lost and forlorn behind Jenn, hesitated, took another piece of yarn and attached it to my wrist. No conversation or explanation. When done, Delphi pointed back to the front of the store.

We were nearly home before I realized that upon meeting me, Delphi had called me Hannah Rose—without Jenn telling her it was my full name.

Bill Smith was—mercifully—nowhere to be seen on our walk home.

When we walked in the house Izzy said she wanted to take a nap. Headaches, normal ones—not fire-breathing ones. Jenn went up to the studio to talk to her mom, I trudged up behind Izzy.

"Do you always get headaches, too? Is it being outside? Around people?" I asked as we walked up the stairs.

"Not always," she said, then added, "maybe it's the heat today." She waved a little wave at me as she closed her door, not unkindly. I headed up to my room.

It was nice to have ventured out of the house—even in the heat—to start to feel like myself again, instead of a caged animal. But meeting Delphi had left me with knots in my stomach. Over and over, I mentally replayed her use of my real name without being told, and her reaction to my shawl. By the time I'd knit a few rows and listened to most of my *Fuel* disc, I'd convinced myself that Jenn had actually *told* Delphi I was Hannah Rose, and that her reaction to my knitting had been a gasp along the lines of "*gasp*—that's gorgeous" instead of "*gasp*—*what the . . . ?*" I managed to hold off my own approaching headache, and I was pretty proud of that. Next thing I knew, I was waking up from a nap, feeling like myself again, and hungry. I headed downstairs where I saw Izzy, as bright-eyed as ever.

"Okay Rose, can you show me some more?"

"Some more what?"

"Knitting!"

"Uh, sure. Let me go get my stuff."

I ran back upstairs. No, I didn't. I started to run upstairs, but slowed down as I passed Mina's floor. Without daily swimming, I detected my body falling out of shape. Before my foot hit our landing, though, I froze. Something was wrong this time. Or not wrong, but *different* than when I was up here before my nap. I stood there, one foot hovering in midair like an idiot flamingo, listening. Trying to feel what was out of place. I didn't think I was in danger or anything crazy like that—this was Mina's house after all—but it unnerved me that I couldn't identify what felt off. It was hard to breathe, and not just because of my awkward position. I tried to sense if it was Justin messing with me, but that wasn't it. And it wasn't something *bad* necessarily, but it was *new*. And weird. I shivered and hoped this wasn't a sign that I was acquiring freaky *Sixth Sense* "I See Dead People" skills. I raced into the room, grabbed my knitting bag, and spun back around to the stairs.

Making the turn to go downstairs, I saw it. The door was closed. I mean the door to the front room on our floor was closed. That door was always open, and the sunlight from those windows brightened the stairwell. It had been open when I'd been up here before, but right then, the floor was pretty darn dark. I stood there like a goon, trying to use my Spidey sense to identify what had happened, and I came away with this profound truth: *someone had closed the door.*

I almost asked Izzy about the door when I got back downstairs. Almost.

"I want to do what you're doing." Izzy wasted no time, but then, that was how she approached everything: bouncing.

"Um. You want to do lace?"

"Yes. Lace."

I'd hung around yarn stores enough to know that you don't tell someone *oh, sweetie, that's too hard for you,* because if a knitter wants to knit something, they'll knit it. It's the motivation thing—just like diving. *You want to dive from there? Go for it! Just, you know, tuck.* So I wasn't about to tell Iz that the kind of lace I was knitting was too hard for a newbie.

"Is there paper down here? To write on?" I asked.

"Yeah, in that end table," she said. I looked over my shoulder at the round antique table with a drawer blending into the curved side and leaned back to tug it open, like I was backstroking. "It's our Euchre paper," Izzy added.

"My great-grandma played Euchre," I said, grabbing a page out of the drawer.

"No kidding? You play too?" Izzy asked.

"Nah." I dug a pen out of my bag. "I forgot how. There was no one to play with."

"Too bad," Izzy said, "but we can re-teach you."

"I'd like that," I nodded, then started to sketch on the paper. "So the only trick about lace," I started, "is that every time you make a hole, you're adding a stitch. That means that unless you want something to be monstrously huge you also have to take away a stitch."

"What if you want a triangle?"

"Then you usually add stitches at the edges, or in a column up the middle, or both. You've seen a triangle shawl that looks like there's a seam up the back?"

"Yep."

"That's what I'm talking about."

"Got it."

"So here," I drew a little diagram of circles and diagonal lines. "This would give you an 'O' and this . . . would give you an 'X' in your lace."

"Can I do that?"

"Sure, but use these needles," I pulled out a set a size or two larger than her needles from the Knitting Garden and handed them to her, "It'll look more lacy right away if you use needles bigger than normal for your yarn."

"Gotcha," Izzy said, and started measuring out for her cast-on.

"Oh, Izzy," I remembered.

"Yeah?" Iz paused.

"I forgot to tell you. Lace looks a mess until you wet it, stretch it, and pin it. So don't be freaked when it looks like a pile of yarn barf."

Izzy laughed and continued knitting. I watched her, amazed at how fluid her movements had become in such a short time. "Oh, um, wait. Rosie?"

"Yeah?"

"Is . . . was this the way you did your cast-on?" I watched her fumble a bit.

My eyes moved from her hands to her face and back again. "Yep, you got it," I said, trying not to sound as suspicious as I felt.

"Oh. Great!" She bounced a little and continued.

I kept one eye on her while I worked on my piece. My pattern was starting to show. I hadn't knit too many lace pieces, but I needed a new challenge as I finished my mittens. Normally, you have to chart lace like crazy to make sure your stitches come out even. But after years of knitting, even designing free patterns for my Tucson yarn store to give away, I wondered if I could knit a design free-form. So far, it seemed to be working, as long as I stretched things out after every few rows to inspect my progress and kept count every row. I knit a center column for growing the triangle, like I'd showed Izzy, then on each side of the column, I knit semi-mirrored shapes. I couldn't yet see what was emerging, but every time I pulled the fabric, the motifs were a little clearer.

"So, were you born in South Dakota, Izzy?" I asked, once I knew she was comfortable enough with her work to talk a little.

"Yep, right outside of Sioux Falls."

"I know where Sioux Falls is," I laughed.

"You don't know where Trent is." Izzy knocked me with her shoulder.

"Um. Nope."

Izzy sobered, "Actually, you might be the only one out here who *does* know where Sioux Falls is."

"Seriously?"

She nodded. "It's bad here, coming from a flyover."

"Flyover?"

"States everyone else flies over."

"Oh," I was embarrassed, "I guess Arizona's a flyover too, then."

"Nah, you're the Wild West. Everyone knows Tombstone."

"Everyone *thinks* they know Tombstone."

"Really? What's different? I always figured it was a dusty little town dressed up for tourists."

I laughed, "It really is a dusty little town. And, yeah, the main street's been kept all ye olde westerny, but the rest of the town itself is . . . you know . . . the roads are paved."

"Well, yeah."

"I mean, it isn't like everyone's gunfighting in the street." Izzy looked at me, so I double-checked my shields. "What?"

"Nothing," she said, and returned to her knitting. She'd created enough rows of her little sample that she approached the spot where the two lines of the X touch each other.

"Geez, Iz. You're flying along."

"I pick stuff up pretty fast."

"Is that a . . . psychic thing too?"

"Nah. It's a 'good with my hands' thing. My grandfather was an engineer. He built cars. Most of my grandma's old house. Stuff like that."

"That's cool! We built part of our house too."

"You did? I didn't think anyone did stuff like that any more."

"Well my family's a little . . . um. Odd."

Izzy stared at me over her knitting.

"What?" I asked.

"Department of Redundancy Department."

"Huh?"

"Being odd here is more like normal."

"Oh," I felt my face flush. "Right."

"Oh, look Rose!" She startled me, but I followed Izzy's finger toward my knitting where it was stretched over my knees. "It looks like a bird's wing!"

"Hey cool!" I grinned at her, "I didn't even know I was doing that! Thanks, Izzy."

"It's what I'm here for," Izzy smiled at me. Sort of. She had a hard time dragging her eyes back to her own knitting.

21 CAVES

I CONTINUED WORKING ON my shawl over the next few days. Once the mittens were washed and blocked, I started to package them up to send home with a letter to Mom, but then I decided to just send the letter. I might need the mittens myself; it occurred to me that, at the rate I was going, I would probably still be here when the weather turned cold.

We all sat around the parlor room after dinner. I listened to Izzy and Mina cleaning up—Izzy was on post-dinner kitchen patrol for the evening. I'd been on pre-. They sounded so easy together, like family.

After a bit, Iz came in, aiming her blue spiky head at the end table with the cards, and started shuffling. Justin made room for her on the sofa, and they started to play. At first, as she dealt, it looked like some kind of Rummy, but, as with most things here, it was a little off. I glanced over at Jenn. She smiled at me and tapped her forehead.

"It's good practice." She nodded at Justin and Izzy, then went back to her book.

I couldn't follow whatever mystical mind-reading game they were playing, but watching them had made me jumpy. Every time they slapped down a card, I wanted to leave the room. The flipping cards, the muted sound of Jenn turning pages, and my needles softly ticking made the house sound alive, but muffled. Every so often, I heard Mina clank something in the other room while she hummed a tune. Kitchen sounds were usually comforting, but not so much tonight. I couldn't help thinking I heard something else. Something new. It made me want to call Lindy.

My hands stopped, my knitting in midair, as I tried to remember Lindy's number. At home, I'd punched those numbers millions of times, but now I couldn't remember them. I felt my eyes start to prick and get hot, so I took a deep breath and made myself continue knitting. So what if I couldn't remember her number? So what if I couldn't call her right now? It wasn't like I could tell her about any of this. It wasn't like I could talk to anyone else about any of this. I tried to resettle into my pattern and breathe. Ground and center. Ground and center.

The sounds of the house were still there, now keeping pace with my deep breaths. I felt Jenn's eyes on me and knew that she had noticed my struggle, but I didn't look up. Instead, I focused on locating each noise. It took me awhile to plot the newest and oddest noise, but finally, I found the source in the basement. There wasn't anything psychic about that—I was sure we all could hear the sounds. The psychic part was that I knew it was Uncle Bill. I hadn't seen Bill the whole time I'd been here. He was leaving early and getting home late or at least after dinner. Or off traveling. Or both. But now he was downstairs, and I wanted to see him.

This changed everything. I looked around and then, all blasé blasé, I put down my knitting, stood up, and stretched—remembering at the last second to check my shields. I didn't need to make the effort; no one cared. So I walked around the corner, not to the bathroom, but to the basement door. It was one of those weird moments where, looking back, you can't quite recall the order things happened in. Either I opened the door and this strange guy blew past me, making me jump, or I was *about* to open the door and this strange guy burst through the door and past me. Either way, I jumped a mile and I probably squealed, though

I'm not really sure I want to admit that.

There were a couple of buggy things about him. One, I couldn't tell if he was angry in general, or angry at me, or angry at being scared by me—or just naturally charming. He was at least six inches taller than me—which is saying something—and to call him "intimidating" would have been a wicked understatement. I gave him my best, "Oops, sorry!" when I'd recovered a bit, but he'd already whooshed by. He mad-dogged me as he rounded the banister, then he moved upstairs so fast that I hardly had time to fully turn and see him disappear. I did glimpse, though, that he hesitated, looking back at me for a nanosecond. He looked confused—or constipated—then was gone.

The other weird thing was that this was the guy who had been kissing me in that vision I'd had.

My stomach didn't like that so much.

Though, honestly, why I'd want to kiss someone so rude was beyond me.

After standing there in shock for a good long time, with the door wide open, I slowly descended the basement steps. Uncle Bill called, "Mina?"

"No, Uncle Bill. It's me." I turned at the bottom of the stairs and walked into my uncle's workshop. It was a jumble of spare parts, hand tools, small power tools, and books. Lots of books. I turned around to see every wall had built-in bookshelves. Dark? Sure. A little claustrophobic? No doubt. But I loved it.

"Nice cave, Uncle Bill!"

"Hey Rosie!" He got up and gave me a bear hug. Without warning, mid-hug, I needed tissues. "Long time no see! Sorry I've been . . . " He held me away to look at me. "You okay?"

I nodded and sniffed again. He handed me the Kleenex box on his table. I shook my head at first, then rolled my eyes and took two tissues. Bill laughed kindly and sat back down. He pointed at the chair next to his desk for me to sit in.

"Sorry," I said finally.

"No apologies. It's hard to be away from home for this long. Everyone goes through it."

"Everyone?"

"Yep."

Without thinking, I asked, "Even the guy on the stairs?" Bill didn't hear me, though, since he asked at the same time, "Can you hold this for me, Rosie?" He was holding together the pieces of something that looked like a radio while reaching for his soldering iron. I stood to help.

"Sure."

"Thank you. I like working down here. It's quiet and easier to think, but once in a while, a second set of hands really comes in handy."

"What are you fixing?"

"Making. It's, ah, not really ready for prime time. I'll show you all when it's done. When it works. If it works."

"Oh. Okay."

"You've been to the Knitting Garden?" It was almost a statement.

"What? Yes. How did you—"

"The bracelet?" I looked at him, trying to figure out what he meant. "The red yarn. It's her thing. Some kind of protection device."

"Oh! *That's* what it is." So, Delphi thought I needed protection.

He soldered something on the back of his contraption very deliberately before saying, "I talked to your dad the other night."

"You did?"

"Yeah. He misses you. He wishes you'd call more." Bill glanced up and put down the tool to hand me the tissues again. "I'm sorry you're not happy here."

It took me a minute, but eventually I was able to shake my head. "It's not here or you or anything like that." Bill returned his eyes to his work. "I just. I don't like calling home. I guess . . . you know . . . if they wanted to know what their freak daughter was up to, they'd call *me* more."

Uncle Bill put down the tool carefully and looked up at me. "You're not a freak, Rose. You're an extremely special young woman."

"An extremely *dangerous* one. Or they think I am."

"Well . . . you're that too. But I'd give anything to have been born like you."

"You're kidding."

"No."

"*Why?*"

"Rose, I've spent my whole life researching and trying to master what you and Mina and your . . . what all of you were born with."

"How's that going for you?"

"Eh." He wobbled his hand horizontally, then ruffled my hair and took something off a shelf behind me. I could feel him searching my eyes as he sat back down, but he wasn't flipping through my memories the way Mina did. After a bit, he picked up his iron again.

"So, you research this stuff? To make up for not being born like . . . like us?" I asked.

"Yup."

"Did you ever come across how to stop it? Or at least control it?

Bill paused without looking up this time, "Honestly?"

"Please."

"Is that what you really want?"

"Yes! The sooner I can get a grip on this stuff, the sooner I can go back home. No offense, Uncle Bill."

"None taken."

"I just . . . what I've always done, known, it's just . . . it just *is*. You know? It just happens. But the new things—"

"The physical things?"

I nodded. "That stuff freaks me out."

"It'd freak anyone out, Rose. In fact, I'd be worried about you if it *didn't* freak you out."

"You would?"

"Yes. Look. A normal person facing this might be excited by the newness of it all, the idea that maybe they could—I don't know—ace a test without studying."

"We can do that?"

"No, but a normal person might think so."

"Right," I tried not to sound too disappointed.

"But something's wrong if you're not at least a little scared by what you can do. You've lived with precognition for so long, I'm willing to bet it would be very hard for you to try to live like the rest of us. But moving things? Hurting people? Breaking things? That's a level of power we haven't seen before."

I had to deliberate before I asked the next question. "Are *you* scared, Uncle Bill?"

"I . . . " He looked up at the pegboard of tools in front of his work table. "Can you hand me that socket wrench?" He nodded the direction.

"This one?"

"Yep, thanks."

"Because Justin moves things, too."

"Justin? You saw him? What did he move?"

"He was moving flowers in a vase."

"How heavy were they?" Uncle Bill never took his eyes off his work.

"I . . . they were flowers. Light, I guess."

Bill sat still, then turned to look at me. "That's because Justin sees them as a normal person does. They're lightweight, therefore he believes they should be easy to move, therefore he believes can move them with a 'psychic' finger, if you will, and so he can. You, evidently, expend the same amount of energy as he does with the flowers, but you do it when you're throwing a body."

"Or torching an ex-boyfriend."

"Or shattering glasses on a table."

"Justin's right," I slumped in my chair. "They never should have sent me here. I *am* too dangerous."

His eyes locked onto mine. "How scared are *you*?"

I shrugged, worried I was going to need the tissue box again.

He paused before he spoke. "I won't lie to you, Rosie. I'm unnerved by what you can do." He sighed. "But I can't see the future. I can tell you this, though. *Mina* can see the future, and she's convinced. She wouldn't have let you in here if she thought you were a danger to us."

"Yeah?"

"Yep. So, listen. Let the fear protect you for now, but don't let it control and overwhelm you. Go up. Go to bed. Get some extra sleep, and focus on staying calm and learning everything you can. Tonight I'll dig up some books that might help a little, okay?"

"Okay." I leaned over the side of his chair and hugged him, "Thank you, Uncle Bill."

"Love you, kid," he one-arm hugged me again. "Your dad does too. You should call him."

I nodded and walked up the stairs, wondering if there was a tissue box in the bedroom and vainly hoping he would find a book that would tell me what I wanted to know—how to have a normal life with my old friends, when I knew that I could maim them in a second of anger. Or how to make a world where I wouldn't need red yarn to protect me.

Or was the yarn put there to protect everyone else?

22 Smiths

"SO I'VE BEEN THINKING." Jenn was in bed, reading herself to sleep, when she started talking and startled me.

"You okay with that?"

"Yeah, but I've been thinking about you."

"You *sure* you're okay with that?"

She smiled, got out of bed, and pulled a small stone box with a pretty inlaid flower off of her book shelf and handed it to me. It looked like mother of pearl, all shiny and iridescent. "I have something that might help you." Jenn's fingers lingered on top of it, like she didn't want to let it go.

"Um. You're giving me a rock? The Fateful Rock of Destiny?"

Jenn smiled, then moved around the room collecting a pen, paper, and a hardback book. She handed those to me too.

"We're really not all fateful all the time. And I don't know that I'd go so far as to use the word *destiny*. But . . . yeah, kinda. It's a stone box, but the stone it's made of is special. You can make a wish with the box."

"I tried that already, didn't I."

"Not really."

"I don't want to think about Mr. Smith again."

"No, I know. I think I messed you up with my instructions and joking. I

155

thought it might help for you to have a more . . . direct way of getting the universe to listen to you."

I considered my options before relenting. "Okay, so how does this work?"

Jenn pointed at the writing tools in my hands. "Write down a wish."

"Really? This is like a tiny wishing well?"

"Yeah, kind of."

"Okay. So, what? Any wish?"

"Sort of."

"Sort of, or . . . ?"

"Or weird things happen."

"Define 'weird,' Jenn. Weird like Bill Smith, or weirder? The summer hasn't really been 'normal' for me so far."

"Right, well, you've already seen some of the weird in action. When you write down a wish, you don't want to make it too unreasonable or the Universe will play you."

"Like with Bill?"

"Like with Bill."

"Alrighty then. No names. Check."

"And it isn't just 'no names'—It's no *Will Smith*. Unless you're about to star in a movie with him, it's too far-fetched to ask for that."

"The universe isn't into miracles."

"Not like that. The universe is nudgeable, though. It's that whole thing about luck—ninety-five percent being prepared and five percent being in the right place at the right time. So instead of something insane—"

"Like Will Smith falling in love with me. Which would be fine, you know, to be clear."

"I know, right? So, yeah, instead of that, think of something you'd like to have happen.

"Like I want to go home?"

"Waste. You *will* go home."

"Right . . . "

"No, like to win your next swim meet. Then back off a step from the specific and think of the general idea. See the *result*, but ask for the general. Like *I want to always be the best swimmer I can be.* Write it, roll it up, put it into the box."

"Because being *the best* swimmer—"

"When you've already worked hard at it—"

"Is a reasonable nudge that the Universe can do. With no downside." I was feeling better.

"Because the universe doesn't see size like we do."

"So I could go for winning the Olympics?"

"Well, not in archery," Jenn said.

"Well, duh."

"But yeah. For me, being the best swimmer I could be would *never* win me a meet. It would mean I didn't drown while jumping waves in the ocean."

I laughed. "Okay, I think I'm getting this."

"Like . . . you know that old joke, when someone is sick, most people pray for a miracle. Jews pray for a good doctor."

"Hadn't heard that one."

"Maybe it's a Brooklyn thing."

"True, though."

"Oh, completely."

"And smarter to wish for the doctor."

"More plausible," she nodded.

"Gotcha. So, figure out what I want, focus on the end result, know what I want but not crazy specific. Make a wish. Write it down. Put it in the box. Stir and let stand for three minutes."

"Lather, rinse, repeat." She smiled, "actually, it usually takes a little longer than three minutes."

"Okay. And then it appears on the doorstep in a bow?"

"Never with a bow. But, yeah. That's the basic idea."

"That sounds easy." I lifted my pen, then looked back at Jenn. "But the only thing I can think of is how much I miss my friends at home."

"I know you do." Jenn's voice was sympathetic.

"But I can't wish for a visit from Lindy."

"Nope."

"There was this guy—"

"You can't wish for him."

"Right, I know. But I could wish for how I felt . . . or how being around him made me feel, right?"

"Well, that could be dangerous and get you into some sort of unrequited thing."

"Ew."

"Yes."

"I can't wish to be happy."

"Too vague," she shook her head. "And you're often happy."

"Can't wish to be rich," I looked up.

"Might wind up in jail."

I sighed, "I could wish for . . . love? Or finding the right guy, so when I'm back home he'll be all in love with me?"

"If a boyfriend is what you want, then that's closer. But love is a tricky thing to wish for, and you might find that someone even better for you is the one you fall in love with. It's kind of like you're giving the Universe a birthday wish list. But the Universe is tricky, right? And infinite. So it might know that there's something better—but similar—that would be an improvement. Like let's say you really want chocolate cake."

"Oddly, I do."

"Right, but you're too smart to put that in the box, so you wish for the *best cake you could ever desire.*"

"Which for me would be chocolate."

"Yes, but then someone brings over the most amazing *vanilla* cake."

"Bummer."

"Well, it's a bummer if you don't take a bite. Because if you do eat it, you find out that it *is* the best cake you've ever had in your life."

"But it's not chocolate."

"Turns out chocolate didn't matter so much."

"But I love chocolate."

"Me, too. But I'm pretty happy to find the *best cake ever.*" Jenn waited for me to briefly grieve the loss of chocolate cake. "Usually, it all starts making sense after you've tried it."

"I'm stuck on the cake."

"I know," Jenn laughed. "I shouldn't have picked that example."

"No, it's good," I said slowly. "So I go back to how I like to feel?"

Jenn's eyes sparkled. "That's good."

"I always feel good when I swim."

"Just good? That's kinda vague."

"Good, at peace, happy."

"That's a start."

"And I like how I feel when I'm around Rob. I laugh a lot around him. It's just like when I swim—I don't worry about stuff like how my hair looks or whether I have lip gloss on my teeth—my friend Lindy does that for me. When I'm around him I feel . . . like me."

"You, but happy and laughing."

"Yeah."

"Then you know what to write."

I looked down at the paper. It wasn't lined paper; it was thicker and fancier than that. The pen wasn't a ballpoint either. It was a marbled green and black fountain pen. I took a deep breath and held it in as I wrote, "I want to be happy, laughing." I paused, then added, "and in love." I blew on the paper to dry the ink, rolled it up and placed it in the bottom of the little box.

23 CALLIOPES

WHEN I WOKE UP the next morning, I had hoped to find a stack of books from Uncle Bill, but instead I found a note: "Still looking. Don't give up. I didn't tell Mina about our talk—wait until I have books. Keep knitting," with a smiley face and the letter "B".

I skipped breakfast and stayed in the room, knitting, until Jenn dragged me down. "Everyone's off work today," she said. "C'mon, I'll practice with you." She waved her Tarot deck at me.

When I got downstairs, I saw everyone draped around the living room using various pieces of furniture and rugs to support their heat-exhausted bodies. It was supposed to be cooler today, but that turned out to be one more lie adults perpetrated on kids. Things like, "your hair looks darling that way," or "I saw other kids wearing this," or "tomorrow will be better."

Izzy, blue hair stretching towards the ground with her head hanging upside-down off the edge of the couch, was so tiny that the rest of her folded up on the cushion easily. One of the rare times I've wished I were shorter.

Mina popped her head in. "Kids? I have an idea." We all adjusted so we could see her. Izzy remained upside-down but turned her head. "It's time for another little test," Mina added.

"Test?" my heart sunk.

Mina held up a nearly-pinching thumb and finger. "Little one. Like the knitting store. Nothing you need to study for."

"What do you want us to do, Mom? It's pretty miserable today, even in here."

"That's why I wanted you to go outside."

"Seriously, Mina?" Justin sounded as unconvinced as I felt.

"Seriously, Justin. Rosie needs a chance to get out, and you need to see if you're getting any better at controlling your environments."

"*We* control our environments just fine," Justin snarked, looping a finger to include Izzy, Jenn and himself. "*She* may have a bigger challenge." He inclined his head at me.

"You seem to have forgotten that you're all in this together, Justin. If one of you can't maintain control, what do you think will happen to the rest? You complement each other. You need to work with each other. You're not a fortress, any of you."

"But she can barely shield!" Justin protested.

"I've gotten better!" I defended, "I did fine when Mina and I were at the library. The whole time!"

Justin shrugged, but Mina persisted. "Today's a weekday and the park won't be crowded with people. I'm starting to think that being outside and in contact with the earth will help Rosie ground more effortlessly. It's also a good time to have a little stress-free fun."

Today, the thought of leaving these protective walls made me sick. Doing it without Mina was worse.

"Do you think that's a good idea, Aunt Mina?"

"Yeah, do you really think that's such a good idea," Justin echoed.

"I think Rosie's been practicing non-stop since we taught her the first principles, and she's not confident about her progress. And who can blame her? She hasn't had many chances to check herself against the real world," Mina went on. "And I think a day like today is a good time for you to get out and work together—when it's not crowded and when you're feeling less than one hundred percent from the heat. Normally you're fine. Today you might need help. It's like spotting in gymnastics. With you there to back each other up, I have a feeling she'll gain confidence in her abilities more quickly. Then we can move on to the next steps."

"Did you have something specific in mind, Mom?"

"I thought maybe you should all go to the carousel."

Judging from everyone's reactions, I guessed this surprised them, too.

It took some time and effort to get us all out the door at the same time, but we managed. I barely remembered to coat myself with bug spray before Izzy opened the door.

As we walked slowly up the slight incline towards the park, I took advantage of the semi-privacy to ask a question. "Jenn?"

"Yeah?"

"Something's been bugging me."

Jenn's eyes momentarily flared a little wider than normal.

"Not bugging me *angry*," I said quickly, "just making me wonder."

She relaxed, embarrassed. "Sure. What is it?"

"I saw some of the book titles in your dad's basement."

"Yeah, he's like the public library down there."

"Yeah, well . . . are we some, like, freaky secret cult? Or witches or something?" I asked.

"No! No," Jenn was very firm. "I mean, I know it can seem like that, and some of those books are ridiculous. But Wiccan is the term for what some people call witches. We have Wiccan friends, but no. We're not, like, Goddess people, right? *We*, Rose, we're Jewish. Period. Jazz is Born-again . . . something, I forget. Justin is Pentecostal. Izzy is . . . who knows," Jenn tapped her on the shoulder where she was walking ahead of us. "What are you Iz? You Buddhist this year? I can't keep track."

Izzy smiled over her shoulder, "I'm a BuLu—a Buddhist Lutheran—but," she turned around and walked backwards, holding onto Justin's arm lightly, "you get that all of this is *not* a religion, right Rosie? It's more like . . . um . . . more like a team of skilled professionals."

"Mission Impossible," murmured Justin as he looked off into the park and took a bite of an apple I hadn't noticed he had.

"Or, you know, X-men," Izzy laughed and turned back around.

"But not mutants," Jenn said, firmly. "I think of us more like a baseball team. It's kind of like we all have our parts to play. We're all good at different things."

"Izzy's playin' *Short*stop." Justin patted the top of her much-shorter head.

"Fuh. Nee." Izzy said, poking his side, making him jump.

"Snap!" Justin laughed, and for the first time, I noticed he had a beautiful smile.

It was nice to be outside, even in the heat, and it felt good to hear someone laugh and mean it. I asked, "So, what are you all good at? What did you start off being good at, I mean? I know you're good at everything now."

"Well, even I had to get good at shielding," Jenn said. "You don't have to be born psychic to ground, center, and shield. But aside from that, Justin and Izzy can do the real stuff."

"It still comes down to the shields, though. Look at Izzy," Justin said over his shoulder. "She chats with dead people."

"It's true," Izzy smiled at me, turning a 360 while walking.

"Now, think, girlfriend." I didn't have to see Justin's face to know he was looking superior. "In a city like New York, can you *imagine* the level of noise for this girl if she couldn't block all that out? *All* the people who have died here?"

Izzy nodded, "I'd go nuts in ten minutes."

"Y'already did," Jenn snorted. Izzy stopped walking and Jenn plowed into her back, laughing.

"But yeah," Izzy got serious. "It was really hard my first couple of months, Rosie, before I could trust that my shields were up all the time. I know how you're feeling. I couldn't go out of the house hardly at all, at first."

"You were younger, too," Justin said.

"That's true, but it's hard work to learn to protect yourself and *keep* protecting yourself even when you're distracted or tired."

"Is that why Mina sent us out today? To practice outside on a work day?"

Everyone nodded at me, and Izzy said, "That, and we all slept well."

"How did Mina . . . never mind. Was it that hard for all of you to learn how?"

Justin shook his head, "Nah, I got it right away."

I looked over at Jenn, who shook her head *no*. Then she said, "Even only doing defense, it still took me a long time to learn how to shield for all of us. Just in case someone needs backup. We all had to learn to work like a team."

"So." We'd crossed the street and entered Prospect Park, trying to stay under the trees as we walked further into the grounds. "How long have you all been here?"

Jenn put on her best documentary host voice, "Jennifer Lynn Green, has been in Park Slope since 1984. At her birth, it was reported that—"

"Oh, nuh uh," Justin groaned.

Izzy took over, her fingertips reseting on her collarbone, "Well, I, Isobel Marie Swensen, was born in '84 too, but Justin here is just a wee tyke. He was born in '85—"

"But I skipped a grade—"

"But he skipped a grade," Izzy smacked his arm. "I was getting there. You have no faith."

"I have lots of faith. Speak for yourself, LulyBuLu."

"*Any*way. Casey was the first to come here. He came when he was, what, 12 or 13, Jenn?"

"Something like that," Jenn nodded.

"Casey." It clicked. "Our floor's front room?" I asked, looking at Jenn.

She nodded. "He's older. He comes and goes." I started to ask if he was the jerk in the basement, but Izzy kept talking.

"So he was here for a while already when I finally told my Mom about all the dead people," Izzy said.

"Wait, *how* old were you when you started seeing, um, dead people?" I asked, fighting the gypsy-fortune-teller-vibe.

Izzy turned around again, still walking, and looked at me. "How long have you known what was going to happen next, Rose?"

In a heartbeat, it all crumbled.

That one question from Izzy—sweet Izzy who you couldn't lie to if you tried—toppled my house of cards.

I knew better, but I'd still been successfully pretending to myself that I could be normal and go back to Lindy and Rob like nothing had changed, if I learned how to control everything and not get angry—as if. But here I was, surrounded by people who really only had each other—each other and some pretty scary skills. Lying to myself, to Mina, and my new psychic friends network wasn't going to fly anymore. If I was ever going to get home, I had to start being honest with myself. And with my crew. I managed to whisper. "All my life?"

"Me, too." Izzy nodded seriously and turned back around.

"You?" I cleared my throat. "You saw . . . Did you *know* what was happening? I mean, when you were little?"

"Nah, I realized at some point that not everyone could see my friends.

My grandma could, though. I liked spending time with her, and I was lucky that my Mom let me—"

"Even though she didn't understand," Justin added.

"True. But still, it wasn't as bad as some kids have it. And I knew better than to talk about any of this stuff with the rest of my family—"

"Or friends—" Justin broke in.

"Or friends, but yeah. It started to get bad, the older I got. When we moved to a new house, the school in our new district was very old. Very, very old. And there were . . . a lot of . . . kids. All around there. Who were mostly . . . You know . . . really sad . . . "

We were all quiet.

"But I was lucky," Izzy perked up, "because my aunt—Casey's mom—saw what was happening and told *my* mom to send me out here. It was an easy sell, because by then, my grandma was dead, my mom was getting freaked out by me, and Casey was already here, so no one was very worried."

"No, they'd already lost it on Casey," Jenn said.

"So, wait. Casey's your cousin?" I asked. Izzy nodded. "He's about this tall?" I indicated with my hand the height of the guy at the basement door.

Izzy nodded.

I filed this for later. "Okay, so how old were you when *you* came out here?" I asked.

"Thirteen, maybe? I guess? It was eighth grade, so that was . . . '97? Yeah, '97."

"That sounds right," Jenn nodded.

We'd crossed a wide meadow, picking a path close to shady trees, and were now heading onto a park road sprinkled with a few insane runners and bicyclists who didn't seem to notice the crazy heat and one thousand percent humidity.

I girded my loins, "How long have you been here, Justin?"

"What? Our baby?" Izzy dragged a finger up Justin's spine, making him jump.

"Oh yeah, play the baby card." Justin rolled his eyes.

"Justin doesn't like to talk about himself," Izzy said, making Jenn turn pink from trying not to laugh, "but I will. He's been here the least, aside from you, Rose, but he's good at pretty much everything—"

"Like *you*, Iz," Jenn interrupted.

"Aw, thank you. But no, really. Justin's good," Izzy said. "But what sent him here was that he sees the shadow of death. It freaked out some of his mom's friends."

"It freaked his *mom* out," Jenn corrected.

"You can . . . *what* can you do?" I asked Justin.

Justin sighed, "It's nothing really . . . "

"Oh, for the love of Dave!" Jenn broke in, exasperated. "He can tell if someone's gonna die. Jazz can do the same thing. In fact, she's been tutoring Justin—"

"Not that I *needed* help."

"Drama much?" Izzy put her hands on her hips and stopped walking, staring at Justin.

"It *is* dramatic!" Justin insisted.

"Well then *you* tell it!" Izzy threw up her hands and walked past him.

Justin sighed deeply and tragically, slowing his gait and holding his clasped hands in front of himself like he was wearing a cassock. "When I was a young boy going to church, every once in a while I would point out someone in the congregation and say, 'Mama, you need to say goodbye.' It didn't take long before she noticed that they were all dying after I said that. So," he tugged on the back of Izzy's shirt, "that *was* dramatic." He sniffed.

"Um . . . " I was almost afraid to ask. "What did you . . . how did . . . how could you tell?"

Justin remained serious. "They were gray. They were, like . . . like they were in an old movie. All black, white, and gray. As a kid, it didn't faze me at all. As I got older, I was all, 'nuh uh!' And I didn't get why no one else could see what I saw—"

"Like all of us," said Izzy.

"Word," Justin admitted reluctantly.

"The people look . . . gray to you?"

"Yep."

"And then they die?"

"Well, not in front of me."

"Though that would have been a clue in the beginning," Jenn said.

"No doubt. But no, I told Mama to say goodbye, but I didn't put together that they were all gonna die soon, not until I was older."

"Wow. That had to be . . . " I was speechless. Somehow seeing that someone was *about* to die bugged me more than talking to dead people.

"It was," he said, proudly.

"So we all had a weird start, not that you'd expect different," Izzy said. "But the interesting thing, *I* think, anyway, was that once we were here, we found that we could do more—"

"Much more—" inserted Justin.

"Yes, much more than we thought. And way more when we're together. We've all learned tons from Mina and Bill."

"I got to see Uncle Bill last night in his office, but I didn't ask him much. When is he home, usually?" I asked Jenn. "Things have changed since the last time I was here."

"Well," Justin cut in, "when Casey's here, Bill is exclusively with him. For us, though, he plays backup. I mean, the man has an *actual* job running the theater, so he doesn't work with us all the time like Mina does, and he travels a lot, but he's around."

"He worked a *lot* with me," Izzy added. "In the beginning I had such a hard time keeping my shields up."

"I have a hard time picturing that."

"Oh sure. He and I used to ride the train together, going into the city or to the theater when it was quiet during the day, which had me terrified. But Bill, you know, he kept me calm. His colors are *so* clear. It's like he oozes protection."

"It's true," Jenn said. "He's always been like that. Even when I was little, I can remember being with him and just *knowing* that everything was okay and I was safe."

"Is that a psychic thing? Geez, I thought that was a dad thing. How do you tell what's psychic stuff and what's normal?" I asked.

"Just because it's psychic doesn't mean it's not normal," Izzy said, adding, "for us."

"Check." I said, then asked, "Is Bill, you know . . . psychic now? Like everyone else? He said he's been studying."

There was a pause, and then Jenn finally answered, "He's not like . . . you all. He learned on his own. He read a lot, experimented a lot, studied a lot, and practiced a lot. He can do some things."

"So you really can learn this stuff from books?"

"Well, to do that," Jenn said, "You have to be really, *really* disciplined, right?"

"Oh yeah. And smart," Izzy nodded.

"And you have to get ready to see some strange sh . . . spit," Justin added, recovering.

Izzy thwacked him again. "As though we don't know that. Geez!"

"But, like . . . *what* books? Where would you find stuff like this? He talked about getting me some books the other night."

"Well," Jenn said, "he spent a lot of time traveling and researching and visiting really, *really* old libraries in Europe when he was just out of high school.

Here too. But here," she sounded like she was quoting Bill, "the books are mostly limited to the late 19th and early 20th centuries. To get to the good stuff, he says you really need to go to Europe."

"And read Greek and Italian and French and—" Izzy counted languages on her fingers.

"Yeah, that helps a little too," Jenn laughed.

We rounded a bend in the road and off to the left I heard children's voices. I looked over at fences and tops of odd-looking buildings.

"Prospect Park Zoo," Jenn said, inclining her head that direction.

I nodded and refocused. "So, Bill studied all this stuff? What's in the books? Is it all the same as what Mina's teaching us, or is it about something more?"

"Um . . . geez, Izzy. You know more about his studies than I do. Same or different?"

"Well, same I guess. He did figure out—"

"Extrapolate," Justin cut in.

"He did *extrapolate*, thank you Mister SAT, that there are two rules that seem pretty universal."

"Rules? Like 'stand to the right, walk to the left?'" I asked.

"You're only saying that because you heard Mina complaining about tourists on the subway last night." I didn't much like how good Justin's memory was.

"So?" I said, brilliantly.

Izzy ignored us. "No, rules like, well, I guess they're kind of 'apply to life' kinds of rules. Sort of."

"So, right," Jenn agreed. "The first one Dad said is like a cross between Karma and the Golden Rule—what you put out there, comes back to you. Put out good, three times the amount of good comes back to you. Put out bad stuff, three times the amount of bad comes back to you. That's why we don't mess with the bad stuff."

"What do you mean, 'comes back to you'?" I asked.

"Well, like, if you decide you really want someone to leave you alone, but instead of shielding yourself so they don't really even notice you, you decide to do something to stop them from being around you . . . like you make them sick so they have to stay home from school," Izzy said.

"After doing something shady like that, you might get hit with some virus that hospitalizes you. Or worse," said Justin.

We turned off the park road and onto a dirt path. For the last few minutes, the cover of the trees had grown thicker and thicker. Now, walking on the dark, cool dirt, protected overhead by the deep green leaves, I was getting some picture of why people might be willing to tolerate the summer weather here.

"But how do you know if what you're doing is good or not? I mean, if I'm kind and gentle to a . . . what . . . like a masochist, is that being nice to them? How can you ever tell if what you're doing is the *right* thing?"

"Well, you know," Izzy said, "some of it is judging by what happens *after* you take focused action."

"English?" I sighed.

"I mean if you're reacting to a situation, you know, like someone bumps into you and you say, 'sorry!' that's not going to give you points for or against. But if you actually decide to *focus* your intentions—"

"Your power—" Justin added.

"Okay, your power," Izzy shrugged, "at some problem, and your decision is, let's say . . . you know, not so nice. Well, you'll hear about it from the universe. Something will go wrong for you—and pretty quickly, too."

"Really?"

"Yuh-huh," Justin nodded. "If you decide to take someone out just because you *can,* you know, someone who's tap dancing on your last nerve," he raised an eyebrow as he glanced over his shoulder at me, "you can wind up with a whole world-a-hurt raining down on your head."

"Experience?" I asked.

"I'm just sayin.'" He focused on the trees.

"You said there were two rules?"

"Yeah, kinda," Jenn said. "Like 'Do no harm' is the other biggie. Then there's little stuff like, 'don't bind yourself to another person'—that's like a love spell or something like that, um . . . 'don't use this stuff to show off.' Oh, and 'don't charge money.' "

"Spell?" I raised an eyebrow of my own, thrilled that all my practice finally paid off.

"Well . . . sometimes it's easier to think of the way we work in terms like that," Izzy was hesitant. "But you shouldn't get too Dumbledore about it. It's not all *Wingardium Leviosa.*"

"It's more like how you can wave a wand all you want, but without focus, intention . . . um, or concentration, it's only waving a stick," Jenn said.

"And looking ridiculous," Izzy giggled.

"Okay . . . and you said no money?" I asked.

"Like, don't charge crazy rates," Justin said. "You can make a living helping people by using your talents, but you can't get mad rich, or you shouldn't, anyway. Everyone should have access."

"It's not right. It's a gift. If someone were gonna charge huge rates, it'd be God, or the Universe or . . . something. Not you. Y'all are just a . . . what was the word Dad used?" Jenn asked Izzy.

"Conduit?"

"Yep," Jenn nodded, a finger aimed at Izzy, one eye closed, "that's the one."

"There are a few other things," Izzy said, moving next to me as we turned again and walked through a little post rail gate next to a Ye Olde House. "Don't try something new unless you really, *really* understand it. Don't get all full of yourself because of what you can do, and assume you can do something harder without guidance. That's why, to learn stuff, you really need to be around people who know what they're doing. That's why us being together is so important."

"Sorcerer's apprentice?"

"Something like that," Izzy smiled.

"And if you're going to do something weird or different or super hard, make sure you really take your time to prep, even do a Tarot spread or something. Make sure you get an independent opinion before you try something . . . dangerous," Jenn looked straight at me.

"That's a lot to remember," I said.

"You'll get used to it. It'll all, you know, be in you soon." Izzy gave me a quick arm squeeze and ran to catch up to Justin at the ticket office for the carousel.

"Shields up?" Jenn asked.

I rechecked myself. "I think so."

"I think so too." She smiled and we headed over to the booth.

If you haven't been a teenager in a while, you might not think we'd like a carousel ride.

And you'd be so wrong.

For one thing, it's fun. For another, this carousel was gorgeous. And old. And for a third thing, riding it cooled us down, or at least let us feel some breeze for a change.

Without talking, we each bought a set of tickets so we could ride a few times—why was I surprised—and we all switched animals at the end of each ride, so little kids who wanted the horse or lion or giraffe or deer that we'd been on could have a chance too. Even in motion, in the air, above the ground, I'd been able to keep myself shielded and centered. For the first time since I'd arrived, I felt like I really had a grip. I could talk, laugh, and still feel like I wasn't going to torch anyone.

It was the second-to-last ride when everything went wrong. I'd been riding an outside horse, happily bounding along and joking with Jenn about missing the brass ring. In San Diego, where my dad's side of the family lived, there's a carousel with a brass ring thingy. If you sit on an outside horse and are tall enough, you can stand up in the stirrups and lean to grab a ring that comes down from an arm. Get the brass ring—get a free ride. It's fun, and I was pointing to a perfect place for a ring arm, when I noticed this guy standing in the brick archway.

The sun shone from behind him, so he seemed to radiate light, which wasn't a surprise, since he was dressed in white, head-to-toe. That sort of made sense, what with it being summer and all. What was a surprise was that he was in white *leather*. And a helmet. I looked at him as long as I could before I had to turn away and search for him on the next go-round. He didn't move, this statue of a glowing astronaut. Just as I started to ask Jenn who that dude was, we came around again, and he put his finger up where his lips would be and shook his head, or his helmet. When we came around again, he wasn't there at all, but that guy from Bill's stairs was, and he looked like he was laughing at me. We zipped around again, then he was gone too.

For the last ride, I climbed down gingerly and got onto one of the bench seats being pulled by a dragon. My brain needed a break and my hands needed to knit a bit if I was going to keep the vague headache from becoming not so vague.

I gave myself whiplash looking, but neither of them showed up again.

I didn't tell anyone about my Strangely Glowing Spaceman or his sidekick Psychic Rude Boy, so everyone thought the carousel jaunt was a success. I hadn't fried anyone like a fish or gone all Jedi warrior on them, and Justin hadn't exploded my brain. A good day all around. So we lobbied Mina that night for approval to go for round two out in the big scary world. Izzy dragged us to Two Boots, this funky little place not far down 7th Avenue from Mina and Bill's. It's called Two Boots because they have Cajun food—that would be the Louisiana boot—and pizza—the Italy boot. In the main room, there was a cutout window looking into the kitchen so you could watch the guys throw the pizzas. I'd never seen that before, so there I was, standing up with all these little kids, oohing and aaahing at the pizza dough. I think Justin thought I was a moron, but *Ma Nishta Na*, eh? Why is this night unlike any other? Answer: it's not.

It was good to be out again, though, and have a whole day of feeling almost normal. That meal marked the first time I really started to feel like I belonged with our little psychic posse, even more than I did today at the carousel. I wasn't having any problem grounding, though Jenn and Izzy had to remind me a few times to keep up my shields. Maybe dinner felt normal because, aside from the state of my shields, we didn't talk at all about being psychic or anything like that while we were out. Normal with quotation marks, I guess, is better than nothing.

"Jenn?" I tugged at her sleeve as we were heading home, "I wanted to stop by that bookstore."

"The Community?"

"Yep."

She didn't miss a beat. "'Kay, see you at home." She kept walking with the others. For a second, I was stunned that she was so okay with leaving me on my own. But maybe I'd been doing better than I thought. Maybe I *had* learned something. Maybe she knew something I didn't.

I hung back, grounded myself, checked my shields and ducked into this cute little bookshop with a garden in back and a little coffee bar and couch area. I didn't really want to get a book, but I did want to prolong my break from the house. So, I wandered around and looked at the Brooklyn Authors' section. Some stuff sounded pretty good, but I wasn't in a buying mood. I wandered over to the empty journal books and thought I really oughta keep a better journal during this whole psychic-summer-palooza. I turned and wandered over to the psychology books . . . and the ESP books. Just looking. The ones at eye level sounded so goofy, *Love Your Psychic Inner Child* and *A Woman's Healing Nature* stuff. It was embarrassing. Celestial this and soul-mate that. These writers didn't get it. It's not like that at all. This was work—hard work—and the books treated it like it was all angels and dreams.

I looked closer to the floor and there were some much more boring psychic books there, sitting smugly on their shelf, spines staring at me, taunting. I pulled one out that looked knowledgeable, written by a Theosophist. I thumbed through it but it was all *metaphysics* this and *esoteric* that. Nothing I was doing seemed either metaphysical or esoteric, but maybe that was because I didn't know what either of those words meant. No pictures or diagrams, either. Mina was right. These books were definitely not *Psychicness for Dummies*, and even though I'm a good student, I really wanted to find a book that explained *to me* what the heck was happening. *Why* it was happening. And, if possible, how to make it stop.

I found a book from India that had beautiful color plates of a guy sitting cross-legged with different parts of his body color-coded. He had a ray of light shooting out of the top of his head, and it occurred to me that I sometimes felt like that—like the top of my head was coming off. I read a few pages, but it made no more sense to me than the Theosophists did.

All told, I must have opened twenty books before giving up. Everything I found was about *growing* your psychicness, expanding your consciousness, astrally projecting yourself to your lover, or magically drawing to you whatever you desired. None of it was about how to control or prevent your ability to talk with dead people and see the future—and burn folks. The right side of my head started to throb and I massaged it while taking a breath. That should be a book title, I thought, "Control Your Inner Flame Thrower: Breathe Deep, Breathe Often" or something. My brief research led me to understand that either what was happening to me was new, or no one experiencing it had taken time to write about it. I stood up, sad and achey and ready to go when one of the books fell off the shelf and landed on my toe.

I tried really hard not to say something bad in response to the unprovoked book attack, and at the same time closed my eyes so I wouldn't see the title. I was no longer in a mood to be enlightened by a psychically motivated book, since I was pretty sure I wouldn't understand anything in it anyway.

I groped for the book and put it back randomly on the shelf, and left that section pronto. I didn't need some soul-mate book to tell me that I'd left Rob behind in Tucson. I already knew that, and I didn't really care any more if the Universe was trying to tell me something about how much more I still needed to learn. I knew that too. Instead I looked at the new fiction for a nanosecond then left to walk home, thanking the pale guy behind the counter. The air smelled damp and the night was dark and I wasn't afraid being on my own at night in Brooklyn at all. In fact, it never occurred to me that I should be.

That night I dreamed.

I'm on my flight out here again. Only this time I board and find my seat next to the guy with the face that was kissing me in that vision I'd had—it's Casey, I guess—in the seat next to me. I stow my bags and kind of climb over him in that awful way you have to do when you come late to a window seat. I check out the window to see if we're close to pulling back and work up some nerve but when I look back at the guy to talk to him about the music that was playing, he's gone and the seat is empty. I look back out the window and see vines, these beautiful vines with white, star-shaped bell flowers growing over the window panes. That's fine, I think, but I keep noting how weird it is to have music on the plane PA. I think it's the song from Casablanca.

I check the plane for the guy as much as I can from my seat, but he isn't there. When I turn back to the window we're already flying. I can see water in the distance through the vines and a hazy sky. It's really pretty. I can see the Washington Monument and the Capitol building. I look down and guess that the pentagonal building below us is, in fact, The Pentagon. Then everything is blue as the plane turns and banks.

I woke with a start, bolt upright, cold sweat dripping down my back and the sides of my face.

It took me a long time to get back to sleep.

24 Runoff

I'D BEEN LIVING IN Brooklyn for close to two weeks, and the lack of monsoon rains was really getting to me.

Let me rephrase that. Many things were getting to me. Lack of monsoons was one of the items on that list. It *did* rain here, but it rained wrong. It was already so humid, the rain felt like more ick, not welcome relief.

Rain in New York just made it all worse. And it was raining today. Hard.

The lousy weather amplified my lousy mood. Two weeks, and I didn't feel any better about what I was doing than I did the day I started. I mean, I hadn't thrown anyone lately, nor had I torched Justin, though he was the most likely candidate. But I still struggled with shielding, especially when I was distracted in any way. It wasn't that I couldn't do it. It was that I had to keep checking. I couldn't shield habitually, naturally, the way the others did. When we were lucky enough to leave the house, I could once again see where the day was going and had a pretty decent vision of the future—just like normal for me—but in the house, it was all fuzzy, which confused and frustrated me. And it was weird, because I would have thought that the house should have helped focus me on exactly this stuff I was learning. I thought the house protections prevented us from doing stuff we weren't supposed to do. I knew I should talk to Mina or Bill about this, but I was so sick of being the one playing catch-up. The humidity was frustrating enough. I really didn't want them reminding me what a failure I was.

That morning, I took as cold a shower as I could stand, just to feel something other than heat on my skin, and thanked God for air conditioning, magic or otherwise. Stepping out of the shower, I could smell Bill's breakfast bacon and coffee. Bill the beloved.

I slowed my gait when I entered the kitchen and saw Mina on the phone, all concerned and, I thought, looking a little nervous. When she saw me she held her hand over the mouthpiece and mouthed, "Get Izzy?"

Leaving the bacon, I turned and jogged upstairs. I rounded the top of the second floor stairs and saw Izzy lying on her bed, making tiny puffs of, I don't know—steam? Or clouds?—appear and dissolve in the air above her.

"Hey?" I started.

"Yeah," she sighed, "I know." She rolled off the bed.

That's the annoying part about living with psychics.

I followed her, clattering down the stairs. We turned at the bottom and swooped around the banister by holding onto the pineapple-shaped finial that I *knew* would bust loose one day and send me flying across the room, not because I saw it in the future. Just because it was crazy loose. When we reached the kitchen doorway, we both stopped. Mina was holding up her hand to us, index finger up, nodding and listening to the voice on the phone.

"Richard Wilson," Mina said, simply and quietly to Izzy.

Izzy walked to one of the wing-backed chairs and sat down. She carefully placed her feet apart on the floor, wrapped her arms around her middle, and gently rocked back and forth. Then she stopped. Everything. It looked like she stopped breathing. I kept watching and was relieved to see that her breath had simply slowed—a lot.

"Big guy? Dark hair?" she whispered with her eyes still closed.

Mina relayed the information back through the phone then nodded, realized that Izzy's eyes were closed and said, "Yes . . . oh, but not dark hair. Gray."

"*Was* it dark?" Izzy asked with a smile, one eye open on Mina.

Mina asked, then chuckled. "Yes . . . that's him."

Then to the phone, Mina said, *no . . . no . . . she . . . well, no . . . Izz's the medium, I'm just . . . the low.* Mina shrugged at us with an "oh well?" expression. We could hear the laughter through the phone and Izzy smiled. It was an old joke. Gotta put the panicked searcher-for-psychic-solace at ease, right?

Mina put her hand over the mouthpiece. "Okay Iz, what else've you got?"

"Geez, this guy's pushy!" Izzy put her knuckles to her forehead and leaned over.

Mina removed her hand and translated into the mouthpiece, *He's a very strong presence and making himself known.*

"He's kinda frantic about the way he left things," Izzy mumbled.

Mina into the telephone: *he's very concerned about you.*

"There's some kind of insurance trouble . . . life, not medical. The medical seems to be taken care of . . . and . . . there's something about a pen . . . ? She found it at the back of a drawer yesterday?"

Mina relayed, then paused. "She's crying," Mina whispered to Izzy over the covered mouthpiece. Izzy added more and Mina spoke into the phone, *Izzy sees a chair, a table, and you, but the important thing is there's that pen . . . and . . . you shouldn't feel silly about paying attention to it. He wanted you to find the pen. It's one of his ways of showing you that he's still there.*

Mina paused, and whispered to Izzy, "Oh, she's really crying now." Izzy opened her eyes, inhaled, exhaled, stood, and walked to the kitchen cabinets and got herself a glass of water. Mina whispered a direct relay to Izzy's back as she headed back to her chair. "Yeah, that's him . . . the pen thing. That's him."

Izzy returned to her seat, carefully placed her water on a coaster on the side table and resumed her blank stare, sometimes closing her eyes, sometimes not. "He's very clear about this: he knows it was heart failure, he knows why, he knows they did everything they could, he's not in pain. His *only* concern is her. He has tried to make it clear that he's with her, but she keeps blowing it off. The pen thing should help her."

Izzy paused to let Mina translate, then Mina whispered back, "Yes, it has. She's rattling off a list of coincidences."

"Great. Okay, I need a nap. I . . . wait . . . ask her where they met."

Mina relayed but watched Izzy, eyebrows down.

"They met at a mutual friend's house. At a party."

Izzy was still. Then she asked, "Has the friend passed?"

Mina waited for an answer. "Yes," she said finally.

"Um . . . " we all waited for Izzy to finish, "I've got that friend with me. Don't tell her that yet. Stall."

He might be pulling back, Mina said slowly into the phone, watching Izzy's every move.

Izzy collapsed, leaning her head into her hands, shaking her head, "Oh, no no no no no . . . " she whispered.

I went and sat next to her chair, "What? Can I help?"

Izzy turned her head to look at me without looking at me. Her eyes weren't focusing on me or anything else in the room. Instead, Izzy was seeing other people in other places. This is the thing I never did. I just knew things in my head, like future memories. She was *seeing* things.

"Rosie?" Izzy whispered. She sounded so sad. So, so sad.

"I'm here?" She reached out and took my hand, and I saw it all. I saw what the friend was showing her. This guy who was returning to comfort his wife wasn't trying to comfort her at all. He was trying to placate her so she wouldn't start looking and discover all of his lies. He'd cheated, he'd lied, he'd played her like a cheap violin. And now Izzy and I knew it. We could see his whole lousy life stretched out in front of us. I was outraged. Outraged for the wife and how fooled she'd been, and outraged that this guy had sucked Izzy into it all. I struggled to regain my breathing and ground myself, but while the friend who had introduced the couple was giving us more of the same, I started to feel something else. Izzy's grip on my hand got tighter and the pressure in my head got stronger.

"What is *that*?" I whispered.

"Wilson," she said. "He's back."

Before I knew what I had done, I could feel everything—my anger at this guy, the pain of watching Izzy get battered by this jerk, and my moral outrage at all of the lies his poor wife had lived through—all of it lashed back at him. It felt like a fireball of rage left the top of my head and aimed itself right for the target this guy had put on his ghost's chest.

Wherever he was, I knew he got zinged.

And I felt pretty good about it right then.

"Pull out," Mina said. I heard her in the distance. Her hands seemed to stretch from miles away to reach our shoulders and pull us back. "Come on, you two. Out!"

Once again, chilly blue washed over me. I opened my eyes slowly, looking at the world through ice-tinted filters. I was on my knees next to Izzy, who was sagging against the side of her chair.

"I made up something vague and hung up." Mina answered my unspoken question, then inclined her head. "You're safe."

I couldn't tell if she was asking or telling but she seemed to want acknowledgment. "Oh. Good."

"Where's Izzy?" Mina asked and at first I was confused. When I looked again, though, I saw what she meant. Izzy's body was resting against the side of the chair, but her eyes were open and her jaw was slack.

"What did I do?" I whispered.

Mina didn't hear me. "Can you go in and help Izzy back?"

"This happened before?"

"Not this bad, but. Yes."

I had exactly zero idea what I was doing, but I had to try. With Mina's hand on my shoulder I didn't need to worry about blowing up anything—or smiting already-dead liars—so I closed my eyes and focused on Izzy, starting with our hands. I felt our hands, where they touched and connected, the light and heat they created. I followed that light like a path, a glowing path of red heat payed out like a cord that connected me, eventually, to Izzy.

"I don't know what I'm doing, Mina."

"You're doing great, kiddo. Try to call her. Like you did before. But," she added quickly, "quietly, remember?"

"Right," I raised one eyelid and saw Mina smile.

Izzy? I whispered. *C'mon Izzy. It's Rosie. Let's . . . let's go back?*

It hurts, Rosie.

I know, Izzy. But I didn't know. I didn't know if she was talking about her head or body or if she was hurting for the poor woman who'd married a lie and lost him. Or if I'd hurt her. But I couldn't think about that right now. *C'mon, Mina's waiting. She'll know how to help.*

I tried to feel the room and kitchen smells and Mina more strongly than I felt anything else, but I kept ahold of Izzy's hands the whole time. In a moment, I opened my eyes and saw Izzy's fluttering open, too. She slumped back against the back of the chair, releasing my hands.

"Thanks," she whispered.

"Anytime," I said, relieved, sitting flat on the floor against the couch. Mina was at the stove, pouring something.

She brought us two mugs of steaming goodness. "Let this cool enough so it doesn't burn you, but try to drink it hot. It'll help." She sat on the floor across from me. Izzy cradled her mug. "You okay?" Mina put her hand on Izzy's knee.

Izzy lolled her head towards Mina and nodded. "It'll take a minute."

"You're going to need a nap," Mina smiled softly.

"You're not kidding." A smile flickered on Izzy's face and she raised the mug to blow on it.

I held my mug tight till it seemed the heat would burn my hands. I didn't want to let go. It was solid. It was here. It was real. And it kept me from worrying if I'd been the one who hurt Izzy.

"Well," Mina said softly, trying to change the mood, "that's something you don't get to see every day . . . unless you live here." She smiled weakly at me, keeping her hand on Izzy and breathing deeply. "You okay?"

"Yeah," I nodded, "but . . . "

"Go on."

I decided to ask a different question, "How did the caller find you? Find Izzy?"

"Ah . . . that's not what I thought you were going to ask—Shielding?" Mina asked. I smiled. She nodded and continued quietly, "the calls we get like that are word-of-mouth mostly. We have some friends who are . . . sensitive but not trained. Sometimes they find people contacting them as a way to get to us. Spirits can tell they're conduits so they get . . . well, they get used that way. That sounds really horrible, doesn't it?"

"No," I shrugged, "it makes a lot of sense." I took a tiny sip of Mina's tea and let the warmth roll down my throat. "I mean, if I'd crossed, I would want to get to someone who wasn't scared. Someone who could handle it. So I suppose I'd do what it takes to find the right person."

"Yes, that's exactly right. I'm a good example. I'm not a Medium. I know and can do other things, but I *understand* mediumship and I know how to funnel people and their loved ones to the right places."

"So, will *I* be able to . . . ?"

"That depends, doesn't it? It depends on you and what you learn about yourself this summer."

"I mean, I saw . . . with Izzy."

Mina nodded, but corrected me, "You piggybacked on Izzy. You didn't initiate the contact. Izzy can do both."

I sipped more tea. I'd hoped that being able to get what Izzy saw would be a sign that I was a little closer to getting the hang of this stuff and going home.

"Aunt Mina?" I asked.

"Yes?"

"Those times when I've seen Mom get really edgy and she absolutely *has* to call you...?"

Mina nodded, "Sometimes it's because I have a message for her. Sometimes it's because she needs to funnel someone to me to get to Izzy or sometimes...she wants to talk."

I smiled. "Wow, what did you guys do before mobile phones?"

She laughed, "We had expensive long distance bills and a lot of frustrating afternoons."

"And..." I started to ask about this particular phone call we just dealt with.

"I don't know." Mina shrugged. "Like you, I can sometimes piggyback, but I needed to help the weeping woman on the phone, so I let you ride with Izzy. She's a very stable medium, so I wasn't worried about you. But I don't know why this guy was trying so hard to contact his wife when..."

"When he was nothing but a lousy liar?" I started to tell her, "You should —"

"Well, people are complicated." Mina responded to my first comment. "He may have been trying to keep her from the pain of learning the truth. We can't know *why* he did what he did if he doesn't tell us. But it makes our job harder when we encounter a situation like this."

"Our job?"

"I like to think we all have these gifts for a reason. That we have some purpose in bringing solace to people who've lost loved ones or offering counsel to people who are lost. When situations like this happen, well . . . ," Mina rose to her feet, "even I get stumped sometimes."

We heard footsteps on the stairs.

"The hordes emerge." She smiled at me, squeezed Izzy's knee and moved to get me more hot water.

"Y'all freaked out, Newbie?" How did I know Justin was going to make a crack? Hint: it's not because I'm psychic.

"Freaked out, how?" I did the eyebrow at him again, to no effect.

"Izzy? Phone call? All that?" Justin moved straight to Izzy and took her hand without saying a word. I scooted back onto the cushion behind me.

I shrugged. "Dunno, Justin. Did it freak *you* out the first time you saw her do that?" I worked hard to control my shields. Of *course* Izzy had freaked me out. *I* freaked me out. I'd be lying to say any different. Dead people? When I actually thought about what just happened, it seemed completely creepy to me, but I sure wasn't going to admit that to Justin.

He was studying me closely, then he *tsked*, pulled a paperback out of his back pocket and aimed his nose at the back cover while keeping hold of Izzy with his other hand, effectively dismissing me. I breathed again. It seemed my shields worked. I wondered if anyone would notice if I shoved Justin in the dumbwaiter and sent him to the basement. Could you leave a shield on someone else so no one could detect them?

Outside, the rain was stabbing down, pummeling the back windows. I moved to the window seat and gazed into the backyard. It was pretty in a humid-green-gray-drippy-depressing kind of way. But then, I felt kind of gray and depressing so this worked for me.

Dead people.

What would it be like to see dead people? To have them bang on your head so much that they hurt you? So far, my ho-hum, day-to-day, seeing-the-future thing had never given me a headache. My headaches were warnings of something I was about to do, not what harm the universe was about to inflict upon me. For me the future caused me no more pain than rain drops did. Relentlessly falling on my head, sure, but it didn't usually hurt. Watching outside I wondered: was it possible to count raindrops? Had anyone ever tried? Could someone like us slow the rain enough to count drops? Were there limits to what we could do?

I watched. The rain drops were hitting the deck too furiously for me to even pretend to see individuals, but the big bloppy drips coming down from the eaves were better. They were larger, more solid. I concentrated on counting them. I reached forty when I noticed the drops were clearer. They were refracting the green of the trees, the gray of the sky, the red of the brick house behind ours. I could see the colors change in the drops on their way down. It was beautiful. And it was slow. Too slow to be normal. I glanced back to the room and looked at the kitchen clock. The second hand was moving in normal time.

But the drops.

I looked again and they were definitely falling in slow motion. I held my focus on them and watched. I had no idea how many hours I sat there, but I finally got the drops to fall slowly enough that I could see myself, looking through the window, reflected upside-down on their surface.

When I had slowed and watched all I could, I decided I would privately ask Mina about this later. She would laugh and remind me that I'd see many odd happenings in Brooklyn, then move on to other things.

I would just wait for another rainy day.

25 SORTILEGE

JENN SLOWLY FLIPPED THROUGH her new Tarot deck. It was a sunny morning after breakfast and we were sitting in the parlor room at a little game table she had cleared. Jenn's back faced the pocket doors and my back faced the fireplace. I had a perfect view of the stairway, which was reasonably fun to watch because today we were an active bunch. Justin had loped out and back, returning with gorgeous flowers for the table, and Izzy—the blue-topped blur—had been up and down the inside stairs at least seven times—the last time sliding on the banister. This was normally a big no-no, but she was so tiny, I figured even if Mina caught her, she wouldn't get busted. There wasn't much risk, though. Mina was in the kitchen with Jazz, so she was distracted.

That was all peachy, but the next time the front door opened, I couldn't sense the person who entered. I started to tell Jenn about the intruder, as unlikely as that seemed, but before I could say anything, there was that strange, tall, dark-haired figure standing at the edge of the pocket doors, scowling.

Jenn turned and said, bored, "Oh. You." She turned back, then indicated over her shoulder, "Casey, Rose. Rose, Casey." I hesitated, then half-waved at him. He wasn't any more pleasant than he had been coming out of the basement or laughing at me at the carousel. This time, though, his stare pinned me like a butterfly to a board. He stood there for forever, watching me. His eyes went from

191

scowl to *you-need-to-leave* to *boring.* We stayed like that, frozen, for hours, staring at each other. Too late, I remembered to shield. And ground. And center. All of which were hard while my hands were trembling so badly. He might have nodded at me right before he took off up the stairs, his backpack bounding behind him. Jenn was trying not to watch me.

"What was that?" I managed.

"Casey? That's Izzy's cousin. The one we told you about who started the whole psychic day camp thing. He's a pain." She looked at me. "Yeah, he's cute, but he's a pain. Don't worry, I won't tell anyone. You totally lost your shields when you saw him."

I tried to pull myself together and decide whether or not I should ask Jenn more about him. Jenn smiled, blushed, got all shifty-eyed and dropped a card, then went back to teaching me. I really did try to repeat everything she said, and worked hard to apply enough focus to figure out how the Magician could logically connect to the Empress, but really I was sneaking looks at the stairway

"So why is he a pain?" I asked finally, straining to sound casual.

Jenn looked up from the cards. "Oh, he's pretty antisocial, thinks he's better than the rest of us."

"Is he?"

"Yeah," she laughed, "but he's still a pain."

Great. Now I was trapped in a house with two pains. Terrific.

I tried to refocus upstairs to see what this Casey was like, to see exactly what kind of pain I was in for since I had a pretty clear picture of how life with Justin was panning out. I kept poking around like a rat in a maze to see if I could find the same feeling that had walked in the door. I couldn't.

For all I could tell, he'd vanished into thin air up there.

No doubt, Casey's presence in the house threw me. I mean, I knew he'd been there before, but now that I knew who he was—and how he'd appeared in my head before I ever saw him in person—I got all squidgy about him. I tried taking a break from Tarot, going upstairs, and listening to music. I tried knitting. I tried reading. Then I thought about the books Uncle Bill promised to find for me. I dragged my knitting bag with me and headed downstairs to the basement to see if he was there. Jasmine, enjoying a weekend off of her super-pressureful job was taking advantage of the downtime by teaching Mina how to cook something rolled in dough that smelled heavenly. I already knew that frying onions and garlic will make the house smell like you're Emeril, but there was a sweet edge to her food that I didn't recognize. I could tell it was going to be like when mom made Chili Sauce every fall. There's this sugar and vinegar smell that infuses everything—clothes, hair, air. It was worth peeling the tomatoes for her, just to have that smell lingering in the house for a couple of days.

Bill wasn't downstairs. I poked around his desk a little, looking to see if he had left out some books that might help me, but I didn't see anything. Instead, I wandered around the long basement, looking at his books, his gadgets, his turkey bacon freezer, his whole world. When I reached the front of the basement, I noticed there were bicycles—not enough for everyone, but a few. I turned away from the bikes and saw a door to the street. I paused and thought for a second—not long enough to stop myself, just long enough to pretend I was responsible—and I tried the knob. The deadbolt above was the only lock on the door, and the gate on the outside could be closed without locking it. I tested both, crossed the threshold, and closed them behind me.

I was free.

I had never done anything like this.

Let's be honest, I'd never *needed* to do anything like this.

Looking up, I snuck a glance back at the front of the house before slinking up the area steps and heading towards the park. What I really needed was to swim, but I'd settle for a nice walk by myself.

At least I'd be free for a little while.

Just before I crossed Prospect Park West, I saw a corner pay phone. My newfound freedom meant I only hesitated for a nanosecond. I picked up the receiver and dialed "0". I didn't have my phone card memorized, but I figured I could call Lindy collect—she'd told me to before. The line rang and rang, but no one picked up.

Just as well, I convinced myself.

What would I have been able to say?

Prospect Park is huge and beautiful and nothing in Tucson compared to it in any way. I liked it a lot—aside from crazy spacemen who hid near carousels in there. Approaching the park from the outside, you see occasional roads cut in, even though driving was restricted on some days, and then every so often there were little entries in the low exterior walls. I picked one and followed the path into the park without much attention. It was quiet and cool in the shade and I felt myself calming down. The Casey thing was definitely starting to bug, but Justin was under my skin worse. The further I got from the house and the more I let myself think about it the more angry I got about his patronizing attitude. I knew I had to let it go and not get so riled, but the things he said—and the way he *said* them—just got in there and festered. *Noobie.* Yeah. Whatever. I stopped, closed my eyes, and took a deep breath.

Deep breathing, patron saint of all firestarters.

It was easier to keep grounded and centered when I wasn't surrounded by people reminding me that I was a dangerous psychic renegade. It was nice to feel my heart rate slow, my shields take hold, to really feel like I was in control. Like I was finally learning what Mina wanted me to learn. I opened my eyes to the lovely world, smiled, slowly inhaled the beautiful greenness—as opposed to a deep breath to keep from hurting someone—and walked on.

One of the other things I really like about New York is that there's always stuff happening. You didn't need to be psychic to know that I was heading towards some event or other. First I heard a murmur, you know, like regular crowd noises, but every so often there was a cheer and squeals from what sounded like kids.

Or pigs.

But probably kids.

I came around a series of bends in the path to see a large playground with a crowd in it. The throng was mostly little kids and parents but there were some people who could probably go to school with me there, too. We were all in a circle around a guy who was doing magic tricks. He had a trunk open on the ground with its back facing me and a hat in front with some money sticking out. He was good with the little kids. Keeping them interested, not talking too much, but gliding from one part of his act into another seamlessly and getting a lot of "oohs" and "ahhs". He had a nice mix of up-close magic, the slight-of-hand stuff, and then bigger tricks using props he'd pull from the trunk. I was really starting to enjoy watching him do the "and your card is . . . " fake-psychic-tricks—I know, irony, me getting a kick out of someone pretending—when he turned to me.

"And you, my lovely lady," he gestured my way.

"Um."

"For this next trick I could use your assistance."

"No," I froze. "No, thank you."

"Oh, come on—"

"No, really," I tried to back away.

"Come on, ladies and gentlemen. A round of applause for our shy beauty." Why was he saying that? Couldn't he see I wanted to be left alone? "Are you from here, m'dear?"

"No." I looked down to check if I was wearing UofA gear, "I'm from Arizona."

"Ah, a desert flower," he winked. "Missing the dry heat?"

"Every day."

"Well, it's about to get a little hotter," he said and the crowd murmured appreciatively. I was lost. He turned back to me, "If I could have you hold this for a moment." He took a pretty well-beaten brown leather wallet out of his back pocket.

"Oh . . . fine," I squeaked.

Then he was fiddling with something else from the trunk, "Pretty hot day today, innit?"

I felt like a dork stuck there holding this wallet and not doing anything else. "Yes," I hissed.

"Okay darlin'," he stood back up with some magic stuff in hand. "For this trick I need a bill. Would you please open the wallet and verify that the money is real."

"Sure," I said, relieved that I was asked to do so little. I turned slightly, so most of the rest of the crowd could see the wallet, then I opened it.

It burst into flame.

"I didn't do it," I choked and dropped the wallet. The fire went out.

The magician came over, laughing, picked up the wallet, opened it—and nothing happened. "Wow," he drawled, "you're hotter than I thought, gorgeous! You free after the show?"

I squirmed while the crowd laughed and he handed the wallet back to me. He backed up to where he'd left his magic tools, "Okay, try again. Just one bill. There aren't that many in there . . . yet," he playfully eyeballed the adult audience.

I really needed not to be there, not to be doing this. Calling attention to myself wasn't smart. I knew that, now. I could tell I was starting to blush and felt the sweat dripping down my back and a throb in my temple, but I was stuck and everyone was watching. I took a ragged breath and slowly opened the wallet. There was a tiny click, and the whole thing burst into flames again.

Now I was mad.

"I think you'll have to get someone else to get your money for you," I said, teeth clenched, holding out the now-closed wallet with my left hand while pressing my right into my temple.

"Yes," he said grinning at the crowd, not picking up on my voice. "You sir. You're not nearly as attractive as she is. Perhaps you're not so hot that you'll light my wallet on fire." He handed the billfold to the laughing father who opened it without any incident.

What a jerk.

He continued with his routine and I vainly tried to let go of what he'd done. It was harmless, right? Just innocent entertainment. But he wasn't paying attention to what I was saying and that got under my skin. While I seethed about his wallet's trick-lighter mechanism he moved on to larger feats and eventually to juggling. Grudgingly, I had to admit that he was pretty good. Then he announced his grand finale.

"For my final trick," he called out to the ever-expanding crowd, "I will juggle not three, not four, but *five* flaming torches."

I started to back out through the crowd and heard him laugh, "Wait, don't go! I need your pyrokinetic powers to ignite the flames!"

If he had welded my shoes to the ground he couldn't have done worse. I couldn't move. "My . . . you what?"

"I need you to light my torches. Don't we," he gestured to the crowd, amping them up. "We need need a hottie to light our fire!" Some idiot in the crowd started chanting, "hot-tie, hot-tie, hot-tie."

"Here," the magician said, beckoning to me. "You won't need to use the wallet, instead, use this," he handed me a beaten up barbecue lighter while the audience tittered. When I got closer to him he whispered, "You can use a lighter?"

"You have no idea."

He laughed, but I watched the tiniest bit of concern flicker behind his eyes.

Good, I thought.

"Okay then," he said aloud turning to the audience, grandstanding. "I will hold the torches . . . like so. You, my lovely desert flower, will kneel . . . there," he pointed to the ground in front of him while some chuckles rippled around the crowd, "and hold the lighter below, right about . . . there . . . perfect. When I give the word, you will click the trigger—and then back up. Very quickly."

Everyone laughed again while I wondered how a show like this was legal. What if I'd burned myself on the wallet? What if I burned myself on this kerosene-soaked torch-lighting maneuver? None of this seemed very safe or very smart and he seemed far too smug. Staying in the house in the future seemed better and better.

"All-righty, are you in position?" He looked around his sheaf of torches.

I nodded.

"Very well, one . . . two . . . *sh—whoah!*" He stumbled back hard as a fireball engulfed the torches—and nearly his eyebrows. "Don't you know how to count?" he growled at me while he began jerky and frantic juggling.

"I didn't do it," I said.

But nobody heard.

I could tell he was angry with me, but I was pretty mad at him, too. Handing over flame-making equipment to me was not his smartest move and not expecting the unexpected when you're working with fire made him seem that much dumber. I mean, you don't know what people are going to do with it, right? I could have been a complete psychopath and used the lighter to light *him* on fire. I could have been a really dangerous person and lit a kid on fire. I could have

—

A fireball exploded in the air above the head of the magician where three of his torches were arcing through the air. The crowd screamed and started to back away.

"Nothing to worry about, folks," he said while his face said something else entirely. "It's all part of the act, see?" He spun around, catching a torch behind his back when a second fireball ignited closer to the front—closer to the crowd.

"*Wha*—" I heard him say and now his face registered total fear. Every time he started to slow down to finish and catch the torches there was another explosion, some smaller, some bigger, that forced him to keep going.

Good.

The crowd couldn't get out of there fast enough with only occasional fathers scuttling in low to drop a buck in his hat.

I was frozen on the ground, still holding the stupid lighter, watching his face and slowly getting that this wasn't him having a torch malfunction.

This was me.

As fast as I could I grounded and centered and breathed deep, pulling up ice blue calm and projecting it out of me and at him. Slowly the torches diminished, sputtered, and went out. The magician was nearly in tears when he finally, gingerly put them down on the asphalt. "Can I have the lighter back?" He cleared his throat, hand out to me.

"What? Oh. Yes," I handed it up to him. He took it, and for a moment I thought he was going to give me a hand up. Instead he looked me in the eyes, face still full of fear for a second, then started repacking his truck.

I got myself up and turned to walk back home and nearly plowed into Justin's chest.

Tsk. "And they all think you're smart."

"Justin, this is not the time." I tried to push past him.

"Oh, this is *so* the time," he blocked me with an arm out holding a cold bottle of water. "We're gonna go sit under that tree on that bench there and we're gonna have a little sip of some nice cold water and we're gonna have a little chat is what we're gonna do."

And so we did.

"Let me start here: *what were you thinking?*"

"I wanted a break." I dug around in my bag to take out my knitting. Soft yarn is calming, so they tell me.

"Happy now?"

"Yes," I said defiantly. "No," I sighed.

Justin relaxed, "Okay. Good. Now, look—"

"You're not going to tell Mina are you?"

"We haven't yet."

"You . . . we . . . *yet?*"

"Mina may be blind, girl, but we're not."

"But . . . but I've learned. I mean you saw, right? You *saw* how I put the fire out?"

I'd never seen Justin laugh so hard. Embarrassed, I opened my bottle of water, smiled and raised my bottle at confused passers-by, took a nice long drink —and he was still going.

"I'm glad I amuse you so."

"Oh, *oh oh oh oh oh* . . . you have no idea. Ahhh . . . " He finally wound down and wiped his eyes. "You think that *you* put the fire out?"

"I know I did. I was grounded, and centered, and drawing up blue and projecting it and could *see* it and—"

"And was that before or after the flare-up and explosions you caused?"

"I—"

"Y'can't lie."

"No."

"And y'can't hide."

"Right."

"You *cannot* sneak out."

"Clearly, I wasn't as sneaky as I thought," I snapped back.

Justin snorted, "Your shields aren't as good as you think."

"I got that."

"Yeah, well . . . "

"But Mina doesn't know?"

"Uh-uhn."

"And you won't tell her?"

"Uh-uhn."

I thought for a moment, "Why not?"

"Because she has enough to worry about. And because as good as she is, *she* can't control you." He hesitated, "We haven't been sure that *we* could stop you, either."

"But you're saying you did today?" I could hear defeat in my voice.

"Containment. Not control."

"Oh."

"But he *was* being pretty stupid with you," Justin said after a pause.

"I know, right?" I perked up.

"We should go before Mina notices."

"Okay." We stood up. "I think that was the nicest thing you've ever said to me, Justin. About the magician being stupid."

He *tsked* at me. "Don't get used to it, Weej," and walked ahead of me down the path.

That night, I ate dinner at the end of the table, next to Jenn. Bill sat at the head with Tyrik, who was over for dinner with Jasmine. Mina and Jazz sat on opposite sides, facing each other. Obviously, they didn't spend enough time together. They looked like Lindy and me when one of us returns from vacation—hardly a sliver of breath between our words. My end of the table was heaped with the usual mountains of good food to share. There was Jazz's fried, spiced chicken things and Mina's huge salad with some kind of crumbled cheese and these little bright red oranges—tangier than mandarin and so good. The mounds of food never seemed to diminish, though I wasn't watching that carefully. I was distracted by that Casey guy, sitting all the way down next to my uncle on the other side from me, talking earnestly and quietly to Bill, with Tyrik leaning in and hanging on every word.

It was impossible not to stare at Casey. He had brown floppy hair that spent a chunk of time in the sun—and needed a trim—with lightly-tanned skin. Not like he sat out with *Bain de Soleil* on, but like he walks his dog every day. He looked healthy—healthier than the rest of us, anyway. He had a delicate mouth that gave away nothing. I couldn't tell whether or not Casey had a sense of humor; he sure didn't laugh. What completely messed me up, though, were his eyes. He had the loveliest eyes I'd ever seen, same as in that vision. Brown, deep brown and slightly turned down at the edges—sad eyes—with lashes barely within the legal length for a guy. Lashes so long I could see them down the table. They were hidden partially from me by the frames of his glasses while he talked to Bill. The glasses were cute, but not so hip that he looked like a Calvin Klein model.

"What?" Jenn said. "What's so funny?"

"Huh?" I said.

"You're smiling."

"*And* she's blocking," Justin nodded at me.

"Yay, Rosie!" Izzy high-fived me across the table.

I tried to shift the conversational focus off me and my shields—my new trick. We meandered to talk of the President, local politics—more of a sport in New York than it is in Arizona—and a girl named Chandra Levy who had gone missing in Washington D.C.

"No way is she still alive." Justin was adamant.

"Well then, why don't you call the Feds?" Izzy nudged him, "Pass the salad?"

"Oh yeah, like I'm gonna make *that* mistake." I was surprised to see Justin glancing down towards Casey. I followed his eye, but Casey hadn't moved or done anything worth watching, so far as I could tell.

"I'm just saying," Izzy started, "better to help the family—"

"I *know* what you meant. *I'm* just saying, there's no way to make that good—no way to bring her back, no way to help, and calling the Feds only gives them a chance to know what we're doing here and that ain't good for any of us."

"That's true—sadly," Mina leaned in, looking at all of us, "It's better not to call attention to ourselves if we can help it."

"What do you think about the creepy senator?" Izzy broke the quiet, finally.

"Creepy," Jenn said. "Makes me totally think that he'd *eighty-six* her."

"Jennifer!" Mina looked surprised.

"I don't know about that," Jazz said, quietly. "It's sad, though, that—"

"It *is* sad because it's going to ruin his career," I broke in. My voice sounded funny. Too loud. Too wrong.

"Rose . . . " Mina was staring at me.

"It's going to ruin his career—and he's a rep, not a senator—but he was stupid, not a murderer." My throat was tight and wouldn't let me swallow. Sweat slid down between my shoulder blades.

"And?" Casey's voice came barreling at me from the end of the table.

I shivered, "And what? He . . . he didn't do it." I stared right back into those eyes.

"And what else?" asked Casey.

"And . . . nothing else. She's dead and it's awful."

"No. Go back to the beginning. Trace it back. And *what*?"

"And . . . and that morning there was this little mean guy, some crazy guy from South America . . . no, not there . . . " I closed my eyes, "from Central America . . . somewhere . . . "

"And? Don't let go."

"Why are you *pushing*?" I wanted to hit him but I pushed at my forehead instead. "I told you what I know."

"Chicken. You're broadcasting the whole thing." Casey looked around at the table. "Don't you all see it? She's like a sparkler with all this stuff flying off her, and she's just sitting there with her hands covering her precog like a little monkey refusing to listen." Everyone looked at him, silent. "Oh *come on*. I'm not the only one who sees this. You *must* be able to—" He stopped mid-sentence, then his eyes speared me again, exasperated, "some sociopath did *what* that morning? Pick up the thread and *follow it*."

"I don't see why you have to be such a . . . " but Casey was getting blurry and more important things came into focus. "He . . . he'd been really angry with his girlfriend and he's been busted before for hurting her, but never for doing something like . . . he did that day. He's going to leave his apartment angry, and he's going to see that poor girl jogging on this horrible hot muggy day and . . . he's the one. He's the one who kills her." I felt sick.

"And?" Insistent. "Follow the thread . . . *And?*"

Why wouldn't Casey go away?

"*And* . . . and he's not going to care because he's gotten away with it. It'll be years before the cops figure it out. I mean, they know it's not the congressman, but the news teams are having too much fun ruining that guy's life, so they don't really listen when the cops are all, 'Look, he *didn't do it* . . . .'"

"*And . . . ?*"

"And *that's it.* They'll keep printing dirt and selling papers and sleeping fine at night. But it won't really matter, because she's dead and everyone's lives have been changed forever. And her parents will never be the same . . . And she's gone . . . " If the heels of my hands dug into my skull any deeper they would touch.

"*Thank* you," Casey said and dropped it. Then, like nothing happened at all, he turned back to Bill.

In the echoing silence Casey's quiet whispers sounded like the voices from that old *Poltergeist* movie.

"She's right," Jazz's Caribbean accent whispered into the emptiness. "As soon as Rosie began, I saw the newspaper story. It takes almost ten years. And the follow-up story is buried *pages* into the paper. Like no one cared about the truth."

"I saw the guy's face," Izzy shivered. "Once you said it, Rose, I saw the guy's face."

Mina was bouncing back and forth, staring at Casey, then me, then checking in with Jazz. I didn't know Jasmine well, but I bet she was regretting bringing her son to dinner. Justin was studying his salad.

I could hear the gears whirring in Mina's cuckoo clock. I heard the oven clicking while the metal walls cooled down. I heard the ice-maker dump cubes into the bin. I heard a car idling on the street. No matter how I resisted, my eyes kept straying to Casey, who had gone back to eating. Even *he* thought I was a freak—and such a bad one that he didn't even have to pretend to be civil to me. A useless, hopeless freak.

Regular conversation eventually resumed, but I couldn't talk. What did Casey think he was doing? And out of *nowhere.* Trying to stab him with *my* eyes didn't do me any favors, because as everyone went back to their dinner, Justin muttered across to me, "You can try with him, but nothing will happen. He is not interested . . . in you or in me. He's all about the books and the mountains, girlfriend."

"Umm . . . " I was surprised to feel myself blush. Justin tried to hide a smile.

"I see you lookin' down there. You may have your shields up, but I can tell you right now—you are wasting your time."

"You think I'm . . . ? Are you crazy? I don't think he knows how lucky he is I didn't accidentally torch him."

"Luck's got nothing to do with it, girl. Don't pretend. We were all over you like a wet blanket. Your throat still sore?"

I reached up and felt my neck, "No."

"Was it?"

"Yeah."

"Just sayin."

I glared at Justin, which didn't change anything so instead I focused on slowing my breathing, "Look, I'm just trying to figure him out. I thought you three were everyone. You're trying to tell me he lives here but he doesn't talk to any of you . . . *ever?* He's never flipped out on you and done something like that before?"

"Neh. Ver. Oh, sometimes he lets us speak to him—royalty with his subjects. You know," he shrugged, "but he ain't my problem. He's Bill's."

"How old *is* he?"

"Nineteen? Or . . . whatever. He's doing some long distance college or something. I really don't know much, girl—he dances on my last nerve by breathing. Don't waste time or energy there. Y'ain't gonna win."

I nodded and let it drop. He could sleep with the fishes for all I cared.

Mostly.

Jenn and I had worked so much on Tarot cards for the last two days, I was sure I was going to spend the night dreaming of chariots pulling me in different directions with cups falling off the back. But I didn't.

I fly over Brooklyn, over the beautiful brownstones, over the promenade at the Heights, over the water, and then I swoop up to meet the tops of the Woolworth building and City Hall. It's glorious. I feel so free and it's so beautiful. A full moon guides my way and clears the air for me. I can see forever—way past Staten Island and the Verrazano Bridge. I can't believe how bright everything is in the moonlight. The city glows. It is heaven. Then I swing over the lovely, verdigris roof with all the fiddly bits up there, and suddenly I'm falling. I'd hit a wall—an invisible wall. And I can't go any farther. And I can't stay in the air. And I can't stop or wake up or scream. And the light of the moon disappears as I fall down faster and faster in between the anonymous buildings.

And then I was back in my room, Jenn sleeping quietly beside me.

I waited until my breath slowed to a more regular rhythm, then I tried grounding and centering. I laid back, pressed my head into my pillow, closed my eyes, and managed to hook in. I started pushing all of the dream and fear and frustration out and down, but when I tried to reconnect and draw up clean energy, I gasped.

"Dammit!" I whispered and bolted upright.

I glanced over at Jenn. She turned, pulling up the sheet, sighing, still asleep.

I went to the bathroom and looked in the mirror. The moonlight was coming down through the air shaft and into the bathroom window, making the room a ghostly blue. I stared at myself in the mirror, then cupped my hands under the cold tap and plunged my face in. Over and over.

I couldn't get rid of the vision of Casey holding my face tenderly and kissing me. Again.

26 Art

"WHAT *ARE* YOU DOING?" Justin broke my—well, I'll be polite and call it concentration.

We were in the parlor and I was looking at books from Mina and Bill while Jenn and Izzy were at work. I thought we'd reached some sort of truce after yesterday's meet-up in the park and last night's showdown with Casey.

"I'm reading." I pointed meaningfully to my book.

"No, you're oozing pain about something. Are you still upset about last night? Girl, do us all a favor and shut it down or walk it off."

I shut my mouth and went back to my book.

"It. Is Not. Working."

"Well, what would you like me to do, Justin?" I kept my breathing regular, as I was pretty sure Mina would be disappointed if I incinerated her antiques.

"Calm *down*. Just chill. Knock yourself out. Whatever. Just do it far away from me, okay?" He left and went up to his room.

That, I was thinking, was probably not a bad idea.

I doubt Justin noticed or cared, but I was out the door in no time, shouldering my backpack with my book, knitting, Discman, and some money. I didn't know what Mina would do to me or if Justin and the others were trying to tail me and I didn't care. Mina hadn't protected me from Casey last night. Didn't seem to care at all, in fact. So why should I?

I made for the train.

It felt good to be out again. I was alone but this time I knew I was in control. I was angry, sure, but I was ice-angry. It especially felt good to be away from a house full of people who don't care when someone's as big a jerk as Casey was. Even Jenn shrugged when I mentioned it, getting ready for bed the night before.

"Yeah, well . . . that's Casey in a nutshell, isn't it?" was all she had to say. I thought about informing her that she was a lousy babysitter but didn't know if Justin had said anything to her about my incident with JerkMan, the Flaming Magician, so I kept my mouth shut.

I had even tried to talk to Mina about it at breakfast, but she wouldn't budge. "Casey was right," she said. "You need to learn to trust yourself and follow the Sight where it leads you. You got there, didn't you? He wasn't telling you to do something you couldn't do, was he?"

Explaining why that wasn't the point turned out to be useless.

How an entire household full of psychics could be so blind—and rude —was beyond me.

On a whim, I took a left on Fifth Avenue and soon found myself in front of the Knitting Garden. I didn't need anything, but I did want to check in with Delphi about my lace. The more time passed, the more I was convinced that she had indeed hissed at my shawl and I wanted to know why. I didn't see her through the window, but I pushed the door open, clinking the little bell.

No one there.

"Delphi?" I called softly, peeking around the corner into the back.

No one there.

I waited for a few minutes, then gave up and headed toward the trains. I'd ask Jenn later.

I knew that even though I had myself in a jaw-clenched, sparkling-blue lockdown, I had to take it easy today and not do anything that might provoke me —or anyone else. The air conditioning on the subway was too cold for what I was wearing, but the chill felt good after the sticky walk down to the station. I pulled out my knitting and leaned back against the cool orange plastic seat. It was a relief to have some downtime and finish a row. The loose seed stitch center and openwork panels were coming along nicely. I could feel all the garbage of the last 24 hours flow out of my finger tips and into the yarn. As much as Justin annoyed me, he was right. I needed to escape everyone to calm down and get focused again.

The train car remained mostly empty, which seemed perfect for me. I stayed on this particular line until we reached Times Square, honing my skills of looking at the subway map on the wall by the door without *appearing* to look at the subway map on the wall by the door. I didn't want to be pegged as a tourist. New York may be safer these days, but a girl can't be too careful, right? Especially a flame-throwing girl. And I didn't have my "Music to get Mugged By" CD in, so it would have been inappropriate to push it.

Following what I gleaned from the map, I switched to the Times Square shuttle, which was a lot more crowded, so my knitting progress stopped. I stood near the doors on the left, holding a pole with one hand and clutching my knitting with the other, looking out the door as the train flew through the short tunnel. Somehow, someone had gotten out there and tagged little bits and pieces of I-beam and concrete. If only they'd used their power for good rather than evil.

I was one to talk.

Following the hordes at Grand Central—and the signs—to the 4/5/6 trains meant I had to wait awhile for a seat on a connection, but there was a blower above the platform near the stairs, so I stood under it and kept knitting. The artificial breeze cooled me and rustled my yarn. No one here cared whether I knitted in public or not. In Tucson, I'd have gotten comments, questions, or at least looks. Of course, in Tucson, they don't have a subway. Maybe that was the real problem.

Exit at 82nd and walk over to 5th Avenue, then head south to the Metropolitan Museum of Art . . . as instructed by *The Mixed-up Files of Mrs. Basil E. Frankweiler.* When I was a kid I was in love with the idea of being let loose inside the museum for a whole day and night. I'd only been to the Met once before with Jenn, Mina, and my mom, but on that trip I'd fallen in love with a particular painting. I had no idea where it was, who it was by, or what it was called, but I was definitely going to find it.

It's good to have goals.

So, I started with the museum map.

I had to guess where the most likely locations would be, and this was tough. I hadn't taken any art classes after eighth grade, so I didn't have much to help me. The first eliminations were the easiest, because I knew I could skip Greece and Egypt. After that, I was pretty much guessing. I didn't think my painting was medieval, but I didn't know how to tell, so since that section was nearby on the ground floor, I decided to head that direction.

The gallery was dark, and cool, and . . . old. I didn't remember this wing of the museum at all, and was sure my painting wasn't here, but I got all twisted around and found myself in front of the doorway to the oddest room ever. I suppose you could call it an optical illusion, because it was like a fake 3-D room.

All pieced together from different colors of wood, this little room looked like a studio with window panes and ledges, tables, all sorts of musical instruments, little knick knacks and details on shelves . . . but it wasn't. It was a little flat-walled room by some Italian guy named Gubbio. Or he was *from* Gubbio. It would probably have helped to know some Italian. You wouldn't think that an illusion made of wood-colored wood would be that real but it was. Like those old fashioned photographs that are all brownish; they still look like real people, just real old. This place was like that.

I left there reluctantly, but people were crowding and I didn't want to hog. Outside the room sat an enormous stone table that reminded me of a special someone. *Casey is exactly like this huge immoveable object. No one is willing to push back except me.* Which then led me to think, *but who's dumb enough to try to push an enormous stone table?* I decided to ignore the table and looked up to see the armor room ahead of me. I also remembered the armor from my trip before.

I remembered that it wasn't anywhere near my painting.

I tried to focus on how cool the armor looked, but kept wondering if maybe Casey was right to push me. Maybe my problem was that too many people let *me* push. Maybe I need someone to stop me.

Or maybe he was a jerk.

I didn't have enough brain capacity for handling any of this while surrounded by the knights. All the metal man-shells were gorgeous and old and really, *really* smaller than you'd think. Some of them were famous—one king wore this suit of armor and a different one wore that. I stood there comparing my knitting to the chain mail, wondering, *how did they make this stuff back then?* Even the horse armor was amazing to see. I made a full circuit, then backtracked to the grand staircase, but this time I headed up. I started by veering to the left, since there was a special exhibit to the right and I didn't remember my painting being part of a special anything. There was a limited showing of prints by somebody—Dürer I think—in some little room that seemed like a museum afterthought. My painting wasn't there either, but Dürer was and his stuff was cool.

Outside of Dürer's afterthought room, I rounded the corner into a brightly lit, white-wall and marble-floor hall which *did* seem familiar. I slowed as I walked, looking side-to-side. There were some really nifty statues in there, and then I saw her.

A young woman with a roundish face and rosy cheeks pushed a tree branch away, walking toward and past me, with an upturned face and a messy dress. She looked like she was listening. Behind her, between her and this poor little cottage, were three angels or ghosts or . . . something.

"You like Joan? Sorry, didn't mean to make ya jump." A security guard who might have been born when the painting was painted had snuck up behind me, "Yeah, a buncha you kids like Joan. Dunno why, but you do."

I picked up my knitting from where I'd dropped it and had to clear my throat a couple of times, "Joan?"

"Sure. You want the schpiel?" the guard asked. Without waiting he continued. "This is a painting of Joan of Arc, circa 1879, painted by Jules Bastien-Lepage." I started to ask, but he went on. "Yeah, I know. You never heard of him. No one's ever heard of him." The guard took my shoulders and moved me two steps to the right and one step back. "The painting itself was not an immediate hit either, however, because—you see—the art critics at the time thought it was a little weird to have ghosts in a painting from an artist who worked in Naturalism."

"So they're ghosts?"

"What the hell else would they be, floating offa the ground like that?"

"Angels?"

He turned back to the painting and appraised it. "Nah. Ghosts. Personally, I think it's okay to blend the two schools. I dunno what they were upset about."

"You're a guard here?"

"Yeah. What's it to you?"

"You know a lot about art."

"You pick stuff up."

"Right. So. Joan of Arc?"

"Yep. Joan. You okay kid? You look like *you* saw a ghost."

"Me? Oh, no. I'm . . . fine. Just a long day."

He looked up and down the hall, then leaned in so close I could smell his Doublemint. "You're not supposed to, so . . . you know, get up if it gets crowded . . . but go ahead and sit against that wall so's you can look at her. But I didn't tell you that you could."

I smiled as he ambled away to his post and I slipped back against the wall opposite Joan. I was hidden from his view by the pedestal of a statue of a running couple. Perfect.

I tried to memorize every last bit of the painting—color, composition, all of it. I even made a pathetic attempt to sketch it in my journal. Looking back, I wasn't surprised that this was the painting I connected to as a child. I wondered if Casey had seen it. There was something so haunting about her face. She had this look. I guess you might expect her to look like she was . . . *gone*, you know, with her hearing the voice of God and all. But she didn't. She looked like she was there—*really* there. She's concentrating so hard, but not angry. She's at peace. She's just . . . listening.

I wonder if that's what I look like.

I wonder if it *is* the voice of God?

"You went *where?*"

"I cannot believe you would be so irresponsible as to put *all of us* into this kind of danger."

"*What* danger? There was no danger! I was looking at a *painting!*"

"And if someone had argued with you?"

"Or you'd missed a train by a second?"

"Of you'd gotten mugged or hurt?"

"But I didn't. You two are *way* over the top. I've been out to dinner and at the bookstore and the yarn store and the library, and like, twice to the park and nothing's happened. I can keep it together now. You know. Ground and center city! I'm all over it." I was *not* going to think about magicians.

Bill and Mina looked like they were going to burst a series of veins in their necks.

"What about magicians?" Bill asked as Mina coldly asked "Twice?"

"What?"

"You've been to the park *how* many times?" Mina owned the "override" voice.

"Uh, once, twice," I thought quickly. "The carousel and . . . to the kiddie park with you, Aunt Mina. My point is—"

"The point is we're responsible for you."

"I don't see what was so bad. I left a note. I wrote down where I was going. I even wrote down when I left. I went out all the time at home, by myself, in a car, which has to be way more dangerous. I was shielding. I was calm. It was fine. Big whoop. No blood, no harm, no foul, right?"

"Rose," Mina sat carefully on her bed next to me. They'd brought me up to their room for a little let's-yell-at-Rosie session. "Rose, try to look at it from our perspective."

I stared at her, shields on full. "Okay."

"You're our niece."

"And we love you," Bill added.

I tried not to smile at Bill. I was supposed to be all surly right now.

"And we don't want anything to happen to you."

"Or to anyone else, right?" I asked.

Mina examined my face carefully before she said anything else. "Right. We don't want *any*one hurt."

"Well, then maybe you should have stopped Casey at dinner last night."

They looked at each other, eyebrows up, "I'm sorry?" Bill asked.

"You sure let Casey stomp all over me."

"Is *that* what this was about?" Mina asked.

"Rose, that . . . that's Casey. He's . . . " Bill tried to find the words.

"He's not very good with . . . people, Rose." Mina stepped in to help, "Perhaps we're just used to it after all this time." She shrugged, looking at Bill for help.

"Well I didn't light anyone on fire when he was making me mad." I didn't want to bring up what Justin said.

"That's true," Mina said slowly.

"But you were focused on a problem," Bill said. "It wasn't purposeful control on your part. It was probably circumstantial."

"That's true," Mina said with more conviction.

Bill moved to my "naughty" list.

"So, what? Am I grounded? Like I can't leave the house? Like what else is new?"

"You're not a prisoner here, Rose. It's just—"

"Not *safe* for me to be out?" I asked. I couldn't remember the last time I sounded that snotty.

They looked at each other before they answered simultaneously, "Yes."

"Great!" I got up and started pacing. "So, I can sit in the house and I can read and study and practice the things you teach me and meanwhile all of New

York is out there and I can't see *any* of it?"

"Not without us," Mina said.

"You know, Aunt Mina, it's possible that togetherness is sometimes the thing that *gets* me angry."

"I understand that, Rose. I don't mean you have to be glued to us, just be where we can see you and help you if you get stuck."

"Lovely," I muttered.

"Rose," Bill blocked my path, "Rose I want you to think about something."

"What?" I looked up at him. He had on his Dad face.

"Think about you getting angry."

"I don't have to think hard." I kneaded the back of my neck with my fingertips.

"And think about how much power you've already demonstrated." I couldn't respond to that, so I nodded. "Now think about how wise it is to let a 17-year-old into a series of century-old tubes, underground, in the angriest, most aggressive and stressed city in the world."

I looked at Bill for a long time, then at Mina. They knew they'd won.

"I hadn't thought about it like that," I admitted.

"It's not that we don't trust you," Mina added. "We don't know how consistent your control is out there. We *do* know that you haven't had anyone try to get in."

"Except Casey."

Bill reminded me. "But, again, last night you were focused on a solving a problem that was frustrating. Everything was redirected to your sight, not your anger."

"Oh," I said.

"And remember how your work with Justin turned out," Mina said.

"That's not fair. It was my first day!"

"You even lose your shields when you're in the house."

"That's only when Justin gets on me."

"And you're doing better with that, but you *expect* to be antagonized by him. We haven't seen you surprised outside of the house yet." Mina lost me there.

I bit my lip.

Mina looked up at my uncle, "Bill and I will sit down tonight and make some plans of places we can go and things we can see together that will get you out and get you some practice."

"Safely," Bill added.

"Well, of course," I said. If they heard the sarcasm they didn't show it.

"And," Mina looked at Bill, not me, "there are some places in Park Slope that I think you can go to on your own. We'll work on that too, tonight."

"But not by subway."

"I think it's best to avoid solo trips by subway until we're more certain of your . . . strengths, don't you?" Mina asked. I nodded, impressed that I hadn't lit the house up. Maybe they were both there to put a psychic fire blanket on me, not because they both wanted to talk.

"You okay?" Bill asked, giving my shoulder a squeeze.

"Sure." I said, with my shields as strong as I could make them.

It's always been a mistake to tell me what I can't do.

I was already making plans.

27 Islands

"WE'RE TAKING YOU OUT."

"What'd I do?" I asked.

"No," Izzy laughed. "We're taking you to Coney. Tons of people, chaos, craziness—all the good stuff. If you can shield there, you can do it anywhere—"

"I'm allowed?"

"With all of us?" Justin asked. "Why not?"

"I thought I was all America's Most Wanted now."

"Not by me," Justin shrugged, opening the fridge.

Izzy laughed, "It's a great place to practice, and it's fun, and it's grungy enough that no one pays too much attention to us."

"But I'm on lock-down. Bill and Mina won't let me out."

"Coney is on your 'safe' list," Izzy said, "because the train doesn't leave Brooklyn—"

"And it's partly above-ground—" Justin added.

"And no one rides it in the middle of the day on weekdays."

"So as long as we report back—" Justin pointed at my nose, "that you kept calm and didn't break anything, or light anyone on fire, then Mina'll know you finally learned something."

I squinted at him in a particularly menacing and brutal way. "Why are

221

you helping me?" I was suspicious.

"So you'll go home sooner. It's not like anyone at Coney will even notice us . . . " he said turning back to the refrigerator, mumbling. "Plus there's plenty of water there, just in case . . . "

"So, what? You guys are going to babysit me?"

"We don't mind." Izzy said, missing the point while fishing for something in her backpack. "It'll be nice to—"

"Where are we going?" Jenn came down the stairs. I loved it when she did something even a little psychic. It made Justin squirm.

"Coney. Let's go, let's go, let's go, let's go. Kay?" Izzy was bouncing again, like the first day I met her. "Hats! Sunblock! Money! Let's get outta here . . . " I could hear her voice fade as she raced upstairs.

I followed my cousin up. "Hey, Jenn?" She looked at me as we rounded the banister on the second floor. "Is it, like, *real* ocean there? I mean . . . can I swim there?"

Jenn shrugged, "I always see people swimming. I've never done it, but I think the water's fine. Probably cold though."

"I don't care. I only need water. It's been a long time since I got to swim at all."

"That's right; you were swim-team-enator, weren't you? Geez, it's been awhile . . . "

"I've been distracted." I said, and pulled a hat out of the bottom of the armoire, stuffing it into my backpack.

We must have waited for forty minutes on the sweltering platform. I wanted to say something menacing, like, "Coney had *better* be good after this,"

but I thought that might be the wrong tone to strike with everyone when, as Bill had pointed out, we were in a confined space in the most stressed city in the world. I shouldn't make them think I was going to char them as soon as we were out of the safety of the house.

Plus, you know, I had an easy time leaving the complaining up to Justin.

"I *hate* that! I *hate* watching a train closing its doors when I'm coming down the steps," Justin stewed. But soon the heat got the best of him, and even he stopped talking.

Eventually, the Slowest Train In The Universe appeared. It was an R train, which they told me was normally not so bad, but it was the midday, and the R was a local . . . a very *local* local. We stopped at Every. Single. Stop. And each stop was epic, though no one seemed to get on or off. Even Odysseus reached Penelope faster than this. It was like the subway had taken a sleeping pill, or my dad's old turntable was playing too slow. Time stretched out and pitched itself too low.

Something had to give. We watched Justin get so bored that he started to think things into people's heads. I have to admit, it was kind of funny to see them look every which way, trying to figure out where the bodiless voice was coming from. He wasn't saying mean things, though. It was more like, *Excuse me, is this your purse?* And then they'd grab their bag and look around the mostly empty train car. No one had talked about doing stuff like that before. I wondered if Mina knew, but decided not to ask. Maybe I'd ask Jenn later tonight.

In a couple of years, we made it to the Stillwell/Coney stop and walked the long ramp down to the street. We jaywalked across Surf Avenue with the other passengers and made a beeline for Nathan's. I'd never had a Nathan's hot dog, and Izzy explained that my upbringing was obviously in question and this was simply something that needed to be fixed. A character flaw.

The hot dog *was* pretty good.

I bought the largest lemonade they would sell me, which, by Tucson standards, was closer to an espresso cup.

"Got drink?" Justin laughed.

"Mock all you want. You'll be begging for a sip in ten minutes."

On the street heading towards the beach, the heat rippled off the asphalt, and we walked from shade patch to shade patch, trying to keep the sun from beating down on us. That was when I became The Smart One With The Big Cold Drink. They took turns wearing the icy, sweating cup in the backs of their collars—even Justin. On our death march towards the boardwalk, we had to stop so everyone else could buy bottled water. I just topped off my cup of lemon-flavored ice from a drinking fountain whenever I felt parched. It was my superior survival instinct, born of hard years in the desert.

Finally, the heat was too much even for me. "Why did we come here?"

"Just wait . . . " Izzy was still cheerful but also, it seemed, impervious to humidity.

"Can we go down to the water?" I tried not to beg. "It might be cooler near the water . . . "

I followed Jenn over to the benches along the edge of the wooden path.

"Whoa!" I said, looking down.

"What's wrong?" Jenn asked.

"No, nothing. It's just . . . there really are *boards* in the boardwalk."

"Did she really say that?" Justin asked Izzy, who nodded.

"I . . . I mean I grew up hearing about The Boardwalk, but wood rots fast in the desert and . . . there are boards here."

"Your powers of observation are overwhelming." Justin turned away. "The force is strong in this one," he muttered, because, you know, it wasn't like I was there or anything. All I wanted was to call Lindy and tell her. She'd understand. Well, the other thing I wanted was for Rob to be there. It would have been nice to take a walk by the beach with him.

Instead, we all sat on a hot bench and watched the passers-by.

I was about to ask why in the world we were sitting there, silently, in the hot, hot sun, when Izzy whispered, "Stop turning around, Rosie. The ocean's still there. He's nearly ready."

I waited, then whispered back, "Ready for what?"

She nodded at Justin as he slowly got up and walked to the middle of the crowded boardwalk. I started to roll my eyes—showoff—but stopped, mid-roll. I could see the shimmer of his shields, but this time they weren't blue. They were a kind of silvery gray, like a cloud in the moonlight. I tried to use my senses the way Mina wanted, to see if I could figure out what he was doing. A long time went by before I noticed that he had made himself invisible.

Not invisible like you could see through him, like a ghost in a movie or something. Invisible like he didn't exist. I mean, obviously, he still took up space. But that was the amazing thing. Maybe it was the kind of shield he put up, but people walking along, clearly aiming for him, would veer off to the side, narrowly missing Justin's shoulder or foot. He just stood there, all calm and smiles and grace.

Once I'd figured out what he was doing, I tried to see *how* he was doing it. He was really solidly connected to the ground—it almost looked like his feet went into the wood slats of the boardwalk. But he wasn't drawing up from the earth . . . he was drawing down from the sky! He was getting it all from the air around him.

"Whoa!" I whispered to Jenn. "That is so cool!"

"You see what he's doing?"

"It took me awhile, but yeah. It's so obvious now."

Justin was firmly tied to the earth, letting the earth pull the sky down around him, protecting him, shielding him, but also making him like the wind. If he'd reached out to touch someone, they would have felt him. But the only indication they would have had that he'd been there would have been a new wrinkle on their shirt and nothing more.

"I wanna!" I whispered to Izzy. She giggled.

By the end of an hour, Izzy had successfully turned invisible, or "anonymous," according to her. Even Jenn had tried and was able to hold it for awhile, but eventually someone's shoulder broke through the shield and startled her. I had managed to pull down the sky while I was sitting, but I was too unnerved to step out into traffic, so to speak. Too many people. Too hot. Maybe if we went *swimming*, I hinted.

Eventually the heat got to everyone and they relented. I'd foolishly thought that all of us would swim, but I was the only one with a suit on under my clothes, or a towel in my backpack. Caving to pressure, I goofed around in the waves with them, getting our shorts damp at the hem, digging holes in the tidal sand with our feet, that sort of thing. It had to be ten degrees cooler by the water, so I didn't care what we did, as long as we stayed there for the rest of the day.

If I had a dictionary, encyclopedia, and a thesaurus, I still couldn't come up with enough words for how good it felt to be in the water. My parents tell me I was a fish when I was a kid, always begging to stay in the pool, ocean, or lake for longer than anyone else. I even loved floating on my back in the bath when I was little. Everything was muffled—not silent or weird. Just quiet. Whenever I touched water, I felt calmer.

Either way, it was wrong today, because as good as it felt to get my feet wet, something wasn't working. I wasn't calming down. I wasn't feeling connected. The opposite, if anything. Maybe it was being in the Atlantic Ocean when my body is programmed for the Pacific. Didn't matter. This low-grade hum that I felt seemed to be for me only, and it was as aggravating fingernails on a chalkboard.

I was trying to suss out what this all meant, when Justin pushed through the tide to me. "So, you ready to go the other way?" He asked.

"I have no idea what you're talking about," I said.

"Well," Izzy called over, dodging a little wave, "you've done anonymous. You've done shields and grounding. You can talk into other people's heads sometimes, so we think you're ready for the next bit."

"Like . . . ?" I drew the word out as long as I could.

Izzy turned and headed back towards the boardwalk. I followed, grabbing my backpack from the sand and threading myself through the huddled masses yearning to be tan. If it weren't for her hair, Izzy would have been hard to follow. Her shields were up like she was Bill Gates' house.

"Wow," I said to Jenn, looking at the stretched shadows. "How long were we down at the water?"

"Awhile," Jenn smiled, reclaiming our bench, which was as empty as when we'd left it, even on this crowded beach day.

Izzy took a moment, then walked out into the middle of the boardwalk, blue hair and all, and kind of . . . struck a pose. She almost looked like a supermodel, but not really.

"Jenn," I whispered, "What's she doing?"

Jenn smiled, "What do you think she's doing?"

"Well, I don't know. I mean, all I can see is that she's really pretty, but I always thought that. This time she's . . . I don't know. I've never . . . did she do her hair differently today? Or get different lip gloss?"

Jenn giggled. "Well, you're on the right track."

Izzy generally attracted *some* attention wherever we went—the cute, waify girl with the bright blue hair is bound to get some stares. But she was getting whistles now. One guy stopped and whispered something into her ear, but she smiled, shook her head, and he reluctantly walked away.

After a few minutes of this, Izzy dropped whatever she was doing and slid back into the seat next to me.

"So?" She was all bubbly. "What'd you think?"

"I ... that was wild ... what ... "

Justin snorted and got up, slowly walking over to the deep-fried-everything stand in front of us, picked up a single napkin, then slowly strutted back. I swear, the man could have been Kate Moss on a catwalk. He looked great —better than I'd ever seen him. He positively glowed. Then I got this idea in my head: he'd thrown a fishing line over his shoulder into the middle of the boardwalk and was slowly reeling it in.

Someone bit.

As Justin sat down, a big beefy guy came over and sat down on the other side of him. I couldn't really hear the conversation, but it was clear that this big guy thought Justin was hot. Jenn, Izzy and I barely avoided aneurysms from stifling laughs. The guy's face was so earnest, and Justin ignored him. Soon I saw the gray shields go up. When that happened, good ol' Earnest stood up, puzzled, and drifted away.

"Okay." I let the laugh slingshot out. "What! Was that?"

Justin looked over with that smile again, "That, girl? That was turning on my glamours. Anyone can do it—and Izzy's one of the best," he said, gently knocking his shoulder into hers. "But it takes a hell-a powerful adept to turn a straight guy like him into wanting a fine specimen of a man like me."

"Justin, that was amazing," I said, honestly. "No offense, but I'm sure that guy would never have looked at you before."

"Not unless he was wanting to kick my ass," Justin said proudly, happy to be out of the house's restrictions.

I nodded, excited. "Okay—with the anonymity thing, I could see what you were doing. I could tell where the intention was coming from and where it was going. This, though ... I have no idea how you pulled that off."

"It's all about where you get your energy from," Jenn said, "and where you want the energy to go."

"Yeah, okay," I turned to her, "so bringing down the sky, got it. But I couldn't see this one."

"Really?" Izzy was surprised. "But you've gotten so much better at seeing auras."

"Well, I could tell when Justin put up his shields and the other guy got bored and went away. That time I saw the gray."

"And . . . " Justin asked, helping the poor, slow girl out a little, "And what did you see when I was all gorgeousness and light?"

"I . . . I saw . . . you . . . Just you. And it's true. You *were* gorgeous. *Both* of you. I didn't see color or energy or intention or anything. Just you."

"Oh no," Izzy and Jenn were giggling.

"What?" I was disappointed. "What'd I do wrong?"

"Nothing," Jenn finally said. "You didn't do anything wrong—it's that they're really strong with this stuff and no one told you how to block glamours. It's kinda like . . . you were falling in love with them."

"So, you're saying, I was just as susceptible to them as the muggles?"

Izzy and Jenn nodded. Justin looked superior.

"Okay, we *have* to fix this."

For the rest of the afternoon we took turns alternating between anonymous and gorgeous. Within half an hour, I had worked up my nerve and had anonymous down cold—even standing in the middle of the boardwalk—but the glamour thing was killing me.

"Look," Izzy said, "If *you* don't believe it, no one will. You have to see yourself being extraordinary. Then you draw up from your anchor like normal, but all the energy goes into your solar plexus and your heart."

"Think gold. Think bling if you have to, but girl, you have *got* to get a more positive outlook into your head. Do you have any idea how pathetic that last try was? You could wilt a flower just by looking at it."

"Thank you, Justin. Very helpful way to get her confidence up." Izzy turned back to me and kinda whispered, "Okay, so part of what he said was right, you *do* have to think gold. You also have to think Red Carpet or Super Model or . . . something."

"I feel so lame . . . "

Justin sighed, "That's the problem."

But Justin was wrong. My problem was that I was distracted by a guy near one of the food stands. I knew I'd seen him before, but I couldn't place where. He was standing next to the lemonade tank, and it felt like he was laughing at me, but it was hard to tell, since the visor on his motorcycle helmet kept flashing reflected sunlight into my eyes. I couldn't follow Izzy's and Justin's instructions while also ignoring this guy in riding leathers.

Helmet and leathers!

The carousel!

But with that thought, Jenn pulled me back. "I know," she said quietly. "It's Tim and how he treated you." I tried to interrupt, but she continued, "I know he wasn't, like, abusive or anything, but still, he wasn't good for you, either. If you're still seeing yourself through his eyes, then you're not seeing the real you."

In a rare show of restraint, eavesdropping Justin didn't give me a hard time about Tim, though I was certain he was digging out memories. I was getting tired and my shields were slipping.

"Right." I tried to fight the frustration and anger that was building in my chest. "I need to not think about Tim." Or the creepy guy staring at me from over there.

"No, you need to think about *you*."

"Um . . . " I rubbed my temples. The guy in leather leaned against the drink tank, watching me.

"Don't bring Tim into it. He only complicates things."

"Then why did you—" it was too hot to argue; too easy to get angry.

"To try to show you where the problem was coming from." Jenn actually sounded irritated too. "Rosie, stop fighting! All we're saying is that your view of *you* is coming through Tim's eyes. It's time for you to see yourself honestly."

"That's crazytalk, Jenn. Bad idea to have me—" which is when the lemonade tank exploded. The mocking motorcycle guy was gone and everyone within fifteen feet of the stand was covered in sticky, icy lemonade.

At least it was cold.

Izzy, Jenn, and Justin gaped at me.

"What the hell, Rosie?" Justin's angry whisper, "It's not *that* hard to do."

"It wasn't the glamour thing. It was that guy over there . . . " They all looked and saw no one.

"Really, there was this guy over there making fun . . . of . . . he *was*. I swear. Don't look at me like that."

We watched people react to being showered with lemonade. Some laughed, some were irked by the stickiness, some were freaked out. The guy who ran the stand fell into the latter category. I focused on him and listened. He couldn't understand how the tank had exploded, what with it being half-full of ice, but also couldn't figure out how no one had gotten cut by the shrapnel—it was a glass tank, after all.

Of our group, Jenn was the first to recover, and evidently decided to ignore the whole event. You'd never have known something was up, except she sounded like Mina. "Okay, Rose, refocus." She moved to block my view of the lemonade tsunami wake. "The idea is not to see yourself the way Tim saw you, or the way you think Tim saw you. How would you feel if that other guy, whats-his-name, the nice one—"

"Rob?"

"Yeah, Rob. How would you see yourself if he told you he loved you?"

Almost against my will, I felt a grin grow slowly on my face. I made a choice to go with Jenn's voice and try to ignore everything else. "I can feel it in my feet."

"Excellent," she clasped her folded hands in front of her mouth.

There was a surge up my spine, over my head, swirling around my forehead and shooting back down my front and into the ground. I could feel the buzzing in my chest—this gorgeous, golden humming. And I knew, without a shadow of a doubt, that I was *hot*.

"That's *it*!" Izzy squealed. Even Justin looked happy, or maybe simply relieved that I hadn't lit him like a can of Sterno.

"Well, you're looking good today."

I turned to see what kind of guy I'd accidentally attracted by my glorious, effervescent magnetism, and gagged.

Casey, who appeared to have been bored and leaning on the rail across from us for hours, headed over, already ignoring me and talking to Izzy. "Mina sent me to get you. Iz, she's got someone who keeps calling. I guess they really need you. *None* of you took a mobile phone to report in with?" He was eyeing everyone, annoyed, "Bill's really ticked." That one he aimed at me.

"I brought *mine*," Justin was indignant as he pulled it out of his pocket, but when he showed it to Casey he got quiet again. "Uh . . . but the ringer is off . . . "

"It doesn't matter," like he was dismissing Justin from class. "You were all working so hard, I had searchlights to follow. So. You have all your things, right? Let's head back." He turned to go.

"But . . . " I started. Casey turned, staring. My shields were down, my glamours long gone, and I was wishing I'd had the foresight to go anonymous as soon as he got here. "But . . . I was going to swim some . . . "

"It's not safe to swim alone here, Rose." Jenn apologetically picked up my backpack and handing it to me said, "We'll come back another day. But," she hesitated, "the sun's given me a headache and we've been out in the heat a long time—it's a good time to go."

I looked down at the boardwalk. Like a stupid kid, hot tears stung my eyes. Everyone moved towards the trains. As we started to walk, Casey and Justin were talking just ahead of me. "Izzy's going to need you, Justin; this call isn't going to be easy."

"Bad like before?"

Casey shrugged.

Justin was quiet in a way I'd never seen him. "A mur—"

"Probably . . . that's part of why they're calling."

Justin said something else quietly to Casey, then jogged ahead to catch up to Izzy and Jenn. Which meant that Casey was next to me. Next to and—surprise, surprise—silent.

"Um . . . it's a lot cooler now." I heard myself say.

"It must have been unbearable when you got here, then."

"Understatement. But I know how to drink water. That's why I didn't get Jenn's headache."

"So." He acted like he was speaking a foreign language, talking slowly and carefully, "You . . . you swim?"

I looked at him out of the corner of my eye. "Yeah . . . yeah I do. I'm on the swim team at scho—*was* on the team. At my old school."

He nodded and that was it. We traveled the rest of the way home in silence.

28 SINKING

ALL NIGHT LONG, I dreamt only of the ocean. There was water in my lace shawl, and waves knit into it. Wave sounds were in my ears, and the wind in my wet hair, and I finally felt like myself.

It hurt to wake up.

No one in the house seemed to know anything about public pools, or they didn't care, so somewhere around dawn I decided I was going to go swimming today, and I didn't much give a flying leap what happened. They could ship me back to Tucson. I'd been working hard. I could go anonymous now which meant no one could see me to bug me. I knew that getting to Coney and back on a weekday was easy. As for the problem of beaching solo—dealing with your things while you swam—I'd figured that one out, too. I planned to take a grocery bag and stash my towel in it, then pin a baggie with my Metrocard and some cash into my suit. Towel stays in bag on beach; baggie stays on me. It wasn't like I was heading out there to glamourize someone.

I just wanted to swim.

To prove my point—that I'd been learning and was safe now—I went anonymous before I headed downstairs. I could hear the others talking to Mina about the events of the night before. I peeked into the kitchen. They were sitting at the big dining room table, but I knew some of them would be able to see the kitchen's central island that had the bacon plate on it. The protein sang to me. I rechecked my anonymity and walked very carefully into the kitchen, paying them as little mind as I wanted them to pay me. I took a few pieces, then gently opened up the cabinet beneath the sink. Bacon was nothing. Taking a plastic bag without the sound breaking the spell would be the real test.

A+. Test passed with flying colors.

As I walked back to the foyer, I could hear my blood pumping in my ears and I focused on slowing it down. I patted myself on the shoulder, psychically, then picked up my towel from where I had left it on the landing, I reset my shields and opened the first door. Before pulling it closed behind me, I paused and listened.

No one called out. Their voices didn't even register a change.

After the outer door clicked shut, I checked my watch and headed down the stone steps. I figured I had at least an hour before they noticed I was missing, and even then, only if anything went wrong. If my plan worked, then I had a few hours.

I whistled as I walked to the train. If it was humid, I didn't notice.

I have a waterproof watch from when I first joined swim team. I know, it causes drag, but it also lets me time myself, and I don't wear it at meets. I say this because I had it on in the ocean and looked at it when everything changed.

I'd been swimming laps, kinda—horizontal to the shore, out beyond what passes for breakers here—then came in and body surfed a bit. New York beaches and the Southern California beaches where I'd swam other summers really needed to get together and agree on how to do this ocean thing. I know New Yorkers would fight me on this, but California does the beach and wave thing better. At Balboa Beach, where I used to go, you get in the water and there's this rush and surge upwards that you can feel when you swim under a wave. Something about that moment has always made me happy. No, not happy exactly. Giddy. You're weightless for this split second, and your hair is pushed back, and you can feel sand and the layers of the ocean's temperatures, and . . . anyway . . . it's just one of those things for me, I guess.

Gorgeous sunsets? Happy.

Huge electric storms in the desert? Happy.

A chocolate birthday cake with real buttercream frosting? Happy.

Going under a big wave in the ocean? Priceless.

I was in a wave when the whole world shifted to the right. Or maybe I felt pushed off balance. Either way, something was wrong, and I came up gasping for air, pleased to find oxygen still available. I steadied my breathing, then took a shallow dive under the next wave, pushing my hair out of my face cleanly. I turned to slog back to my towel, checking my watch to see how long I'd been out.

I froze at that border where wet sand turns dry. My towel had been taken out of its classy plastic bag, placed neatly on the sand, and now had an occupant. Sitting on exactly one half of it was Casey.

His arms were encircling his knees while he watched the water. He had sunglasses on, so I couldn't tell if he was watching me. For all I know, we could have stayed like that—me standing mid-step, him looking at me from behind his dark glass—for an hour. A wave or three had to wash over my feet to break the spell.

"So, you haven't played with water yet?" Casey asked, finally.

It took me an abnormally long time to process this. The raindrops flashed through my mind, but I shook my head.

"Ah . . . perfect."

"Um. What are you—"

Casey rose, held up a finger to silence me, and walked past me to the water. The tide was coming in, but not evenly, across the stretch of beach. I followed and we had to adjust our position a few times until our feet were in the water, barely. The wave surge didn't go over our ankles.

"Okay," he said. "Watch."

I looked down where he was pointing—at his feet. At first I didn't notice anything. Water, sand, feet, no biggie. But, soon, the change was unmistakable. We were standing side by side. The water was covering my feet as it rolled up the sand, but it wasn't touching his. In fact, it was giving Casey something like a two inch gap all the way around. The water met up again, above and behind his feet, but he was completely dry.

"Omagaw! How'd you do that?"

"How do you think?"

"Um . . . magic?"

He looked at me, "Occam would be *so* proud of you right now."

"Oc-who?"

"You heard of Occam's Razor?" I shook my head. "Einstein's version of Occam's Razor is the principle that if you face a problem, the correct answer is usually the simplest."

"So . . . magic, Professor?"

"Yeah, that's the simple answer . . . it's not the *right* answer . . . "

"Show me. I mean . . . can you?"

Casey snorted. "Can you concentrate?"

"Yeah," I said, more sarcastically than I wanted to. "Of course I can."

"I don't know if—"

"Water," I said pointedly, "calms me down."

"Subways to *get* to water aren't calming."

"People," I emphasized, "aren't calming. I don't mind subways. They're air conditioned, anyway." Casey watched me for a minute, statue still. I squirmed when he looked like that—especially behind those glasses—but I did my best to keep up my shields and stand my ground.

"Mina's right," he said finally. Then, as if nothing had happened, he continued. "So, first, you should plant your feet."

"Woah, wait a minute. Mina's right about what?"

"Do you want to learn how to do this or not?" he asked, pointing at the sand.

I looked down. It was obvious now; the water was avoiding him. I looked up and shrugged.

"So, plant your feet. Really *plant* them. Let them sink into the sand. *Feel* the sand. Lower your *Ch'i* into every little grain."

"Chee?"

"Later," he sighed.

"Okay . . . I'm sunk." I thought I could feel my feet nudge deeper into the sand as I re-grounded myself.

Casey looked back at me. "Excellent. Now I want you to think of your legs like . . . like they're wax."

"Wax."

"Yes. You know how wax and water interact?"

"They don't?"

"Exactly. That's what you want here, too. As you sink into the sand—still grounded—you need to feel the outsides of your legs . . . no, wait . . . feel like there's a wax *coating* on your legs and as you sink, you can feel that wax melt off a little and down into the sand." He started to say more but stopped, looking out at the water. Then: "Sorry, I haven't taught before."

Funny, I thought, since he talks like a professor.

He looked down, now, watching my toes carefully, and I had to close my eyes to block him out. "Do your best to melt enough wax that you create a good-sized barrier between yourself and the water. This shouldn't be too hard. You don't need the wax to go deep, but you do need it to go wi—hey! Nice work!"

I opened my eyes. It was possible to see—if you were paying *very* close attention—that the water was refusing to touch me.

"Feel that?" Casey asked.

"Feel what?"

"You feel the tension? Between you and the water? The resistance?"

I stopped. I tried thinking . . . *feeling* with my feet. "It's like opposing magnets!"

I grinned over at Casey and watched a real smile take hold across his face. A gorgeous, welcome smile.

And that's pretty much when I stopped breathing. The next wave rode right over my feet—a mini-tsunami of failure.

"What happened?" He sounded disappointed.

"I . . . I don't know . . . I felt it. It was working." I scrambled to focus everything I had into my shields to make sure Casey couldn't see the same vision I had been seeing.

It wasn't until the train ride home that I started to relax enough to actually talk to Casey. After avoiding all of us for so long, it was odd to have him sit there next to me.

"You're a good teacher," I said finally, trying to break the ice.

"I am?"

"Yeah, I mean, I was able to do it. Some."

"It's true. I don't think it will take you much more practice to master it." He spoke deliberately.

"Really?"

"Practice and attention. That's all any of this takes."

I nodded, thinking. "So . . . you're in college?"

"Yeah, I do it correspondence, well . . . on the Web mostly. Not really a conventional correspondence course, but sometimes I send things in by snail mail."

"Wow . . . that's gotta be hard."

"Why?" He looked over at me.

"Well . . . uh . . . because you don't get to see the professor, or, you know, see or talk to other students."

He looked around the subway car, like he was looking for someone else to talk to. "That's not really much of a problem for me," he said quietly.

"But . . . but you spend so much time alone. I mean, Justin said you go off to the woods and stuff. Don't you ever get, you know . . . lonely?"

When he turned to me I felt that whole pinned-like-a-butterfly thing again. It wasn't my imagination. It was like he was trying to find something in me —in my mind. The air conditioning on the train made me shiver.

"I don't get lonely," he said at last, looking back at the subway map, or the wall across from us. Anywhere but at me.

I nodded, weakly. But nature abhors a vacuum, right? So I kept going. "Well, then . . . what do you *do* with . . . I mean, are you, like, *working* when you're out in the woods . . . because, you know, they all say you're the boy wonder. You're the oldest. Everyone says you're the best . . . Do you, you know, like . . . help police find bodies and stuff like that?"

Casey's head whipped around to face me, glaring. His voice sliced me. "Why? Why would you think something like that?"

The anger made me flinch. "I . . . I don't know . . . it's . . . isn't that what people like us do? I mean, Izzy's always helping people—like last night—and since you were gone . . . so much . . . I thought that you, you know . . . were off . . . being, I don't know . . . a hero or something."

If anything, he was angrier now. "Yeah . . . a hero. Is that what I look like to you?"

"Geez, Casey. I don't know. What do you look like to me? You look like a guy who has no idea how to have a conversation. How's that? I just asked—"

"—well then, *don't* ask."

And that was the end of that.

"I called your mother."

"Fine." The ride home with Casey had left me in a foul mood, so I really wasn't excited about the argument I was about to have with Mina.

"Your father needs to talk to you."

I looked at her sideways, "Dad?"

"He wants to talk to you."

"Not Mom?"

"No." She handed me the phone to dial.

"Office?"

She nodded and I punched in his work number.

"Daddy?" I turned away from Mina when I heard him pick up the phone.

"Rose? They found you?"

"Sure, Dad. Of course. I was just swimming."

"At Coney Island?!"

"Well . . . yeah. It's the easiest beach to get to. There's only one train and it's not crowded. I went there with everyone yesterday."

"Rose, what were you thinking?"

"That I needed to swim. There's nowhere to swim here, Dad."

"Rose, you have to clear something like that with Mina."

I turned around and looked at Mina, begging her with my eyes for some privacy. Finally, she nodded once and left the room, closing the door behind her. I sat on the edge of her bed. "Dad, she would have made the others go with me. They don't want to swim."

"So?"

"So they would have just sat there, all, 'can we leave yet?' and I would have been thinking about that instead of the water. I needed some downtime."

Dad was quiet for a bit, "Are you getting along with everyone? Don't you still get along with Jennifer?"

"Sure, Dad. That's not it. I mean, you and Mom even say that sometimes we all need a little time to ourselves. I left a note. I even told them where on the beach I'd be."

"Did you take your phone?"

"No. But I thought about it. I was worried someone would swipe it. That, and I wouldn't have been able to hear it from the water anyway. I was going so I could do laps, not sunbathe."

"Right. Okay. Look, do you understand why Mina's so upset?"

"Yeah, she thought I was going to light the boardwalk on fire."

"Well, honey, it's not only her. We're all a little . . . nervous. She said you've been learning, but she still doesn't think you're really in control of this . . . of these . . . abilities."

"Well, I don't know how she'd know one way or the other, Dad. I sit around the house all day, practicing, but we never really *do* anything. There's nothing here to get angry at," Then I thought of Justin. "Nothing much, anyway, so it's not like I've been tested, except yesterday."

"Right . . . "

"And, in fact, the times I've gone out on my own, you know, which is *kind of* like a test, I haven't had any problems at all."

"That's true."

"Can't you get them to cut me some slack?"

"No. But I can talk to Mina. Is she still there?"

"I'm sure she's outside the bedroom door," I raised my voice and spoke clearly. "And I'm sure she's heard everything we've said."

Dad chuckled. "Put her on for me, Rose?"

"Sure."

The door opened as Dad said, "I miss you, HR. It's not the same without you in town."

He had to wait until Mina was in the room.

"I miss you too, Dad," I managed to get out before I needed to find tissues. I didn't want to hear this side of the conversation, anyway.

"Your father is persuasive."

I waited.

"Here's how we'll work this. Leave a note on the downstairs bannister if you go out alone. You don't ride the subway. You do take your phone. You need to be as specific about where you're going as you can be. Until we know more you can't leave Park Slope without the others. That gives you a pretty big area to hang out in."

"But no water?"

"No *Coney*. But we'll be getting you to water. I promise. We're heading to the cabin soon."

29 BUTTERFLY

I'D BEEN HAVING A lot of dreams lately—dreams that I didn't like very much. Izzy and Jenn had told me about lucid dreaming and that once you know you're in one, you can start influencing what happens.

I tried.

I failed.

So. Another night, another nightmare.

In the dream I sit on the ground in a lovely meadow in the middle of the woods. I am not looking at my hands but I know I'm knitting. It's beautiful there. I hear the birds, feel a cool breeze on my cheek and the warm sun on my head and watch the leaves rustling in the trees all around me. Then, out of the clear blue sky, I hear a loud boom. *Then another. The birds fly out of the trees and straight up into the sky, cawing and screaming to each other. Trying to find each other. A huge gust of wind shakes the trees, knocking me back too, knocking leaves off the trees. The leaves flutter down, down, down on me, on my head, on the ground, but when I look I see they aren't leaves, they're newspapers and pictures of people I don't know. Newspaper after newspaper—from all over the world—pile up around me. I look for my knitting because I need to stay calm and focused but in my lap there is only the ball of blue yarn my mother spun for me. I can't see my needles anywhere. I take the ball in one hand and tug on the strand of yarn snaking away. The knitting is under the pictures and papers. I start inching my way through the piles, tugging, following the yarn, letting the line take me back to my knitting, to my shawl. It is very very important that I find it. It will make the papers go away. I have to find it. I pull and rewind the yarn for hours, more and more desperate to feel the smooth needles in my fingers and know that it is safe. I watch my hand reel in the yarn as it grows easier to pull and wind but the yarn is changing. It isn't sky blue yarn my mother made. Now it is dark and purple . . . and wet. Then I see the corner of my shawl and I cry with relief. I lunge and pull it out from under the papers and I scream. It is blood. The blood is on my hands. The yarn is the blood.*

I woke up gasping, tears on my cheeks.

I stayed in bed for a few minutes, waiting for my heart to normalize, scrambling to grasp the threads of the dream, and trying to fall back to sleep. Giving up, I gathered my things as quietly as possible. Jenn's a hard sleeper, but it's summer, and who wants to get woken up early, especially accidentally, right?

I slunk into the bathroom and showered as quietly as I could in an old brownstone. I towel-dried my hair, avoiding the ruckus of the dryer. Instead, I left the bathroom, twisted my hair up off my neck with a banana clip, quietly tossed my towel and pajamas at the foot of my bed, hesitated, but defiantly grabbed my knitting bag, closed the door gently, and headed downstairs.

I needed to look at this thing in the daylight.

Even walking as gingerly as possible, I couldn't prevent the stairs from thundering in the morning silence. I paused and quickly went anonymous. I had no idea if that would help, but figured it was worth a try. The creaking didn't seem to wake anyone. With my knitting and bug spray, I went out to greet the morning, and the door to the back deck made no further noisy complaints. It wasn't cool, exactly, but it was cooler than it would be the rest of the day. And while it was stickier than I like, with my wet hair up it wasn't as unbearable as direct sunshine. I sat in a chair on the deck, propped up my feet, sprayed myself all over—twice—and watched the sun appear over the tops of the brownstones of

Brooklyn.

Being a desert rat by birth, I am used to those grand, expansive sunrises. Sixteen shades of pink, forty shades of yellow, slices of green, all merging and changing as time passes—and all of it stretching off into eternity no matter where you looked, like the entire sky was wrapped in party paper for some little girl's birthday. Brooklyn's not like that. I felt a little like I was watching a time-lapse film or something. Shadows of buildings and trees grew then shrunk back as they inched up and down the sides of the neighboring Brownstones, crawling across the street then retreating as the sun gradually rose over Prospect Park.

It was spectacular.

I knew what I had to do, though. I couldn't hide behind sunrise-watching any longer. I didn't want to be inside or around anyone else in case this was messy—and I definitely didn't want to try to explain what I might see. So, I breathed the morning in, grounded and centered, steeled myself, and pulled my knitting out of the bag—then opened one eye a tiny bit to look.

It looked like knitting.

I opened both eyes and really examined the shawl. It was blue. It was lacy. It was a shawl. No blood. No weird messages knitted into it in little Braille bobbles. Nothing to freak me out like my dream. It was nothing more than sticks and string. I began knitting slowly as the birds awoke, pushing all of last night's dream into the stitches. Unfamiliar songs filled the air around me. I'd reached five —five new bird songs I couldn't identify—when the back door opened. As far as I could tell, using all I'd learned so far, absolutely no one was there. I stopped knitting mid-stitch, reaching out to sense who, or what, was behind me without turning to look. Was I Izzy now? Was I about to see dead people?

Though I sat frozen for only a second, I still struggled to fight a wave of nausea before I turned around to see Casey closing the door quietly while reading the front page of the *New York Times*. I shivered—the damp morning air, no doubt. My jaw may have actually reached my lap as I watched him walk silently—

obliviously—to the other end of the deck where he sat down, unfolded the paper, pulled out sections and made two piles. The sports section in one pile—I was willing to bet cold hard cash that this was his discard pile. I closed my mouth.

He folded the A section some special way so he could hold it in one hand. Then, while reading the front page, he moved the unwanted pile to the table in front of me, never looking up, and went back to the cushioned bench that ringed most of the outdoor deck. He sat there, sideways, with one leg up on the outside edge of the pad, leaning against the outer wall. The deck itself wasn't more than four or five feet above the ground. It hid the entrance to the basement, so the deck ended where the stairs up from the basement began, preventing you from clocking yourself trying to move from the basement to the backyard. Deck stairs down to ground level were on the opposite side. I hadn't yet ventured into the Midsummer's Night garden.

But now, I was determined to keep knitting my lace and not think about visions, or kissing, or Coney or . . . Instead, I bravely continued working on my shawl. My clean and not-at-all-bloody shawl.

I knitted. Casey commenced reading a new page. He didn't seem at all bothered by the presence of another human being not ten feet away. He offered zero acknowledgement of my existence: not a nod, not a grunt, *nothing*. Now, I've had my moments of being utterly rude, but usually the reason was nerves or ignorance, not deliberate jerkitude. The vision of him kissing me was fading rapidly. Now my heart was rushing for a different reason. I knew I needed to calm down or I'd be 2–0 as a human Zippo.

But after sitting and fuming about Casey for a good bit, I realized I had a new problem. If I said good morning at this point it would be weird and probably sound like I was mad at him. Why play my hand like that? Then again, if I didn't say something I would slowly drive myself crazy.

I didn't like my options.

"Anything good in there?" I asked, finally.

Okay, that was lame, but at least it broke the tension—mine.

He turned his face from the paper slowly, peeling his eyes away last, and shrugged. He looked back down.

I tried again. "Are you taking summer classes?"

He moved his eyes from the paper again, with visible regret, and looked at me for a long heartbeat and, once again, I felt like a butterfly on a specimen board.

He cleared his throat, "I realized last night that I never introduced myself, properly . . . before. I'm Casey Andersen." He made no move to get up or shake hands or anything.

"Ah . . . uh, Rose Tyshler, with a 'Y'. I know." I could feel myself blushing under his gaze, "It's . . . It's weird. It's Russian."

"No, I . . . it's your first name. Rose. I knew you didn't look like a 'Rosie' to me." He was still staring.

I started to correct him but instead said, "Sorry." I shrugged and forced myself back to my knitting. The butterfly thing was creeping me out.

"That was rude," he said, a fact, not an apology. "I don't talk with people often. I'm out of practice. Yesterday . . . I must seem—"

"It wasn't rude." My mouth was dry. "I just really didn't know what to say. It's . . . you're . . . You don't *look* at me like other people." He looked down and away. "No, not bad or anything like that. I'm sorry—it's like . . . I can't explain this . . . it's like your eyes are a microscope. I feel . . . *examined*." He was looking into the garden, nodding slightly. "So, um . . . " I didn't want to lose the chance at a conversation that might end the eternal tension, "how do you do that?" He looked up.

"You . . . what? You want to learn how . . . what?"

"How you look . . . Well, I mean, I am here to learn, right? And you taught me the wax thing at the . . . was it okay for you to do that? Because you're older I thought you could . . . or had permission . . . or are you, what . . . like . . .

allowed to teach? Do you have to get . . . um . . . certified . . . here?"

He laughed sadly and shook his head. "Normally I don't teach. It wouldn't be safe."

Now I laughed. "Oh brother. Have I heard that one *way* too many times before!" Casey's eyes locked on mine like a laser and the laugh stopped in my throat. I coughed. All I could think in that split second was, *no fire!* "Sorry," I recovered slowly, "that's . . . that's exactly what my parents said, over and over again, before they shipped me out here. That they were doing it because it wasn't *safe* for me to stay. That *I* wasn't safe . . . which I think was their way of saying that they didn't feel safe when I was around."

Casey returned to looking out at the garden, not at me. "Yeah. I think that's how it starts for most of us," he said softly.

I was assaulted by wave after wave of silent images of Izzy, Justin, Casey, even Mina, all younger and being scolded at the scenes of various sorts of psychic destruction—broken coffee tables, shredded curtains, flat tires, busted china. Then the backdoor opened and the memories stopped. This time, I knew the person in the doorway was Mina.

"Hey kids. Pancakes or waffles?"

"Either, Mina. Thank you," Casey said without hesitation.

I looked over my shoulder and tried to smile, "Which is easier?"

"Uh . . . probably pancakes."

"Then pancakes." I found I could breathe again. "I'll come help." I wasn't sure if I should ask Mina about the pictures I saw of her as a kid, but I knew I didn't want to be alone with Casey right now.

I sort of waved at him as I walked inside with my knitting. He smiled his weird sad smile, and barely nodded as he turned his head back to the paper. I had to work at not sounding winded as I walked in the house. His smile—that infinitesimally small hint of his humanity—literally took my breath away.

Again.

I was back with Jenn on Tarot duty that afternoon. She's a Tarot Terror, that one. I have no idea how she memorized all of it, but she did.

"So, do you use this on yourself? Are you like a gypsy fortune teller on the side? What do you do with this?"

"Well, aren't we feeling questiony today?" She shuffled the cards, smiling, "I don't do anything outside with any of this. I haven't told anyone I can do this, right? I think it would . . . " she stumbled, "I dunno. I haven't told anyone. So, no . . . I'm not a fortune teller."

I looked closely at Jenn. "But you're so good at this part of it," I nudged. "You told me you were all, 'oh, no. The others do the psychic stuff. Not me,' but you were *so* not telling the truth."

"It *is* the truth. This is just understanding symbols. It's not magic or anything," she yawned.

"You tired?" I asked.

"Yeah," she yawned again. "Good book. But we should get on with this," she pointed at the cards.

"But why don't you let your friends know? I mean, you *do* have other friends at school, right? Or do you hang with only Izzy and Justin?"

"Oh no, I have friends," she shook her head, looking down. "It's just that people get weird when they hear you can do this sort of thing."

I tried to look at her eyes, "Was there . . . Did you have trouble before?"

Jenn paused in her shuffling and sighed, "It wasn't all that bad, I guess, when you look back on it. But when I was in elementary school there was this kid who was . . . he was mean. Even my Dad said so. It was like he would figure out your insecurities and . . . work—really, really hard—to hurt you. To use your weaknesses against you. I guess I must have told one of my friends what was going to happen to him—I was probably bragging."

"You? But you said—" I saw Jenn's jaw tense.

"Yeah, well . . . cards . . . " She flipped five cards in front of her with precision. "Anyway, I learned. He overheard. He was . . . he was relentless. He thought I was such a freak, he would even say things in front of the teacher, but she didn't know what he was talking about so it went on and on. Finally my parents changed my school. I came home crying for weeks before they switched me."

"What happened to him? What did you get from the cards?"

Jenn looked up and straightened her shoulders, "That he was going to spend nearly his whole teen-and-adult life in prison. He was going to break his arm when someone tripped him coming off the stage at an assembly. He was going to be suspended for breaking the nose of the kid who tripped him. Stuff like that."

"And you were right?"

Jenn tilted her head to the side and looked at me.

"You haven't told *anyone* else outside of this house about what you can do?"

She shook her head, straightening the cards.

"Do Izzy and Justin know you saw that?"

She paused, then shook her head. "It hasn't . . . it hasn't happened like that in years."

"Oh."

"Okay," she said, changing her tone. "So, we have five cards. The top three are the *past, present,* and *future.* The bottom two are *advice* and *outcome.* Now I did the reading for me, so come around here and tell me what you can see for *me.*"

I got up and stood behind her. "Um, okay, so I scan all the cards first, right? So, across the top you have The Sun, The High Priestess, The Fool. Beneath you have Temperance and Moon."

"Good. So you start with . . . ?"

"I'm going to start with The High Priestess, which is in the location of your . . . present. That card would indicate that . . . um . . . "

"Yeesss?" she drew the word out into a soft hiss watching me walk back to my chair.

"Wait a sec," I stalled, "I'm trying to figure out how this all fits into the whole ethical thing. Do you use the cards to tell you what to do?"

"Oh no. That would be silly. People can get addicted to this the same way they get addicted to anything that makes them feel good. Tarot can be useful for *helping* make decisions, though. Sometimes it's good to find out if the person you like will like you back, or if you're wasting your time on them. Or if you're misreading a person entirely."

I nodded, happy to let her ramble.

"Plus," she yawned, "you can do what mom calls 'quick and dirty' readings with one card and a pendulum."

"A what?"

Jen fished around at the bottom of her card bag. "One of these," she pulled out a little gold chain with a squiggly medal on one end and a pointy green bead on the other. "A pendulum is . . . well," she giggled, "it's kinda cool. But you have to introduce yourself to it first. Here," she handed it to me to hold then had me scoop up the cards, "shuffle the deck three times. Okay, now cut the deck —focus on a question." She waited as I closed my eyes and thought. When I opened my eyes she said, "Right, now you'll draw the top card and put it down in front of you. Analyze the card. Say what you think the card means out loud. Then, hold the pendulum over the card and ask the pendulum if your interpretation is correct. It'll tell you."

"Um . . . what?"

Jenn laughed.

"Seriously," I said, "*Mas despacio, por favor?*"

"Okay. Slower. Hold the pendulum out. In front of you. Yep, good. You can relax your arm. It's not going to whack you in the face. Good. Better. Okay, now say hello. Out loud."

I looked at Jenn.

"I'm not crazy," she said. "Say hello."

I snorted, "Hello . . . pendulum . . . thing . . . " It was perfectly still, just hanging there.

"Now ask it to show you *yes*."

I lifted an eyebrow but dutifully said, "Alrighty pendulum. Show me *yes?*"

Somehow, seeing the future, talking into people's heads, shoving guys across the room without touching them—that all seemed fine. But having this pendulum start slowly swinging on a perfect line away from me, back and forth: *this* freaked me out.

"Okay, now thank it for showing you."

"Thank you . . . pendulum . . . for . . . showing me what *yes* looks like." I glanced up, "Do I ask it for *no*, now?" Jenn nodded. This time, the pendulum swung right and left. This thing was very specific. I kept checking my hand to see if it was shaking or moving this sucker, but I was rock steady.

"Great," Jenn was happy. "Okay, now analyze the card and then ask the pendulum if your interpretation is right. And you have to do it out loud."

A door slammed behind me and I jumped, dropping the pendulum, my heart leaping from my chest. "What was *that?*"

Casually, Jenn said, "I think it was Casey. He leaves a lot."

I turned around to the foyer. I couldn't feel anything now, and hadn't felt any hint that anyone was there. Jenn was probably right. Casey escaped. I looked back at the card. Jenn yawned again.

"Would it be okay, Rose, if I went and took a nap? I mean now that you have your friend the pendulum to keep you company," she smiled sleepily.

"What were you reading last night?"

"You'll laugh."

"No I won't."

"Yes you will."

"Try me."

Jenn yawned and said behind her hand, "Harry Potter."

I tried not to laugh, I really did.

"See?" She said, walking out, "You can't trust people these days."

"Yeah yeah yeah." I waved my hand at the stairs. "Can I borrow it when you're done?"

"Of course," she said, not missing a beat. "And Rosie?"

"Yep?"

"Don't forget to say 'thank you' to the pendulum after it gives you an answer."

She wasn't joking.

30 STRONGARM

EARLY MORNING.

AGAIN.

I was up before everyone.

Again.

Normally, I'm a crazy late sleeper; go figure. But there it is. I was awake. Something Izzy had said one night about "controlling your environment" was spinning around my head, along with Coney Island, Casey, pendulums, and crazy bloody knitting. Since the house was still sleeping, I decided to go outside in search of environmental inspiration. And yes, I left a note.

Across the way, near the junction of our street and Seventh Avenue, there was a bagel shop. You know how people in New York are supposed to be all rude and "what do *you* want?" Yeah, well, they're not. They just talk fast. I swear to you, the guys at this little bagel shop would walk on hot coals for their regulars. The place smelled *awesome,* like the old school meaning—some serious awe. Baking bread is one thing, but baking bagels, fresh cream cheese, lox, and huge black and white cookies? Yeah—that works.

Soon it was my turn and I was ready. I was *not* going to be abused today for ordering too slowly. Without stumbling, I ordered a sun-dried tomato bagel with a schmear. You have to pronounce that right or they insult you. Not mean,

257

but, you know, an "outsider in our midst" kinda thing. I thought it would be cool to fool them into thinking I was from here, and sure enough, *no one* tapped their toes or snorted at me today. I took my bagel out to the front of the store with a hot chocolate, and sat on the low wall in front of the church next door. The stone was cool and the morning was only sort of humid. It was nice. Even the mosquitoes gave me a break.

Leaning over to set my hot chocolate down on the ground, I saw a marble sitting nonchalantly against the wall. Not a big aggie; just a marble—a cat's eye. After positioning the bagel in my lap, I went to pick up the marble— and it moved. Away from me. Like it didn't want me to touch it.

Now, here I am with a beautiful morning breaking around me and the marble doesn't want to play nice? So I tried again. And again, it moves away from me. I sat up and considered this new wrinkle in my morning.

Strategy. That's what I needed.

I picked the hot chocolate up from my right side and placed it on my left —on the other side of the marble. I took my napkin, rolled it up, and placed it parallel to the church wall where I was perched, making a little cul-de-sac for the marble. It didn't stand a chance.

Slowly, I reached back down to grab the marble, and it moved . . . bouncing against my cup. It wasn't hard to scoop it up now. Unreasonably proud of myself, I wanted to stop people on the street to show them this trick, but then I remembered where I was and what I'd just done and thought better of it.

I half-expected the marble to buzz in my hand or something, but it didn't. Once I picked it up, it was just a marble. I took my drink, my bagel, my New Friend Marble, and I walked back home with a ridiculous smile on my face.

"I have never seen *anyone* so attached to a marble before! What are you trying to do? Fuse yourself to it?"

I jumped about a mile. Casey had walked into the kitchen and I hadn't noticed. Actually, I'd been concentrating on getting the marble to roll again. I was sitting on the floor on the other side of the island with the marble on the rug. It was a smooth Persian-type-good-for-rolling rug, not some crazy shag thing—friction is not a mystery to me. But there was Casey, mocking me anyway.

So, I figured I'd fight back.

I looked at him, really harshly, and I gave him the silent treatment. Then I saw through his eyes—I was sure of it—that I was an enormous geek and a fraud, and that he was about to make complete fun of me, and I'd probably be an idiot and cry and maybe I should go back to Tucson right now because I couldn't get the hang of manipulating physical objects with intent, like all the good psychic kids could. I could only do any of this on accident. My throat tightened.

"Focus," he sat down on the rug across from me. "You're connecting to it. You need to repel it, okay? It's like if someone offers you pop and you want water —you push it away."

This time I could mock him. "*Pop?* Midwest much?"

Perhaps Casey wasn't as good at taking it as he was at dishing it out. He stared silently, then continued, looking back at the marble.

"You need to detach yourself from the marble, focus on where you want it to be, and . . . push. The focus is on the result, not the process or the object."

"Oh!" Suddenly it made sense. "But that's weird." Casey stared. "Because I knit a lot, and the process *is* what matters to me." My nervous talking kicked in. "I love knitting. I love calming myself by . . . you know . . . creating . . . and so it's the . . . process . . . okay, usually I give away what I make, but I understand what you're saying." I really wanted to tell him to stop looking at me like that.

He pointed to the marble.

I took a breath, made sure I was still grounded, and decided I was going to roll the marble into Casey's ankle as he sat there, cross-legged in front of me. I released my breath slowly, focused on where I wanted the marble to move, and . . . pushed.

Glass shattered.

Casey was on his side.

"Wha—?"

Trying not to laugh aloud was turning Casey purple as he rolled onto his back on the floor. "Wow . . . Rose . . . you really *are* good," I could see tears welling up in his eyes.

"Are you . . . " I looked around, trying to find the source of the shattering. "Are you hurt? Did you duck?" There was a picture over the couch behind Casey, and the protective glass on it had shattered. I looked under the couch and way at the back I could see my little marble there, smirking at me.

"Who's breaking things?" Bill called, bringing breakfast meat from his basement stash to fry up for we, the hordes.

I started to say something but Casey broke in, "It was me. I was trying to show Rose a trick and I got a little too into it."

Bill looked amused. Casey shrugged and got up.

"You staying for breakfast?" Bill asked Casey, who shook his head. And without another word, he left. I heard the front door click quietly this time.

I watched Bill as I picked up pieces of glass, but he seemed completely unmoved by Casey's lie and immediate evacuation.

I got the broom and dustpan, because what am I good for? Cleaning up my messes and not much else.

Whatever.

My earlier success made me yearn to go back outside again. The day was still nice after breakfast and low in humidity and I wanted to explore. Jenn asked if I wanted company, but I said no, just wander and think. She didn't hassle me when she saw me grab my phone.

I convinced myself I was *not* going to be out looking for Casey.

I turned in the direction of the bagel store, but this time, I stayed in the shade on our side of the street. I passed handmade clothing boutiques, jewelry boutiques, that bookstore I liked, and then I reached a main intersection. I looked up the street—that way went to the park. I looked down the street, and saw the nose of a shiny red fire truck with guys all standing around.

I love fire trucks, and I'd never gotten to see one up close and personal.

"Hey," I half-waved, trying to look really casual as I approached.

"Howyoudoin'?" One of the older firemen asked.

"I'mgood, you?" I countered.

"S'anicemornin'can'tcomplain."

"Nah, s'notbad, nottoohotyet."

"Nope."

And then we just stood there, looking at the truck; he didn't seem to mind the pause at all.

"So, um . . . " coming back to myself. "So . . . can I look closer?"

"Ohellyeah! That'swhatit'sherefor," he smiled and motioned me around to the other side of the truck.

There was a younger guy, with a square jaw and the bluest eyes ever. I swear he was like a recruiting poster model. His navy blue t-shirt pulled tight over his chest and I thought, *Yeah, this is the guy I want coming in to save me in a fire. This is a guy you can trust to get you down the ladder.*

He smiled at me and asked, "Wanna sit?" while he opened the cab door.

"Really?"

He nodded and I hopped up onto the running board. I looked inside at the dash, the radio, the switches. "How long does it take you guys to learn this stuff?"

He laughed.

I smiled, looking out and enjoying my pretend power. I climbed back down. "So, is it harder to be a fireman in New York than, say . . . some suburb somewhere?"

"Brooklyn's not *hard*, but, you know . . . if you can do it here . . . everywhere else is a piece of cake."

I nodded and smiled. My mom says New Yorkers are house-proud. Drifting around the station house, two guys up front pointed the pole out to me —there really was a pole. And there was a line painted on the floor—the point beyond which I couldn't go, which was fine. I got to see all the hoses and the dials and they told me about the hookup and how big a pain it was when folks double-parked. Stuff like that. It was a lazy summer morning. For them too. We kinda sat there on the stoop for a long while and enjoyed the day.

Even deep within the weirdness that was my summer, that morning I could easily say, "Life is good."

Until it wasn't.

A little kid and his mom walked up, and the guys started showing the kid around the truck. With big wide eyes, the little boy took in the colors so happily, the shiny chrome and red, that it was impossible not to grin like a dork. I started to stand up and say goodbye, but sat right back down again, hitting the stoop hard enough to force the air out of me. Across the street, half-hidden in a morning shadow, I could see the figure of a man in white. On his head was a glossy white helmet. His arms were crossed like he was ticked off, and he was looking right at me. Or it seemed like he was looking right at me, because how could I tell with the visor down, right?

He shook his head. Then he jabbed a finger at me.

When I came-to, the older fireman I'd talked with before was sitting on the stoop next to me, cradling my head in one hand and pressing a cool, damp paper towel to my forehead.

"There you are!" He smiled down at me. "You gave us a bit of a scare, miss. One minute we're shootin' the breeze. Next, you're all slumped over here like a rag doll."

I struggled up from my awkward position. "What happened?" I put my hand on the paper towel to take over for him. He used his newly-freed hand to help steady my shoulder. He kept the other hand on the back of my head.

"Dunno. I looked over and you'd passed out."

"I never pass out."

"Well, you did this time. First time for everything, hey?"

"Yeah."

"S'okay with you if I look at the back of your head?"

I nodded, and put my head down on my knee. I felt him gently move my ponytail from one side to the other.

"Lucky you have thick hair. I think it took the brunt of the hit."

"Hit?" I raised my head carefully, looking at him out of one eye.

"When you fell back. You clonked yourself pretty good. But I don't think you even have a bump. Hard head?"

I nodded slowly, "You have no idea. Wait, can I ask you a question?"

"Shoot."

"You have a lot of motorcycle riders here in Park Slope?"

The man looked at me. "I gotta admit," he said finally, "that is not the question I was expecting."

"Do you?"

"Some," he said hesitantly. "Is there a rider in particular you're looking for?"

"No. Yes. Yeah, a guy who wears white riding leathers. Have you seen him?"

"Leathers? Like racing leathers? Aw, hell no, miss. Mosta the guys ride here, they're mama's boys with too much money or weekend warriors. We don't see much in the way of leathers here."

I took the towel off my forehead. Why this news should make me tear up was beyond me.

"You okay?" the fireman asked. "You still look a little wobbly."

I folded the towel smaller and smaller and smiled up at him. "Nah, I'm good." I put my hand out, "Thank you for rescuing me."

He took my hand in both of his and helped me up, "Ah, s'nothing. You gave me something to do. It's been quiet lately."

"Glad to be of service."

He took the towel from me and headed back into the firehouse as I walked back up towards Mina and Bill's with only one thought on my mind: *I've gotta tell Casey . . . tell Casey . . . tell Casey . . .*

By the time I got back home, Casey was long forgotten. Who I needed was Bill.

I poked around looking for him. I looked in the basement and in the back and upstairs. I found Mina up in her studio, working on an altered book she was making for a local boutique.

"Oh, he's out with Jenn for some father-daughter time."

I nodded.

"And I think Izzy and Justin went for a walk. You were out—yes, I got your note, thank you—and they wanted a break too. They should be back soon."

"Oh. Okay."

"You all right?"

"Yeah. Sure." I strained to keep my shields strong.

Mina watched me, then said, "Okay." But I could tell she didn't mean it.

Later that afternoon, when Bill returned and was down in the basement, I excused myself from a psychic self-defense practice, which was probably not the best practice for me to miss, and went downstairs.

"Uncle Bill?"

"Hey, you. How you doing?"

"I'm okay, but I have a song question for you."

"A song? Okay. Sing."

I sang a song that had been stuck in my head since I left the firehouse. It was on a full loop, starting at the beginning and playing all the way through then starting over again. I had no trouble remembering the melody. It was stuck there permanently as far as I could tell. I had to wait for it to reset so I could sing it to him from the start.

If anything his look intensified, "Huh. Well, okay. It starts with trumpet?" he asked.

"The version in my head does."

"Well, yeah then. It's Louis Armstrong. That opening riff is pretty famous."

"What's it called?"

"'La Vie en Rose'. It's an old Edith Piaf song. It's beautiful."

"'The Life of Rose'? That's kind of creepy, Uncle Bill."

"Not the life *of* Rose, it's 'a life in pink,' really."

"Seriously? Kind of a girly song?"

"No, it's about looking at the world through rose colored glasses because you're in love."

"That's it?"

"Yeah, like the whole world changes color for you."

I stood there trying to put this all together.

"Anything else you need?" Bill waited.

I startled and smiled, "Nope. That was it. Thanks Uncle Bill." I gave him a hug and walked back upstairs wondering why in the world a motorcyclist had delivered Louis Armstrong and his pink love song to me.

31 Strong Arms

THE NEXT DAY I surprised myself and woke up late, trying hard to forget the dreams crowding my brain—car accidents, train wrecks, it was like a 1970s disaster movie marathon. All I needed was a Titanic dream to complete the set. I'd gone to bed early—earlier than everyone else, anyway, though I don't think it was because I had a concussion or anything—so the late wake-up was unexpected. By the time I came down for breakfast, plans were already being made.

"It's important that we fix this. Last night was hard on you two and this morning has been painful for everyone within two feet of you."

"*I* was fine," Justin said defensively.

"*You* are a liar," Izzy said, mimicking his emphasis.

I started to back out of the room. I'd never seen Izzy angry before, and didn't want to get into the middle of this one. But Aunt Mina saw me and pointed to the oven full of a fabulous strata that smelled like it had arrived via angelic delivery services. "You missed the fireworks last night, Rose. We had a very . . . "

"Manipulative?" Izzy offered, with a tinge of snark in her voice.

"Yes, manipulative presence here last night who was *not* playing nice with Izzy and Justin. I thought it would be good for us to do some trust exercises in a little while. Nothing heavily psychic, but important nonetheless."

It felt like everyone was sitting on the edge of a glass knife—you couldn't see it, but you sure could feel how close you were to being sliced. I tried to be unobtrusive so I nodded, grabbed my breakfast and took it to the back deck. It was another nice morning. Jenn was out back too.

"Oh good," she said, "I couldn't stand being in there but I was getting lonely."

"Wow! What the heck happened last night? They're so tense."

"Right? Well, you know how Izzy got called the other night when we were at Coney? Well, they called again, but this time the caller didn't want to deal with it on the phone. She's local."

It took me a second to process. "Izzy left the house?"

"She left the house," Jenn nodded.

"Isn't it dangerous to do this . . . outside?"

"Sure turned out that way."

"Why's everyone telling *me* to stay in the house but not taking the same advice?"

Jenn shrugged, "Life is pain?"

"True, but unhelpful. So what happened?"

"Well, Izzy and Mom and Justin went over to Two Boots to meet whoever this woman was who needed Izzy's help."

"Two Boots? It's so noisy, though."

"Yeah, but it's very public. And when someone's coming through strong, Izzy can get a read on them anywhere . . . the subway even. So whoever she was supposed to be communicating with turned out to be a real jerk. He didn't like something Izzy said so he started talking through Justin. I guess Justin said some really mean things to Izzy before Mom figured out what was up."

"*Justin* said mean things? To Izzy! That should have made it kind of obvious."

"I know, right? I guess his shields were down." I restrained my comments. "Anyway," Jenn went on, "I think that's how Mom figured it out. She's good with auras. So the woman was really apologetic and bought everyone dinner and all, but they haven't been speaking to each other since. It's pretty bad."

"But if it was Justin being manipulated . . . "

"I know . . . I think Izzy understands, but from what I overheard this morning it was kinda personal, like Justin was being hijacked and his memories were being used."

"Has this happened before?"

"Nuh uh. Izzy's never seen Justin used like that . . . Mom said it's her own fault for letting them practice outside of the house, but this friend of hers insisted . . . yada yada yada."

"And so that's why you're outside?" I asked.

"And so that's why I'm outside," Jenn agreed.

We ate in relative silence, not creepy I-don't-know-what-to-say silence, but more like we're-so-chill-we-can-be-quiet-and-thoughtful together silence. Jenn didn't ask why I crashed so early last night and I didn't offer. I was still sorting through it myself, and I didn't really feel like sharing yet. *And* I still couldn't get that song out of my head.

"Okay, you two. Fireworks are over. Jasmine is here, and we're going to work on some healing specifics this morning." Mina poked her head outside cheerfully, but you could tell she was wiped. I looked over at Jenn, who seemed to have heard it too. "She's just upset because Izzy got hurt," Jenn whispered over my shoulder as we walked inside. "She doesn't want any of you damaged on her watch."

"Neither do we," I agreed.

Jenn and I put our dishes in the dishwasher and wandered into the front parlor. Jazz was there, talking to Izzy. Justin was scowling in a corner seat, holding a book, and Casey, Bill, and Mina were having a tense but quiet discussion in the front entry.

I could barely pick up on them, but I did hear some of what Bill said. His low whisper sounded almost angry, or at least forceful. "Look," he was saying, "you get nothing... negative effect..."

"It's not that..." then whatever Casey said sounded like, "*Veyahavta?*" but his back was to us so I couldn't be sure. Plus I don't think he knows Hebrew.

"Yes," Mina said to him, "you have to... humans who are..." I could see Bill nodding and thought I heard him say, "loss takes" or "low stakes" or something like that. Casey's head was down. Bill leaned over and said something else quietly to Casey who shook his head, then shrugged indicating our room with his head. Jenn tugged at my sleeve to stop me from staring. I turned away as I saw Casey face Bill and square his shoulders. He came in and stood, leaning on the doorway, as I sat down next to Jenn.

"All right." For the first time since I got here, Mina sounded forced. And not for the last time today I found myself relieved that I'd missed last night. "Today we need to try to get past all the detritus left over from yesterday, so I thought we'd do some basic trust exercises. Jasmine has come today to help. I wanted to have as many calming presences in the house as possible."

"Is Dad going to do it too?" Jenn asked.

"He's going to spot you. We need backup today, I think."

Bill smiled at Jenn while Mina continued, "We're not going to work on anything specifically psychic, but instead on things that are very necessary if we're going to keep working this summer. So, Izzy and Justin, stand over here." They seemed to want to get to this, which I thought was probably a good sign. It's not like they were mad at each other, I guess. Hurt by a ghost. Who knew?

"Jenn and Jasmine, you two stand here," Mina squeezed Jenn's shoulder.

This left me with Casey. My stomach lurched. That's why he was angry. He could barely look at me, and I was going to have to do some trusty thing with him? The blood was rushing to my head so fast I didn't even hear Aunt Mina tell us where to stand. I moved where she pointed and tried not to pass out.

Standing in front of him on the floor instead of next to him on the slope of the beach, I really noticed how much taller he was than me. He was taking deep, regular breaths—bracing himself for this horrible morning of working with me? I swallowed and focused on not getting sick on him.

Mina's first command was that we stand facing each other, eyes closed. At least I didn't have to see him looking at me. I breathed while I listened to Aunt Mina. I heard the other people. I started to slow down. Down. Match them . . . match him. Breathe together.

Without trying I could feel him across from me—not hear him. Feel. My stomach was in knots while he stood still, right in front of me, breathing. His warm skin, the pulse in his hands as they hung at his side, all of this was connecting to me, weaving through me, wrapped up in me.

So, obviously, I was losing my mind. I was imagining. I must have been. But then he shifted his weight from one foot to the other and it was like he brushed up against me—from three feet away. Again I couldn't breathe. Then I heard *him* breathe deeply and his breath dragged mine along too. He reconnected and matched my breathing again, which must sound like a steam engine about now.

"When you feel that your breathing is linked, slowly open your eyes and look at your partner."

I knew I would melt into a puddle now. When I opened my eyes, his were already waiting. Staring down at me. Not unkindly. My heart skipped a beat, and I saw a flicker of a smile flash across his face. I struggled to stay focused and grounded. His eyes were beautiful. Then something altered on his face. Like when you finally recognize someone you've been talking to for ten minutes. You can't say anything about it but you're all, *Oh, now I remember, THAT's who you are! You were my babysitter a hundred years ago!* in your head. His eyes still skewered me, but differently. He wasn't the same Casey at all, and I stood there, dumbstruck, trying to comprehend the change in him.

Then a new thought clenched my stomach—I had no idea about his abilities. I hadn't asked Jenn. He was supposed to be so perfect, a killer psychic, what if he could read my thoughts? Read my heart? Even if I was shielding!?

He smiled again—I think he smiled. It was gone so fast, and I didn't have time to think because Mina was speaking again. It was hard work to return and hear her.

" . . . want you to focus on moving together. Don't force it. Don't *try*; just let your arms move. Work to have one brain's impulses control two bodies, or more like the two brains working as one to move the bodies as one. Arms and hands first, then we'll deal with the rest."

Then my right arm was drifting up, gently, slowly, more graceful than I'd ever been on land in my life. Casey and I were fingertip to fingertip.

"But don't touch . . . " said my aunt.

Now palm facing palm, without touching, but that didn't matter. My hand was dripping, my stomach a jar full of lightning bugs. Worse, I had forgotten to breathe for the last hour. It didn't seem to throw Casey, though. Right around then is when I heard a voice—it sounded like Casey.

Relax, Hannah Rose, you're doing great.

No one.

No One my age calls me Hannah Rose.

I do, the Casey voice said, *or I* will *if that's all right. It sounds more like you. So far.*

I kept looking at his face and saw the might-have-been-a-smile cross it again. Our hands moved up and left.

I decided to test the voice and see if it really was him. So I thought at him, softly, *So, okay, how did you know that was my name? I never told you.*

I could lie to you and tell you I asked your aunt . . . the ghost smile. We lowered our other hand.

Or?

I could tell you the truth ...

Which is ... I watched his face. Again with the flicker at the edge of his mouth.

I talked to your grandmother.

Ummmm ... my head pulsed.

The one who named you ...

Uh ... the dead one?

That's her, this time he gave me a full grin.

Our hands were frozen in the air, not touching, hovering. My breathing was jagged.

When ... um ... when did you two meet?

Just now. She's pretty devoted to you. I've learned a lot.

Just now? You learned a lot just now?

You'd be surprised.

Not hard to do. My head was spinning. *How can I hear you? I thought I was shielding.* Our left hands started to move up and over to the right.

I'm sending and you don't know how to block me yet.

This is why Mina worries? Because I still can't block dangerous people?

I'm not dangerous ...

But this feels dangerous, I stopped myself from thinking.

We stood now, both hands up, palms millimeters away from each other, and if lightning had struck the top of my head at that moment I don't think I would have felt any different. Every bit of my body was on edge—like the way your hair goes up if you rub a balloon on your head.

Do you really do that to your hair?

I flushed as our right hands slowly moved in a circle out to the right, down, around, and back up. Then the same again with the left. We weren't very exciting with our choice of hand movements, but then, we were a little distracted.

I tried very hard to keep my mind blank. Just focus on shielding while *not trying* to move my hands while moving them . . . while looking into his eyes . . . while . . . lost cause.

So why don't you like your name? The voice jarred me out of my concentration and he smiled for real now.

I love my name, I thought back, *But it's . . . private, and . . . it's too formal for me now. I used to be Rosie, then a couple years ago I managed to move that to Rose with my teachers. Maybe I'll try moving to Hannah Rose now.*

"No," he whispered out loud. Now he looked surprised and glanced over at Mina who seemed not to have noticed. The voice in my head said, *Look, I've been an ass. I'm not good at . . . I want to start over. It's easier for me to start this way . . . here . . .*

Shocked is too light a word for that moment. Stupefied came closer, but I could tell that if this continued, I would have to invent some terms.

I told you that I didn't think you looked like a Rosie. His smile lasted a little longer that time.

"Great, you can stop now," my aunt interrupted. She had a nearly concealed smile on her face. "We'll rotate partners every few days until everyone's back in sync, okay? So, let's check in so we all know what areas still need work. Izzy and Justin—You had the most to tackle today. How'd you do?"

Izzy nodded slowly. "Well, I definitely reached the point where I wasn't in control."

"A human Ouija board," Justin added.

"Yeah," Izzy agreed. "It just felt like it was happening. We haven't done this before. I like it."

"Justin?" Mina turned to him.

"I feel better about it . . . " I'd never heard Justin sound apologetic. "I hope . . . Izzy? You too?"

Izzy nodded, "Yeah . . . we'll get there." She looked from Justin to Mina and nodded with finality.

Mina looked relieved, "Jennifer and Jasmine, How about you?"

"Superior," Jasmine smiled. "I never had such an easy time. I didn't have to think through it at all."

"Same here," Jenn nodded. "But I think that's mostly due to Jasmine."

"I saw what you were doing, too, Jennifer. Don't sell yourself short. What about you, Casey, Rose?"

I wasn't about to answer for Casey, but was very curious to know what he would say. He studied my face and my stomach took a triple-gainer. He turned to Mina. "Pretty good," he said finally. "You know, all-in-all . . . for a first time."

"Well, Rosie," Mina beamed, "You can't ask for higher praise than that from Casey. Nice."

I allowed myself a half-smile and a nod. It was all I could do to keep from bursting out of my skin with joy and tap dancing on the furniture, but it was also completely humiliating since Casey could, in all likelihood, hear exactly what I was thinking.

I didn't want to embarrass you, I heard him say. *I hope that was okay.*

I glanced at him sideways. Who *was* this guy? This was not the Casey I met before. This was definitely not the Casey on the way home from Coney Island. I noticed Jenn watching me. I smiled weakly, waved on the down-low to her. She nodded. Mina gave us new instructions.

"Now, this time, I want you to do the classic falling-back exercise."

"Hey," Bill said to the moans, "If it didn't work, no one would do it."

"We'll add a psychic edge to it, though," Mina continued. I heard Casey sigh, or maybe whimper. "So, Rose, Jazz, and Izzy, turn so your back faces your partner." We did. "Close your eyes and relax into your breaths." I could feel Casey behind me, and could both hear and sense his breathing again. I tried to match it again and let it relax me as much as anything could right now. "As your breathing becomes more and more peaceful, find your center, then lower your center slowly, down further than normal and broader too. Think multi-layered, until your feet feel like tree roots. Solid. Deep in the earth."

This was no challenge. I was already rooted to the floor.

"Now, partners, at your own pace, as you sense they are grounded and completely relaxed, send a signal for them to relax backwards into you. Don't tell them to fall or make a noise. Simply let them know that it's okay to let themselves go."

It was odd to feel both terrified of making contact with Casey, yet also completely and utterly relaxed. Then I felt Casey tense. I panicked—was he afraid of touching me? I breathed, trying to re-steady myself, re-ground. My heart slowed, at least to the speed limit, maybe a little under. I felt, rather than heard, Izzy go—a gentle swoosh in the room, then stillness. "Nice," I heard Mina breathe. My focus at this point was on trying not to try—which was, of course, impossible.

I'm here. I heard Casey whisper in my head and then I released—the air put up no resistance—into his arms. He caught me, my back on his flat forearms and hands at my waist, and I gasped, jolted from my calm, jumping away. I spun on my heels, glaring at him.

"What the hell was that?" I hissed.

"Casey?" My aunt said. A warning.

Casey was staring at me, looking just as shocked as I was.

32 MAGNETICS

"I . . . HAVE NO IDEA what happened," he said—and he wasn't lying. Whatever it was, it wasn't him *doing* something. It was just *something*. He had pulled his hands away from me as soon as I was steady, then raised them in the air like he was surrendering. I could see bewilderment on his face. Evidently Mina could see it too, because she said, "Okay, enough for now. Take an hour everyone and then we'll work on some other things. Back here in sixty," and she motioned Casey and me over.

I heard Jasmine and Jenn talking as they walked to the back porch and Jenn looked over her shoulder at me as they left. Mina motioned for us to follow her into the kitchen. Bill was already there. I couldn't tell if he was irked or what. Casey and I each took an end stool at the island, keeping a safe distance between us. Mina and Bill stood in front of the stove, looking at each of us in turn.

"Okay, what happened? Rose, you first." Bill was firm.

I froze. Why me first? "I . . . it was like this . . . shock? Maybe?" It was more question than answer.

"Did it hurt you?" Mina was concerned and picked up a junk mail flyer from the counter, idly rolling and straightening it.

"No," I thought carefully, "not hurt . . . " but I couldn't explain what I'd experienced. It was . . . everywhere. It was under my ribs, down my spine, all through me. I was starting to feel a dull ache in my middle, as though something had been removed. I needed to feel that . . . whatever-it-was again. I was missing a piece—a phantom limb. I looked at Casey—what had he taken?

Casey filled the silence and asked, "Bill, would it be permissible to try to relay it?" Bill looked at Mina and nodded. I heard, *Can you think back to what it felt like? Attempt,* he paused to think, *an instant replay, so I can see what happened from your side and send it—*

"Wait." I asked aloud, "You want me to send it to you? Can't I just send it to you *and* Bill and Mina? Because I can do that. I've sent to Mina before."

"But this is—"

"Let her try, Casey," Bill seemed confident. "Rose, when you take us through it, focus particularly on how you felt, how you reacted."

"Uncle Bill," I hesitated, "You're okay with this . . . receiving thing?"

Bill smiled kindly at me, "Yes, this much I can do. I'll be fine. You go on, now."

I nodded and closed my eyes, easing back into what it felt like to breathe with him—feel Casey there behind me—then slide through space, back into his arms. Then the jolt again, the shock, the shudder that rolled through my whole body, and I heard my aunt suck in her breath.

"Oh," she sighed, "Oh my."

Casey looked down, "I didn't mean to . . . " he started.

Bill turned away. I couldn't tell if he was angry or laughing.

"No, no, of course not," Mina stopped fidgeting and shook her head. "You can't do that on purpose. Or at least, you know better than to try."

I looked back and forth at them thinking, *Hello! Someone! Can you explain this please?*

Casey said, "Ah, look, Rose. That . . . what you felt—that was . . . unusual. Even for us."

"Okaaaay. Unusual good or unusual bad?"

Casey looked at Aunt Mina and Uncle Bill, who had recomposed himself and was watching. "You call it," he said finally, handing the stage to Mina.

"Well, Casey," she squirmed, "you know that personally I have no problem with—"

"But—"

"Well, She is my niece after all. This does put a . . . new wrinkle on things, no?"

"It doesn't have to. You were right," He was very serious, tense jaw, the whole bit. Casey didn't look nineteen. He looked much, much older—and tired.

"Well, you can't keep doing *that*—"

"I wasn't talking about that, I meant the long-term implications," it all sounded mathematical to me.

"What if it doesn't work out?"

"Then it doesn't. Normal people go through that all the time," Casey insisted.

"You aren't normal people," Mina said quietly.

"No," Casey said, "We're not. We know I'm not. Maybe I'd handle it better than normal people."

I started to ask a question but Bill cut me off by asking, "You don't see it interfering with her training—or yours?"

Casey considered this, but only for a moment. "Not if we don't let it. It might be helpful actually. Maybe I can move her along faster now that we know this. And of course, for me it's even more than what you suspected . . . "

Bill nodded, "Of course. As long as you're sure she won't cause the same problems . . . ?"

"Apparently not. I *want* to see how this works now, Bill. I think you were right. I haven't—we haven't seen this before. Not with anyone. It's . . . well, obviously it's important. To me. For a number of reasons."

Mina and Bill exchanged looks. "All right then," Mina put her hands deliberately on the counter and pushed herself back, "I'm not sure about it, but we don't seem to have much choice, do we? But Casey," she looked hard at him, "She's not only a student to me. Please."

That imperceptible flash of a smile washed over his face, leaving a twinkle in his eyes. "I'll be gentle," he said, with what I thought was mock seriousness.

"I am not talking about *gentle*, you knucklehead! I'm talking about keeping your hands to yourself," and she whacked him lightly on the forehead with her junk mail baton. "By parental standards, this has already gone too far."

He actually laughed. "I should probably explain this to her a little better."

"Yes, you should." Mina and I said at the same time. I was both ticked and triumphant at having been able to say anything at all, finally.

Bill chuckled, "Why don't you guys go for a walk or something—away from everyone else?"

"And don't rush back," Aunt Mina added. "I don't want you two here for the next exercise. You'll only distract them."

"Okay." Casey carefully motioned me towards the door and I felt his hand near the base of my back, not touching, just close. Like the opposing magnets at the ocean, he guided me out of the house. From the corner of my eye I saw him grab my bug spray.

"Hands to your*self*," Mina called after us as the door closed.

33 PARKING

THE SECOND HE TOOK my hand on the street, I experienced the same unbelievable jolt, starting in my solar plexus, then shooting down to my feet, leaving me weak and breathless. It wasn't painful; it was the exact opposite. But it happened so fast it took my breath away. A thousand aftershocks later, I knew he was watching his effect on me through his humidity-fogged glasses. I would have laughed at his owl eyes, but I couldn't talk. He seemed to enjoy my current state, regardless of Mina's instructions. Unlike the first time, and maybe because he didn't let go, the waves minimized, spreading down to my fingers and toes as I struggled to raise my shields. The whole effect left me rubber bands for legs and a head full of cotton.

"What are you *doing* to me?" I was finally able to mumble.

"Taking you for a walk," the smile again.

"That's not what I meant," I said.

"I know," he said, and I could tell he was still smiling. Jerk.

I smiled too. Weakly. I had to conserve my energy for concentrating on difficult things—like walking.

We were drifting through the sticky air along the gradual slope up to Prospect Park. The air smelled . . . green, I thought.

Casey looked at me, amused, "So what does the desert smell like?

281

Brown? Don't look surprised. You're sending. When you send I can hear you very clearly. But only when you send. Or when your shields are way down." He handed me the bug spray. We paused so I could coat myself and half of the surrounding sidewalk—but he didn't release my other hand. I was awkward maneuvering this way, but Casey seemed endlessly amused. I straightened and felt the shudders begin again. When I pulled together the puddle that used to be me, I answered him.

"My desert isn't brown—at least not this time of year." It was hard to talk; even my lips were tingling. "This is when we get our monsoons and the whole place really greens up."

"Would *I* think it was green?"

"Where were you born, again?"

"Sioux Falls. South Dakota."

I calculated while the bug spray melded to my poor, poor, weak skin. "Nope, you'd still call it brown . . . but you'd be wrong." We started walking again. He took back the can and it fell out of sight into a pocket on the other side of his shorts.

"And the smell? Can you think of the smells from your desert?"

The scent of rain in the desert—the Sonoran desert—can be a mystical experience. The first time I remember noticing the rains, I was a kid, maybe six or seven. We were on a big family trip up to the Grand Canyon and the day we stayed in Flagstaff we decided to go to a place called Wupatki Ruins. Basically, picture ancient adobe condos that make you wonder if maybe we aren't as civilized now as we like to think.

Walking through the homes of people long gone by a thousand-or-so years, I noticed the blue sky giving way to heaving, gray-black clouds. I remember standing there in the still, hot air, holding my parents' hands as we watched the clouds boil over us. Then the lightning came.

Thick, metallic bolts hit the desert floor with such force I could feel the air vibrate with each strike. The storm was near to the south of us, but the sound meandered, reaching us several beats after the visual. Then the wind washed over us, blowing my hair off my face. It cooled us off after the hot day. Then the smell arrived. It was damp, a warm and oily smell—like an earthy spice preserved in some ancient jar deep in some cave filled with petroglyphs.

The smell of rain in the desert was my first—and so far my only— addiction. I could never get enough. All summer long, all I wanted was for the rains to start, the rains to stay, the rains to never leave. In approaching storms, I would stand on our ramada roof long past the point of safety. It didn't smell right coming through a screen door. You have to be part of the rain for the season to make sense. Monsoons were designed to be played in—until the lightning gets too close.

That long-ago day in the high desert, the temperature dropped a full twenty-five degrees in seven minutes—my parents still talk about that. We were dressed for heat and all four of us wound up shivering, soaking, laughing, racing back to the truck.

I tried my best to remember this particular memory in detail, to conjure these images and scents for Casey—partly because it was a good rain memory, and partly because it was a good family memory, which mattered to me. I was sure that whatever I sent would leave him completely underwhelmed, but just shy of the park, he stopped and turned to me, still holding onto my hand. I faced him, looking up, waiting.

Finally, he nodded slightly and said with a faint smile, "it took awhile and you were . . . far away at first. However, I have never, *ever* wanted to visit a desert—especially in the summer time—but that was . . . "

I had the distinct impression that he wanted to kiss me. My stomach leaned back in preparation, but a couple of skate boarders shot down the sidewalk and street coming from the park, and I jumped and dropped Casey's hand as they raced by, cracking themselves up. But, before I let go of Casey I knew the skaters' names, where they lived, where they were born, what they had for breakfast. I knew way too much about them. Including that they were stoned.

He pulled back and looked at me, then he turned towards the park again and said, "Well, I don't know what rain in the desert smells like for an absolute certainty, but I think know what it smells like for you. You sold me." He reached over deliberately and took my hand again, this time more gently, but once again, he had to wait while my body adjusted. When the waves were over I was breathless, but able to walk. Slowly.

We continued silently, easily, to Prospect Park, and over to the meadow where we sat under the trees and watched young insane men completely unaffected by heat or humidity playing Frisbee. They ran, jumped, and caught the plastic disk in the bright sunlight. Dogs jumped at their feet. Man and beast performed catches that defied logic and gravity. It was fun to watch, but they made me feel hotter and stickier. The grass was prickly and normally I would *never* have sat on the ground on a day like this, but right now it didn't seem so bad.

Walking and holding hands was hard enough, but stopping and sitting down while still attached was worse. He had leaned back against a tree and held my hand in both of his. My body had less to do while sitting which left more time for noticing what was going on and it took longer for my nervous system to calm itself. Eventually I felt like I could breathe again and started to—deeply. Casey chuckled, shaking his head, but didn't talk.

Finally I said, "I guess I'm the only one in town who can't handle humidity."

"As I understand it, only natives call New York 'town'—maybe you *will* survive here."

I smiled.

"And anyway, summer's a very short season. September will be here and take you by surprise. Everything is better in September. Everything's better in

Brooklyn too. The city—on days like this—really stinks. Literally."

"So you wouldn't peg me as an outsider?" I asked hopefully, then told him about the Music to be Mugged by CD which made him laugh.

"I'd like to hear that sometime."

"Okay," I said, still feeling off-kilter.

"But back to your initial question," Casey continued, "I wouldn't peg you as anything, Hannah Rose. You're impossible to pin down."

"Is that good or bad."

He smiled and looked at the sky.

"It is what it is." But whatever I was, Casey didn't seem to mind and made no move to keep away or leave. I found that in spite of our previous subway ride, I was comfortable with him now. Though patience has never been one of my virtues, I settled in for a long wait. Casey had a lot to explain and I was in no rush.

While we watched, the game of Frisbee broke up and the guys and their dogs began to wander off. High fives and distant waves were the last we saw of them. I felt a breeze pick up and tickle the back of my neck. It didn't feel so sticky now and Casey, finally, turned to me.

"Sorry. I wasn't trying to be dramatic. One of the Frisbee guys could hear us . . . well, you anyway, and I didn't want any eavesdroppers on our conversation. Thank you for being patient."

I turned my head and smiled at him with narrowed eyes, "You gonna fess up now, Bub?"

Casey laughed, "Yes . . . mostly." I sighed and rolled my eyes, looking away. "Look, this is going to be faster if I use some . . . jargon, then I'll speak normally again, okay?"

I started to laugh. His speech was rarely normal. But instead of saying anything smart, I just nodded, "Shoot."

Casey took a deep breath. "The place where you felt—where you're feeling uh . . . *things* . . . that's a Chakra. You know what that is?

"Vaguely," I said, squinting at him. "I saw a book."

He gazed at the distant buildings on the Parkway, "Well, Eastern Philosophy teaches that different parts of the body correlate to different . . . ah . . . vibrations. So, theoretically, baser . . . instincts, forces, Id, those vibrations, would start in the Root Chakra—you can guess where that is . . . ." He blushed. I felt better knowing that he could do that. He wasn't The Teflonator after all and I nodded, blushing a little myself.

"Well," he hurried to change areas of the body, "the top of your head would be your Crown Chakra—that one is the most spiritual—the purest. The one we find that is connected to, ah . . . " he paused.

I waited for a second, then suggested, "Heaven? Angels?"

"That's the right idea." He nodded. "The places you got, um . . . zapped, those are—"

"The heart chakra?"

"Nice. Yes. That's one of them," He smiled sideways at me.

"Eh, lucky guess. I know where it felt like it hit me."

He shook his head. "I don't know, Hannah Rose. How often do you do that?"

"Do what?"

"Dismiss what you do as lucky, or a guess, or ascribe it to coincidence?"

"Uh . . . well, all the time . . . maybe? I mean, yeah, I'm used to knowing what will happen, but that's just the way things are, right? I don't, y'know, *know*. And I still don't think I make things happen—not bad things. Not all the time. I'm not *really* dangerous." I shrugged and looked at the field where the Frisbees once flew wondering why it felt so important that Casey not think I was capable of those things.

"You made the lemonade explode."

I turned purple and turned away, putting my head in my free hand. "You saw that?"

"Yes," He was smiling, but he wasn't being mean. "And I heard about more from Mina and Bill."

"Oh great."

"No, you're not hearing me. I had to find out about it all from them. Stop blinking like that," he laughed, "I mean, I didn't get the information from you. I didn't see it like I would have been able to with *anyone else in the world.*"

I could feel Casey shift to look at me. "Mina and Bill . . . none of us expected—I mean it isn't—look, I didn't do this on purpose. I *couldn't* have done this on purpose. For an opener it isn't ethical—" I thought he was starting to get nervous, and it seemed when Casey got nervous he began talking like an attorney rather than as his normal, patronizing professor self. "Full disclosure, now? I don't know how to do this. Technically I *can't* do this . . . I knew it happened to other adepts when they . . . and I was fairly certain what it was when it occurred, but not that it was going to happen. And I never would have picked you—"

"Whoah whoah whoah." Pulling away from him, I leaned off to my right and stared him down.

Casey wasn't a lawyer anymore. He was a nervous 19-year-old guy—although that didn't make me feel any more charitable. "So, I'm not . . . what? Good enough for you? You wouldn't have *picked* me?"

He tried to recover, "That isn't what I meant—"

"No, it's just what you said!"

He sighed, looked down, and started to pluck grass from the ground in front of him. He repositioned himself so his legs were bent and he was leaning his forearms on his knees, his head dropped, studying dirt.

"It's not you," he started, talking to the grass. "It isn't that I wouldn't have wanted to . . . spend time with you or . . . whatever. You're thinking about this like a girl and you can't."

"Gee, I'm sorry." Now I was fully sarcastic, which, as I may have mentioned, is not my most attractive mode. "I didn't know I was supposed to be thinking about this like . . . what . . . one of New York's Finest? What do you want?" I was getting angry. And that scared me. I didn't want to light Casey on fire.

Not yet, anyway.

I took a deep breath and I felt something else. I was still learning, but I could tell this wasn't me. Something was coming off of Casey in light waves. It calmed and centered me. If he was doing something to me, I didn't mind. It helped. I was still ticked, but soon my head was clearer and I said, "I'm sorry. That wasn't helpful. Please . . . I want to understand this. Everything here is so . . . alien. And not just the psychic stuff, I mean that's bad enough, but I don't have my friends here. There's nowhere to swim. I barely know my way around. I can't drive here. I don't even know where to get ice cream. It's all . . . wrong."

He grinned straight at me and said, "You're absolutely right. We need ice cream." He stood up and held out his hand to me. I knew perfectly well what would happen when I took it, but at that moment, I didn't much care. Whatever line had hooked between us was real. I was absolutely drawn to this guy who I didn't know and hadn't really liked much before, and who, quite honestly, scared the bejujus out of me. So, against what little occasional wisdom I might have, I took his hand again.

The jolt of—whatever it was—shot up through my arm, straight into my chest and down, turning my legs to pudding, leaving me warm and tingling like a raw nerve. Not pain . . . thrumming. I felt a fine mist of sweat on my forehead. I gasped and thudded back onto the ground but didn't let go.

"Are you okay?" He seemed worried. I could tell he was wrestling with whether he should drop my hand or help pick me up with his other hand. Instead he froze. "Does it . . . hurt?"

I shook my head and took a few deep breaths, rising and steadying myself onto my feet.

"Okay then," he nodded, meaningfully, "we have a mission."

"Does it depend on my being able to breathe, or is that optional?" I half-smiled. I was mostly serious.

"Breathing is usually beneficial," he half-smiled back. "Is it too awful? Should I let go? It's . . . it hasn't been like this for me . . . I haven't . . . " he stopped and looked at the sky, running his free hand through his floppy hair, "I . . . you should understand that, for me, I can . . . when I touch your hand I'm . . . I'm . . . it's like I'm walled off from you. I can see if you send. But if you're not blocking, I can only see what you let me see—if you let me see anything. And when any of that comes through—like the rain in the desert—it's this . . . pale . . . it's mist . . . It's this odd pale blue mist . . . I'm sorry, I can't explain this better."

"It's not awful," I said. I couldn't tell him that I didn't want him to let go, while at the same time it was enormously difficult to draw air into my lungs. Or stand up straight. Or see clearly. Everything blurred like a chalk drawing on the sidewalk when it rains, then it would snap back into focus. "It doesn't hurt. It's more like . . . " I had to think about this. It's more like what? I'd never felt anything like it. "It's like it's too much. Too much good. Too much . . . I don't know . . . too much feeling . . . Somewhere inside me there's something that . . . pushes me over the edge and there's this . . . geez, this is hard . . . " I felt myself start to blush, "then it's like I get aftershocks for awhile. It's not painful, but it's . . . overwhelming. It's hard for me to say in words, too. But it's more than just a 'boom' . . . . There are things that I know when you hold my hand—and it was the same at the house when you caught me, only it was stronger that time."

"You *know* things?" We walked slowly across Prospect Park West, down towards 7th Avenue where I assumed our goal was ice cream. "What kinds of things?" He tried too hard to sound casual.

"I can see . . . more. It's not painful, it's like, I don't know. Almost panic . . . maybe? It only lasts a moment, but I can feel . . . Like I'm getting—too much information . . . it's not only people that I'm picking up on, it's also animals . . . trees . . . rocks! Wait!" He stopped and I turned to look at him, understanding for the first time. "Is this what you get all the time? Is this how the world looks to you? Everything? Everything in your head all the time?! How can you live like this?"

He smiled slyly, sadly. "Well, now at least one other person understands." We turned back and kept walking, still holding hands. Still occasionally shuddering through pleasant waves, as well as the intensity of the images occasionally rolling off Casey. We headed down Garfield Place. Every time we passed someone, I got another wave of information.

"I shouldn't say that. Bill understands. At least intellectually."

"How do you *deal* with this?" I finally asked.

"That's what I've been trying to tell you. Normally, I can block it all—all of it—but only for a very short while. It's like I have a lens and I can keep the lens cover on or I can take the cover off and aim that lens at someone. When I aim at anyone, I can see everything—*everything* about them. But, as you probably guessed, I don't like to do that—and I can't keep the lens cover on forever. And I can't stand having it off for long."

"No, I can see that. This is *horrible*. When does it stop?"

"It doesn't. Ever."

I looked at the pretty doorways we were passing, all different colors. "Is this why you're gone so often?"

Casey nodded, looking anywhere but at me.

"Are you going to leave again soon?" I might have whispered. Everything was far away.

Casey shrugged after a moment. "I decide my own schedule. I'm not . . . having trouble with anyone but you—and you're no trouble at all." He smiled sideways at me and I saw his eyes twinkle behind his glasses. I melted all over again. "I suppose I don't have to run away immediately if," I heard him change mid-sentence, "if I can keep the lens cap on for the rest of the world."

"So, when you're with me you can't block at all?"

"No. No, when I'm with you I can't see *you*. You're . . . an image that's blurred around the edges and for some reason I'm not able to see you clearly, sometimes at all."

"Is that good?"

He stopped, started to say something, then started walking again. Finally, looking at the sidewalk he said, "It's better than good. I never thought I'd . . . " he raised our linked hands together. "I can't do this. With anyone. Not for a long time."

"And you're not getting anything from me?"

"Not unless you're sending. Or your shields are on the fritz like back in the parlor."

"Yeah, I was a little distracted," I admitted.

"Just a bit."

"You're such a brute."

"Oh, you know that's true." We laughed. It was the most natural thing in the world.

"So how do you, um, do the lens cap thing?"

"Normally? Well, there are two things that help."

"And they are . . . ?"

"Not being surprised and knowing who I'm surrounding myself with."

"So, the people at Mina and Bill's—"

"—Are known quantities. I can handle them. I've already been overwhelmed by them. I know them."

"Oh! What can you tell me about Justin."

"Not fair," he said seriously, "Really. Would you want me talking to him about you?"

"Good point. Okay, I take it back. So can you keep the lens cap on if you're surprised by someone on the street?"

"Yes, but it's hard. It takes a lot out of me. On a normal day I would *never* risk going down to 7th like this."

"Then why are you doing it now? I don't want you to get hurt!"

He looked over at me, smiling, "I won't. But thank you. Actually, I can do it because of you."

"Me? What am *I* doing?"

"Grounding me."

"Come again?"

"You're giving me . . . you know those plugs you put into the wall sockets?"

"Um, yeah?"

"You know how the third prong is the ground?"

"No, but let's pretend I did."

"The gaps in your education, Hannah Rose, are most bizarre."

"Keep it moving, dude. This is not Abuse Rosie Day. So, the third prong?"

"The third prong is the ground. It's what makes the device work, work well and keeps it from, well, accidentally blowing up."

"So grounding is a good thing." I said.

He looked at me, checking to see if I was joking or not. "Yes. Pretty high up on the good score. But that's it."

"I lost you. What's it?"

"You're the ground."

"Oh! Like Izzy and Justin."

"Yes," he sighed.

"So I . . . I keep you from blowing up? Or flying away?"

"I seem to work better. The lens cap lasts longer and stays on better."

"And that's from me?"

"Seems so."

"Huh. Imagine that."

I thought while we walked in comfortable silence. "You know, my grandfather had macular degeneration. He couldn't see whatever it was he was looking at. He only had his peripheral vision."

"That's a good corollary." Casey thought for a moment. "Except that for me, when I'm with you, I can focus easily on what's really here. It's all the weird ... psychic ... stuff that gets pushed to the periphery. For me it's a relief."

"So are you pushing the rest of the world's problems into me?" I asked, "How is it that I'm seeing this?"

"I'm not certain, yet. That's the interesting part. It's like seeing the dark side of the moon during an eclipse. I can see the bright stuff around the edges, it's still there for me, and I can tune in if I want to, but the signal is fuzzier ... weaker. But it's definitely not as hard for me to block the world out with you around. Maybe I can deflect it. Maybe some of it is hitting you, though. Sorry. And then when we ... when I hold your hand, it's all easy and ... effortless. " He smiled.

I felt my face flush.

"Here." We had arrived at a little storefront on Union Street, a few doors up from my firehouse. It was a Tastee Delight, a place I'd never heard of before.

Casey bought me a cone and we sat down on the little white plastic chairs in front of the shop, licking the melting rivulets and watching the world pass by.

I hadn't felt this comfortable in weeks. Which is when I realized I hadn't heard Louis Armstrong in my head since we left Mina's on our walk. I smiled and relaxed into my weird new world.

Casey and I walked home without talking, but with our hands wrapped tight around the other—with one of us shivering like it was winter.

34 Anticipation

OUR TRIP TO THE family's cabin in the Berkshires was coming soon, and for me, "distraction" was the name of the game — and not only the distraction of having Louis' song back in my head again. The thought of escaping the heat and spending some time "in the nature," as Bill said, which included a lake, was like Christmas in August (an Izzy phrase), and everyone was buzzing around, excited.

"Mina?" It was my turn to help with lunch, so I was making sandwiches with my aunt.

"Hmm?" She was arranging baby carrots on the plates to look like sleeping faces.

"I have a little problem I've been keeping from you."

Mina stopped and looked at me, very calm and steady, "You know you can tell me anything, Rose."

I nodded and said somberly, "I have friends."

Immediately, I could feel Mina elbowing past my shields to see what I was up to.

"Hey, no fair!" I was laughing, "I'm serious. I have pushy friends at home, is what I mean. I don't know what to do."

Mina recovered but wouldn't let herself smile, "You don't know how to have friends? Oh, Rose," she teased, "I'm so sorry, sweetie. Maybe we should find a therapist to teach you how to be a friend?"

I nudged her with my hip, "No, what I *said* was that I have *pushy* friends," I was serious now, "and I don't know what to do."

"Pushy? Is this the girl you get the letters from?"

"Lindy, yeah. She hates email, but she's a really, um . . . diligent writer." I pulled her latest list of questions out of my pocket and handed them to Mina. "I wrote her back a couple of times—not answering the questions, but saying everything's great. Tried to throw her off the scent."

"She didn't take the hint."

"No, and after it got . . . interesting here, I really didn't know what to say. I can't tell her what's going on. Look at her questions. How do I explain all this to her without explaining it?"

"Well," Mina looked out the window, "you don't *have* to tell her anything and you don't have to lie. You write her a lovely letter that includes your *trips*," she emphasized the word, "to the library, museum, Coney Island, and if you need to you can say 'I can't explain for a couple of months, but I promise I'll tell you as soon as I can.'"

"You don't know Lindy," I moaned. "She'll pester. She obsesses."

Mina stopped and turned to me in a way that made me stop and look back. "Rose. You are thousands of miles away. You can't allow yourself any more distractions than you already have. When Chloe did it ruined—" and Mina clamped her mouth shut, shaking her head.

"*Chloe?*" I hadn't thought about her hardly at all since arriving, "Chloe was . . . " Dots connected in my head. "Chloe was *here?*" Mina looked at the ceiling, waiting for the inevitable, "But she was at boarding school because . . . oh . . . *OH* . . . you had her *here?* You're the boarding school?"

Mina shook her head, "No, we didn't have her here that long." Dominoes started to fall and Mina spoke slowly. "Things didn't go so well for Chloe. She, well, she wasn't you. And more than that, she let herself get distracted by home and . . . other things, and you can't. You *cannot* let that happen to you. If you get distracted you—"

"I light people on fire?"

I could feel Mina wavering. "Yes," she said finally. "You do."

I couldn't speak.

"Are you okay Rose?"

I nodded. About a gajillion questions swirled through my mind, but I wasn't going to risk soaking the grilled cheese sandwiches I had so carefully assembled. I gracefully swiped my arm across my eyes.

"I'm sure you have questions," Mina said. I could tell she felt bad. And she was trying to ice me to calm me down. I blocked her. I didn't feel like being manipulated. I also wasn't getting a headache like I was going to char the cheese with my mind. I just wanted to get far, far away and think.

I didn't want her or anyone else in my head, so I swallowed and forced a shrug. "So, I'll write Lindy a letter this afternoon and tell her nothing."

Mina watched me and took a long time to answer. "Why don't you wait?" I felt her trying to get in. Now *she* was frustrated. Good. "You can send her a postcard from Stockbridge," she said at last. "Less writing space but with a postcard from somewhere else. She may let it go, thinking you're too busy."

"Yeah, that's good. But," I'd been embarrassed to admit this in front of everyone else, "where *are* we're going? I mean, everyone's all crazy about going to the Berkshires, but I don't have a clue. Jenn just says they're north of here."

Mina smiled and looked relieved. "It's a little cabin on a lake in a place called Stockbridge which, it's true, is north of the city and then a little east into Massachusetts. It takes a while to get there, so we'll break the day into two trips. You'll love it."

"And I can send a postcard from there?"

"Yes." Mina said. "You'll like it there."

I reserved judgment.

Jenn and I spent chunks of time packing over two days—the day of the park with Casey and the day after—so that way we wouldn't forget anything crucial. Slow and steady, blah blah blah. This packing included collecting knitting projects (me), music (us), hair accessories (us), and books (us), and endlessly lamenting over the current fashion in bathing suits (Jenn). Most summers in Arizona I lived in a suit, so I was less affected by this deep fear of Jenn's —the wearing of the suit. Of course, being five-foot-eight with the metabolism of a hummingbird helped. My mom laughed at me, often. "This too shall pass . . . " she would say and whack her hips.

Against my better judgment, but at Jenn's insistence, I packed one pair of jeans. It was 90° out and at least 880% humidity. Really. The *last* thing I wanted on me was denim. But Jenn promised I would be sorry if I didn't. So the jeans went into the duffel, but I drew the line at a sweatshirt. She clucked at me, "Gonna regret it . . . "

"Yeah, yeah yeah," I waved my hands at her mysteriously, "You and your strange Eastern Seaboard Ways don't scare me."

"Yeah, well . . . you just wait for your first blizzard, missy! *Mwaa hah hah hah hah*."

"Oh sure, play the diabolical blizzard voice card."

"You'll learn," she shrugged and zipped her bag closed. And about then, the song in my head morphed to a new tune.

Once we were packed, I decided to do some "homework." I went downstairs with my journal and a book Bill had given me to learn more about the history of people who were . . . well, like us. A book I'd not seen in the public library.

Downstairs, Izzy was flipping cards with Justin. I sank into a nearby chair and opened my book. But no matter how many times I re-read the first paragraph, I couldn't make sense of the words. The new song wouldn't stop. I'd been making peace with Louis Armstrong riffing in the background of my life, and he was practically silent when I was with Casey. Now, with this new song, I would begin reading, comprehending the first sentence or so, but then I'd notice the new music then see a park, then ice cream, then I'd be walking around Brooklyn with Casey and that was the end of reading.

Izzy and Justin had been downstairs longer than I, but I couldn't think of a clever, casual way of asking them if they'd seen Casey yet. I was blocking like crazy as I sat there, trying to relax, slowing my breathing, reaching out to find him in the house, but I came up with nothing. I couldn't tell if he was gone or only shielded to me. So I went back to my book. Even with my blocking efforts, I could tell that Justin knew exactly what I was doing. He kept shooting looks my way and making disapproving noises.

I switched gears. If I couldn't talk to Casey, maybe I could talk to Uncle Bill again. I had a pretty good idea where he was, but I thought maybe I should practice a different skill to hunt him down. I decided to go with anonymity. I'd grown to be pretty good at being sneaky, but this required shielding, holding the anonymity, *and* looking for Bill—all in daylight when Izzy and Justin already knew I was there. I allowed myself to sink in and root, but I wasn't outside this time, on the ground, so I couldn't really bring down the sky. Leaving the house anonymously had been easier.

Nevertheless, keeping my shields up, I pulled on the dim, cool, quiet of the room, the muted colors and peaceful gentility of the antiques. And I watched Justin.

Slowly but surely, he stopped paying attention to me, stopped looking annoyed at me. When I was sure he wasn't seeing me any more, I started to reach out with my Spidey sense for Bill. I had three places to look for him: upstairs, the basement, or the backyard.

He was in the basement. Not a big surprise. I probably could have just walked over to the door and called down, but since Justin now wasn't paying me any mind, I considered it a win. Maintaining shields and anonymity, I got up and headed to the basement door.

"Rosie!" Uncle Bill jumped and nearly embedded his head in the low ceiling. "I didn't hear you come in. Holy cow, you scared me!"

"Sorry," I grinned but felt bad. He hadn't seen or heard me until I released the invisibility thing—right next to his desk. "I was being invisible."

"Well, yes. Yes, you were."

"Can I talk to you about something?"

He took another lungful of air and leaned back in his chair. "About music or about Casey?"

"Wow! You *are* psychic, Uncle Bill."

"Not psychic, Rosie. Just not stupid."

I scrunched up my face and sat down in the chair next to his desk.

"Music first? Or Casey?"

"Music."

"Shoot."

I sang the opening to my new song. Bill smiled.

"That's a great song. That's 'Take the A Train'—Duke Ellington. A jazz classic."

"Not Louis Armstrong?"

"Not Louis. This one stuck in your head now?"

"Yep. I wonder if it's the universe trying to keep me calm?"

"Jazz is good music," Bill said, "Or at least that Big Band sound is. Good dance music. Maybe you should swing dance with Casey and see if the song goes away?"

"I couldn't stand and dance with him at the same time."

Bill chuckled. "All right, what else do you need to know?"

"Casey."

"Casey. I don't know that there's all that much I can tell you, Rose. But I can listen. What's bugging you?"

"Um, I don't know. Let's see . . . who, what, where, when, how, and why?"

Uncle Bill laughed, "Oh well, if that's all."

"Well, how old is he?"

"Don't you think you should be asking him these questions?"

"He's not here. He's not here much at all and he's not here now."

"Ah . . . right," Bill looked back at his desk, glancing over at the books open on his desk.

"What? Where does he go? Do you know where he goes?"

"Sure, he always checks in with me. He goes different places. He has a couple of spots he likes where he can either practice with minimal people around, or a place where he can be completely alone."

"Practice?"

"He . . . I don't know how much I should tell you. Really this should be coming from him, Rosie."

I stared at him until he broke.

"Look," he said leaning over and resting his elbows on his knees, gesturing with his hands, "Casey's complicated. Not like 'teenager complicated,' I mean *complicated.*"

"Right. That's what I wanted to know. *How* complicated."

"Very."

"That's not helpful."

"It's about the best I can do."

"Well, why is he such a big secret?"

"He's not, Rosie. He's not a secret. He's very private and I think everyone here gives him his space."

"Because . . . ?" I asked, drawing out the last syllable.

"Because he's had a rough time."

"You mean the way he sees everything about everyone he comes into contact with?"

Bill looked at me. "He told you?"

"No. He showed me. Accidentally."

"You actually saw what he sees?" Bill leaned towards me.

"I guess so? Why? Is that such a big deal?"

"Explain this to me. Explain how this happened."

I've only seen cross-examinations on TV, never been in one, until now. It's not pretty. I was going through the skateboarder story for maybe the fourth time, when Bill finally asked, "Wait. Wait. You saw this—you got this flash of knowing—but your head didn't hurt?"

"No. Why?"

"Not even a little?"

"Not even at all? Why, Uncle Bill?"

"Look, Casey and I have worked together for years, but I've only been able to go by his descriptions of what's happening to him. Once, a long time ago, we had him try to send to Mina so we'd have someone with more skill and control who knew what he was seeing, you know?"

"Sure, makes sense."

"Well, Mina was down with a migraine for days."

"What?"

"I know," Bill nodded, "we were all pretty shocked. We'd figured Casey was only a kid, but . . . you know. Hubris."

I nodded. "Did she . . . I mean, I know it hurt her, but did she get anything? Did she see?"

Bill shook his head, "whatever sparked the migraine also wiped her short term memory. She didn't even remember sitting down with Casey."

"So . . . " I paused.

"So," Bill agreed, "the fact that you've seen the world the way Casey sees it —and he wasn't touching you?"

"No. No touch the first time. I jumped and let go of his hand, *then* saw. Later I got flashes while he . . . " I swallowed, "held my hand. When we were walking to get ice cream."

Bill couldn't have cared less. "Huh. Well, the fact that you've seen it and avoided retching is huge. It's better than I thought."

"Better than—? Wait," I narrowed my eyes as new dominoes fell into place. I spoke slowly, "what were you and Mina and Casey talking about before we did the falling exercise thing?"

Bill's face went blank. "I don't know what you're talking about."

"Yes, you do," I laughed in my surprise, "Don't try to lie, Uncle Bill. Your shields aren't strong enough."

He released the breath he'd been holding. "Really? I thought I'd gotten better."

I shook my head, "Why didn't Casey want to work with me?"

"It wasn't you," Bill looked surprised. "No, no it wasn't you. It was the fact of the exercise at all. He didn't want any part of it. As you can imagine, it's a lot of work to be around other people."

"But you were talking about me."

"We were?" Bill's face was innocent. "Huh. I just remember trying to get him to participate because it was a safe environment. We like him to practice with actual people from time to time, to see how he's progressing, and we needed to even out the numbers with Jazz there."

"Really."

"Yep."

I sat there for a long while, looking at Bill. He looked back at me, trying so hard not to lose it.

"Oh, Rosie," he said finally as he melted like a candy house in a monsoon. "You'll see him tomorrow and you can ask him all this stuff then. Okay?"

"Tomorrow, when we head up to the cabin."

"Right." I could tell he really didn't want to talk anymore. His eyes kept straying to the open book on his desk.

"Well, thank you Uncle Bill. And I'll see him tomorrow?"

"Tomorrow," he agreed. "You bet."

35 Trains

ON THE MORNING OF our departure, there was still no sign of Casey, and no one else was talking about him, so I didn't ask. I thought it was pretty rude of him, though, to take off—again—after all that had happened. Forget my talk with Bill, I still had questions.

Ooh! Maybe that's why everyone thinks he's a jerk.

Because he is.

Occam's Razor!

I didn't have much time to be upset. The whole house was turning inside out. Jenn and I were able to coast, though, since we'd done all our packing earlier. We sat downstairs reading (her) and knitting (me) while everyone else scrambled. I tried to look bored, but really I was still feeling around for Casey.

With all the hubbub, I'd expected to see everyone bringing piles of luggage to the door, but when everyone came down—finally—they were all carrying their backpacks, like Jenn and me. Nothing else. Come to think of it, I hadn't seen our bags since Jenn zipped them up and put them by the door of our room. Bill had gone into work that morning, so it was just the four of us in the house plus Mina—maybe Bill had taken the luggage? Mina had been working her way through the house, closing curtains and checking latches, turning taps to be sure they weren't leaking, triple checking to see that the refrigerator was still empty.

Finally, her mental checklist complete, she turned to us. "Done. Out!"

She swept us in front of her, out and through the door. We trooped down the street to the train station, immediately sticky from the heat, the humidity, and the synthetic fabric of our packs on our backs.

Still no Casey.

Still not asking.

We settled in on the train. All of us were quiet and pretty mellow, when it dawned on me that I'd never thought to tell my parents where we were going or what we were doing. I swung around a pole and moved to Mina.

"Aunt Mina? Did you tell Mom and Dad where we're going?"

Mina smiled, "Uh huh. They know. But you can call them soon. I'm sure they'd like to hear from you."

"I can call from the train, really?"

Mina nodded.

"But don't the tunnels block the calls?"

"The next train has no tunnel. We're going up on Metro North," she smiled.

"Metro North goes all the way to Stockbridge?"

"We're going to meet Jasmine, Tyrik, and Casey first, wait for Bill, then we'll head up together in the van."

I hoped Mina couldn't hear when my heart stopped.

So, Casey was ahead of us. I started to ask why, then shut my mouth when it clicked that he must have taken our luggage early—Occam's Razor, you dope. It would have been a hassle to lug bags on the train.

Still, he could have said goodbye.

When we trudged up the stairs at Grand Central, Mina and Jenn led the way, with Izzy and Justin in front of me. I caught up to Izzy when we entered the main concourse. "Is it just me, Izzy, or do you feel the need for white gloves and a hat when you're in here."

"Hat or snood," Izzy nodded seriously.

"Snood," Justin snorted. "Y'all need to stop cursing in the station. That sorta thing is frowned on by The Man."

"Justin, no one says, 'the man' anymore."

"No one white."

"No one under the age of 30."

"Maybe I'm mature for my age."

"Maybe you're smoking crack."

Justin sniffed, but winked at me and caught up to Jenn.

"I love this place," Izzy said, seeming not to mind Justin skittering off.

"I love it too," I agreed. "I thought it was just me being a geek."

"Might be," Izzy smiled, "but you're not a lonely geek."

After standing in line, Mina bought our tickets at the clerk's window and handed them to us. We turned and headed over to the track. "So, Rosie," Izzy started. I looked at her, curious to see why she sounded so funny. "I wanted to . . . I wondered what—"

"Platform 9-3/4," Mina interrupted, motioning us into a car.

"Ha," Justin said, regally, "It never gets old, Mina."

"Nor do you, Just," Mina laughed. I rolled my eyes at Jenn.

We followed Justin's lead and stowed our packs up in the racks near the front seats in the car. Jenn nudged me into a window seat. I looked back at Izzy, wondering if she was waiting to finish her sentence, but she seemed to be in a convo with Mina.

"It's all pretty," Jenn whispered, "but you want to be on this side if you want to see the river."

"Do I want to see the river?"

"Yeah. You do."

Justin and Izzy wound up in the seat behind us. I guess they had made up for real. No weirdness now. I wasn't the only one loving this trip so far; Justin had been in a good mood ever since the day I trust-fell on Casey. Or at least, he hadn't been on my back as much. Mina was already ensconced in a seat in front of us without a window, deep in a book.

The train started with the expected "Stand clear of the closing doors" thing, then the bells, then a lurch. The tunnel for Metro North was different than the subway tunnel. Moving out from the murky underground, we were in a vast rail yard. Old trains, other tracks, and a few scattered lights dotted the landscape outside my window. Then it grew lighter, then another single tunnel and then outside. Just like that. We picked up speed, moving over bridges and through industrial areas in no time.

Mina turned away from her book and leaned the top of her head over her seatback, "you can get a signal now, Rose." And back to her book she went.

I pulled my bag down, found my phone, and dialed my parents.

"Rose!" Mom had answered. "How's your trip?"

"Um . . . the one I'm on right now, or the bigger trip that brought me here in general?"

"How about both?"

"The bigger one is good. We're having a good time. This little one is only starting so I can't tell you much. The train is nice . . . "

Mom laughed, "It's good to hear your voice. Things are quiet here."

"Well, then you should come visit. That'll give you some noise."

"Hannah Rose?" Dad clicked on, "You there? How are you?"

"Good! I'm really good. Things here are . . . interesting . . . " I didn't want to tell them about Casey. Yet.

"Is that a *good* interesting or a 'why do you hate me' interesting?" Dad might have been joking.

"Mostly good, I guess. Yeah, right now it's good."

"No more running away?" Dad asked, laughing.

"*Spuyten Duyvil. Next stop,*" the train loudspeaker said.

"Oh!" Mom squeaked, "I know right where you are!"

"You do? Wow. You *are* psychic," I laughed.

"No, I heard the conductor say Spite-n-die-val. I always loved that name."

"That's a weird word to remember, Mom."

"Eh. The name is Dutch. It stands out."

We talked a bit more, avoiding anything important—like Casey. Mom told me a few things to try to do in Stockbridge. Dad told me what kinds of plants and geological formations to look for. It's a weird way to tell your kid you love her, but it's their way. Then the phone connection became more static than call so we hung up. I turned my attention to the window. Jenn was right; the view was awesome. The river sparkled in the heat and sun; the Palisades across the water were lush and green. Sitting in the cool train car and looking out at the gorgeous world skim by felt luxurious. I started to understand why everyone liked making this trek every summer. Too bad it was still humid.

"You keep forgetting, it's because of the humidity that it's all lush and green," Jenn leaned over and said in my ear.

"I don't forget. I just don't like to remember," I said, still looking out the window. I almost stopped this time to ask how in the world Jenn, who says she's not psychic like the rest of us, was able to hear me while my shields were up.

36 DAM

WE STOOD AND COLLECTED our stuff when they announced the Croton-on-Hudson station. My backpack felt heavy as we came down the stairs to the parking lot and I missed the last step, landing with a thud. Directly in front of Casey. He stood there, leaning against the van in the loading zone, with this little smile on his face, looking straight at me.

Smug.

Jerk.

Damn him and his floppy hair and cute glasses!

I tried not to watch him as we all piled our backpacks into the rear of the van. "Rose gets shotgun," Jenn said smiling over her shoulder at me as we climbed in. "She's never seen Croton."

"Should we have a tour?" Mina asked.

"I can do that," Casey nodded as he opened the door for me, waving me in and bowing like a butler before he slid the back door closed and walked around to the driver's side to start the car. Justin gave me a look, either anger or exasperation. I didn't much blame him, but shrugged at him anyway. He pointedly looked out the side window, away from me.

Mina was in back, right behind Casey. She tapped his chair thoughtfully, rather than tapping him on the shoulder, "Let's do Silverlake, then the Opera

House, then the Dam, then downtown," Justin snickered almost silently and I heard Izzy smack his arm, "that sets us up to head to Jasmine's place." Casey nodded and put the car into drive.

While he controlled the car, Mina narrated, but I had a hard time concentrating. " . . . Swimming hole . . . residents . . . ten degrees cooler . . . turn of the century Opera House . . . Mister Harmon himself for Madame Lillian . . . Dam, built by Italian . . . dam that collapsed . . . Black Cow coffee is better . . . Blue Pig ice . . . Mt. Airy road takes us . . . "

I tried to look like I was concentrating; occasionally I'd hear Casey say something like, *You should be focusing on Mina more, Hannah Rose,* but he'd say it in my head. He looked awfully proud of himself. Cat-that-ate-a-canary proud. I tried hard not to show that I'd heard him and a couple of times I heard him chuckle softly. I wanted to thwack him on the arm but didn't feel like doing it in front of everyone else.

There was no doubt—Croton was beautiful. Green, lush vegetation, cute little houses, adorable Main Street—not really "quaint" in an icky gingerbread house way, but comfortable. And pretty. And quiet.

Basically, Not New York City.

We drove through and out of town, up into the hills. Old stone fences and heavy undergrowth gave way to some amazing old farmhouses and fields that looked like postcard pictures. After twists and turns, Casey pulled into a long driveway that ended in a gorgeous—I'm gonna guess historic—barn-like house. It was painted that old red color with white trim (hence the barn theme) but the structure itself was more like a house—just big. We collected our backpacks and headed over to the door around the side. I could see that Jasmine's place was a lot like my home in Arizona. It was cobbled together—all the same color, but different woods, materials, styles. A Ye Olde Frankenstein house instead of an Adobe Pueblo Frankenstein house.

I loved it before we ever stepped inside.

Inside, it was so beautiful I thought I might cry. I didn't know places like this really existed. Old plank floors, antiques that looked like they'd been in this house since they were new, rugs that were obviously made by hand—and a spinning wheel in the corner. I might have squealed, but if I did, no one made fun of me. Instead I watched everyone relax. Even Justin, who normally carried himself with a straight haughtiness, relaxed here. It was a good house.

Jazz hugged everyone, while her son Tyrik hung behind her, looking shy. I imagine it was weird to have your own house invaded by psychics—I'd be freaked out if I were him. How would he know if we were all reading his mind or something? But during the hugging, I noticed something I hadn't seen in Brooklyn when he visited for dinner. Tyrik was protected. I wasn't sure whether Jasmine had put some sort of shield around him, or if everyone participated in making and maintaining this bubble of safety. But no one was scanning him. I checked his face again, and I could tell that he knew it, too.

I followed Jenn out back to a screened-in porch. Justin and Izzy went somewhere with Tyrik. They must have hung out before; he seemed more comfortable with them. Even though he knew Casey, and talked with him at that dinner, Tyrik gave him a lot of space. I wondered if it was fear of or respect for Casey's situation. Mina and Jasmine were talking over by a pitcher of lemonade. Jazz had a light sweater over her summer-dress shoulders which got me thinking. I walked over with my knitting bag and pulled out the shawl, holding it against her skin.

"What is that, Sweet? It's lovely."

"It's a shawl I'm making, and it's the same color as the sweater you're wearing."

"Look at that," her eyes danced in the light.

"I think this one's going to have to be yours, Jasmine."

"But it's so much work," she protested.

"But it's so cool to see my knitting on someone who looks good in it. I'll have it done before we come back to the city. I knit pretty fast."

"What a treat for me. Thank you, Rose." And she gave my hand a squeeze.

With a dopey grin on my face, I took my knitting over to the empty fireplace where Casey and Jenn were already planted on old, creaky chairs I wanted to take home with me.

"So, um . . . " I'd never seen Jenn so nervous, "so, uh . . . Casey, I was wondering, you know, what happened the other day when you and Rose . . . when you caught—"

"No idea," Casey broke in. He sounded really tense, which was a big change from how he sounded in my head in the car.

Be nice, I aimed at his head.

"I mean," Casey tried again, glancing at me, "I mean I have no idea. Neither does your mom. No one does. Even Bill's at a loss. He's actually in the city researching today. He should be back in a little over an hour, though." Casey checked his wrist.

That was news.

"Did Dad say what he thinks it is?"

"He thinks Rose is an anomaly. Or I am. Or when you put us together we are."

"Meaning, you're even vastly more awesomely differenter than we thought you were?" She raised her eyebrows.

I was relieved when Casey laughed, "Yes. Or Rose actually makes me most astonishingly differentest."

"Well, it wouldn't be the first time I've had that effect on a situation," I shrugged.

And for the next couple of hours Jenn, Casey, and I sat there talking like it was the most normal thing in the world—even though I'd never seen the two of them say more than three civil words to each other at one time.

I'm a togetherizer.

It's just how I roll.

After a spectacular barbecue dinner, to which Bill barely made it before Tyrik snatched the last couple of ribs, everyone piled into either the van or Jazz's car to head down the hill into town. We arrived at the Blue Pig ice cream shop at the same time as a bunch of high school locals. We had to stand in line behind the unruly mob of whippersnappers for a mighty long time, but Jenn promised me the ice cream was worth it. Casey didn't line up, though. He sat over by the edge of the parking lot in the early evening twilight. I could only see his shoes and an occasional glint from his glasses from where I was standing.

"Is this why y'all didn't want me going out on my own?" I whispered to Mina. She looked at me. "Because I can hear what they're thinking about us and it makes me want to smack them."

Mina smiled, "That's part of it."

"Mob mentality," Jenn nodded.

"Always ugly."

"Well what do you expect," Izzy whispered over her shoulder. "You know . . . they're *teenagers.*"

We smiled our superior smiles until we got the ice cream and stopped caring about the other people at the shop amid our nummy noshing sounds. I saw Bill walk over and hand a cup to Casey and wondered why Casey hadn't asked me to get him something.

By the time we got back to Jazz's house, ice cream partway gone, I was completely wiped—which was hilarious because I'd done exactly nothing that day, no studies, no reading, no work. But I decided not to argue with my body. Casey was talking to Bill and Jenn was talking to Jazz, so I said *bye* at Casey's head, more as a test than anything else. His eyes flicked at me with one of those here-and-gone smiles. And that was it. I went to bed.

I didn't dream at all.

37 MAGNIFICENT SEVEN

WHEN I AWOKE, THE sun was barely up and everyone else was still asleep. I crept downstairs to see if I could find something to eat. Before I was fully awake, or even fully downstairs, I heard a noise. When my legs turned to rubber as I rounded the corner at the bottom of the stair, I knew it was Casey.

"Hi," he said softly, "you left before I could say goodnight."

"You're making—" I couldn't remember if I'd brushed my teeth before I came down, which seemed really important, "—you're making pancakes?"

"Is that so wrong of me?"

"No, it's just that . . . You're the quietest pancake-maker I've ever seen."

"It's a gift," he said, swirling his spatula in the air. Then he laughed once, shaking his head.

"What?"

"No, it's nothing," he put the empty bowl in the sink, silently.

"So? Share the nothingness," I took a step closer to the counter.

"It's . . . we're having a conversation."

I stared, "Why, yes. Yes, we are."

"I know that's not much for you, but for me. To be able to be this . . . normal. It's odd. It's great," he caught himself quickly. "But it's new for me."

"It looked like it was new for everyone to have you talking to them last

317

night," it sounded snarkier than I meant it to. I think.

"What do you mean?" Casey looked confused as he flipped the last of his pancakes.

"Nothing. Seriously." He lifted an eyebrow at me. "I just knew that last night was the first time Jenn's actually had a conversation with you."

"It's true." He looked up and flashed me a million dollar smile, "With you near, I can talk to people. Even more than one at a time!" He made it sound like he'd climbed Everest. Goof.

"Well," I said, and couldn't think of anything more so I stood there, looking at him, feeling like a complete dork.

He smiled over at me from under those lashes, glasses sliding down his nose, as he bent down to put the final pancakes in the oven. "I wanted to show you my room."

I started to say something smart, but surprise finally registered and I switched to, "You have a room here?"

"Uh huh," he nodded. "I have . . . things here I think you'd like to see."

I couldn't tell if he was joking or teasing or what, but how could anyone lie while making pancakes? I took the bait. "But you have your room in Brooklyn?"

"Yes, but the one here is my real room. This is the place I feel like . . . it's like home. Stockbridge feels safe—and it's peaceful, but it's still work for me when I'm up there. This is a home. Jasmine and Tyrik are here on the weekends and sometimes I stay, sometimes I go back to Brooklyn or up to the cabin. When I'm up here during the week I maintain the house for Jazz."

"Maintain? Snow?" I said hopefully.

"Sure, in the winter. But, you know, Jasmine and I have had some similar experiences and she can see as much future as I can—and block more than I can —so it's easier being around her than most people."

I wanted to know if she was easier than being around me, but he was on a roll.

"Talking to Bill is great because he's easy to work with. He's relentlessly positive and a great researcher, but still . . . Jasmine is a friend. She's helped me through some really rough times."

"I don't even know her very much and I like her a lot already. I want to be her," I said.

"You're not the only one. She's pretty much the only person I know who was born with her glamours on. That helped her to work her way into her job, that's for sure."

"What does she do?" I pulled out silverware for breakfast, trying to count enough for everyone while listening.

"Well, what she used to do was nanny work." I thought to make a Mary Poppins joke but pressed my lips together. "But while she was nannying in the Slope, she was working her way through night school. If she hadn't had glamours I don't think she would have been able to get her hours rearranged so she could go to school. But she did. Worked harder than anyone I've ever known, too. And now she's a big financial honcho on Wall Street."

"That's fantastic. Is that how she—" I'd come around Casey to the refrigerator to see if there was some juice I could put out when I felt him behind me. His breath moved my hair gently and I shivered.

"I'm not touching," he whispered.

"I don't think it matters," I sighed.

He chuckled. "Just checking to see where the boundaries are."

I looked up over my shoulder at him. "What?"

He smiled. "Just checking," he said, and he turned away to replace the pancake mix box in the pantry, then walked towards the back stairs. "C'mon," he said, indicating that I should follow, but I held back. "It's not like you're breaking a rule. You're allowed to walk around the house."

I couldn't put my finger on it, but it seemed strange to be going to

Casey's room, only the two of us. I'd never felt the need for a chaperone before, but I was shaky just being near him and the thought of being that alone with him, that far from everyone else, that private with him . . . it felt like we were crossing a line.

I followed, though.

Slowly.

When we got up to his door, which was mostly closed, he pushed it open and held it that way, meaning I had to walk very close to him to get into the room. He really seemed to enjoy his effect on me.

But his room was worth it.

He didn't have posters of bands or sports stars on the walls. Instead he had tacked pages from books, quotes that he'd copied down on napkins, scrap paper, paper towels, whatever had been handy when he read or overhead something. There were postcards of great works of art from the Met and MoMA. There were pictures he must have taken up in Stockbridge or home in South Dakota.

There were no pictures, as far as I could tell, of his family. Not even Izzy.

But Joan of Arc was there. My special painting was on his wall. I pointed and looked at him, speechless. He shrugged.

Casey followed me, standing almost safely near-far, watching me as I read his walls. He loved philosophy; that much was clear, and a little of everything else, too. There were quotes from Twain, Brecht, Göethe, Plato, Aristotle, Kant, Machiavelli, Berkeley, Nietzsche, Jung, Vonnegut, and the Bible. I could have read his walls for days. I made one entire circuit, reading only the pieces at eye level, when I noticed that he'd also started to cover the ceiling.

"I ran out of vertical space."

"Jazz lets you put tacks in the wall?"

"What?"

"Um. Nothing." Stupid, sure, but what else could I say? Because how do you turn to someone you've known for such a short time and tell them you love them?

And I did.

Casey may have been infuriating sometimes, but now I saw his mind—and he was so beautiful. I loved the person who decorated this room. Deeply. I was afraid to open my mouth again. Afraid that something so revealing, so huge that it would leave me wide-open and unprotected, would come tumbling out of me before I could stop it.

Then he was behind me, where he'd been the whole time I'd been reading his walls, but closer now. "That's why I wanted you to see the room."

I thought very carefully about what I was going to say next—and I made sure I thought it while I was blocking—like a linebacker.

"You said you couldn't hear me," I squeaked.

"I can't if you're not sending. But . . . you were sending . . . "

Not for the first time around Casey, I thought I was going to throw up, or lose my shields, or more likely both. If this is what love is—many nauseated moments strung together—I would need to rethink this relationship thing.

I heard him chuckle and could feel him raise his arms to put his hands down on my shoulders; then he stopped himself. I was riveted to the floor.

"Turn around." It was more question than command. His voice was soft and apologetic. "I don't want to touch you . . . since it bothers you."

I turned around. He'd put his hands back down at his sides.

"Hannah Rose," he was smiling peacefully, so calm. I, on the other hand, did not feel calm at all. "I don't think you comprehend what it means to me that you . . . that I can . . . that we can stand this close to each other. I don't think I've properly expressed the joy of not having to block out everything when I'm with you."

I nodded.

"I can't do this—anything like this. Except with you."

"You can't ... stand ... in a room?"

"No," he looked up, shaking his head, impatient, "no, be this close to—"

I heard a noise downstairs, "Casey?" It was Bill's voice.

"Oh no," I moaned, "busted."

"Coming," Casey called down, then looked at my face. "You're not in trouble. Bill knows."

My first thought: Bill knows?

And second: Bill knows *what*?

I hesitated but followed Casey back down to the kitchen. Bill was cooking his bacon and had put the butter and syrup out for Casey's pancakes.

He nodded at Casey, then asked me, "So? What did you think of his walls? Pretty good stuff, eh?"

"I ... it ... I think I have a lot more to read. It's pretty packed in there."

"Well, sometime you should read it all. It's quite intense. There are some quotes you found, Case, that still haunt me."

"Yeah, well," Casey smiled at Bill, "I have a lot of time for reading." He started the last tasks of preparing breakfast for the hordes. I moved to help. The smell of bacon and coffee seemed to draw everyone down to breakfast in slow, eye-rubbing waves.

"How many are we now?" Bill was counting out more strips of bacon. "Jennifer, Rose, Izzy, Justin, Casey, Mina, Jasmine, and me and Tyrik ... hey! You guys are the Magnificent Seven! Seven Magnificent Psychics, all in one room. Harmoniously, too! Go figure."

"I'm only a sidekick, Daddy—the Nearly Magnificent Seven. But what does that make you and Tyrik?" Jenn asked, giving her father a little hug.

"I think that makes me the driver and Tyrik the chaperone." He kissed her forehead and laid the fresh bacon in the pan, then delivered the plate of cooked bacon to the table. Casey presented the pancakes and we all sat down to eat, like the surreal but happy family we were.

38 SECRET HISTORIES

THE WHOLE CHLOE SAGA that Mina mentioned back in Brooklyn had been scratching around my brain. I volunteered for clean up with Jasmine while everyone else went for a cool morning walk. It gave me a chance to talk with her alone for the first time, which was important: I wanted to ask her a question.

"Jasmine?" I couldn't bring myself to call her "Jazz" to her face.

"Yes?" She nodded to a location for the dishes I brought over from the table. Her hands, carefully placed in rubber gloves, were sunk deep in the soapy sink water.

"I just wondered . . . Mina said something about my sister the other day. I —"

"Yes," not interrupting, more like stopping my growing nervousness. "I was here when your sister arrived. I know your parents haven't told you. I know Mina only told you very little. I also know that it is absolutely fine for you to ask me questions. So please. Ask."

I felt like a balloon deflating. All my tension oozed away with Jasmine there. Being around her was like a cool drink of water on a Tucson summer day, or a friend reassuring you, when you think you've really messed something up with her, that everything's going to be all right. I don't know how else to describe her. She's peace in a person. That's all.

"Okay . . . well, obviously I've been able to figure when Chloe came here, but I don't know why. I know that in my case, I was, well, causing trouble so my parents sent me here to help me control all this stuff. But Chloe . . . I don't remember her doing any weird stuff."

Jasmine didn't look up from the dishes. "When your parents and Mina decided to bring her out here . . . you understand, Mina had not tried to do anything like this before. They often helped sweet Casey as they could—he was so fragile—and of course at the time, they thought Jennifer held promise as well." She sighed lightly. "Mina and I had met, thank the Lord, a few years before but the idea of creating a safe-house for children, for young adepts, hadn't really occurred to any of us."

"So what did she do?" I hoped Jasmine couldn't hear how desperate I felt.

"She's really never talked to you about his?" Jasmine tried to hide her shock.

"We hardly even speak to each other. But, you know, she's eight years older than me. It's not like we have a lot to talk about, right?"

Jasmine looked out the window, her hands resting on the side of the sink, "When Chloe was sixteen, she was in a car accident. You remember that?"

I nodded.

"You remember *why* she had the accident?"

I wasn't sure how to answer that. "I remember what I heard but what I *knew* was that the adults weren't telling me the truth. I remember that my parents were whispering about it a lot, but I knew that when they talked to me—or anyone else for that matter—that they were lying."

"That is correct. They couldn't tell anyone else the truth."

"Why? What is the truth?"

"Your sister, she had a vision while she was driving. She lost control. She was very, very lucky she only went into the ditch at the side of the road. If she'd gone into the oncoming lane . . . " I shivered and deposited more plates, moving more slowly, concentrating.

"So . . . what was her vision about, Jasmine? Do you know?"

"It was . . . " she turned and looked at me standing next to her, "Well, my Sweet, it was about you."

"She had a vision about me? What, like, she saw what I was doing at school?"

"No . . . " Jasmine paused for a long time, turning back to the window, her profile lit by the soft outside light, "I'm sorry, Rose. I am not at all sure how I should say this . . . "

"Well, then I suppose you should come out with it. I can take it."

Jasmine gave me a funny look that I couldn't read. She wasn't trying to get past my shields; she was moving far away. Her eyes defocused and her face wasn't slack exactly, but it was . . . glowing . . . relaxed. That beautiful face stopped in time—stopped time. And then she was back and her eyes were like coal black stars again.

"Your sister saw you in danger. In a dark fog. She didn't know when it was, nor where. But she felt death all around you—an older you. And she panicked. And then she crashed."

"Where did you go just now, Jasmine?" I whispered. "Your face . . . "

Jasmine carefully removed the gloves and went to sit in a chair. I cautiously began to dry the dishes she'd stacked on a towel to the side of the sink. Something to do while I waited for her.

Jasmine sighed, probably because it's ridiculous to keep secrets in a houseful of psychics. "I went to Chloe. She never learned to block—at least she never learned to block me. I went and pulled out her vision."

"You can do that from here?"

"I can."

"Did she know you were there?"

"Probably not," Jasmine was being honest, not mean. "Chloe was nothing like you, Rose. When she came here she was scared. Understand, there were no other young people here—Jennifer was eight, like you. Casey overlapped with Chloe briefly but he was young too. Yes, I know, that must be very odd for you. You and Casey have a very special, a remarkable and . . . unique bond. Chloe and he had nothing of the sort. They barely spoke.

"Your sister spent most of her time pining for her friends and your family. She didn't attend to her studies—I always wondered if it was because she had no one to study with. She went to the local high school and didn't fit in. Not at all. And she arrived in the winter, mid-year. It was a hard time for her. And she missed you a great deal."

"Me?" I choked, "Chloe hates me!"

"*Au contraire*, dear. She loves you desperately. She worried that this horrible thing would happen to you while she was away. It distracted her. It didn't matter that you were much older in her vision. She felt as though she had been given the responsibility for keeping you safe." I saw the painting of Joan of Arc in my mind. That poor girl who heard a voice tell her to ride into battle to save France. And Chloe felt that way about me?

"Justin isn't much different." I looked at her, blinking. She continued, "He's not. He, too, has had a hard time adjusting. He hasn't had the support of his family as you have, and in that, he's like Chloe."

"My family didn't . . . support her?"

"They weren't being mean to her. They didn't know how—and they were so far away. Justin's mother also doesn't understand."

"She understood enough to have him come here to learn."

"No." Jasmine said, "She won't let him back in her house until . . . until he stops."

"Stops? He can't stop. It's not like he chose this." Jasmine looked at me, purposefully. "He can't go home?" The light was dawning, "He can't *ever* go home."

"Not as long as his talent is intact. Not unless he can fool his mother into thinking he's lost his gifts."

"That's . . . That's so messed up."

Jasmine nodded. "It's one of the reasons I try to work with him when I can. He sees patterns visually the way I do, so we complement each other. But I'm no substitute for his own mother. She's . . . not ready yet."

"I'm going to need to think about this, Jasmine."

"I know you are." Jasmine rose and began putting away the dry dishes. "These things take time to sift through us. Like water into soil. It goes through eventually, but it takes its own time to do it."

Without thinking, I gave Jasmine a hug. "Thank you," I whispered over her shoulder. "Thank you for telling me the truth. And about Justin, too."

"It was a pleasure, my sweet. You can ask me anything, anytime."

"Thank you."

"You can also, I believe, find me as I just did your sister. You have many gifts. Some of them are similar to mine. Casey and I have enjoyed playing games and testing different theories with each other. Perhaps the three of us —" her face clouded for a moment then she smiled her lovely smile at me. "I look forward to working with you, Rose."

"I would love that, Jasmine." We finished the dishes in silence; the happy, calm silence of two friends. Jasmine wasn't going with us to Stockbridge, which I thought stunk. She said she'd try to get away for a long weekend or two, but couldn't promise. She worked a lot. But, of course, because of her work, she and Tyrik had both a place in Brooklyn and this "cabin," she called it, up here.

I'd barely exchanged ten words with Tyrik and felt awful about that, but I told him I was looking forward to seeing him on the way back, if not in Stockbridge. And I was. Casey said he was a great kid, and Casey wouldn't lie about that.

Later that morning, we stopped on our way out of town at that coffee place called The Black Cow. Bill was friends with the owner, a big, sweet guy with a long gray pony tail. It wasn't just a social call, though. Bill also said he needed caffeine before "tackling the Taconic." Bill had an alliterative attitude in the a.m. We had crazy competitions of inventing incredible alliterative anomalies during our daytime drive . . . oh never mind. I lost the competition anyway.

And so we went, six-sevenths of near magnificence and our driver in the crazy huge van, heading out and up and away to the Berkshires.

Water

39 BOWLING

"EVERYBODY OUT!"

WE STUMBLED out and around to the back of the van, then dragged out our bags. I followed Jenn into the cabin. Everyone else had been there before; they all stormed past me purposefully, while I stood near the front door, like a lemur, big eyes staring.

The room was huge, with a massive cathedral ceiling. Built like a giant lean-to, a diagonal wall, which became the ceiling, was one nearly continuous skylight, giving the place a kind of holy feeling. Shafts of light glittered down through trees then through the glass and dappled the floor. While the bedrooms were secreted away up and downstairs to the left, the main room served as common room, dining room, and kitchen. Through the wall of glass we could look out through the trees at a lake. It was breathtaking in a simple way. If Nature could build a house in which to perfectly appreciate itself, this would be it.

The others were already putting away stuff in the bedrooms. I could hear laughing. I had lost track of Jenn, but had no desire to hunt her down. I dropped my bag and flopped onto one of the overstuffed couches. Someone, at some point, would tell me where to go. I closed my eyes, kicked back and enjoyed the clean and green and not-as-humid-as-the-city air.

I was not relaxing for more than a minute before something was behind me. The door was open. I could hear Mina and Bill outside at the car, talking pleasantly. The back of my neck prickled and—like those old Rolodex things you see in 80s movies—my mind flipped quickly through everything that could be there: bear, cougar, rabid raccoon, venomous squirrel. I tried to control my breathing, ground and center, and focus on seeing what was really there without using my eyes. Whatever it was, it wasn't moving, so I figured I was either safe or it was waiting to pounce and I would soon be dead. As I cleared my mind I found it—over and over—filled with images of Casey. I tried to erase him and see what was really there, but I couldn't. Ridiculously, I started to feel tears prickle the inside of my eyes. Then I heard his voice say, as though from the vision in my head, "Good grief, woman, would you trust yourself?"

I jumped up and there he was, hands in his pockets, casual as the sky is blue with a Grand Canyon smile on his face, his glasses reflecting the patches of light on the floor. I could have growled at him myself, but it's hard to growl at someone when they're looking kind of adorable.

"You knew," he said easily, coming around the couch. "You got it right as soon as you grounded. You really have to learn to listen to yourself. You need to be able to tell when you're focused and accurate, and when you're off."

I was still breathing too hard and couldn't think of a witty reply, so I returned to my comfy spot on the sofa. Casey came around and sat next to me gingerly, keeping enough distance to avoid any sparks.

"Everyone's a critic," I said finally, and far too late to have any impact.

He was quiet for a moment, no doubt processing my scathing response. "So? Nu?" Casey finally said, laughing with his eyes. His fall-into-them, long-lashed, brown eyes.

"What new?" I asked.

"No. Nu? It's Yiddish. It's sort of, 'So what's going on and when are you gonna get around to telling me about it already,' or something like that."

"Ahhhh, Yiddish from the Midwestern boy?"

"You're one to talk. I thought you'd know."

"Nah, I didn't do much Yiddish at home. For a second I thought you were practicing some alternative, 'Who's on First' routine."

"Impossible—if there was one, you'd be the one who knew about it."

"That's true. I love my movies."

He smiled, "It's just one of the many reasons . . . " and he stopped.

"What? What reasons?"

"Rosie?" Jenn called from upstairs, "You ever gonna bring up your bag?" Casey gestured, open palm up towards the staircase.

I scrunched my face at him—effective flirting maneuver #107—carefully climbed over his feet, leaned down to grab my bag and started to stand up. He was behind me again but I couldn't tell how close. I was afraid to stand up all the way. I could feel his warmth on the back of my neck—how did he do that? Silent *and* fast. And warm.

He whispered, "Do you want me to carry your bag?" but he thought at me, *I can't stand this much more. I need to talk with you.*

I sighed, "Okay," and moved aside, reluctantly, so he could take my duffel since my legs were getting rubbery again. I let him lead the way—he actually knew where we were going. Plus, I thought my knees were going to stay on the couch, whimpering.

We climbed up the rough-hewn staircase made of timber so solid it didn't creak at all. I was impressed after Brooklyn. *It's better this way, Casey thought at me. Easier to sneak out at night.*

"Casey!" I whispered, "You . . . cheat?"

He smiled over his shoulder at me and winked.

I was going to need oxygen if he kept this up.

We turned left into the upstairs wing. There was really no other way to describe it. It was a wing. Way bigger than Jazz's place. Casey led me down a short hall to an open door on the right. Jenn and Izzy were already there, laughing.

"There you are!" Jenn smiled, "that one's yours." She pointed at my bed. This time Jenn and Izzy and I would all be in the same room. New blood is good. I smiled.

Casey dropped my bag on the bed, bowed at me cheezily, made an excuse to Jenn and Izzy, and went back downstairs.

Izzy and Jenn looked at me for about fifteen seconds before they fell apart laughing.

"What?" I felt myself blush.

"Oh. Nothing," Izzy couldn't have kept a straight face if her grandmother's life was at stake, and fell all over herself, rolling back on her bed.

Jenn saved me. "It's nothing bad. It's, you know, for as long as I've known Casey—"

"for as long as *I've* known Casey," Izzy interrupted.

"Right. Both of us. We've never. Ever. *Ever*. Seen him like this."

"Like what?" I was worried.

"Like . . ." Jenn started.

"Human?" Izzy offered.

"Civil?" Jenn added.

"Normal," they said together.

"So thank you, *Rose*," Izzy said more seriously, "for getting Casey to . . . *bloom*—" and she fell into another heap of hysterics.

"Oh brother," I muttered, opening my bag.

"We'll have used it all up pretty soon," Jenn laughed, wiping tears from the corners of her eyes with the edges of her hands.

"All right," I said glumly, "holla' when you're ready to talk like regular mutants," I left my bag where it was as I walked back downstairs.

"C'mon," he flopped his hair at the door.

I looked around and everyone else was either napping or reading—or, you know, cracking themselves up in the upper reaches of the house. I caught Mina's eye from her reading place on the couch and she waived us away. I guess she looked into Casey's heart and saw nothing to fear. That or she was almost done with a really good book.

I grabbed my knitting and ducked out quickly after Casey. He was already most of the way to the woods walking a path that was known to him but completely invisible to me.

I could almost sort of hear Casey narrating nature for me, " . . . Milkweed . . . black-eyed Susan . . . Queen Anne's lace . . . oak . . . maple . . . "

The trees gradually released us and a lake blocked our way.

"Stockbridge Bowl," he nodded at the water.

I stood there for a second, then it clicked. "Oh brother."

"What?" he looked concerned.

"I thought it was a football game or an amphitheater," I said, "*This* is the bowl?"

"Yes," he nodded, speaking slowly, "because the water fills the bowl . . . "

"Yes," I said, "I got that . . . now."

He laughed and continued towards a small dock protruding from the end of his path. He walked all the way out and sat carefully, taking off his shoes and socks, putting his socks deliberately into the appropriate shoe. I sat next to him. Not touching.

"So," he said.

"So," I said.

"Look," he started and stopped, then started again, "this is really . . . odd."

"You're joking," I deadpanned.

"No, I mean you . . . you let me . . . you don't . . . not since my Dad . . . "

He put his head in his hands. "I don't know how—"

"Did . . . " I overlapped, feeling that horrible impulse to fill dead air, "did you get along with your dad?"

Casey was silent and I started to think this had been a mistake. This was all a mistake. My heart started to beat faster and my lips were dry. I should never have come to New York. Mom didn't know what she was talking about and Mina was only being nice to me. I was a complete glass-smashing, fire-flinging failure. Casey obviously realized that something had gone terribly wrong and he had made a mistake opening up to me at all. He was going to tell me he needed me to leave him alone. I'd wrecked everything.

"I don't talk about my Dad much," Casey said cautiously.

My breathing started up again. I sighed a little, weighing my reactions carefully. "Do you still talk to your mom?"

"Oh . . . sure . . . sometimes. She doesn't really . . . get . . . She's . . . I mean, she's proud of me, I guess," he shrugged.

"Is she, er, gifted?"

"No. Not even a little."

"Oh."

Silence.

"I was in the newspaper. That's how Bill found me."

"Really?" I was surprised. "Bill 'found' you?"

"Yeah, he—uh—look, are you sure you want to hear this? It's not a happy story, but I feel like you have a right. You need to know in case . . . in case you want to leave."

That was, perhaps, the stupidest thing I'd ever heard him say. Candy. Baby. You understand.

"If you're okay telling it?" I was proud I'd managed diplomacy instead of screaming, "*out with it!*"

He looked down at a little fish playing around the dock pilings. "I was twelve. I was still in Sioux Falls and South Dakota is . . . well . . . you know." He shrugged, "South Dakota is only in the national news if there's freak weather."

"True."

"So, there was this horrible thing . . . At the Empire Mall. This girl. She was maybe eight. I can't remember exactly . . . she, um . . . she disappeared."

"She was taken?"

He nodded. "Snatched. It was awful. Her mom literally turned her back for five seconds and this guy dangled a toy or a cookie or something in the girl's face and she followed him. You know how those clothes racks are mazes at the stores." I nodded. Casey went on, "Anyway. It was . . . it was as bad as you imagine. He didn't know what to do . . . He was . . . he was an idiot. An evil idiot. She kept crying. He . . . he tried to stop her and put his hand over her mouth to quiet her but his hand was big and her face was so small . . . So small." Casey stopped. I waited. "He would have done so much worse to her. I guess it was," he choked on it, "better for her . . . or something . . . by the time he realized what he was doing, it was already . . . "

A lump grew in my throat. I wanted to take Casey's hand, but I knew it would stop him. And my heart.

"Anyway." He wiped his palms on his jeans. "So there's this huge search and no one knows where she'd gotten to. And it's awful and the Mom is on TV pleading for her daughter to be returned. Offering money. Offering anything. But she's already gone. Which I knew, because . . . because the girl was with me. She'd been with me since she died. It's as if she wanted to find a friend—someone who could see her—so she did and she just . . . stuck to me.

"I was only twelve. But I understood what had happened to her. Mostly. Then finally the mom . . . she was so sad."

As Casey gazed out at the water. I looked over at him and saw the lake reflected in the silent tear tracks on his face.

"She needed to know. And the girl, Kerry, wanted to talk to her Mom.

So." He took a breath, like he was making the decision all over again. "I called the 1-800 number that was on the TV all the time. I had no idea what was going to happen to me. To her. I thought the number belonged to the mom." Casey took a deep breath and ran his hands through his hair, looking up. "I told the woman who answered the phone that I knew where Kerry was, and that I wanted to help. I thought I was talking to the mom.

"Kerry never left my side—ever. I think she was scared for me too. We rode in the police cruiser together, sat in the interrogation room together, and eventually I translated from her to her mom."

He leaned back onto the deck, lying flat. I sat there, cross-legged, waiting. My ankles hurt pressing into the wood of the dock, but I couldn't move.

"Put your feet in the water," he said from his back, looking up at the sky through the trees, "it feels nice."

I followed his instructions quietly as he continued. He was right. I sat, wiggling my toes, waiting for him to resume the story.

"Right away the news people went nuts because, of course, I knew where she was—where her body was, I mean. And I could describe the guy. I knew his first name and I saw his house, inside and out, and part of his house number. So . . . so I was right. And they found her . . . body. And her mom—" His voice cracked. "Her mom thanked me for the . . . " he shuddered when he inhaled, "the 'peace of mind' I'd given her." He had to stop. I took my feet out of the water and curled up on my side next to him, my forgotten knitting for a pillow, looking at his face in profile.

"And I felt like crap. Because all I did was make a phone call. I didn't do this on purpose. I don't see dead people on purpose. I don't—" He stopped again.

This time I slid my hand, palm up, on the dock between us. I projected how I felt, gently but clearly. He reached over and held on. We both gasped, but softly, prepared. I was glad I was curled up on the dock because there wasn't a chance of my being able to walk in the near future.

But I didn't let go.

His breathing steadied and his face calmed. While he collected himself, I looked beyond him to the few cloud patterns the horizon. I listened to the birds, though I had no idea what kind of birds they were. Then he drew a deep breath.

"So. That's how Bill found me. The newspapers. He flew out, spoke to my parents, and I started to come here in the summer and any break I could. Eventually I stayed here full time with them. Then I found a way I could go to school without having to go to class with other people."

"Yeah, what's up with that?" I regretted the words as soon as they were out.

He hesitated, "Well, you've seen it . . . And I've told you how different things are with you. I mean, you know I can't really handle being around other people constantly. I know everyone thinks I'm just really shy—"

"Shy?" I nearly choked. "Casey, they don't think you're shy. They think you're arrogant if they think anything." I gasped. "Omigod, Casey. I'm so sorry. I didn't mean that."

"Yes, you did," he said quietly, "and . . . you're right. That makes . . . well, that makes a lot of things make more sense," he mused. Rather than being hurt or angry, as I would have been, he was instead synthesizing this new information. Weighing it against memory and filing it into its proper place.

We were quiet for a long while, holding hands, a covalent bond of loneliness. I listened to the water lapping the little shore. I watched birds circle and vanish, replaced by new ones. I let the breeze blow my hair around and into my face and breathed it all in. It was so lovely here. Lovely and still. I hadn't realized how busy New York and Brooklyn really were. Tucson was gonna feel so slow when I visited in December.

Even in the peaceful calm of the afternoon, something was worming around in my brain, "I'm sorry, Casey, but I don't really get it. Why can't you be around other people? I mean I know why you don't *want* to be—it's too much to take in and it would get exhausting. But you keep saying 'can't'?"

Casey rolled all the way onto his side and looked at me. "I can only tell you what Bill told me."

"Okaaay."

"According to Bill, well first, Bill did a lot of research on me and others like me right after we met. It wasn't only this little girl who found me. After her it was . . . it was everyone. I could hear . . . the people. The ones who died and still needed to talk, or the families who got left behind and heard of me from the news. Well, all of them, living and not, they all came after me, trying to get information and . . . I guess to say goodbye."

"That must have been horrible."

"It was. It was also really frustrating because I was a kid, and you know, at first it was rather cool to be the center of attention?" I nodded. "And not only that, but also it was wonderful to feel like I could help people. But it got surreal and frightening very quickly. The more people I helped, the more clearly I could see their pasts—every time I met someone new. Their whole past. It was like getting hit in the memory with a textbook of every new person's life. I acquired their memories—good and bad and sometimes . . . awful, but as that whole thing got . . . stronger I guess, I also started doing what you do. I saw things. I knew things. The older I grew, the harder it was for me to keep my own thoughts in my head when I was around other people. It was like I picked up their . . . oh, I don't know, their energy, their memories, just, you know . . . *them*, and I amplified it. If they were happy, I got manic. If they were sad, I was depressed for days. I started to lose me.

"But there was Bill. He noticed what was happening to me that first time he came out, but I guess he couldn't convince my parents to let me go with him full time—he told me later that he'd wanted to take me right then. But we managed to convince them to at least let me go for the summer. Eventually they noticed that I wasn't . . . happy at home. And I certainly wasn't normal. So . . . so, I stayed here."

"How did Bill know what to do?"

"Well, as I said, research. And I think what he found scared him enough that he wasn't willing to take 'no' for an answer from my parents."

"Why? What'd he find out?"

Casey looked at me, very serious. Almost stern.

"If I can't control this, I'll die."

The drama of it made me start to laugh, but he wasn't kidding. He was more serious than I'd ever seen him, and I'd seen him plenty serious before.

"*Die?*" I tried not to sound snarky. "Die? Like seeing someone's past will kill you?" He let go of my hand and put his head up on his bent elbow, looking down at me on the dock.

"Someone's past won't kill you. But that's not what happened to me. I saw pasts, presents, futures, and dead people—all of that, all at once. You saw it in the park that first day, for a second. With the skateboarders. I know what you saw. You saw everything. And that was just for a split second, and *that* knocked the wind out of you.

"I was a kid when this all started. I couldn't filter it. It was too much." I could hear rising panic in his voice and reached my hand over to his cheek to quiet him. He surprised me and grabbed my hand, not hard, but fast and I gasped. "That is why *this* is so important." He indicated my hand. "I can't do this. I can't do this with anyone. I can't do this with my own mother. But you. You're a blank to me. I can't see anything about you on my own. Not unless you send—or unless I work really hard. I get glimpses of your past, but they're happy ones. I see no more future for you than I see for myself. I see no dead people with you. No clouds hovering. Nothing. You, Hannah Rose, you are it. You're the only person I can actually have any kind of contact with."

I didn't know what to say. What *could* I say?

"That is what kills people like me," he went on. "On some level you can learn to still the voices and find some peace, but you can't ever, ever love someone. And we know from rhesus monkeys and failure-to-thrive studies that this isn't healthy. You wither and die. Even something this simple, this natural," he nodded at our hands, "the intensity of any contact, all the memories, past boyfriends, successes, failures, *everything*, everything slams into you. All the time. It's horrible. It's impossible. And it stops us from making contact, from making real connections. From loving anyone."

"But not with me?"

"Not with you." I saw tears in his eyes. "Not ever with you."

40 PHYSICS

THEY DIDN'T CALL IT Boot Camp for nothing.

For a little over two weeks, we practiced the fundamentals in the morning: grounding, shielding, that sort of thing, then broke into partnerships to work on controlling inanimate objects together. Think of those games where you use a spoon in your teeth to pass an egg back and forth, or hold a balloon in between your and another person's bellies—no hands—while running crab-like down a track. But do all that with your mind. It was supposed to be more for fun than hard work, and some days were successful, but generally, I wound up swimming laps from our dock to the next and back again to work off my frustration. Luckily, I was usually partnered with Izzy; at least she's patient. The days I worked with Justin weren't as fun. Most of the time Casey was off with Bill somewhere, at least in the mornings if not all day, so we never got a chance to reprise our first stunt.

After lunch one day, I had some free time. I knew the city must be roasting, but up here it was lovely and actually cold in the shade. Well, cold to me, and cool in the sun as long as you were near the water. Casey was gone, so I took my knitting and headed down to our dock. *Our* dock. I laughed at myself. A few times sitting there talking to Casey and it was already ours. Silly. Dumb. Case hadn't even said goodbye—again. He and Bill weren't at breakfast most mornings, though the bacon was.

My lace had been developing nicely, though. As the shawl extended up from the lower tip-point I could distinctly see the two birds—maybe they were doves or love birds—flying towards each other. Since I'd decided on a Faroese shawl, I wanted to make the center shaping clearly carry the borders of the middle panel. I didn't want the elements to look accidental, since the center was quite distinct—two parallel columns. I don't much like shawls with yarn-overs running up the middle. They look creepily spine-like to me. I already have a spine; I like to keep it *inside* my skin, thank you. I held the knitting stretched across the circular needle up to the sky, trying to see the pattern. The background motif was very open and soft, and I tugged at the finger-like edging, impressed at how long I was able to extend the points.

I sat, purling back a row, looking at the trees and the lake, breathing in the clean smells of soil, water, and sky. My visible progress was slowing as the shawl widened, so I had a long row ahead of me. I don't have to watch my hands when I purl, which freed me to look up. A breeze conducted nature, blowing the trees around. The leaves rustling, the wind playing on the water, and the light dancing: it was a little mini-symphony all for me. I sighed, loving the display.

"Don't tell me you find all the beauty depressing."

I jumped a foot and scrambled to keep my knitting from landing in the water.

"Argh! You scared me!"

Casey laughed, "Clearly. But I gave you fair warning."

"Did not." I tried, with minimal success, to recover my dignity. And my yarn.

"Did so." Casey sat down next to me and looked up. The trees were very, very still. I looked down: not a single ripple on the water.

"That . . . that was you?"

Casey winked. "It's nothing but practice. You could do it too."

I shook my head and returned to my knitting.

"What?" he elbowed me lightly. My stomach didn't flip so much that way. "You're talented. You can learn how to do it too."

"I dunno, Casey," I started, "there's a big difference between knowing the future and moving stuff without touching it. I'm fine at the first part. But . . . the marble? And especially nature. I dunno. Stuff out here seems to be particularly hard for me. Remember my epic failure at Coney."

"That wasn't epic. Trust me. After all," he couldn't suppress a grin, "it's not like you lit the water on fire or anything."

"Jerk," I grounded and elbowed him back, but I was laughing too.

"Maybe you're not thinking of it right?"

"What's right?" I stopped knitting.

"Well, essentially, we're all one, yes?"

"Sure. Okay."

"I mean, we all come from the same stuff, 'all flesh is grass,' that sorta thing."

I squinted at him. "You mean carbon-based life?"

"Sure, basic idea. So if we're all the same stuff, and the matter we're made of is known to influence other matter without necessarily touching . . . you see where I'm going with this."

"Ummm . . ."

"Then it stands to reason that *we* can influence other matter without touching it."

"Ummm . . ."

"Okay, let's start again. In science class you learned about electrons and protons and stuff like that, right?"

"Yeah."

"Okay, do they influence each other?"

"You mean like the attraction thing?" I asked.

"Yes," he said patiently.

"Then yes, I remember that, professor."

Casey started to say something, stopped, rolled his eyes at the sky with his palms up for a moment, then continued his lecture. "Okay, well, this isn't any different than that. Particles have energy and they influence other particles.

"Check."

"We, *we*," he wagged a finger between us, "have energy—our abilities— that we can focus and have influence over . . . well . . . easiest for you has been accidental influences. You *have* been able to get matter to move, but usually that's been moving humans, like flinging Justin across the room without touching him. Which, by the way, I loved."

"But the marble thing . . . "

"I was just getting to that. When you're paying attention and not going on instinct—"

"Or reacting to some jerk—"

"Or that, you seem to have a hard time figuring out where one thing ends and the other begins." I nodded. "Most of that is because you're over-thinking. You're acting like the marble and you are two different things."

"Well . . . because they are, aren't they? You *said* I need to know where the marble ends and I begin." I was starting to wonder if maybe, just *maybe*, Casey might be nuts rather than psychic.

"No. It's no different at all. Look, on . . . uh . . . on the sub-atomic level, you can know where a particle *is* or you can know how fast it's *traveling*, but you can't know both at the same time, because the very act of measuring influences the whole thing." The professor thing was not his most attractive side, I decided.

"I remember that from science, but it never made any sense."

"It's the Heisenberg Principle and it's true for what we do, too."

"It's the *what?* and . . . *how?* In that order, please."

"Heisenberg, a physicist from the 30s, and . . . umm . . . okay, so, hang on.

I need a metaphor. Uh . . . you can see the past, clearly, right?"

"Generally," I batted my eyelashes at him.

Casey grinned, pushed his glasses up and went on. "Okay, so we all—we, us here—know the future. But not the *getting there*. We don't see the getting there. We see the future *outcome* when we look for it, and may even see how the outcome goes on from there in skips and jumps. But I can't, for instance, see myself, right now, heading towards . . . uh . . . dinner. Yes? Making sense? I can't see *everything* that will happen between now and dinner . . . to me."

"Okaaay."

"That's because this isn't some kind of forward-moving déjà vu. This is physics."

"I thought it was magic . . . psychic . . . stuff."

"Physics *is* magic, Rose. . . think what would happen if you took a solar-cell light bulb back to 1910. It's magic. It *was* magic."

I wanted to stop and think about this, but he kept going.

"Anyway, this is simply a long way to prove a point. You can—no. We *do* affect physical things. All the time. Blow on hot chocolate and your breath—which you create—will move the steam. You create something you can't see, which affects something you can see but can't hold. You are *constantly* affecting and changing things. And because of that, because of free will and all the problems that arise from having free will, we can't precog how we get from point A to point B—even when you can clearly see point B. And that's where you come in."

"Why?"

"Because you actually have done it. Most of us go event to event, but you have these flashes where you control physical space *and* you have episodes where you see a whole arc like at dinner that night. You were sending. That's why I was so annoyed with you—you weren't following the whole arc."

"It was scary," I insisted.

"Scary, maybe, but important for you to notice. *You* see the particles move. And you don't appear to be affecting them by seeing them. Not all the time, but you have done it. And that, Hannah Rose, is . . . weird."

"Well, that's a new one. No one's *ever* called me weird before . . . "

"Ha," he said.

And we both looked at the water.

"Okay, there's the metaphor. Look at the ripples my foot makes in the water."

"Y'huh." I looked.

"You can control those. *You*, Hannah Rose, can control those, from the moment I touch the water to the moment the ripple dies out, far from us."

"Nuh'uh," I glanced at him sideways. I was actually watching the ripple to see how far it would go. It was going a long way away on the glassy lake. The Casey breeze was gone and the water was undisturbed.

"Try it. I *know* you can do this. Even *I* can do this, and I'm usually lousy at manipulating physical space."

I sat up and looked at him. "You—you who waxed off the ocean—you should know that's the worst thing a teacher can say, Casey." He looked at me surprised. "You never ever say anything like 'c'mon, this is easy' to a student— or 'just look harder'—because if I'm having a rough time, then it *isn't* easy. And looking harder is just gonna hurt my eyes. So give me some real instruction or let me sit and burn through it *veeery slooowly* on my own."

Instead of looking like I'd given him a smackdown, Casey looked more excited, "Right. Okay, yes! You're right. Absolutely. It's not easy. But it *is* doable. So, look. You naturally understand the rhythm of people-futures. You seem to pick them up effortlessly. Which is great. And you were able to move Justin— which, again, I thought was great." I laughed and he smiled. "The things that have been hard for you when you're not angry are non-human objects. So. Look at the water, just water-water. No ripples." I found it difficult to pull my attention from his face, but I managed, finally.

"All right, focus now on how the water breathes. See how it's rising and falling almost microscopically? The lake is a living thing, Hannah Rose. It has its own ecosystem, its own relationship with the air—a relationship that we do not share. So you have to learn water. It shouldn't be as hard as the marble—don't look at me like that; there's a reason I said it—it shouldn't be as hard as the marble because you already have a relationship with water. You are already so in-tune with it. It's something that holds you and protects you . . . and . . . it loves to touch you . . . " he stopped, looking away.

"You there?"

Casey took a deep breath and turned back to me. "Yes. I'm here. Hang on." I started to reach my foot down to the water, but Casey put his arm out to stop me. "Don't touch it yet!"

I pulled my leg back.

"I'm sorry, I want the first contact to actually mean something so it'll help you with this."

I nodded, "Okay. So water likes me and I like it. But I don't see it breathe. I don't see it living. I mean, the *fish* down there . . . they're living. But the *lake*?"

"You have to see it as a . . . host."

"That is *totally creepy* and very *Alien* of you. I don't want to think of my lake that way."

"No, it's not creepy, it's like . . . it's like when your mom was carrying you, before you were born. Babies in the womb are a perfect parasite."

"Well, that's romantic."

"They are!" He was adamant. "They take all their food, oxygen, and immunities from the mother. If the mother gets sick, the baby still takes what it needs. It's a parasite—a parasite the mother loves and wants and all that. But it's still a parasite. The mother is a host. So if you think of the lake like a host—"

"Then everything that lives in it and off of it is all part of the system. Very natural. The lake is the mother that feeds the fetus."

"There you go. And like any mother—"

"She breathes."

Casey nodded. "So now, look. Um . . . okay, wait, *don't* look at the surface that looks so smooth and glassy. Really try to *see* the lake . . . the mother . . . the host. And watch how it lives. It'll take a minute for your eyes to shift . . . "

It made sense in my mind, but I wasn't seeing what he wanted me to see. I did, however, see that Bill was barbecuing the most amazing blue cheese hamburgers for dinner that night, but I decided not to share that tidbit with Casey. I'd gotten much better at shielding around him—or at least not projecting at him, I guess.

"I dunno, Casey, I can't see it. I know you're right and I *know* the lake is what you say it is, but it's just too calm out there and . . . it's . . . nothing but glass to me."

"Try not looking with your eyes. Close them and look that way."

I was skeptical that this would work, but I tried it anyway.

And I failed.

"Okay," he tried to sound upbeat, "Don't get down on yourself, okay? I'll think of another way to communicate this. But you must, *must* take this seriously. No more *Alien* jokes."

"Not even little ones?"

"No. Only serious scholarship from you from now on."

"What about jokes about Justin?"

"Well . . . maybe those . . . " he began to look thoughtful. "You *know,* this trip is the first time since I can remember where I was able to sit in a van full of people without losing my mind."

"You mean you didn't drive up with everyone before?"

"Of course not. Justin *alone* would have killed me. I drove the other car while Bill drove the van."

I nodded. "Well, that is some real news. We should have had a party or something! Piñatas, cake, presents, *some*thing . . . "

Casey turned to me, very serious. "Hannah Rose, *you* are my present."

While I was trying to figure out if he was serious or joking, because—let's be honest, that was majorly cheeseball—he fell apart laughing. I followed, feeling tears come to my eyes. He had to lie back on the dock, he was laughing so hard. I did too and we stayed there, panting and calming down for a while. I even forgot I was lying on my shawl.

"Sorry about that," he said, finally.

"Don't apologize! That was a great laugh!"

"True. But," he rolled onto his side and rested his head on his hand, "it's kinda true."

The sun had moved and I had to shield my eyes with my hand, and squint, which I'm sure was everso charming. "You're not kidding now."

"I'm not kidding," he was smiling. "You're the best thing that's ever happened to me. You are the person I thought didn't exist. And then . . . there you were."

"Here I am."

And he kissed me.

My heart stopped. My breathing stopped. And I was lucky he was holding my face with his free hand, because I couldn't hold up my head, either.

I had to lie back on the dock for a while before I regained my legs. Then I had to work up the courage to sit up, lean over my knees and breathe for a few minutes. Casey was trying not to crack up.

Sweet.

Finally he stood and tapped my shoulder—which only made my arm and part of my neck feel funny.

"Let's get you out of the sun, Hannah Rose."

We walked back together, following our invisible wooded path home again, home again, jiggity-jig.

41 NIGHTSWIMMING

I NEEDED TO SWIM.

Casey and Bill had disappeared again, and everyone else was taking afternoon naps. The temperature outside hovered close enough to "warm" to convince Mina that it was okay for me to dive into the chilly lake. At the dock's end, I slipped off my flip-flops and dove in. The shock of the cold water was like sandpaper on my skin, but I kicked hard and felt warmer after I passed the second dock. I flipped onto my back and swam gently for a while, just drifting along. I lost count of the docks, but our cabin looked distinct. It would be easy to find again.

Drifting on my back, I watched the clouds move across the sky. My head cleared and I really, truly, relaxed as I slid past houses, cabins, docks, and boats. The stillness filled my mind, allowing me to forget everything but Casey and the surrounding beauty. At one point, I thought I heard my name, but that was ridiculous. Fish don't generally talk to me. I kept swimming.

The cloud patterns were amazing and morphing rapidly. Quite a breeze up there. I saw long, tall, shapes, then a running rabbit, then a camel—or dromedary, actually—then a dolphin jumping, then a plane, then a church with a super long steeple, then another plane, then a tall mast ship. Then my head hit the wood.

It hurt, but not crazy hurt. I turned and pulled myself up on the diving platform that marked the space between the shore and a little island. It wasn't very big, maybe ten feet across each way with vertical posts at each corner, but I would have expected every inch of it to be occupied by splashing kids. Why there were no rugrats out here on such a beautiful day was a mystery.

I didn't spend much time worrying about that, though. Instead I sklathed out and enjoyed the warm sunlight and the air's crispness. The breeze was much lighter here than it was in the sky where the clouds were speeding along My breathing slowed, and soon I was asleep.

Then it rained.

It wasn't a heavy rain, but it felt good on my sun-warmed skin.

And then it didn't feel good at all and I was drenched, sitting up, and sputtering. Casey—without his glasses—was laughing his butt off.

"What was *that* for?" I shook the water off my arms.

"Fun?" he squinted, though it was more question than answer.

"For *you*!"

"Well . . . yeah . . . " he was still laughing at me as he sat and leaned against one of the corner posts.

I turned back onto my stomach with my head facing the edge of the platform, letting the warm wood take the cold-water feeling away. Casey scooted over and sat next to me, swinging his feet over the side.

"Nice swim?" he asked.

"Uh huh," I said. It was hard to talk with my head pressing my jaw into my arms.

"You burn?" he asked.

"Don't think so. Put on Bullfrog. You should get some glasses."

"Funny girl. I only ask because you're looking rather . . . rosy."

I lifted my head and looked at him. "Ha. Ha. You're so—wait, how long have I been out here?"

"Long. Hour. More?"

"Oh no," I moaned. Even Bullfrog couldn't stop that burn. I burn easy and have to work up to a tan. I was going to feel hideous for a couple of days.

"Should we get you back inside?" Casey was playing with the hair that escaped my braid, which made me shiver. In a good way.

"Yeah," I sighed and sat up. "I better go put on some aloe."

"Okay," and Casey dove in, splashing me with his wake. I knew the water was going to be super cold with a burn, but I took a deep breath and dove in after him. After the shock, it occurred to me that this was how I was going to be feeling most of the time I was with Casey.

May as well dive in.

"Night swim," Jenn whispered in my ear after dinner as she passed me on her way up the stairs. I nodded wisely, with absolutely no idea what it was she was talking about. But, not feeling feisty, I followed her.

Izzy was there, too, when I got to the room and she closed the door behind us. "What are we doing?" I whispered conspiratorially.

"We're all going for a swim." Izzy bounced, "It's a full moon. You won't believe how gorgeous it is. We're usually lucky when we're up here and get one—"

"Actually, we *always* get one . . . I should ask Mom," Jenn drifted off, then refocused. "Anyway, we'll take the rowboat out to the platform, then swim a bit. We'll sneak out around 10:30 or so."

"Sneak out? In *this* house?"

"Well . . . " Jenn shrugged, "I'm pretty sure Mom knows what we're doing, but I think it makes her happy to think we get to be 'normal teenagers' for awhile." She smiled. "So the drill is—put on your suit, then put your pajamas on over it. We're good about keeping up appearances."

"Right." I nodded, "Suit. Pjs. Check."

I pulled a dry suit from the drawer and my pajamas from the hook on the back of the door and went to the bathroom to change, brush my teeth, and deal with my hair. It had been in a perpetual braid since we arrived. I wondered how much it would hurt my scalp to brush it out now. Maybe when my hair was wet. Yeah, I'd wait until we were swimming.

Why we were going to swim at night when the water was so cold was beyond me, but I'd come to expect weird answers to perfectly normal questions. Instead of bugging Izzy, I stayed on my bed knitting and listening to my Discman until Jenn walked over and tugged on the hem of my pajama leg.

"Time," she whispered as I pulled off the headphones.

I knitted to a safe stopping place, rubber-banded the needles together, tossed them aside, and grabbed one of Jenn's extra sweatshirts. The cool night air was going to be mighty cold on my pinked skin. I followed Jenn, who nodded at my borrowed sweatshirt and muttered, "Toldja."

Izzy, Justin, and Casey were already waiting under the trees. Unlike the place in Brooklyn, the stairs here don't creak so it was much easier to sneak out—especially easier since Mina and Bill apparently knew we were doing it. Casey was leaning against a tree, well away from Justin and Izzy, and he was looking—I must be honest—gorgeous in the shadows. Tall, mysterious, handsome. And really, really psychic.

Psychic: the new sexy.

We all headed, silent and single file, down to the dock. The rowboat was already in the water and ready to go. Casey held the line while the rest of us climbed in and positioned ourselves. There were already towels and soda and chips in the bottom of the boat, so our feet and legs had to invent some odd positions to fit, but we accomplished the task and pushed off.

Casey rowed us out to the diving platform, which felt closer when you weren't swimming. He tied off to a platform post and, again, held the boat steady for us. Izzy and Jenn pulled out the towels and snacks and put them in the middle of the platform. Me? I just sat there and watched.

Within minutes everyone but me was in the water. Splashing and laughing quietly. "Aren't you guys afraid of *Jaws*?" I asked from my Buddha-like perch on the platform.

Izzy said from down in the depths, looking over her shoulder at me, "I thought you were the fish? Why aren't you in the water?"

"*Jaws* at an early age," I shrugged. "I know . . . it's irrational, but it's night and it's water—"

"*Fresh* water," Justin pointed out, "not salt water . . . where *sharks* are . . . "

"I know I know I know, I'm not saying it's realistic. It's just—"

"Nuts?" Justin asked.

"I also got burned today. It's gonna be freezing."

"I think you should try," Casey was lazily backstroking circles around the platform.

Jenn nodded. "I think you'll be surprised . . . "

I started to shake my head, but something in Jenn's voice made me reconsider. She was grinning at me and she wasn't *usually* mean. So I shrugged and took off the sweatshirt, then pulled off my pajama bottoms. The night air was cool but not cold. It felt good on my skin, actually. Not unlike the aloe I put on earlier. You could count on Mina to have a medicinal plant around—even one from my part of the country.

I started to dip my toes in, but Casey stopped me, "Ah ah ah . . . you can't toe-in. You have to dive."

"Uh, you *do* know how to dive don't you?" Justin snarked.

I looked up at the heavens, asking them to smite Justin, but I was denied.

I braced myself and dove in.

It was warm!

Not bathtub warm, but warm enough for comfort. My sunburn felt better. Much better. Someone had done something to the water.

I surfaced. "Okay, who did that?"

I heard laughing as I swiped the water off of my face. "Gotcha," Justin sounded happy. Izzy was touching the dock ladder with her fingertips while she treaded water, cracking herself up. "Oh, Rosie! You should have *seen* the colors your aura went through when you dived in. You were so surprised!" Only Izzy could say things like that and not sound like a dope.

Casey continued his circular laps. "You can't come past here, Hannah Rose. It'll get cold again. I mean, come out here if you want to, just know that the water will change."

I nodded and dove down a bit. The water didn't get colder the further down I swam . . . it was uniformly warm. Amazing. I surfaced and breast-stroked my way over to Casey as he maintained his circles. "You guys always do it this way?" I asked, making a circle interior to his.

Casey's eyes sparkled at me, "Yup. Pretty good trick. Izzy and I learned this at our family's place on Lake Okabogee. When we were kids we had no idea what we were doing, but it works as long as she stays in the water near the middle. Then I can make a perimeter for her to bounce off of."

"Pretty nice, what two-sevenths of magnificence can do, eh Rosie?" Izzy called.

"The best."

Sitting on the diving platform later, eating chips and drinking soda, we were all quiet, smiling, and listening to the night around us. I watched the ripples play with the moon's reflection, creating different shapes. Just like clouds, I saw images glimmer in and out in the water. I breathed deep.

"I don't wanna go back," Izzy said quietly.

"Me neither," I agreed.

"We have time. School doesn't start yet," Jenn said.

"I know," Izzy said, "I really love it here. Brooklyn's great and all, but this is where I'd spend my life if I could."

We could hear animals rummaging on the shore, the water lapping the edge of the platform, and I could have sworn we could hear the stars.

Soon it was announced that the time had come for Justin and Casey to enact their summer tradition: they "had to" race to the island and back while the moon was at its brightest. I'd never seen Justin do anything that physical—especially not with Casey. You could have pushed me into the water with a leaf.

"You're not the only swimmer, girl," Justin said at me and dove in first.

"Cheater," Casey muttered, carefully setting down his glasses. He followed Justin into the dark.

"They always do that," Izzy said, shrugging, "it's the only time they ever got along before—the annual race."

"Guys," Jenn sniffed, looking up at the constellations.

"I tell you what," Izzy twanged in agreement, knees up, leaning back against one of the corner posts. Towels and chips were scattered. We were calm and we were happy. I couldn't remember the last time I felt like this. Like I was in control.

I was wrong.

I smiled generally in Izzy's direction when her blue hair—made blue-black in the moonlight—started to reflect the moonlight not so much like hair, but more like . . . a snow cone . . . or an egg shell. It got whiter. So white it was almost solid. And the white shell thing was bigger than her head.

"Iz?" I got a funny feeling in my stomach. Without looking over, I could tell Jenn was sitting up and paying attention too.

"Izzy? Izzy, are you still there?" Jenn asked, but Izzy didn't answer, because she *wasn't* there. Or rather, Izzy's face wasn't exactly there anymore. Her body was, but her face was fading in and out of being someone else's face too.

"What. Is. Happening?" I whispered at Jenn, never taking my eyes from Izzy.

"Um . . . well . . . Izzy can channel . . . but . . . " Jenn shook her head, "but not like . . . usually voices, not . . . "

The face that was taking over then letting go of Izzy appeared to be male, but the eyes were hidden. Like the guy had a hood on over his head.

Icy cold shot up my spine.

Izzy—or the face on top of Izzy's — swung from me to Jenn and back at me. Izzy's finger pointed at me.

"Rose?" the Not-Izzy voice rasped.

My frozen brain wasn't thinking straight.

I nodded.

"Rose," when Not-Izzy spoke I had to watch—even if I didn't want to. His not-a-face was a magnet. "Rose, you must pay attention."

"I'm . . . I *am* paying attention," My eyes still searched for some piece of Izzy in the face.

"No," Not-Izzy's mouth said, "No. You need to focus on what you're here for. You're getting . . . distracted."

"I'm learning," I protested.

"No. You're not . . . devoted. You aren't diligent. You have no purpose."

"Look, if I wanted a lecture—"

"Quiet. You've been reckless. You haven't learned fast enough. You must learn control."

"Why is everyone telling me I'm reckless?"

The face-that-wasn't-Izzy's stared at me, as if everyone on the planet knew the answer but me.

"Because you are," Not-Izzy said matter-of-factly. "Because you killed me."

All the air left my lungs. It took me a moment to compose myself. Long enough to see Jenn looking down at her hands. "I ki . . . I did *what*?" I didn't know spirits could be confused.

"I am not confused. Here . . . " He reached up to the sides of Not-Izzy's head and lifted the white glow. I had to think—to *decide* whether or not I was going to retch off the side of the diving platform. Half of the top of his head was red and gray and shiny in the moonlight. While I stared, rudely, I heard Jenn gasp. It wasn't a white glow or a hood he lifted off—it was his helmet.

The helmet that the guy at Coney Island wore, right before I exploded the lemonade, and the guy at the carousel, and across from the firehouse.

I shook my head, "I don't understand."

"You, Rose, you told me to kill myself and so I did." He said simply.

"No. I would *never*—what are you talking about? *When* are you talking about?"

"In your car. With your friend. I passed you on my bike and you told me I was going to kill myself."

"I told . . . That was *you*?" I could feel Jenn glance at me, "But I didn't do *any*thing to you. You were driving like a nut! You were swerving through traffic."

"I wasn't swerving. Traffic was stopped. Motorcycles can ride the line when traffic is stopped. I was *fine* Rose."

"No. You were . . . oh God . . . you were asking for . . . asking to wipe out . . . " My words stumbled while my mind raced.

"That's what *you* said. And right after you spoke that aloud, I crested the hill and my wheels were yanked out from under me. I went down, into, and under the truck that had stopped traffic in the first place. You laid me down so hard you swung me into the pole and shattered my helmet."

I worked hard to breathe. "You crashed."

"*You* crashed me."

"Did . . . did it hurt?" I sounded wrong. Squeaky.

Not-Izzy looked thoughtful in a transparent sort of way. "My pride. But it was fast. My neck snapped—better that way maybe . . . "

"I . . . I did that . . . *to* you?"

Not-Izzy nodded.

"Why are you telling me this?" My nose was running and I brushed at it with the back of my hand, like a three year old.

"Because You Must Pay Attention, Hannah Rose. You need to be prepared. Don't let my death be a waste. Learn. You cannot keep tugging at fate. *Follow* the cord, don't pull on it. You do damage. You kill."

"Others? I've killed more than you?" my throat burned as the tears started.

"You have pulled the strings on many things. But you didn't pull me off my bike . . . you yanked."

I saw Justin fly across the room.

I saw Tim catch fire.

I saw the magician's explosions.

I saw the glass break, the marble hit the frame, the water move around my feet . . . the . . . the . . .

In the end, I *was* sick over the side of the platform.

When I could sit up again, Izzy's head rested in Jenn's lap and Jenn was stroking her hair.

"Jenn?" I whispered, "What happened."

Jenn kept her eyes on Izzy's face. "Later," she murmured back.

I heard quiet splashes behind me. Casey swam around to Izzy's spot. Justin was behind him. They pulled themselves up onto the platform. Justin crawled over to Jenn and Izzy and Casey scooted over to me after checking on his cousin.

"We saw everything," Case leaned in so he could whisper, "mostly. You okay?"

I started to nod yes, then stopped and shook my head. "I want to go home."

"We can't move Izzy yet. Let her come around."

"Is it always like that?" I asked, "do you pass out after . . . "

Casey shook his head, slipping his glasses back on. "Not always. That one was . . . new for her. She doesn't channel faces. She's always been a vocal medium. I never saw anything like that."

"Do . . . you do that too?"

"She's coming around," Jenn reported. She and Justin helped lift Izzy gently to a sitting position. She leaned against Justin's shoulder and rubbed her face.

"Girl, don't do that to me again. You had me going!" Justin's voice was soft and soothing.

Jenn held her hand, "Iz, that was massive. Are you okay?"

"I don't know . . . I don't know what happened." It was more question than statement.

"You channeled," Jenn was petting Izzy's hand, "and it was amazing. But I'll give you the run-down tomorrow. Now we need to get you back to the cabin." Jenn sounded like her Mom.

Izzy nodded and Jenn, Casey, and Justin maneuvered her into the boat while I held the line. "Climb in, Rose," Casey said over his shoulder.

I hesitated. "No. I can't . . . yet . . . maybe I'll swim back."

"That's nu—" Casey glanced up, "I'll row back out for you in a few minutes okay?" I nodded. "You'll wait here for me."

It was a command. I nodded again and sat down to wait.

When Casey returned he had a thick blanket with him, which he wrapped around me. I didn't realize I was shivering.

"I thought you *wanted* to go back? I thought you said?"

"Home," I said, "I want to go *home.*"

Casey pushed away from the newly-cocooned me so he could lean back and look in my face. "Did nothing you just heard sink in?" He sounded angry. "You're going to run away? After all that—after learning all that, you're not even going to pay attention to what the man said? Toss the poor guy a bone, Rose. He came all that way to get through to you. Learn to control this stuff. Whatever it is that sent him back here was pretty massive. We've never seen anything like it. So, no. No, you *don't* get to go home. You don't get to run. You get to learn how to control yourself and you start now. You understand me?"

I felt the tears on my cheeks before I realized I was crying, "I'm not blowing this off. I'm here, aren't I? I'm missing the start of my senior year, right? I'm trying, aren't I? Every day. Every. Day. I try to get a grip on this stuff without feeling like a complete freak. The words and the cards and the shields and the . . . stuff . . . and the . . . control . . . and . . . But you don't get it. I don't *feel* out of control. I don't *feel* like I'm doing anything. God, are you listening to yourself? How can I control something I can't feel? Or see? How do you know it's there when you can't tell it's there? You're all asking me for the impossible! All of you are, every day."

Casey started to speak but took a breath instead and pulled the blanket around both of us. He must have been blocking mightily because I didn't feel a thing.

"This is one of the reasons to work on the water." Casey began again, softly this time, "I need you to focus on that. I need you to go back to where we were when we were talking on the dock before. See the water in your mind. Feel the water. It's easier out here because you can feel the platform moving with the water if you let yourself reach down."

I started to argue, but it was Casey. And I was scared.

I tried. I focused.

"Now, when you feel the rhythm of the water, I want you to relax into the surface. Get the rhythm of the ripples. Let that motion take over your own rhythms. Keep your eyes closed. I'm going to move you in a minute."

And Casey stopped talking. He let the water talk for him. Gradually I began to feel the lake breathe. The gentle swelling and release of the water was constant and even. I was drowsy.

"Focus," he whispered as he lowered me forward onto a rolled towel on the edge of the platform. I heard a voice from far away, above and behind me. The voice said, *watch the ripples*. Balancing my chin on my folded arms and towel, I opened my eyes and saw slow, gentle mounds of water move by below. *Breathe with them* the voice said. So I breathed and the water breathed with me. *Now make the ripples come closer together*. As I breathed it, it happened. Somewhere inside me someone was happy. And impressed. *Now stop the ripples*.

Glass. There was nothing but glass. Black obsidian glass in the moonlight. My teeth rattled.

"Rose!" Casey called, "Rose. You're not supposed to stop breathing! Rose!" I looked up at Casey, shaking me. Then he let go and sat back, sighing. "You stopped breathing."

"I stopped the ripples," I croaked.

"Yes. That you did. You also stopped *breathing*."

"I stopped the ripples."

"Yes. You controlled the water. Do you remember where you went when you got control?"

"Uh huh . . . "

"Well, that's why we come here." He calmed down some, "It's easier for you to stay grounded on the water and get control—and easier to do at night because you can't see that it shouldn't be happening. That it shouldn't be possible."

I nodded. He mostly made sense.

"You want me to take you back?"

I nodded.

I slept until nearly noon and woke up with that blasted Louis Armstrong song playing in my head again.

"You okay, Rose?" Izzy sounded concerned when she saw me on the couch the next day. She was right to worry. I felt lousy. My stomach was unstable and my head throbbed like my brain was going all *Alien* on me.

"I should be asking you that instead," I said, embarrassed.

"Naw, I'm fine," she shrugged, "sleep is all I need after something like that. Sleep and Tylenol. And chocolate. Let me get Mina for you." I started to protest, but Izzy was already on her way to the back of the house. I heard talking. I reached over to the side table for my big cup of water. I remember in Arizona I got dehydrated once and had a similar headache, but not the stomach. I was sure this was from the sunburn. It had to be from the sunburn.

Plumping her damp hair as she followed Izzy back to me, Mina looked serious.

"Alright, kiddo," Mina pointed to the floor in front of the window seat. I looked at her. "Lie down."

I wobbled my way over to the rug and found a way to get down onto the floor without squishing the middle part of me that hurt so much. Once down, I closed my eyes. The throbbing in my head had to be audible to everyone in the room.

Mina positioned herself at my head. I felt her cool hands on my feverish brow and I sighed.

"Just relax," she said quietly, like I could do anything else with her working on me.

Mina repositioned her hands over my eyes and kept them there for a long time. Then she moved them to the sides of my head. Cool breezes radiated from her hands, over my temples, moving like silk, smoothing out the pain and neutralizing it.

External Psychic Alka-Seltzer.

"No jokes. Breathe," Mina murmured.

I took a deep, slow breath.

The waves of silk wove through my head and down my neck, surging through me and out of my arms; then they found my stomach and calmed it, flowed across the sunburn and coated it in cool, soft, lack-of-pain.

"Better?"

"Much," I whispered.

"Then stay here and rest, kiddo."

I took another breath and felt Aunt Mina get up and walk away.

It was the last thing I felt for awhile.

I have no idea how long I slept, but when I awoke, the light slanted differently and the house was silent. I stood up gingerly. No pain. My head was better—no trumpet solo blaring over and over in my brain. My stomach showed no signs of its previous imbalance, but I still wasn't ready to eat. I walked, carefully, waiting to see what would happen in my head and gut. Nothing happened, and my skin, which was still pink, didn't burn at the touch or stab me with pain at every movement.

My knitting sat at the corner of the couch. The magazine I'd been half-heartedly reading was still on the coffee table where I'd left it. But I wasn't interested in either.

I looked out the windows for awhile, then walked over to the door, found my flip-flops, and wandered outside.

I walked the opposite direction from the water. We'd been here awhile now, but I hadn't really explored the woods. The terrain wasn't strenuous, but it did wend up and down a bit, creating little hollows and culs-de-sac that hosted surprise houses. It was quiet; even my flip-flops were muffled by the forest carpet.

I came to the top of a rise and stopped, holding my breath, hoping I hadn't been too loud. Jenn sat at the bottom of a ravine. A squirrel was on her head, eating a nut, and a young deer curled up with its head in her lap.

I tried to sit on the rise without scaring them, but the squirrel heard me and bolted. Jenn looked up, smiled, and motioned for me to come down. The deer continued to sleep. I tried to sit super-quietly where Jenn pointed, but the deer lifted its head. Rather than being scared, though, it licked its lips and put its head back down.

I was boring.

"He's hung out with me before," Jenn whispered, "and sometimes Izzy comes too, so he's used to other people. The squirrel was new. She didn't know any better ... but you know how it is with squirrels."

I started to nod, then said, "No. Actually no, Jenn. I don't know how it is with squirrels. I didn't know you could do this."

"Oh, this? It's ... nothing. I just come out here sometimes to calm down and the animals find me."

"Sure." I nodded, "that's *all* it is."

Jenn smiled.

We were quiet while Jenn petted the deer's head. She picked up my hand and showed me how to do it without waking him again. It felt like a Rottweiler.

Very smooth. Very sleek. Very strong.

"Wait. You come here to *calm down*." Jenn looked up at me through her bangs without lifting her head. "Jenn, You're always calm. I've never seen you get upset . . . ever."

"Well," she shrugged and thought before she answered me, staring all the while at the deer, "that's what everyone expects, right? It's not like I'm lying—" she glanced up, "or that I've been hiding . . . " she petered out. I waited, watching her squirm and avoid my eyes. Her shields were up, but faltering and soon I'd know what she was going to say whether she told me or not. She knew it too. "So that's not really true either," Jenn concentrated on her deer's head. "I have hidden things." She was very quiet.

"What kinds of things."

Jenn looked at me, trying to get past my shields to see what I was really thinking. "Um . . . some things."

"Big things?" I asked. Jenn nodded, haltingly, not taking her eyes off the deer. "How big?" I asked.

"Pretty big?" She answered. I looked at her, waiting. "Pretty darn big?" She added, looking sheepish.

"Psychic things?"

Jenn nodded.

"You can do more than you let on, can't you?"

Jenn smiled this crooked little smile but other than that she didn't move.

"I knew it!" I almost didn't whisper. The deer sighed in its sleep.

"I didn't want anyone to . . . " she started, "but I've known about," she hesitated, "a lot of things . . . about you . . . for a pretty long time now."

"What things? Jenn? . . . " I waited, "Jenn? Come on, you can't leave me hanging."

Jenn straightened her shoulders without disturbing the deer. "Well, I've known about how . . . how you get when you're angry." Now it all tumbled out, gaining speed. "I knew about your boyfriend before you told me. I knew about the motorcyclist. I knew about —"

"The *motorcyclist*?" I interrupted. "How did you know . . . ?"

"I saw it." She shrugged. "How do *you* know things?"

"But I didn't show it to you," I protested. "I didn't even know it had happened!"

"Well, I guess you're not the only one who can pull stuff out of the air." There was an edge in her voice I'd never heard before. "I saw it. I guess it was in your subconscious because it came to me very clearly. I almost said something, but I wasn't ready for the dominoes to fall yet. But looking back that was a mistake. Like not telling you about Cas—"

Jenn shut her mouth so fast her jaw had its own sound effect.

"What about Casey." My stomach hurt.

The deer looked up at me again, struggled sleepily onto its spindly legs, licked the side of Jenn's face, then turned and walked away.

Jenn sighed, "I knew."

"Since when?"

"Since you saw him kiss you. While we were working when you first got here—when you first learned to ground-and-center. I knew whose face it was . . . you didn't." She couldn't look at me.

"And you didn't tell me?"

"I didn't know what to say . . . I tried to tell Mom."

"Your *Mom* knew?"

"Well, no, she didn't really listen. She doesn't think . . . "

"You told her about the motorcycle *and* Casey?"

She nodded. "I told her Izzy knew."

"But it was you. You *are* psychic?"

She hesitated, then nodded. I couldn't speak.

"Please don't be mad," Jenn said finally, "I didn't know what to do." I shook my head and started to get up. "Don't," Jenn tried to grab my hand. "What would you have done if you were me?"

I turned and looked down on her, "I would have *told you*."

"Really?" she asked, "really? You would have?"

I nodded.

"I don't believe that for a second," Jenn said, leaning back, hugging her knees to her chest. "What do you think you would have done—how would you have felt if you knew that I knew stuff about you that you didn't know yourself? You're supposed to know everything. And I'm not supposed to be able to do any of this, right? I'm just Jenn."

"Why have you been hiding what you can do?"

"It's . . . it's complicated."

"I think I can handle it." Jenn was silent. "I think you might owe me this one, Jenn."

"Owe you," Jenn muttered. "Yeah, I owe you."

"What?" I said. "You've been keeping secrets. Big ones. I think it's time to explain."

"Fine," she played with a piece of grass. "I want to be normal, okay? I was a kid when Casey showed up and I'd already started seeing things, but when he got to our house, that first summer with your sister? That just scared the crap out of me. Yeah, well, we're not in the house. Words don't matter so much out here."

I nodded and she continued.

"So I hid it. And I listened to what they were teaching Casey and what they were trying to teach Chloe, and I did it myself. Then covered my tracks."

"You're better than any of us," I whispered.

"Not Casey," she shook her head. "He still has way more control than me in most things. But I remember what it was like in the beginning. That's why I gave you and Justin so much space. You have to find your way through this and it's hard. Justin needs to be the prodigy to gain some confidence after the way his mom treated him. You need to figure out how to control yourself, and get comfortable with what you can do. All of that has to come from inside.

"You *gave me* space?"

"I pulled Mom off you when I thought she was pushing too hard. I boosted your shields when I could. I helped you get glamours the first time." My head hurt all over again, but not so much that something didn't become clear to me.

"You. *You* made me blue when I was in Tucson?" Jenn was quiet, but I wasn't. "*You* iced me after Mom told me I had to come. You kept me from fighting her. You made sure I came here."

"You had to, Rosie. You were going to hurt yourself or someone else. I couldn't let—"

"When was it ever your decision?"

"Are you sorry you came?" I looked at the leaf in my hand. "Listen, I knew this was hard enough on you—and you haven't exactly had an easy time even with backup . . . breaking frames and throwing Justin . . . " she choked, and I couldn't tell if she was starting to laugh or cry. I couldn't tell if *I* was going to laugh or cry, but the image of Justin flying prevailed.

"I did do that, didn't I?"

"Yeah," she put her hand over her mouth. "Yes, you did."

"Yeah . . . good times."

I breathed deep and tossed the leaf. "So?" I asked. "So what else do you know about me?"

"That's it," Jenn said. "I knew you'd be good for Casey, though."

"You . . . is that why you gave me that wish box? Don't try to squirm out of this, Green. Did you give that box to me to get me to draw Casey so he'd finally have someone he . . . " I was sickened at the thought that this may all have been a trick and not reality.

"I gave you the box to make sure—he needed a nudge. But trust me, you were meant to be with him."

I shook my head, "I dunno Jenn. You told me not to mess with that."

"I told you that you could nudge the universe but it would only work if it was meant to go that way. It's good. Trust me."

I snorted. "Please. You gonna tell your mom what you can do?"

She looked at me, eyebrows creased, "No. And neither are you."

"Jenn—"

"No, I'm serious. I want to stay normal. I don't want to be extraordinary. And I don't want to shift the balance."

"But you're—"

"But I'm *stable*. Don't you get it? I don't need special attention. I can channel just as well as Izzy, but I can block like Casey—better. So I block. All the time. No one sees what I'm doing, and that's fine with me."

"But the Tarot cards?"

"Are fun, but you don't have to be psychic to use them. You could deal out any deck of cards randomly and make up a story full of symbolic do's and don't's based on them. No one is surprised that I'm good at them."

"What about the animals? Do they know that deer come and use you as a pillow?"

"Nah, but animals being drawn to people isn't all that uncommon."

I made myself shrug, "Fine. But don't you, y'know, don't you hate having your parents spend so much time on everyone else?"

"Sometimes. I still go off and do things with them by myself. Our life is a whole lot less messed up than bunches of kids I know."

"Does Izzy know?"

She shook her head.

"I know Justin doesn't."

She nodded.

"Casey?"

Jenn paused. "He suspects."

"He can keep a secret."

"He'd better." She looked at me seriously, "You'd better, too," she said.

I looked up at the trees and tried to ground myself, nodded at her and said, "Of course. I know nothing." Then, "What if Casey figures it out?"

"You can tell him yourself as long as it stays between the two of you."

I looked back up at the sky and the green puzzle of branches above. "You want to walk back?"

"Nah. I want to see if the squirrel will come back. I still have nuts."

"Don't we all." I turned and started walking. The return trip was longer than it had been coming here, but a new song didn't start in my head until I'd almost made it back to the cabin.

Before dinner we sat on the dock and I hinted to Casey what Jenn had said. I was surprised to find that he was completely unfazed.

"Yeah, I always knew she was better than she let on," was all he said.

It's hard to hold a grudge when the guy who just got charmed isn't bugged by it.

I dreamed that night.

I am on a plane and the guy reading my graphic novel is in the bathroom or something. I turn and look out the window at the gorgeous cloud formations next to us. I feel my seatmate sit down. I turn to ask him how he likes the book.

It isn't my seatmate. It's a man in motorcycle leathers and a white helmet. He won't look at me, but instead I hear, "Don't get distracted, Rose. Don't get off track again. Focus on where you're needed. Find the thread and let the rest of it go."

When I woke up, I remembered a talking egg that told me, "let it go."

43 Homebound

I slept for most of the trip back to Croton. That might have been because I was lulled to sleep by Casey reading a book as thick as my head—which is saying something. Izzy and Justin were playing a new game to see if they could make the horns honk in the cars next to us. They were intermittently successful, which is why I didn't sleep the whole way. Jenn was up front with her dad and Aunt Mina was in the way-back, out cold, car horns or no.

Jazz's place was empty. She left us a note telling us she'd returned to the City for work. The group's disappointed sigh was audible. Everyone had been looking forward to showing her the new things we could do. We dragged in our backpacks and left the rest of the bags in the van. Then, pretty much all of us went to our beds and called it quits. Before I passed out, I ate a couple handfuls of Cheerios, got what I needed for the next day out of my bag, read a little more of Casey's walls, shuddered a few more times, and passed out on my bed. I don't think I even put on pajamas; I slept in my shirt. The last few days in Stockbridge had exhausted me.

Just as before, Casey was in charge of returning the luggage to Brooklyn. And, as before, he departed before we woke up, as did our bags. I'd wanted to ask if I could go with him, but he was gone before I emerged. We left after breakfast, armed with our backpacks and transported by a couple of gypsy cabs. Of course, there was Bill's required detour to the Black Cow, where we loaded up on Black Calf chocolate milks and those super-flaky sweet elephant ear pastries.

"You wear more than you eat, but they're so good," Izzy said, brushing crumbs off before she got back in the cab.

"They'll be better if they stay outside the vehicle," Mina helped brush crumbs off Jenn.

"Hey, what about the former driver?" Bill asked.

Mina lightly brushed the front of his shirt, too. "The former driver is smart and has a bagel instead of a crumbling monstrosity," she smiled. "I think he can handle not leaving crumbs in the nice man's cab without too much help." She kissed him and he held the door for her, getting into the cab last.

Ew.

Then, as the train took us back to Brooklyn, I watched the Hudson River flow by outside my window. As we clattered along, I wondered about the people who lived here hundreds of years ago. What did they think of the river. To me, it was beautiful and slow and magnificent. To them, was it a big problem? Just something in the way? Was it a challenge? A terror? A terrible beauty? How many things are like that, their meaning changed by the passage of time? Like us —what would have happened to people like us a couple hundred years ago?

I shut myself up.

We rolled peacefully towards Brooklyn: our island off the coast of an island off the coast of North America. Once we reached Grand Central Terminal, however, Aunt Mina lost her mind. She was watching me closely—hovering actually. Finally, I turned and surprised her as we walked across the large hall to the 4/5 train.

"What?" I turned, looking right at her, walking backwards. "What is wrong? You're watching me like a hawk."

Aunt Mina jumped when I spun around, but her voice was smooth and hard as glass. "I'm watching your shields. For backup." She stopped walking and nodded at Bill who led everyone else to the clock to wait. Mina turned back to me. "Look, kiddo. You learned a lot in a relatively short period of time. Up at the Bowl, you didn't need to protect yourself at all because you were surrounded by water and people who weren't dangerous. People able to protect you if you needed it. Now you're back in the city. You don't have water. You're surrounded by crazies, and I'm concerned. I knew we should have made a game plan last night, but everyone passed out, myself included. I'm sorry; that was my mistake. I know that coming back to the city is a hard transition for everyone, but everyone else," she indicated Justin, Izzy, and Jenn, "has done it before."

As soon as she said it, I realized that I was, indeed, feeling unsteady— not quite nauseated, but unsettled. Jumpy. I looked around then back at Mina and shrugged.

"Here," she said. She took my hand and allowed me to see through her eyes, to see why I was so fidgety. Everyone around me was moving in a vertical pool of color. Some colors seemed taller than the bodies, some smaller, some— honestly—a lot more scary than their actual bodies appeared. While some walked with purpose towards a train or exit or ticket window, their colored selves drifted, seemed to check things out, then catch up with their bodies, sometimes coming into contact with other colors, and then those other pools shimmered and changed with the touch. Finally, like ripples on the water, they shivered back into themselves.

The most interesting thing, though, was watching people walking hand-in-hand. Those colors blended and effortlessly wove in and out of one other— usually. One couple walked toward us with one color very pale and, it seemed to me, cowering away from the other, darker color. The lights moved around, one stalking, one being stalked, and it was impossible to tell which color belonged to the guy and which to the girl. I nodded at them and looked at Mina.

"Are they okay?"

She looked, and shook her head, "No. They're not. And they shouldn't be together. They know it too, but . . . " she looked back at me. "This is why I'm watching you. If you'd been too close to them, it's entirely possible that they would have gotten mixed in with you. When you're as wide open as you are right now—yes, even though your shields are up, they're still Stockbridge shields, not city-strength—it's disturbing when that happens. You need to re-ground before we get on the subway."

I nodded, then asked, "I have a . . . color like that?"

Aunt Mina smiled at me, "A very bright and happy one. You look great."

I laughed, "As long as I'm not 'perky.'" Then, "Is that part of what happens to Casey?"

"What?"

"That his . . . colors . . . get taken over by the other people?"

Mina and I moved towards the others who had been waiting, mostly patiently.

"Casey is . . . " Mina was cautious, "he's in a difficult situation. It's more than the colors; it's . . . Casey's very . . . attractive," she smiled at me. "I mean, obviously to you, but on a psychic level, he attracts . . . everything. Troubled souls, both living and passed, people who are lonely, who are angry, who are overjoyed—he's an enormous psychic magnet. And the thing about Casey is that his shields are amazing, truly amazing. You should see him when he has to come someplace like this. He has to move slowly because his shields are like stone and the concentration really exhausts him."

We neared the stairs to the 4/5 trains. "But," she continued, "he can't keep it up forever. He's a giant electromagnet in a hardware store, absolutely everything flies at him. I think 'brutal' is a good way to describe it."

I shook my head. "What did he do before he had you and Bill?"

"Well, he was younger. It's really when you hit puberty that these things ramp up for most of us, and he was no different in that respect. I imagine he's told you about the girl in Sioux Falls?" I nodded. "Well, she was the first. Or at least the first he noticed wasn't with us," she said. "There may have been others, but he sees them so clearly it's sometimes hard to tell that they aren't living. Regardless, they found him, though it started slowly enough. Bill wasn't able to get there right away, but he reached Casey before he had another significant episode. Within a couple of years, though, it was becoming clear, even to his mom and dad—who *hated* this—that they couldn't keep him at home without helping him somehow. So they let us take him. And thank God."

"He told me they didn't . . . get it. That's gotta be hard."

"It was," Mina nodded, "it is. I don't know if you understand how important you are to him. I hope . . . I hope it turns out that that's okay—for both of you. It's a lot of responsibility."

"That's a weird word to use for 'dating,' Aunt Mina."

"Maybe. But it's accurate. Look, I know you two . . . like each other . . . but relationships are . . . well, they're complex under the best of circumstances."

"Aunt Mina," I said quietly, "You don't have to have The Talk with me."

She laughed, "Not even attempting that. No, I know I'm speaking for your mother when I say that neither of us want our girls to feel, or to ever be . . . trapped in a relationship at all, much less so young." She must have seen the look on my face because she quickly added, "I mean, Rose, I've seen lots of people who met young, got married young, and are very, very happy together. That's not what I'm saying. I'm saying that Bill and I can see what you mean to Casey. He cares about you, no question. It's transparent. But you're also much, much more to him than simply a girlfriend. He honestly thought he would have to live isolated, in the mountains, like a hermit for the rest of his life. You . . . you opened a whole world for him."

"I know. He doesn't get anything off of me."

"No, Rose." The train doors opened and we walked on and sat down, the others not far from us. She turned and looked straight at me. "No. When he's near you it's not simply that he gets nothing off of you—he gets nothing. Well, nothing he doesn't want to get. You unwrap the coils and turn off the electricity. Nothing in the hardware store is coming at him. You stop the noise for him—unless he wants to listen. And, thank God, just having you near him helps."

"I know. We figured out that I don't have to touch him for it to work. So that's good . . . " I blushed.

"And, on that note, I've seen what happens the few times you've made contact when I'm around. I know what it . . . does to you. And that *is* a conversation for another day. But for Casey, it's like his colors—what you're seeing on other people now—go from an agitated orange-red, to a smooth, rippling light blue. Actually, almost a periwinkle." She was looking up, thinking and remembering.

I laughed. "I want to see you tell Casey that he's 'periwinkle.'" She laughed too.

"Well, maybe that's between us. Anyway, where I was going with all of this is that even though you do all that for Casey—and it's truly a wonderful thing to watch—you cannot, absolutely *cannot* feel responsible for him and stay with him longer than is good for you—for both of you. If you fall in love and it's lasting and you live happily ever after, someday, then wonderful. I'll be the first to open the champagne. But if you weary of him, I do not want you to stick around purely because you feel badly, thinking you're the only way he'll survive. If there's a You for him then there's bound to be someone else—another You—who can do the same thing. This isn't all on your shoulders. All right?"

I nodded soberly, but the thought of life without Casey was too much for me. I had to be with him. When we were together, maybe *he* felt normal, but *I* felt extraordinary. And more than that, all of this craziness—Tim, the motorcyclist, Brooklyn, all of it—made more sense with Casey around. He never judged me or got mad at me when I didn't grasp something fast enough. I felt safe. Why in the world would I ever, *ever* want that to stop? Casey would have to leave *me.* I couldn't imagine ever leaving him.

"Shields up. You're slipping." Mina winked and left me to myself for the rest of the ride home.

44 FIRSTS

SEPTEMBER 6TH.

FIRST DAY of school in a new town . . . which happens to be New York City.

After the requisite racing around, racing back, losing, finding, then losing my earrings again, finally I was able to make it out the door. Izzy and Justin were already partway down the street.

"Come *on*, Rose," Justin whined. "What did you forget *now*?"

"What *is* that?" I murmured.

Jenn walked up next to me. "What is what? C'mon. We're gonna be late," and she passed me to catch up with Izzy.

"What is that . . . smell . . . feel . . . What's up with the *air*?"

Over his shoulder Justin said, "Hello? September? You don't have Autumn in the desert?"

"Oh, we have September. Just not like this. How'd this happen so fast? It's not humid anymore."

"Yeah," Jenn was practically skipping and turned around to walk backwards in front of me. "Some people say spring is best, but they're wrong. Autumn is."

"I like the leaves," Izzy said.

385

"I like the slant of the light. It comes down through the trees different in the fall," Justin said thoughtfully.

"Oooh, poetic," said Izzy. Justin lazily slugged Izzy on the arm.

"I like the start of school," Jenn said to me. Izzy turned and thwacked her on the back of the head with a finger. "Hey! I do," Jenn protested, turning front. "The classes are easy in the beginning, and I like being in the city and out of the house."

We headed to the N/R station between President and Union Street. I liked this station, not because it was so cool, but because it was under an old Brooklyn bath house. None of us knew the history of the place, but it was fun to imagine what it was like when people came here to cool off in the summer . . . in their oxymoronic wool bathing suits. A totally different world.

I stood there, looking at the funky geometric colored tiles lining the track walls for only a couple of minutes before the train pulled up. We were having too good a time, though, and completely missed the Rector Street stop. Luckily the World Trade Center Concourse was next, which Jenn said was super-close to school, too. There were guys on my high school football team in Tucson who could have thrown a pass from one stop to the next.

"We'll come back this way after school," Izzy said conspiratorially. "There's good ice cream over that way. And I absolutely feel the need to treat ourselves to Ben and Jerry's after such a difficult and challenging first day."

"You think it's going to be difficult?" My stomach flopped.

"Nah," Izzy shoved me playfully, "but it makes a great excuse for ice cream."

The concourse was packed and one hundred percent in motion—so many people moving so fast, so many stores. Some I knew, like the Gap and Limited, but some I didn't, like Papyrus and Sephora. "I need to get lipstick there, later," Jenn said. "Remind me?"

I doubted I would. But she would remember. She always did. We walked out a corner exit and into the morning again. The buildings surrounding us cast shadows big enough to keep us chilled until we got to the school. We walked through a little farmers' market with awnings pitched in the parking lot. I was tempted to buy some bread that smelled like heaven in a bag. But Jenn told me they were there every Tuesday and Thursday so I'd have another chance.

Unlike Arizona, my new school was right in the middle of the city—right in the middle of the downtown financial scene. It was surreal seeing guys in suits instead of cheerleaders in skirts. Another good thing? No school parking lot. No dumb kids smoking in the corner, no annoying groups of guys, no even more annoying gaggles of girls. Everyone was heading somewhere on purpose, and most were adults.

I had to revise my opinion when we passed a Burger King and a deli and a small group of boys—they had to be freshmen or sophomores—hiding in plain sight at the front corner of the school, out of the line of the windows—smoking.

"Hey Nathaniel," I heard a woman dressed like a teacher say to one of them, "you're gonna be a very handsome, very *young* corpse." She kept walking into the school without looking twice. One of the kids looked down, then back over his shoulder in the direction she'd gone, stubbed out his cigarette, half-waved at his friends, shoved his hands into his pockets and slouched into school.

We walked in to find our principal in the foyer, greeting the kids, some parents, the new teachers and the returning teachers. A handsome, soft-spoken, African-American teacher stood next to the bank of elevators, guiding kids in. Elevators! Seriously! Everything—let me emphasize that—every thing in Tucson is one story tall. My new school was *vertical*.

We entered when it was our turn. The older man operating the elevator had a thick accent and it took me a while to understand that the only two stops would be the seventh floor and the twelfth. My first class today was on 12. Lucky.

I started with AP English every day but Monday. Our teacher seemed nice. He was this tall musician guy. I figured we would do a lot of poetry—that's

387

what I remember everyone complaining about in Tucson—but he started our class with a pretty tough analysis paper. We had to read a short story and analyze the use of metaphor. I'd never heard of the writer, so it was a bit of a challenge, but it was good or at least interesting. I worried a bit that I would be way behind; Arizona was not known for its stellar educational system. But after class, Justin, Izzy, Jenn, and I all compared notes, and I didn't seem to have missed anything major.

The views out the windows of this school were amazing. From my first period seat, if I looked to my left, I could see these two huge black buildings. And if I stood right at the windows, like I did after the bell rang, I could see the World Trade Centers—well, one of them, anyway. If I really leaned, face up against the glass, I still couldn't see the top.

"Come on Dreamy Girl," Izzy said.

"So, Iz," I asked, "if you guys get stuck on work in class—"

"No." Izzy shook her head, "Not even sort of."

"Totally unethical," Justin scolded.

"I was just checking," I defended, "I don't know how well I can block when I'm thinking in class."

"That's exactly why we won't go there," Izzy put her arm through mine, "will we?" She led us to our next class.

Mina had "arranged" it so Izzy, Justin, Jenn, and I would all have the same schedule. This was mostly for my protection this year, but it was good for them too. There was always the possibility of one of us losing our shields or having something unexpected happen. This way, we all had each other's back. The side benefit of this was that I had friends in every class, including lunch.

It was Burger King for lunch the first day, which wasn't thrilling, but it was near the school. We had more choices for other days. Seniors get to leave campus at lunch, which was the same as at home. What wasn't the same was what it felt like to go to school in a city the size of New York. Even with the windows closed on the 12th floor, you could still hear the occasional car honk, or a passing siren. In Arizona, if I had my windows open at night I would hear crickets, maybe a coyote, and if I was lucky, I'd get a whiff of some Javelina, snorting around a prickly pear in the wash. The city was to Arizona as Earth was to Pluto.

I forgot Izzy's earlier instructions and expected to take the train home right after school, but instead we went back to the Concourse. First, we had to buy the required start-of-school lipstick and ice cream. I asked if we should also get first-day-of-school paper and first-day-of-school pens at Duane Reade. They laughed and walked the other direction.

We wound around enough that I knew I'd need them as guides to get out, but at last, near some noisily thwapping revolving doors, we found a Ben and Jerry's stand. Izzy ordered Chunky Monkey first while Justin shook his head, "I don't know why you don't branch out."

"Say what you mean, Justin," she eyeballed him, "You know why I don't like your Scary Garcia."

"It's good."

"It's creepy."

"Frozen chunks of cherry aren't creepy."

"They are if they squeak on your teeth."

"You're a freak."

"That doesn't change the fact that Cherry Garcia's whack."

"Cherry Garcia, sugar cone, please." Justin ordered, pushing next to Izzy. She sighed and turned away with her monkey.

"What're you getting, Rose?" Izzy stood next to me looking at the board.

"Dunno yet."

"You don't have a favorite?" she asked. Jenn ordered Phish Food.

"Nope. I just like ice cream. But I think I'll try Mint Chocolate Chunk."

"Really?" Izzy asked

"Yes, really. Why?"

Izzy shrugged. "No reason."

I asked for my ice cream in a cup and turned back to Iz with as serious a face as I could manage, "I know I've disappointed you by not having found my perfect and extremely odd flavor yet, but I want you to know that I'm willing to work hard to conquer this deficiency."

"I'm sorry about your shortcoming," she said.

"I think you'll have to find a way to stand by me as I embark on this difficult journey."

"I appreciate your commitment, soldier," she nodded crisply before she started laughing.

We headed back to the trains with our ice cream, passing another thousand guys-in-ties. As we got closer to the platform, the crush of bodies made me glad I got my dessert in a cup. "Why is everyone leaving? It's only, like, 3:30."

"Bankers' hours," sniffed Justin. I guess he didn't like bankers. Or maybe it was still just me.

We walked in the front door to the smells of amazing cooking. Casey and Mina were up to something, locked in the kitchen making a celebratory dinner. We weren't allowed in, but they did let us set the table in the dining room. We were efficiency personified, another benefit of psychic-ness: exchanging thoughts when shields are politely lowered. I set water glasses, Izzy set forks, Jenn set spoons, and Justin set knives.

"Appropriate items," Izzy giggled, poking Justin with a fork.

"Fork you," he Brooklynned back at her. "Don't break those glasses, Weej."

The room was quiet.

"Better to warn me not to break *you,* Cap'n."

The laughter was cautious at first, but kept coming. This looked like the beginning of a beautiful . . . well. I didn't want to get carried away. We didn't kill each other, and that was a good start.

At dinner, Casey sat next to me. While we ate, I heard, *Okay, really, how was it?*

It was hard not to smile while I sent, *It was good. I really like my physics teacher. He cracks me up.*

Yeah, no. I know that part. You've been thinking about him and the history guy since you walked in. I'm talking about the culture shock. New York schools? I mean, they weren't like South Dakota schools for me. I'm guessing they aren't like Arizona for you.

Oh, that. I'd have been terrified today if I hadn't been here all summer. If I hadn't walked in with Four-Sevenths of Magnificence I guarantee I'd have lost it.

And how was everyone else? The other students? Nice enough?

Yeah, especially because they all love Izzy. And Jenn's friends were nice. The guys were less suspicious of me than the girls—

Casey looked at me.

But none of them like me. *Don't worry.*

He stopped, mid-spoonful.

What?

They don't need to like you to be . . . problematic. You're like . . . fresh blood. New meat.

Thanks.

I didn't mean it that way, he sighed aloud. *This is—it's difficult to make my thoughts sound nice or polite when they aren't. Guys are . . . guys. We're all basically the same.*

You too?

He paused. *Well, sure,* he answered deliberately, *to an extent. It's one of the reasons I kept away from you for so long, Hannah Rose. One of the reasons I was afraid to work with you. I knew the first time I walked in the door that I received nothing from you. I knew there was a chance, and . . . look where my bedroom is. I'm no idiot. And I have the advantage over the boys at school. I know my limits.*

"Oh," I whispered, "I don't know what to say."

It's fine. It's okay. Never mind. I won't bring it up again.

"No!" I got a couple of looks from the table, *Whups. No. The last thing I want is for you to feel like you need to, I don't know, censor yourself, especially in your head. That's messed up. Do you . . .* I wasn't sure what to say. *Do you want me to stay away from the guys at school?*

"What?" Now it was his turn to get looks, *Sorry. No.*

Mina looked hard at Casey and long at me. Conversation gradually resumed.

Look, I'm not interested in that. I don't ever want to . . . You're in charge of you. I trust you. This wouldn't be much of a, he stumbled, *a . . . relationship . . . if we didn't trust each other.*

I reached my toe over under the table and touched the back of his calf. His eyes darted at me and he smiled slightly as he leaned over his soup bowl.

Me? I shivered.

After dinner Casey sat with a book on the other side of the kitchen window seat from me while I did my homework—English writing, then a little history, and physics reading. Easy stuff. Jenn was curled up in the chair near me and Izzy and Justin worked at the dining room table. Every once in awhile I'd glance up to see Casey looking at me with that funny half-smile on his face.

"What?" I whispered.

"Nothing," he mouthed back.

"You know, every time you do that it takes me an hour before I can work again?"

"I'll stop."

"Lie much?" I couldn't help smiling at him. You'd think after all that time in Stockbridge the reaction situation would have settled down.

Things continued like this until bedtime. Slowly we all peeled off from the downstairs workspace and made our way to bed. Casey walked up with me, clicking the lights off without touching a switch. I couldn't stop the grin whenever one went out. If my friends back home knew . . . *oy.*

Casey walked me to my door, kissed me gently, but briefly—momentarily stopping all my signs of life—and headed to his room. As he opened his door he turned, waved, and kinda dork-smiled. I waved back, grinning like an idiot.

I had a hard time getting to sleep once I got into bed. The thoughts in my head kept swirling around and around. I couldn't believe I was so lucky. I couldn't believe Casey—of all people—said we were in a relationship! I couldn't believe I was dating someone who could turn lights off with his mind. I couldn't believe this was all real.

I couldn't believe something hadn't yet gone horribly, horribly, wrong.

In my dream I am sitting down, my legs hanging over a ledge. I hear a foghorn. Or a boat. Or something. And I hear water. Like when we were at Coney Island, or maybe like at the dock. Lapping water. And I keep thinking, "Open your eyes!" because I can't see anything. Then I keep saying back, "They are open!" I have yarn in my hand and I'm winding it wet, pulling it out of the water. I try and I try

to get away from there—from the place where I can't see, but I can't leave. I'm tied to it.

> *I can't see how to get away.*
> *I can't see the thread.*

45 FRIDAY NIGHT LIGHTS

THE NEXT SCHOOL DAY passed much like the first—still learning the drill and trying to feel comfortable in a very different environment. We went to Steve's Deli for lunch and Ben & Jerry's again after school. It was fine, but Casey's not going with us meant it was all a little less bright and cheery. I'd grown used to his near-constant presence in Stockbridge. Still, no homework gave us some freedom that afternoon. We left school and walked west to the Hudson, south around the tip of the island, then up to South Street Seaport and up over the Brooklyn Bridge to home.

I had never been on a bridge like that. So big. So beautiful. So old. It didn't take much to imagine carriages and Model T's crossing the span. The water was bright with diamond flashes from the slowly sinking sun. I tried sending to Casey but had no idea if anything reached him. We stopped to gaze passively at historical markers but didn't really pay attention. Off the bridge in Brooklyn, we briefly got lost looking for a train, and finally boarded an accidental series of buses. One took us onto 5th Street.

"Hey?" Jenn nudged Izzy, looking at both of us. "I'm gonna stay on and run to the yarn store." Izzy nodded. "You wanna come?"

Izzy shook her head but I said, "Sure," shrugging. I didn't have much money with me, but I did have my knitting in my bag to show Delphi. I thought my lace might impress her this time.

The bus dropped us off only a few stops beyond where Izzy and Justin left us, and a half-block from the Knitting Garden. We crossed the street and walked in. Delphi wasn't visible anywhere, but an older man in a baseball hat was there. "Don't worry, you're in the right place. She'll be back in a sec."

Jenn smiled and nodded, heading to the crochet hooks, while I browsed the shelves.

"Can I buy these from you?" Jenn asked the man, holding up two hooks.

"You got money?" He eyed her.

"Yes."

His face widened into a grin, "Then *sure* you can buy them from me." He rang up her hooks and she handed over her cash. We had turned to go when Delphi entered.

"I rushed back," she said breathlessly, "because I had to catch you before you left."

I looked at Jenn; she was completely unsurprised by this.

"What's up, Delphi?"

"Your bracelets," Delphi pointed to our naked wrists. They must have fallen off up in Stockbridge. I couldn't remember the last time I'd seen one on either of us.

"You raced back here for yarn bracelets?" now Jenn was surprised.

"Not just yarn," Delphi made her way to the back of the store like the first time we were here, "yarn blessed at the Kotel," she looked at me. "The Wailing Wall . . . In Jerusalem."

"I know," I nodded, trying not to look miffed.

She returned to talking to Jenn. "So the yarn was blessed, then brought to the Rebbe's grave, then given to you." She pulled down her box. "Just yarn," Delphi muttered. She motioned for us to present her our wrists, which we did. "And this time you need to keep these on!"

While she tied a bracelet on Jenn, I started to pull my knitting out of my bag to show her, but she nailed me with such a look that I put the knitting back without missing a beat. I would have asked what that was about, but honestly, she spooked me. I didn't really want to know.

I tugged at Jenn's sleeve. We said otherwise pleasant goodbyes and left.

"So, that was—" I started.

"Delphi. Yep." Jenn said with finality, and I didn't say a word more about it on the way home.

When we finally walked through the door, Mina and Casey had dinner nearly ready for us, but tonight with the addition of Jasmine and Tyrik. "Did you kids come home by way of Staten Island?" Mina almost sounded worried.

"No," Jenn deadpanned, "Jersey." She flopped on the couch and dropped her backpack on the floor. Mina shot her a Mom Look that made Jenn sigh, get up, and put her backpack with the rest near the back door.

"The bridge looked nice," Casey said as a greeting.

"It worked?" Jenn asked, brightening.

"It did."

I thought I was the one sending to Casey. I was going to have to talk to Jenn about this tomorrow.

Dinner Friday night was a candlelit affair with everyone taking turns putting the flames out and relighting them—without a match. Candles, challah bread, and wine. Even the under-agers each had a mouthful of sweet wine—for a sweet week. It was good—it felt like family. And every once in a while Casey would brush the side of my leg or touch my hand under the table, then smile when I shivered.

Why didn't we do this over the summer? I asked. *Friday's like this?*

Too hot. Mina says God understands.

After dinner, Bill fired up his record player. Justin teased him, but spent the whole night poring over the album covers and sleeves, tsking at whatever he was finding out about what he called "mad old" and Bill called "totally hot" music, making Bill laugh. We sat in the front room, relaxing and talking quietly. Now that the hard work of the summer was over and the emotional high of starting school was fading, we could feel how drained we were.

I had my knitting bag with me as I sat on the floor in front of Casey who was on the couch and lifted out the pile of yarn that was still not a complete shawl. Too much Casey. Too little knitting.

"I'm not quite done with your shawl, Jasmine. I'm sorry." I said, probably interrupting her and Mina's chance to talk to each other.

"No apologies needed," Jasmine smiled. "It's not even winter yet."

"No, but it's been cool in the mornings. I'll finish it this weekend and get it to you."

"She works near our school," Justin noted.

"No kidding?" I looked from him to Jazz, "Great! Maybe I can drop it by next week?"

"I would love that," and she flashed me that glamour smile leaving me all cool blue and happy for the rest of the night.

Eventually Justin migrated over to Izzy where she was on the floor with a couple decks of cards.

"Seven!" Izzy said and flipped a card.

"Ace!" Justin flipped his.

"They're seeing if they can make that number card come to the top of the deck." Jenn told me.

Justin showed off with a mighty, multi-deck shuffling job and Jenn, Bill, and Tyrik joined in a very basic poker with them until, at last, my eyes started closing. Casey tapped my shoulder lightly with his book to wake me up and whispered, "C'mon, I'll walk you up."

I knew Aunt Mina and Jasmine were watching us as we walked upstairs, side-by-side—with Casey lighting the way before us. Tonight I didn't care. I felt great—tired but great.

"You know," I murmured, rounding the landing of the second floor, "Mina's in kind of an awkward position with us."

"How so?"

"Well, I mean, how would your mom react to me living under the same roof as you? Or you living across the landing from me?"

"Oh. That."

"Yes, that."

"Well, it's not like we can actually hide anything from Mina and Bill."

"No, I know they can read me like cheap fiction, all psychicness aside."

"It's true," he smiled, "I can always tell when you're ticked at me."

"Yeah?"

"You have *that look*."

"I'm going to go out on a limb and assume it's a particularly withering look?"

"The witheringest."

"It's a gift."

"Indeed. But it's also why I'm not that worried. No lines can really be crossed, can they?"

"No, I suppose not."

"I mean it still takes you fifteen minutes to recover from this," and he kissed me.

I had to hold onto the banister for a full minute. "Unfair," I croaked.

We got to my door and Casey was still smiling. "Prepare yourself," he murmured. He gingerly wrapped his arms around my back, barely letting them press against me. It took everything in me to ground myself, but I managed and felt only the slightest pleasant buzz. Who said I wasn't learning?

He sighed as I rested my head against his chest. It was nice to find a perfect fit. For a minute we just breathed together. Just us. I'd never felt this safe in my life.

I love you, his voice was in my head.

I lifted my face, sleepy, and stared into his face. "I think I knew that," I half-whispered, half-croaked. I cleared my throat, "I mean, I think you clarified that earlier."

"It's nice to be able to say it," he said aloud. I smiled up at him. It was nice to hear it, but he already knew that, too.

"It's weird, though, isn't it?"

"What is?" I asked his chest.

"How fast . . . ?"

"Yeah . . . well, we've had mitigating circumstances telling us that we're a good fit."

Casey moved his hands from my back and I took a deep breath as he cradled my face in his hands, leaned towards me, and kissed me so tenderly it brought tears to my eyes. He was nothing like Tim. Casey was so *normal*—for me, anyway—it felt like we'd been together forever.

"I know," he said aloud, "That's why I can do this." And he kissed me again. And it felt like . . . like a normal kiss. A perfect kiss. A perfectly normal kiss. He must have been grounded like an Oak.

"Is it hard to keep from—"

"Zapping you?" he murmured.

"Yeah." I put my head sleepily back on his chest.

"It's getting easier—thank God. I thought it was gonna kill me. I've been working out." In his chest I felt him laugh lightly.

I smiled.

His breath rustled my bangs. "I love how your hair smells."

"I think I've been stealing your shampoo."

"Yeah? Just more proof that I have great taste."

I strengthened my shield, aimed, and gave him a quick bear hug. He gasped.

"Gotcha," I smiled, proud that I'd found a way to send back to him a little of what he did to me—a psychic relay.

He lifted my chin to kiss me again. I shuddered and Casey sighed, "You'd better go to bed. This is getting . . . difficult."

I looked at him.

"I'm psychic—not inhuman."

I continued to look at him.

"I'm male," he finally said with a smile.

"Ah," I said. "Good-night."

He kissed my forehead and pushed my door open for me, holding my hand, then my fingertips, until the last possible second and then he closed the door softly. I could hear his footsteps creaking towards his bedroom.

Finally in bed and drifting off to sleep, it occurred to me that Casey and I had a mighty difficult year ahead of us. If this is how we felt *now*, and we were living in the same house, across the hall from each other—Mina and Mom be damned—what in the world would it be like for us in a month? In six months?

Instead of dwelling on that, though, I drifted back to the feeling of his arms around me. His hot breath on my hair. And with that, I fell asleep. And this time, I didn't dream.

When I woke up, the room was as it had been the night before. I was alone. Jenn wasn't there, but the sun was up. I blinked in the bright morning light, trying to determine what was different.

I didn't smell bacon.

Something was wrong.

I quickly showered, dressed, and clomped down the stairs. I slowed and quieted when I reached the lower landing. I knew everyone was in the kitchen; this time I knew because I was psychic, not because I could hear them. They were all silent as the grave. When I entered the kitchen I saw coffee mugs in most hands and an untouched plate of biscuits on the center island. The room was still so I hung back against the sink counter, watching and waiting to learn what was going on.

Jenn was on the couch; Casey and Izzy were near her. All three were concentrating so hard that beads of sweat formed on Jenn's forehead, trickling down her temples. She looked unsteady, like the bridesmaid at my cousin's wedding who locked her knees during the ceremony and passed out.

I shivered.

I'd seen Mina look worried before, but not Bill. Not like this. I was afraid to sneak over to get coffee. Breathing sounded too loud.

After what felt like hours, Casey broke the tension. He opened his eyes and looked straight at Mina. Izzy fluttered onto the armchair weakly and Jenn, who looked green for real, was guided over to lie on Justin's lap while he stroked her hair and fanned her face with a magazine.

Casey shook his head, "That's it. That's all. Just a plane."

Mina looked down and sighed. "It's okay. That's enough."

"No," Casey said, "that isn't." Jenn looked up at Casey with an odd mix of admiration and relief.

Mina looked at Jenn, worried, while Izzy agreed, "They know. They *all* know. Everyone on the flight knows. It isn't an accident." Her voice cracked on the last word. She cleared her throat, leaned back, and folded her hands on her stomach while closing her eyes, exhausted. Even her hair had wilted.

Mina looked back at Casey. He said, "I think that must be why this scared Jenn so badly. We've all seen disasters before, right?" He looked around the room as everyone nodded.

"Earthquakes, fires, trains, car breakdowns, buses with flat tires—even dead people pop up on our radar—but most of them are because of accidents. This was *not* an accident."

"It's bad," Izzy added, "I'm gonna be shaking for days."

Bill and Mina looked at each other. "All right then," Bill finally started, "we have a problem. Let's be systematic about this. Casey, what do we know for sure?"

"We know it's an airplane."

"What were people wearing?"

Casey's eyes looked blank for a moment, then snapped back. "Nothing to indicate a season, no shorts or sundresses, no coats or hats."

"That doesn't mean anything," Mina added. "The coats could be in the overhead."

"No turtlenecks," Izzy's eyes were closed. "It's not winter. The light is wrong for winter."

"Any old 70's clothes, or current . . . or too future-modern?" Bill asked. Izzy shook her head.

"Could be the Southern Hemisphere," Justin shrugged. Everyone groaned. "I'm just sayin'!"

"Okay, so we've got not summer, not winter, not long ago or far future, and . . . nothing else." Mina supported herself with the island counter as she sat down on a stool.

"And no one had a newspaper out," Izzy added. "I couldn't catch a date from anything. Not even a ticket."

"Isn't there someone we should tell?" Jenn whispered.

"Tell them what?" Bill asked. "That we think there's going to be a plane crash? That's hardly useful information." He was gentle when he said it, but Jenn looked hurt.

"Nor sane," Mina added. "Don't forget the Y2K thing. Everyone panicked and dumped tons of money into fixing a future problem that hadn't materialized yet. Then, when nothing bad happened everyone said, 'well, *that* was a waste!' rather than noticing that the problem never happened *because* it had been fixed!"

"Right." Bill paced. "If we go public with this, either people say you're lunatics right off the bat and do nothing, or we stop the crash and people say, 'What a bunch of lunatics! There wasn't any crash!' "

"Or, if we tell them and it happens, then they say we *caused* it," nodded Justin, speaking softly while watching Jenn. "It's jacked up." No one else moved. His words hung in the air.

I noticed the clock ticking. Birds were making a racket about some seeds they found in the back garden. A car honked at a guy turning left down on 7th Avenue. I didn't take my eyes from Casey. He was the steadiest person I knew, and if he was shaken . . .

"I say we get out." Casey's voice made us jump. "The city is crazy. We're not going to figure this out here. Let's get out to recenter Jennifer and make a plan. At least for the weekend."

"Stockbridge?" Jenn asked hopefully.

"No, it's too far and already too late. Just trying to return to the city on a Sunday night will be a four hour traffic jam, minimum . . . and that's only from the end of the Saw Mill." Bill shook his head.

"What if we come back on Monday night instead?" Casey asked.

"Miss school?" Justin was hopeful and helped Jenn to a sitting position, still stroking her hair to keep it off of her damp face.

"I'll call the school right now and leave a message for them to hear on Monday morning." Mina walked towards the hallway phone.

"What will you tell them?" Bill called after her, "It's nuts for the kids to have an unexcused absence on the third day of school."

Mina ducked her head back into the room, and for the first time that morning, I saw her eyes twinkle. "Who said they'll mark it unexcused?"

Bill clapped, "Okay! Saddle up, troops—grab a bag, toothbrush and underwear. Let's blow this 'Burgh!"

Everyone scrambled. Mina and Bill whispered together on their way out, but Casey, Jenn, and I hung back. I sat down where Justin had been and snagged Jenn's sleeve as she started to get up. Jenn relaxed back into the cushions. "Jenn, I'll pack for you. You stay here and rest," I said softly. "Any particular clothes you want me to grab?

"Thank you," her face was still pale. "I want something warm. It'll be cool up there."

"And she's been shivering all night." Casey knelt down and gently, visibly grounding himself, took her hand, rubbing it to warm her up. He watched her face closely and I felt my stomach twist. Ridiculous. They'd known each other longer than I'd known him. Envy was stupid, I told myself. "You sure you're strong enough for this drive?" he asked her. "We won't be there until after lunch and there aren't many places to stop on the Taconic."

"No, it'll be good. Knowing we're going to be up there instead of . . . I want to try to get away from the dream."

"Good enough. Do you want me to stay here while Rose packs for you? It won't take me two seconds to throw my own bag together."

Guys I thought, *have it so easy . . .*

Casey looked up at me and smiled, "Not in everything. Some things are pretty tough." I think he winked at me. Jenn agreed with him, though, so Casey settled in while I trotted up the stairs, pulled out my overnight bag and started packing. I did the same for Jenn, grabbing from the bathroom whatever toiletries I thought we might need, and heading back down to sit with Jenn while Casey packed.

Once Bill had retrieved the van from its recent opposite-side-of-the-street-parking exile, we all piled in and crept silently towards the Brooklyn Bridge, then up the FDR, over the Willis Avenue bridge, making our way up to the Deegan Expressway and New York Thruway, finally reaching the Taconic Parkway.

Once out of the city and onto the actual open road, I felt like I could breathe again. Casey noticed and nodded, smiling softly. The same thing had happened to me when we'd come up here last time. The Taconic was the first place I'd felt like I could see the sky. In Arizona, the sky is immense. And the sunsets? Spectacular. Maybe someday I'd drive the Taconic in the evening and get to see a real sunset in New York. Maybe we wouldn't be the people on the plane. Maybe I'd live long enough for one more really good sunset.

Casey put his hand next to my leg on the van seat—not touching me, just letting me know that he heard me. I looked over at him.

I'm sorry I can't hold your hand right now. I'm at the end of my endurance.

It's okay. I smiled weakly. I really wanted to feel his hand in mine.

No, it's not. I really want to. I want to feel . . . contact or a connection with someone else or . . . I'm not sure what. But I really want to touch you.

My stomach heard him. *I'd like that too. But I'm not . . .*

It's that after last night and this morning I don't have enough left . . . I don't think I can stop from hurting you. It's taking everything I've got to sit in the van with everyone.

You're just tired. Lean your head against the window and try to sleep. Get your hand-holding mojo back. I smiled.

What I was really looking for was a place to have Bill stop and get a coffee.

No. Sleep, Case.

Yeah, you're probably right. You're not going to be . . . bored if I sleep?

I almost laughed out loud, then thought *I've survived 14 hour West Coast car rides for almost two decades without you. As much as I love having you awake, I think I'll be fine.*

His eyes sparkled at me, or maybe it was the reflection of the morning sun. Either way, he looked dreamy. Forgetting all about the reason for our van trip, I leaned my head back against the seat and drifted off myself, with—I'm convinced—a big cheese-eating grin on my face.

46 PATTERNS

WE ARRIVED AT THE cabin a little after one o'clock, dumped our bags, and drove back into town to find some food.

"Alice's?" Jenn asked hopefully. Alice's Restaurant—the song-ified version of which Bill took to singing (in its entirety) each time we had set wheels on the Massachusetts Turnpike, except today—was a little too pricey for us.

"Too much," Mina shook her head.

Bill started humming the song then addressed part of our posse, "Boys who eat more than anyone even though you are skinny rails—?"

"Yes," answered Casey and Justin together.

"I'm thinking maybe we should drive up to Pittsfield to get lunch?"

We all shuffled back into the van and headed north to Friendly's which was open. As it was rather late in the lunch rush, they had no trouble finding tables for all of us. Our silence persisted through lunch. Justin brought a magazine inside to read while he was eating. I'd never seen someone do that when in this group. But, rather than getting miffed, we knew exactly why he was doing it. We all wished we'd thought of it too.

Lunch had no taste. The indoor lighting was enough to make me feel queasy. I'd slept fine in the car, no tortured dreams or anything, but the weight of everyone else's mood was souring my stomach. Re-grounding and shielding helped some, but it seemed that we were all crowding one another. Egon the Ghostbuster said to never cross the streams, but that's exactly what we were doing. Even Izzy was accidentally sending from time to time and though everyone's eyes were on their barely eaten plates of food, the psychic fracas made any concentration impossible. Casey sat across from me with Izzy, and Jenn sat between Justin and me. Every once in a while Casey looked up at me and smiled apologetically. I mirrored him and wondered if I should try to see Jenn's dream too. Everyone else had connected with her—well, maybe not Bill—and had seen the nightmare. I felt left out.

Don't do it. Casey sounded angry.

Why? I feel like I can't help her without seeing it.

It's a plane crash. Everyone knows they're going to crash. It's not pretty. Just stay away from it. He looked straight into my eyes, *Rose, it's not that you* can't *do it. It's that you'll feel it. You don't only see this one—you* experience *it. Like . . . You know how it feels when I zap you? Imagine that same thing but it's fear instead of love hitting you. Everyone on the plane is terrified and you . . . mainline that.*

Protecting, not patronizing? I sent back to him.

Yes. Your heart rate will change or you'll throw up or you'll be depressed for days or . . .

Casey would know this better than anyone. Jenn's dream must have been hell for her, and I was sure that even with the amount of psychic capacity she'd been concealing, she wasn't prepared for this.

Bill paid for everyone's food and we all slouched out to the van again. The light was heading down earlier in the day, now, letting me know that Autumn was definitely here and I was not in Arizona. Though the air was still warm in the sun, it was easy to tell that it was cooling off as our edge of the world prepared for night.

We headed back towards the Stockbridge Bowl and meandered down Lake Drive to our cabin again. All of our bags were still piled on the floor inside the front door. We each dug around to find our own; I grabbed Jenn's and my overnight bags and headed to our room. Casey caught my eye on the way upstairs.

Meet me outside.

I put the bags on our beds and headed back down the stairs. I passed Mina on my way and it had to be obvious that I was headed towards the door. She didn't bat an eye, but sort of waved me away.

Casey was waiting on the porch, hands in pockets. "The dock?" And he started walking.

I followed him down the path to the water and we walked out to the end of our little dock where we'd sat together before, forever ago.

"It's still here," I said, quietly.

"You thought it would be gone?" he asked as he sat down, keeping his shoes on.

"I dunno, Case." I sat next to him. "Doesn't it feel like everything has changed?"

"You mean today? Because of the dream?"

"Yeah. That and things are . . . different. It's like, I remember hearing adults say, 'don't try to grow up too fast,' which made no sense to me before." Casey smiled at me and looked at my hand. I regrounded and nodded as he took it and held it in both of his. "Now I'm thinking, *Oh,* this *is what they meant! This sucks. Everything is different now . . . Now we're . . . responsible!*"

"You weren't responsible before?" his glasses glittered in the dusky light.

"For me, sure. For other people? For people I don't even know? Everything since the motorcycle guy . . . naw, this is different."

"Maybe this is what the motorcycle guy was telling you. Get ready to feel responsible."

"Maybe." I changed the subject, "Pretty light on the water."

"Uh huh," He nodded and followed my gaze. "Brace yourself?" he asked, but I didn't have enough time. He released my hand with one of his and put that arm around my shoulder instead. While I was jolted a bit, it wasn't nearly as bad as before.

"Better?" he smiled without taking his eyes off the water. "I think the water helps. It's grounding you . . . and you're grounding me. Are you okay?"

"Yeah, I think I am . . . Is that why I have an easier time kissing you on this dock than anywhere else? The water?"

Now he looked at me. "Is that true?"

I nodded.

He kissed me suddenly, but not quickly. I had enough time to think that he was going to have to embarrass me by performing CPR right there on the dock.

Eventually Casey pulled away with a ridiculous grin on his face. He was staggering, with all of his geek-boy charm and Midwestern, solid, good looks. When he looked at me like that I wound up dizzy. He chuckled, "Geez, I wish I had a camera."

I punched him in the arm. He lolled over like a child's punching-bag clown and bounced back—and kissed me again. We both started laughing at the same time, lips still touching, which made me laugh harder. Then I snorted. Casey lost it and I folded myself over, trying to stop the tears from running down my face. He was curling into a fetal position and we laughed hard until the laugh became a chuckle and then a sigh. And then we were lying on our backs on the dock, holding hands and looking up at the sky.

"Feel better?" he asked.

"Mmhmm," I said.

"Me too."

The sky was changing color and the darkness of the sunset moved faster now that summer was done.

"I wish I was a painter," he said finally.

"Why?" I asked.

"I wish I knew how to capture color like that. The way the sky fades from one color blue into a completely different one. I'm always amazed. The sky can be thick with really heavy rain clouds and you can look at the sky and say, 'wow, it's gonna rain.' Or you can look at a sky that's the same—really thick with heavy rain clouds and say, 'oh hell, a tornado's coming!' It's all in the color. I think that's phenomenal."

"Wait, back up. I have no idea what you just said," I rolled to my side and supported my head on my hand so I could see him. "Why can you tell it's a tornado?"

"Haven't you ever been in one?"

I blinked at him.

"Oh. No tornados in Arizona?"

Blink. Blink.

"Okay, so you know what rain clouds look like."

Blink blink blink.

"Don't get annoyed." (Blink.) "When a tornado is coming the sky turns green."

I started to blink, then said, "Seriously? *Green?*"

"Yup. I have no idea why."

"Weird."

"Yup."

"Green green?"

"Dusty green."

I rolled onto my back again and saw that he'd been right. The sky was yet another shade of blue. I loved that. I loved this moment. I loved Casey. And then I remembered why we were on the dock.

"Do you think Jenn's going to be okay?"

"Oh sure. She'll sleep it off."

"You think? What if she has the same dream again?"

Casey was silent for a moment before becoming a professor again. "I don't think she will. I know I have no empirical reason to say that, but I don't believe she'll have *that* dream again. I think it's over. It's whether we can get her laughing enough before bedtime to get her to sleep. She's not a great sleeper to begin with and that dream . . . " he shuddered.

"She's a bad sleeper? For someone who didn't talk to any of these people until I came along you sure know a lot about them."

"I didn't have to talk *to* them to learn about them; I watched. I listened, when I was around. I didn't need to do much more than that."

Animals rustled in the trees behind us.

"You're quiet," he said finally.

"Yes. I'm *listening.*" He chuckled in the dusk. "My dad always told me I needed to listen more and talk less. I guess that's what he meant."

Casey nodded. "Your father is wise. I learn plenty."

"*And* you become an International Man of Mystery in the process."

"It's a nice byproduct, but not the main goal."

"You had a goal?" I asked.

"Nah. I suppose it's just the way I am."

I smiled at the sky. "We should get back. I don't think anyone knows we're here."

"They know," he said, but he started to get up anyway. "Maybe we should try to get everyone active tonight, maybe play a board game."

"Okay, but nothing that needs us to keep secrets or anything. You guys would be lousy to play *Taboo* with, or *Mastermind* or *Clue* or—"

He laughed, "I get the picture. C'mon." He stood and offered me his hand. I hesitated and he said, "It's okay. I'm back."

I took his hand and it was fine; very minor buzzing. We walked back to the cabin hand in hand. I was sorry when he let go at the doorway, but he was right. Now was not the time to let Mina and Bill see that Casey could touch me without me having a complete seizure.

Jenn wasn't downstairs but everyone else seemed to be—except Mina. "She went to the store," Casey whispered. I nodded, grabbed my backpack from next to the door and went over to a couch, slouched down, and following the lead of everyone else in the room, pulled my feet out of my shoes and put my heels on the coffee table. I took my knitting out, trying to concentrate on something other than how Casey made my heart dance.

We didn't really have dinner that night. Mina, wisely, bought snackish foods; hummus, naan, cheese, fruit, carrots—things we could grab and pick at with no real cooking involved.

I spent most of the evening knitting while playing a half-hearted game of Monopoly. I was continuing the shawl, transforming the wingtips and tails of my birds into a complex labyrinth. Life was complicated right now, and seeing my pattern grow helped me feel like I had some control.

Casey sat across from me, reading some huge tome when the game finally caved to disinterest. Jenn was lying next to me on the couch looking at the ceiling, but calm. Izzy was slowly flipping through her deck of tarot cards, but it didn't look like she was paying attention. Justin sat on the floor, swinging a pendulum over the coffee table. Every once in awhile Izzy would toss him a card and he'd hold the pendulum over it and shake his head. Bill had positioned himself on the window seat, trying to give us some space, I think, while whittling or something. Mina had gone to sleep early . . . or at least, she'd gone to the bedroom early. She had the worst job. She had to call the mothers and retroactively tell them where we were. Some would ask why. Since Mina and Bill weren't really our legal guardians, they had to clear every major move with our parents. Day-to-day things like going shopping for clothes or going into the city, that was fine. But when we came up here for summer Boot Camp—that got cleared by the 'rents. I guessed she must have done the calling when she went grocery shopping. I had no idea what she'd say to everyone. "One of the kids had a bad dream. We've left town. They'll miss the third day of school . . . but don't worry . . . " It would sound like crazy talk to an outsider.

Izzy sighed and flopped back in the chair. "Case, read us something. I don't care how boring you are. Just pick a place and start reading."

Casey sighed, turned back a few pages, then forward, then back, then began reading, "Okay, so this is an American guy in London. It starts with him walking around the city."

"Got it." Izzy said.

Casey started to read about "cross-section curves" and how the sidewalk-to-street curbs were sharp and vertical. While his voice continued, I watched the faces around me fade away into that slack, "I'm checking out, now," look. But Casey seemed to like the book, so I tried to attend. He went on about how the up-and-down-ness of the curbs when seen from the side might look totally random, even to a scientist, "'But if he had depth and ingenuity, it would be a different matter.'"

Casey took that moment to glance up. Everyone else looked like they were asleep. When he saw that my eyes were still on him he gave me a smile that would melt gold and kept going.

"' . . . Some deep part of the mind, adept at noticing patterns (or the existence of a pattern) would stir awake and frantically signal the dull quotidian parts of the brain to *keep looking* at the pile of—"

"Hold it." Izzy interrupted when my own eyes were starting to roll back in my head whether I wanted them to or not. "Hang on, Case. What's this about finding patterns?"

"It's about *Finding. Patterns.*" Casey looked scornfully over the top of his book. He needed reading glasses perched on his nose to really achieve the look he was going for.

Izzy glared at him, "No. I mean, 'say that in English, dopey.' Something in that blob of words is important. To us. Right now."

Casey stared at her for a moment, then looked back to his book.

"Well, I think it's that patterns are always there. That if you keep looking from different approaches to try to see the patterns . . . " Casey stopped and looked up.

"Or if a group tried . . . " Justin was leaning forward.

"Who else has been having disaster dreams?" Izzy asked. "I know I did earlier this summer . . . "

"Me too."

"Yep."

But none of us had seen the same thing.

None of us saw when anything took place.

We saw plane rides. We saw dark days. No one saw what Jenn did.

For the remainder of our time in Stockbridge and the journey home, we practically Venn diagrammed our dreams.

No one else mentioned hearing music, seeing vines, being stalked by comic-reading seatmates, or being haunted by motorcyclists.

We found no patterns.

Air

47 May You Live in Interesting Times

BACK IN BROOKLYN, TUESDAY morning was beautiful. Even better, I woke up looking forward to stepping outside to greet the chilly morning air. The sky was clear and blue—the way Arizona skies look after a rainstorm. We walked to the train together and something, the weather maybe, made me forget all about the bizarre weekend. Maybe it was the kiss Casey snuck me on our way out the door, but Jenn seemed to be buoyed by the feel in the air, too—and I'm pretty sure Casey didn't kiss her. Even Justin was in a good enough mood to surreptitiously play hopscotch with the sidewalk cracks as we left the house. I glanced back at the huge front window and saw Casey there, smiling at me. I walked backwards, grinning at him until he blended into a tree reflected on the glass.

The train traffic seemed lighter. Izzy thought it must have something to do with the election. "Maybe people are taking their kids to the polls and going to work late? There were a bunch of dads with kids out this morning walking towards the school."

"Dad used to do that with me," Jenn said. "I always loved the sound that handle makes when you finish voting."

Someone had left a *Daily News* on the seat next to me. It turned out to be yesterday's so I thumbed through it to see what we'd missed. Not much. No crashes, no accidents. Just lots about Giuliani, Bloomberg, and the election. I was starting to think our weekend run was silly, but seeing how Justin held Jenn's hand the entire train ride made me remember the implications of her dream. Once I let those thoughts start, they soured my stomach and I started feeling sick all over again—as though the weekend wasn't bad enough.

This time we didn't accidentally miss Rector Street. However, I skipped it on purpose.

"Going one more stop to the farmers' market," I said to Izzy. "Gotta get more bread."

"Carbivore," Izzy smiled a small smile as the train door closed behind her. I found my way up and over to the farmers' market, located my bakers, got my challah loaf, and headed back to the school. The rest of the group was skulking about outside, looking dour.

"Ready?" Justin asked as though I'd told him to wait—for hours.

"You didn't have to stay here," I apologized, following the stream of students and voters into the school.

The second I crossed the school threshold, it took all my effort not to get the phone out and call Casey. The music in my head slammed in, much louder than before, louder than the lobby noise. I closed my eyes, whacked the side of my head with the heel of my hand, but couldn't dislodge it. The elevator to the seventh floor didn't change things, either. I was back to "Take the A Train." No one else seemed to register that anything was wrong.

Izzy handed in our excuse note in the 7th floor office, then emerged and paused in front of the north stairwell—the "up" stairwell. "Let's take the other one," she said, and wheeled around. We trudged along compliantly in Izzy's wake as we headed to the south. Having her blue hair and chipper voice out in front meant people parted for us like we were in a pond with Moses leading our line. No one even grumbled that we were going the wrong way—and none of us were about to argue with Izzy's instincts.

"It's just lack of sleep," Justin said over his shoulder to me on the way up. "No one slept well this weekend."

I tugged his sleeve, "You can hear it?"

"What?" he looked confused, then shook his head. "Bread," he explained, "settles a no-sleep stomach."

"Oh, okay," I said, disappointed.

We reached the 12th floor without further traffic problems. Jenn, Izzy and Justin went into class. I followed them slowly, perched on my seat, and noticed Justin eyeing me.

"What?" I asked defensively.

He shrugged and wouldn't meet my eyes, "Did you get the bread?"

"Yeah, why?" I studied his face. "You want a piece?"

He paused before nodding. I pulled the bag of bread out of my backpack and didn't say another word as I handed it to him. He pulled off a chunk and closed his eyes, practically sucking on the fresh morning goodness.

Our teacher was sitting on the edge of his desk reading our note on top of his attendance book with Izzy in front of him. I wondered what Mina put on the excuse. *Absent due to Psychic Trauma* probably wouldn't fly. There was an assignment written on the board, so I pulled out my folder and knitting to help me percolate on the topic. The bell rang, Izzy sat down behind Justin, and Mr. Grayson told us to start writing, if we hadn't already, while he took attendance. Knitting to the lap, pencil to the paper.

The assignment was one of those personal inventories. You know, *what do you like, what do you hate, what's your favorite book*. But our teacher threw in a twist—no "to be" verbs. It was harder than it sounds and I was just getting into it when the world stopped.

Casey in my head yelled, *Stay!* and my head snapped up to look around for him.

Then I heard the soundtrack to an old World War II film, the whine those planes make as they're dogfighting and divebombing in the movies.

I looked at Mr. Grayson's face—he was looking out the windows.

So I looked out the windows, north, towards the skyscrapers.

A beautiful sky hung outside that window, a framed postcard picture beyond the shadow of the towers.

Then a plane, too low. Much, much too low.

They really shouldn't fly that low in a city with buildings this tall.

My eyes rattled.

Huge, heavy pieces scattered, arcing, falling, falling slowly, suspended in oil.

I heard things.

Far away, farther than screams, Casey's voice, *I'm coming to get you all, just stay put! Don't —*

There wasn't any air.

Don't *what?*

Casey?

Casey!

He's *here?*

I need to run. My hands are shaking. I need to find Casey, but I can't speak to tell Jenn.

I hear, "*Holy Sh . . .* " and we are all at the window to see. To look. To witness.

Paper shreds float down gracefully, caught by competing air currents.

"Look Mister . . . the paper's on fire . . . "

"Did the Yankees win?" a whisper.

"No . . . It's not . . . it's . . . they . . . haven't played the series yet . . . "

Mr. Grayson's radio clicks. Static first, then, " . . . commuter plane . . . accident . . . such a clear day . . . "

The teacher next door talks to Grayson in the doorway.

Quiet.

Serious.

Frowning adult eyebrows.

Creased foreheads.

Lips straight lines.

Eyes dark.

Shaking heads.

Nods.

Glances over shoulders.

Drifting paper.

Sparkling diamonds in the air.

Sirens far away.

Teacher's voices replaced by the intercom. "Don't worry . . . wait for instructions . . . safer inside . . . "

A noise in my head, like a fly buzzing. Then tinny Louis Armstrong again, just in my left ear.

Izzy's voice said, "Is this it, Jenn?"

Jenn frozen. Not blinking.

Take Jenn's hand.

Keep her calm.

Focus.

Ground her.

Ground her. Pull her back.

Grayson at the window tuning the radio. Sobs soft behind.

Jenn, Izzy, Justin, and I—surveillance camera eyes.

Watching.

Watching.

"Oh my God. Rose," Justin had picked my knitting off the floor where it must have landed when I jumped up. He had it spread over his desktop, stretched the way you need to stretch lace to see its pictures. "Rosie," he whispered insistently, now, "there's another plane."

We weren't looking at lace birds in the sky.

We were looking at the tower-wide central spines of my shawl with clouds and two huge plane-birds, at different heights, flying towards the center.

Justin is frozen.

"What?" I ask. He's looking in my eyes. He has lovely eyes. "Can you hear it too? The music," I said, "won't stop."

The building spoke: "No reason to panic ... listen for further ... "

"Jazz," his eyes are pooling water.

"I know," I whisper. We are anonymous. "I can't make the jazz stop."

"No," he croaks, pointing up to the unmolested tower. "*Jazz*."

Jazz?

"Take the A Train"?

Jazz!

Jazz*mine!*

"Where is Jasmine's office?" I'm holding on to the window frame. "Justin. Where. Is—"

He pointed again. Up.

"No." I shook my head. "No. I mean, where's Wall Street? You said she works on *Wall Street.*"

"It's *all* Wall Street, Rose," he says, pointing at everything outside the windows.

No! I hear myself, "No no no no no no no, Justin." My hands are on the sides of my head, holding it in.

Now my hands are flat against the window, my forehead pressing on the cool glass. *Casey,* I yell at him wherever. *Stop!*

I hear him, far away, *I'll get you as soon as I can. I've got to get to Jasmine first. She's waiting ...*

426

"Casey?" Justin, now next to me, whispers.

I point out the window, towards the street, buildings, church, towards City Hall and the Brooklyn Bridge.

"He's coming here?"

I nod.

"He can't go in," Justin clears his throat.

"I know." My voice is small and shakes more than I want it to.

We look out and down at a little chapel graveyard on the other side of a big black building. A little place across from the Borders. Its colors are bright and green and safe while everything else can only be seen through the haze of drifting burnt paper—gray and dangerous. I can hear the shuffling and crying around me fade out while I concentrate outside. Outside of myself.

Casey? Casey, you have to hear me. I know you're coming. You have to stop.

And then, sounding like he's yelling at me through one of those 1920s megaphones, I hear him again. *Stay inside, Rose. I'm past City Hall and almost there. I'll be able to get you soon!*

I shake my head and watch Justin focus on the tower. I know he's trying to get through to Jasmine. Then he turns. "Mister Grayson," Justin clears his throat again and pops back into the visible world, "Mister Grayson I think you should get everyone away from the windows."

"It's okay, Justin, it's only paper, now," Grayson points at the debris slowly meandering by the windows. I am already shoving people away from the glass.

"Now!" Justin yelled.

"Casey Stop!" I spin to see out, to stop him for real.

Justin yells, "Get back!" to me, to Casey, and to Jasmine—and everyone in the room.

I hold onto the window ledge and close my eyes, turning to focus every ounce of my intention on Casey. On sticking him to the spot. On rooting him to the sidewalk wherever he is. On grounding him so long and hard that he'd start to grow leaves. I hit him with everything I can muster to keep him from going into that building.

The shriek of another plane overhead shakes our world.

The building rocks around us.

The horrible slow motion dance again.

Chunks of building, twisted girders longer than Mina's house, desks, flames, glass—all pass our heads just outside the windows.

Flying east.

Flying down on office people running away and emergency crews running in. And the Farmers' Market. And Borders. All down below us. All down.

In silence.

No music.

A silent, falling, arching, aching, slow dance.

I look across the room at Izzy, Jenn.

Faces white. Not pale.

White.

But not gray.

I stand at the window with Justin. Splitting our world between Jazz who is gone, Casey who isn't anywhere, Izzy and Jenn who are frozen, and us.

Insignificant us.

We watch it all drifting around from what we thought was our invisible world.

"Rosie! Justin!" Grayson snapped, "Hallway! Now!"

Knocked from our failing anonymity, the worlds merge and we follow. Grab backpack, go to hallway, look around. Teachers closing blinds, ushering kids, hugging kids, remaining calm.

Tears.

Holding hands.

Then silence.

Then breathing.

Then questions.

"Miss—who did this?"

"Mister—what happened?"

"Are we gonna . . . die?"

Teachers answered.

Carefully.

"Well," lady teacher said, "I think it's probably the same guys who did 1993 . . ."

"Planes were . . . what? . . . hijacked probably?" He shrugged.

"You think, Mister? Really?"

"What else could it be?" she said.

"Yeah, yeah . . . no doubt . . ."

Lady teacher said quietly to Grayson, "Strange. They didn't demand anything . . . they just . . . crashed."

"Miss, this is messed up . . ."

"But," they both said to the hallway full of students, "but we're fine, okay? We're *fine*. The principal's in touch with the Supe's office? They're in touch with the mayor. He's in touch with the governor, got it? So don't worry. You're safe."

They lied.

They didn't know anything.

We knew more than them.

Not by much.

Behind them, Justin and I could hear Grayson mutter, "You really believe that crap?"

"No," she said, hiding her mouth, "but keeping them calm is more important right now ... maybe?"

Cell phones out.

No signal.

Didn't stop trying.

One caller in tears, connecting.

A mother.

An aunt.

A grandma.

A sister.

The building spoke again, "—South Stairwell, that is *Stairwell B*—do *not* leave your floor until cleared ... starting at the top ... Be patient. You are safe ... *turn right* and head south to Battery Park. *Do not* turn left or go north ...."

We sat and waited.

Good kids.

Good little scared kids.

The north stairwell door opened and two men walked towards us. The AP we'd met the first day stayed and spoke to Mr. Grayson, but the Dean started moving us off the floor.

"C'mon, move out!" He smiled. Sort of. "Turn *right* ... If you get caught going north or ... "

He pushed us ahead efficiently.

"I'm taking *roll* when we get to the park!" called the lady teacher in front of us. One of her kids laughed. Sort of.

She trailed her students down the stairs.

Wait your turn.

Silence.

New noises from rooms and windows.

Calm stairwell.

Quiet kids down all twelve floors to the street.

The fire doors held open by teachers.

We blinked.

Wrong to be this bright.

Wrong for this to happen on a beautiful day.

Just wrong.

I shook it off. I had to turn left. I had to go north towards the craziness.

Casey was there.

I pushed to the left and was pulled back.

"Are you high? We go this way."

"Justin, Casey's out there. I have to go—"

"You have to not die, girl."

I pulled my arm out of his grip. "I *have* to get Casey."

"You think he's going to want you to walk into that?" He held my shoulders and turned me, keeping a firm hold. "You think he would forgive me for letting you walk into that?" I looked towards the north and watched. Watching made the color wash away and drain out of the towers. The trees had turned gray. Borders was gray. Then the whole scene flickered like a silent film and the color returned.

"You're staying with me. Casey is a big boy—stronger than any of us— and I'm not lettin' you die. The hell I'm going to face him with that on my hands."

"Justin . . . I *grounded* him."

"Good, then he has half a chance."

I twisted out of his grip and started jogging north. I could hear voices, angry, aimed at me. But I had to get to Casey. I had to take him with us. Shoulders bumped into me, the salmon in the stream of scared faces. It wasn't far. I knew if I ran I could—

Pulled back, spun around. Hear the slap before you feel it.

"Rose!" Justin. Angry. "Rose! You are coming *with me*. This isn't the end. Do you see?" He pointed my chin at the farmers' market, now in view. "Do you see anyone there at all? No you do not. Because they're not stupid. And they're not dead. They're all going to live. Casey will be fine and you will be, too, if you come with me."

"You hit me."

"And I'll do worse if you don't move it."

"Justin, you don't get it." I struggled as he pulled my backpack strap to get me to move towards Jenn and Izzy, waiting. "Justin, listen to me. Casey *won't* get out. He can't. I grounded him there. All these people are running past him and they're scared and he'll soak it all in and he won't be able to get away."

"Rose, the man blocks like a champ. Right now we have to get Jenn and Izzy out of here. He would *want* us to get them out of here."

And he put one of my hands in Jenn's and held tight to the other, dragging me south.

48 SALMON

THERE WERE SCREAMS, THEN popping.

There was popping, a rumble, then screams.

And shoving.

And a louder rumble-roar like Hell was here and not happy.

And people pushed.

And Justin clawed at me, trying to keep contact. I had a second—less—to look and say, "Sorry," before I turned and ran.

North.

Who runs towards collapsing, burning buildings and disasters? Firemen, the police—and stupid people like me.

Casey was there, stuck because I'd grounded him, and I'd be damned if I wasn't going to go get him. If his body wasn't crushed, his mind would be unless I could get him out of there.

Casey? I tried to locate him him, find a way to release him, listen harder for him as it became impossible to see. *Casey?*

The street was a mosh pit of shoulders and noise and sweat and panic. Arms reached out to me, to stop me, to turn me, but I dodged, I ducked, I struggled. I got myself to the ancient stone retaining wall next to the churchyard across from school and I slid north along it by feel—out of the way of the main throng.

Justin, Jenn, and Izzy would be fine together, I told myself.

Casey wouldn't be.

Not after what I did to him. Not after I forced him to stand there and take this, all of this.

The ash was everywhere.

The roar hadn't finished before the darkness rolled in. Predatory and dank, roiling clouds of concrete and debris pushed over us, choking us, blinding us.

The waves of runners continued on and I stopped, feeling along the wall for any information.

An edge.

A doorway alcove.

I hugged it, pressing into the space, turning away from the sounds and the ash and the crazy wrong world I'd wandered into today.

I wanted to take a deep breath to calm and ground myself against the feelings in my stomach and the ache in my head but didn't dare. I hadn't breathed in awhile and fumbled around my neck. I had a polo on and pulled it up and over my nose and mouth, gingerly testing it's use as a filter.

My eyes remained closed, though. I couldn't shake the image of Indy yelling, "Don't look, Marian!" while the Ark's contents spewed around them.

I didn't want to look.

I didn't want to think.

Now that I could breathe a little through my shirt I could start to pull my shields up and as they came up, I saw a red line.

Saw is usually the wrong word in these moments. My eyes were tightly shut, and I don't have visions.

But there it was, a red line, glowing and leading from me, out of the alcove, and heading north.

Follow the thread.

The bracelet on my wrist led out and away from me.

Towards Casey?

Follow the thread!

So I did.

I didn't have to use my eyes.

I only had to follow the thread.

Right hand out on the building, left hand keeping the shirt over my nose; keeping myself grounded, centered, and shielded as much as possible, I moved north again. Focusing on Casey, following the glowing red line that connected us.

The fingertips of my right hand grazed wall, then window glass, then nothing.

I had to cross a street.

Preparing to let go of the only solid thing in my world—the wall—forced me to focus outward more. Things were still rumbling and creaking and screaming on my left begging me to look, but I won't open my eyes. Open your eyes and you're dead. Open your eyes and you won't see the cord. The gray air continued to coat my skin. It stung and burned and itched but I couldn't pay attention to it. I reached way down, connected myself with the core of the earth —as much as was possible when the earth was as scarred as it was now—and stepped forward.

With my eyes closed the human side of me wanted to shuffle along safely, but everything else in me screamed to get to Casey as quickly as possible.

I took a step.

Then another.

Then another.

Then I put my foot out and hesitated. In my mind's eye, the pulsing red cord sloped down and got darker. I let my foot fall slowly this time and it kept going down, past the level of the ground.

I was walking off the curb.

I knew where I was, now. Liberty Park with the statue of the Briefcase Man, was on my right. A big building with a Brooks Brothers was coming up next, after the park, and had a low wall, at least at the corner, that I could use to guide me. The parking lot with the farmers' market—or the place where the farmers' market had been minutes ago—was on my left with all the sounds I was not going to pay attention to.

Off the curb and onto the street I focused more on the brightness of my red cord. A darker red cord meant step down, a brighter red cord meant step up and the further I went the more it became a contour map for my feet to follow. I wasn't going to think about what I was stepping on or over or just how much this wasn't flat sidewalk and road I was crossing. Instead, I made it across the street and by the time I got to the retaining wall in front of the Brooks Brothers shop I wondered if I would ever need my eyes again. The red thread was lighting my way and I was able to "see" dark gray shapes beyond what the red pulse was showing me. I could tell that the wall was about to stop and stairs were going to start. I could tell that I was going to have to climb over something pretty big that shouldn't be on a sidewalk in a few more steps.

I could tell that I had a long way to go.

If it hadn't been for the choking dust and ash I might have reached my goal sooner, but between the blown-sideways cars, the chunks of building on the street, the thick, slippery powder covering everything, and my inability to breathe, I wasn't quick. More than once I came close to another person, moving along like a snail through the wasteland. The first one I encountered was inching along, hugging a building like I had been doing, one hand on wall, one over mouth. I almost called out. Almost.

I had to get to Casey.

I was able to move pretty quickly past the Century 21 store—its long smooth wall was easy to follow. The few times I went too fast and caught my toe on the rubble I was able to stop myself by falling against it instead of onto the jagged ground. Subway entrances were to my left. I could tell by the holes that appeared deep and dark and I nearly dropped my shirt when one of them rasped, "Help? Someone? Help. Help me find my daughter?"

"What?" I managed through my shirt, mouth tasting like the inside of a rock.

"My daughter. I can't find my daughter. She was with me, then . . . "

I started to walk towards her but moving off my path made the red thread die out and I could see nothing again. Focusing on Casey, the cord pulsed brighter and I could see.

"I can't. I have to save someone. But I see others heading this way. I'll tell them."

"Thank you," she sobbed. "She was right . . . she was here . . . " I could tell she was leaning against the stairway wall, staring at her hand.

I kept going and found that the people I thought I'd sensed were just pillars of debris that had landed close to my glowing red cord.

The smooth wall ended. I crossed another street to a hotel entrance which was trickier to get past. There were more iron stairway railings, more open space. Then someone appeared from inside. He was tall, dark, less fuzzy looking, which may just be that he was cleaner than I was.

"Hello?" I called. "There's a woman . . . "

"What?" He choked and pulled at his shirt to get it over his mouth.

"There's a woman. Back in the subway. Needs help."

"Everyone does."

"No, she lost her daughter. A kid."

"Oh God."

"I couldn't . . . I have to get . . . "

"No, it's okay. See? Radio . . . I can . . . " Click. Static. "I'll go see," he called and headed back where I'd come from.

And then I was at the graveyard behind the little chapel. The place I thought Casey was when I grounded him.

"Case?" I started to call softly.

I heard creaking metal and sirens and crying.

"Casey?"

I could "see" more now, more real light was out there beyond my eyelids. I was pretty certain I could have opened my eyes all the way awhile ago, but I hadn't. I was afraid of what was going to get into my eyes if I did. I wished I had a bottle of water or something to wash off with. The closer I got to Casey the more I noticed the stuff on my skin, in my ears, down my back. So I was going to have to stop thinking like that and focus, instead, on finding him.

I tried to peek out of squinting eyes, "Casey?" I called louder.

Coughing answered me.

"Casey?" I screamed. "Where are you?"

More coughing then a barely audible, "Rose?"

"Oh my God. Casey? Where are you?"

"Rose? . . . Rose . . . " his voice was weak and indistinct.

I tried to call again, but in order to say anything I had to inhale and got a mouthful of dust. Shapes resolved themselves out of the haze, and my eyes opened on their own. The dusky light was enough to see by, now, and more people drifted by. I could hear voices, "You okay . . . You okay? . . . You okay? . . . " others crying, others talking quietly to each other. My red thread was still my compass, so I clamped my watering eyes and kept moving in that direction.

"You okay?"

The voice was in front of me and something cold was pressed onto my hand.

"I'm—" I looked down at the water bottle being pushed at me.

"My boss said . . . " he shrugged over his shoulder to a Duane Reade across from the chapel.

"Oh." He turned to move onto the next needy person. "Thank you—a . . . another?" I reached for his sleeve and watched ash puff off of my arm. He turned back, "A friend."

"Sure. They're heavy."

"Thanks." I pulled the hem of my shirt up and deposited more bottles there. I turned back in the murky light towards where I hoped I'd find Casey. I called again and nearly tripped on him, huddled on the ground up against the railings of the chapel graveyard.

"Casey?" I was afraid to touch him.

"You—"

"Yes, it's me. I'm here."

"Rose . . . took . . . "

"What? I can't hear you very well, Case."

"Took . . . long enough," he croaked.

I laughed and cried and opened a water bottle and found his hands and helped get it to his lips. He finished it and I helped him with a second, then drank myself from the third.

He coughed more. I couldn't see if his eyes were open or not. His glasses were coated with ash.

"They came . . . "

"I know they did. I'm so sorry. I didn't know—"

"They all . . . " he faded out.

"Casey," I said. "*Casey?*"

He roused and rasped, "Jasmine?"

I couldn't say anything or I knew I'd start to cry, but I started to cry anyway.

"I know."

"Jasmine . . . gray . . . "

"I know. We tried . . . I have to get you out of here, Case."

"Gray and . . . called . . . "

"I need to move you, Case."

"Can't."

"Sure I can, Casey, I'm strong—"

"Can't move . . . can't move feet . . . "

"I know. That was me. I can . . . hang on . . . " I went deep and found the place where I'd locked him to the earth to keep him from running into the building that would have killed him. I cut the connection, opened my eyes to smile at this guy I was so in love with and instead of seeing his smiling face in the brightening world I saw him slumped against the railings. Not breathing.

49 AFTER

THURSDAY I WOKE UP, brain fog lifting, sad, angry, but more normal.

Which wasn't necessarily good.

It was another beautiful day, which didn't help. Today I could recognize people and I watched Jenn and Izzy surface every once in a while. Justin was unchanged—in flashes I remembered that we worked together pretty well on Tuesday—until I ran away. I sat near him in his room with his TV on most of the day, and was surprised to find it so easy. We had a little chat about my leaving him and running north, but in hindsight he agreed I did what I had to do to get to Casey. And that he would have done the same if he were me.

And where was Casey?

Casey was missing.

Bill was missing.

Yesterday, I couldn't argue.

Today I could.

"Mina, where is he? The medics said St Vincent's when they took him from me. I should be there. You know he's better when he's with me—he might come-to if I'm there. You know it will help him to have me with him."

"All I know," said Mina, her eyes red-rimmed and bloodshot as she made lunch for everyone, again, "is that you found him. You roused him. You got him to safety. Beyond that I only know what Bill is telling me. And Bill and Casey are not here. Period. Not even you can change that. *Finis.*"

"No! I see your face. You know where they are. I can't—" I swallowed, "I can't feel him Mina. Tell me where they are."

She shook her head, "No. Don't make this sound bigger than it is. You were never able to feel him in the house—"

"But I couldn't feel him *out there*, either!" I pointed emphatically nowhere. "Not after—"

"Stop asking, Rose," Mina begged. "When you *can* talk to him, you *will*. Bill knows how you feel. He knows what you can do. You got Casey out. That was great. Now you have to trust Bill. Don't look at me like that. Please, drop this until Bill thinks Casey is ready."

I thought about—then started to worry about—barbecuing the house and all in it, so I went and sulked on the window seat with my journal. The hell I was going to knit. I tried to breathe and remind myself to cut Mina some slack. She'd been taking care of all of us since we got home on Tuesday. Plus she'd just watched the whole event happen to her daughter, and Jenn wasn't one hundred percent yet. At least those were the reasonable things I told myself while I breathed.

I had to see Casey. It was ripping my heart from my chest not to see him. Not to know he was okay.

So.

Breathe.

Breathe. Focus on the light outside. Focus on breathing. In through the nose, out through the . . . The light slanted differently in the fall and made the backyard even prettier. Everything was softer in the light. Or the ash cloud worked like a lens filter for the sun light. The sun, the ash, the sun fading through the ash on Tuesday, letting us know we were alive. The ash. The ash coated the trees in the backyard. How long would it take to clean. How long—

The phone rang. It was Mom. She was worried yada yada yada. I tried to sound unbroken and strong even though I wanted to yell and make her force Aunt Mina to tell me where Casey was. I could tell that she was keeping something from me, though, all through the conversation. I wondered if Mina had told her about me and Casey? Then I started to wonder if she knew about Jazz, that she felt bad but didn't know what to say. Whatever it was, a phone call can only last so long and then it was back to the void.

Everyone continued doing what they had done all morning: nothing. Jenn had moved down to watch TV with Izzy and Justin in his room. Justin was pretty much holding Izzy up. She wasn't back yet. We'd all tried to help her, give her shield backup, but we were weaker, too. Mostly she slept, which I suppose was the best thing she could do. Standing in the doorway, watching them watch-not-watch TV with the zombie faces we all shared, I wasn't sure how good it was for any of us, but none of us could stop looking. Crack for the recently traumatized. Every once in awhile one of us would get up to go check the Web on my laptop to see if new information was there.

It wasn't.

Aunt Mina was making something for lunch that smelled spectacular, but it didn't seem to rouse us at all.

"Soup's on," she called up, finally, her voice flat. She put out matzo ball soup in a tureen, fresh chocolate chip cookies, tiny spinach and cheese puffs, and a pitcher of iced tea. "The tea is especially good."

Obediently we filled plates and bowls and meandered, converging on the dining room table.

"I miss opening the windows," Justin complained. "It looks beautiful out."

I looked out the front, "Why can't we?"

"Smell," he said shrugging, and looked down at the soup he wasn't eating.

"I thought the . . . smell had calmed down," I said, more of a question

443

than a statement.

"I went out and sat on the stoop this morning."

"Oh."

"How long," I cleared my throat, "How long do you think it's going to keep burning?"

Jenn never took her eyes from her soup. "For awhile," she said finally. "There's a lot there to burn. Not just building stuff but desks and computers and carpet—"

"And people," Izzy broke in. It was the first connected, spoken word I'd heard from her since Tuesday.

"Yeah," Justin was quiet. "But there aren't as many as we thought at first, are there, Iz? Giuliani keeps taking the number *down*. That's good. Most of the people got out?" It was a question.

We sat there, looking at our soup. If it had color we couldn't tell. Or didn't notice.

"Eat!" we heard from the stairwell as Mina went by.

Mechanically we all picked up our spoons and took a sip of the broth. Then another. Then more.

Justin chuckled, "Hedgewitch."

"Jewish penicillin," I smiled.

"Sooooup," Jenn added. Izzy was still gone, but at least she was sipping the broth.

"How long you think school's gonna be closed for?" Jenn asked me quietly, taking a pull of her tea.

"I'm not sure," I said, "I can't really see much of anything." Jenn put her spoon down and looked at me.

"Well, that's a first," Justin sounded like his old self.

"Look, I know I'm supposed to be able to see more futures or whatever, but it's like no one knows what to do next, so right now the future looks . . . like an old TV set, all fuzzy and black and white and not tuned-in."

"How is the school?" Izzy surfaced for a moment but went away again before anyone could answer.

Justin looked at me and shrugged, "You seen it?"

"I tried. Last night I tried to go look."

Jenn nodded. "Justin?" Jenn's voice was so quiet, "Is Izzy . . . "

"She can hear you, Jenn, but she's not focusing here much."

"What's happening to her. I mean, have you two heard or, you know, seen anything?" I asked.

"She sees dead people, Rosie. It's not good."

"I know that, but has she," my stomach felt funny, "has she wound up channeling . . . like she did for me on the lake?"

Justin looked up. "No," he said carefully. "She's been visited, but no one's pushed through. Not like that. Mostly they seem to be trying to figure out what happened." Justin changed his tone, "And how you holdin' up, Weej?" He nudged me with his elbow. "You just get to New York and buildings start falling on you. You gettin' a complex yet?"

"Not yet, but if you keep bringing it up I will," I said.

"What're you looking at?" Justin said to Jenn. "The girl can take a joke."

Jenn paused then shook her head, "Nothing . . . it's nothing. Eat up. Mom wants to talk to us." Hopeful for news about Casey, I nodded and finished my soup, carried Izzy's and my dishes back, and put another spinach puff on my tongue as I rinsed and placed the dishes in the dishwasher. I knew we were supposed to be taking turns cooking and cleaning, but Mina had been doing it all since the buildings fell. I promised myself I'd help more that night.

Like magnets we all homed in on the front sitting room, sliding into place silently. Aunt Mina rotated a comfy chair to face us, then settled into it.

"I know," she started, after a pause, "that you—that all of us—have been hit hard by this. Everyone has. The city. Everyone. But more than ever, we have to shield and ground ourselves. Bill and I knew you all were susceptible to receiving, no—," she shook her head, leaned forward balancing her elbows on her knees and her head in her hand, "to being inundated by any trauma, but this is so far beyond anything we ever imagined."

"Or saw," Justin added.

"Or saw," Mina agreed. "Thank you. Yes. So, I thought it might be good, instead of watching TV, for you to talk a little. Get it out. Push it away from you, push it at me if you need to, just so you have room to breathe again. I worry that not talking is hurting you more."

We all nodded, but no one spoke.

Finally Mina nodded at Justin. "You start?"

He paused, then nodded, "I think the first thing we all thought when it started was, 'It's Jenn's dream.'"

I nodded. "That was when we were still in class?"

"When I saw your knitting," Justin agreed. My stomach clenched.

"Your knitting?" Mina looked at me.

"It dropped and Justin picked it up for me just before the plane hit."

"Did you see the plane come in?" Mina asked.

"I think our teacher did," I said, relieved Mina didn't ask more about my lace. "He was sitting in front of the class, looking out the window for the first one."

"We heard it, though," Justin said. "Both of them. Like sitting on a runway—that loud."

Mina nodded. "How did you know what to do?"

We told her about our evacuation and separation, how they boarded a ferry boat and escaped to New Jersey and eventually got a train back. How I'd walked back with the hordes across the bridge after finding and then losing Casey to a team of paramedics. And it sounded just like that. Like a four-year-old telling a story on autopilot.

"Well," Jenn said, finally, "my dream makes sense now."

We all nodded, remembering, when something hijacked my mind. Just like the first day when Mina flipped through my memories like so many index cards, someone—or something—was digging through my past. Images appeared before my eyes.

"Rose, what's wrong?"

Voices came to me underwater. Something was shaking me, but I didn't care. I was watching scene after scene of me, on the plane, flying in to New York, knitting, dreaming. Over and over I saw myself knitting to stay calm, pushing everything bad out of me and through the needles. I saw Jasmine admiring my shawl and I saw the thing that never happened—the thing that was supposed to happen. I saw us spread out and look at the completed shawl and see it for the warning—for the omen—that it was.

No wonder Delphi hissed.

My dream planes never crashed, like Jenn's, but the last image I saw was of Oracle Road, back in Tucson, where a motorcyclist in a white helmet was sprawled on the pavement next to an earlier wreck. His head was at an unnatural angle to his torso, and the ambulance radio was playing *La Vie en Rose*.

I knew who'd just grabbed my dream memories, and my should-have-been-memories, and shoved them in my face.

I buried my fists in my eyes, trying to see stars instead of motorcycles.

"Rose. *Rose!*" I heard Mina's voice, but it was still far away. When I tried to look for her, everything was blurry. Shapes and light and little else.

Someone shook me.

Then someone slapped me.

My eyes cleared and I saw Justin, looking at me, scared, with everyone else looking at him, mouths open.

Justin stood back up. "It works in movies." He shrugged.

"Worked here too," I said, rubbing my cheek. "That's two I owe you."

He shrugged and tried not to smile. "We can negotiate the equation between you throwing me and my slaps later."

Mina insisted, "What did you see, Rose. Where did you go? I couldn't follow you."

"I should have known." My eyes burned.

"Everyone feels that way—"

"No. Mina. *I* should have known." I looked at Jenn and Justin and Izzy, desperate. "The motorcycle guy. Remember? He's been trying to tell me for months."

"How?" Izzy asked, surprising all of us.

"Remember when were in Stockbridge, and trying to see if we'd been receiving patterns? I was. I was getting patterns."

"But we all talked—" Jenn said.

"Yeah, and what did I say? I said I'd had a few dreams, but it was only the airplane I flew here on."

"So?"

"But it wasn't just *dreams*. It was jazz music and the shawl, the shawl that was supposed to be for . . . So, something was always wrong on the planes in my dreams. Creepy angry guys. Every time. And we were heading towards the city. And the big buildings were always too close. I could see the faces of people in the buildings. If I'd finished the shawl . . . "

I heard the clock ticking.

Justin's stomach growled.

Far away I heard a siren. A shiver ran down my arms.

Finally Mina spoke up, gentle and quiet, "Rose, I know that you feel awful and that everything is . . . everything feels wrong for the entire city, probably the country. But I also know that you can't put this burden on yourself. You just can't. No one knew."

"I did."

"No, you didn't. Or more to the point, Rose, what could you have done?"

"I could have saved—"

"We all want to feel that way, Rose," Justin interrupted.

"I should have known not to go into the city on Tuesday. And I'm supposed to be ready, right?"

"I suppose we all should have known not to go in," Jenn said.

"But wasn't that the Motorcycle Guy's point? I was supposed to have stopped this. I can tug on the future. If I'd realized and we hadn't gone in—"

"That's expecting a little much of yourself, Rose?"

"I saw the plane," I couldn't speak aloud that I should have at least known Jasmine was going to die. That Louis Armstrong, the great jazz musician, had tried to save her. That Casey and the Motorcycle Guy had been telling me to follow the thread. That the thread was the shawl and the music and the music was Jazz, and if I had just connected my dreams and my knitting and the jazz I would have stopped Casey from running into the city because Jasmine wouldn't have gone to work that day because I would have warned her.

But I couldn't say that.

"I think," Mina started carefully, "I think that if we could have done anything to stop this, we would have seen it coming more specifically. In many ways, you were saved from the torture of living with knowledge but being powerless."

"I knew." Jenn said. "My dream. I knew and I *was* powerless."

"We all had dreams, Jenn . . . " Justin's voice was weak, "but none of us saw this pattern . . . it's on all of us, Rose. Not just you. We all should have known."

I started to try to speak, but Mina interrupted. "No." She was firm. "You all saw A Disaster. But no one—no one saw *this;* no one could predict *this*. If anyone could have imagined something so heinous you would have seen it in one of those awful action movies. This was twisted and sick, designed by twisted and sick minds."

"If I'd seen enough, I could have gone to Boston and stopped those guys from getting on the plane," Justin countered, getting roped into my energy.

"Now you?" Mina said, "Really, you think you could have stopped them from doing this?" She was escalating, too. "This was in the works for a long, long time, and not on a human scale, on a *political* scale. None of you are tuned in to that. You're still . . . you are all still learning. It's like," she fished around, "it's like trying to control a slot machine. There are too many moving pieces. Not even Casey," I flinched, "*Not even Casey* could have tracked this. Obviously. So, Justin, what would you have done? Body-blocked them? Tripped them? Glamoured them and stolen their passports? I'm very, very serious when I say *There Was Nothing You Could Have Done.*"

"But the motorcycle guy said—"

"Izzy," Mina cut me off gently, "didn't you show me the construction workers in New Jersey?" The blue head nodded weakly, eyes still down. "I don't know if she showed the rest of you—I'm not sure how much you've been talking to each other while you're watching TV—Isobel, sweetie, could I relay to show them or . . . ?" Mina reached out and held Izzy's hand.

Izzy inhaled like an oyster diver coming up for air and Mina projected:

Izzy is outside the office building in New Jersey looking for more of our teachers by the place where the ferry came in, the place with the wooden wall with the Mike Mulligan holes you can look through. There is a construction guy standing there, too, shaking. He says they were all up on the building they were working on behind that fence, and they saw the first plane go in. They all panicked . . . calling the cops. Calling 911. Calling the FBI. Calling their pastors. No one got through, mostly. Then he shakes his head and tells her that they saw the second plane fly down the river . . . and they knew. They knew it wasn't just any plane; it was a Second Plane. They all start dialing again, but this time to prevent, not to rescue. The construction guy says he got through to the Feds. All the guys are screaming on their phones to get the people out while they watched the second plane bank and turn over Staten Island . . . and then they watched it go in. They couldn't do anything but watch.

We were all silent. Aunt Mina's point was clear, but it didn't make us feel any better.

"*I* could have helped," I said stubbornly. "I was *supposed* to help. If I'd paid more attention and learned more . . . The motorcycle guy said I was supposed to be ready. I could . . . I could *still* help. I can find things. That's something I can do. I should go down there and help . . . and help *find* people."

The entire room—the whole house—held its breath.

Then Mina said softly, "Rose, honey. There's no one to find."

My sobs surprised me. Justin put his arm around my shoulder and I wept into his chest like a baby.

I cried for the first time since the ash fell.

50 On the Road Again

THE GREEN AND BROWN blurred past me. I wondered, somewhere in the back of my mind, I wondered why I wasn't carsick.

"You doin' okay, Rose?"

Dad was far away, far away in the front seat, driving me away.

Away from danger, he said.

I hurt. My stomach. My head.

Don't think.

My cheeks were warm and clean and wet.

"Let her go, Dad." It sounded like Chloe. The back of the head in the seat in front of me looked like Chloe. But Chloe hates me. The green and brown spun past my eyes. Count the white blips. Again and again and again and again and again and—

Thursday night.

2 a.m.

The rain smelled wrong during the storm. Lightning flashes outside the windows revealed the shocking green of early September in Brooklyn, the beautiful, turbulent sky, and the stain of smoke drifting over the East River onto us.

And the smell.

Always the smell.

The rain smelled wrong.

It smelled like ash.

I noticed the smell before I heard the screams.

Casey was screaming.

Screaming and insane and terrified.

My heart scrambled out of my chest before I was fully awake. The house was absolutely silent. All I could hear was my quick breath and my pounding heart. Jenn sighed and turned over in her bed. Casey wasn't here. Casey wasn't anywhere I knew. He wasn't anywhere I could reach him.

He needed me. That much I was sure of. With his screams echoing in my head, I focused for a long time, trying to suss out what I could do. Finally I arrived at, *well, if I can't be with him, and I can't find him, then at least I can create how I want to help in my head. Make a picture of what I want, and let the universe take it from there.* Jenn, my happy-thoughts guru, might even be okay with that decision. So I imagined Casey resting peacefully on his bed. I imagined me in the chair next to him, holding his hand. I wanted to purge the bad. I did what I thought Justin would do—I went deep, pushing blue-green healing light through his soul, pulling the bad with me when I moved on. Every place he tried to hide himself, every frightened corner, I pushed and forced my way in, trying to take the worst of it all and force it down, and out, and away from him.

Brillo and Clorox.

I thought, *I'm sorry. Casey, I'm here. I'm here with you. We're here and it's going to be okay.*

Eventually I slept again, feeling a tiny bit satisfied, like maybe I'd actually done something.

The green-brown blur was taking me away.

All wrong.

Very, very wrong.

Chloe and my Dad were talking about me. I think. I don't care. An air horn could not have made me pay attention.

My mind was far away.

Far from here.

By Friday morning, something that had been banging around the inside of my mind for a full day, demanded attention. I couldn't really talk to Jenn, she wasn't fully returned. Izzy was out of the question, and Mina would think I was asking for something else entirely.

"Justin," I stood in his doorway, "Justin, did the people in the Towers— did they *all* find Izzy?"

"What do you mean?"

"I mean, is she still checked out because thousands of dead people, like, broadsided her?"

"Kind of, yeah."

"Oh God," I had to fight nausea. It *was* as bad as I thought.

"What?"

"I made him stay there, Justin."

"English, girl."

"When I stopped Casey, I was trying to keep him out of the buildings. I was trying to keep him back, so the falling glass and desks and . . . stuff wouldn't hit him."

"Good! Then you saved him."

"No, Justin," I was crying in front of him and I didn't care, "Justin I . . . It's exactly the thing he can't handle. It's what Bill had been worried about. I made him stand there and take it, take in all those souls . . . When I tried to disengage him so I could move him, he stopped breathing. Not for long, but enough. He couldn't take it.

Justin, I killed him."

I thought the rocks we passed were pretty. Some gap. Some river. Pretty rock. Almost like home. Almost like the West. *That* home.

But I won't be home there. Not now. Casey's not there. Everything was wrong. I shouldn't be in a car. The car isn't safe. What state is this? Is this New Jersey? Everyone says New Jersey isn't safe . . . or is that just Newark?

I thought about asking where we were when Chloe opened the window. She stuck her head out a little. "That smells so great!" The words whipped by with the wind and her hair, tangling and warping, making her sound mechanical.

Robotic.

The air rustled my own hair, blowing it across my face, in my eyes, over my lips, sticking to my cheeks.

"There's a memorial tonight, Mom." Jenn said.

Mina nodded. "I saw. I wondered if you guys wanted to go."

"I do," Jenn said, after a pause. "I think we should."

"What about Casey?" I asked.

"No," Mina sighed. "Rosie, for the millionth time, he's with Bill. He's safe. Bill is perfectly capable of taking care of Casey."

"I *need* to see him," I said.

"I know you want to—"

"Not want, Mina, *need*. I . . . I know what happened to him."

"She does," Justin and Jenn said quietly at exactly the same time. I whipped around and looked at Jenn.

"What do you know," I growled.

"I know what happened. I know how it happened."

"How do you know, Jennifer?" Mina asked slowly.

Jenn was silent while she thought. Finally she sat and said, "Same way everyone else in this crazy house knows everything."

"Do you know where he is?" I demanded. I was the only one who wasn't shocked by what Jenn revealed and I wanted to get my answer before Mina stopped her.

"Yes," she said simply, looking at me, "but it doesn't matter. It won't help. You can't get to him and you can't help him."

"I can . . . I could . . . "

Breathe Rosie, I heard Justin, *don't ignite your cousin*. It was such a ludicrous thing to hear in my head, I almost laughed.

"Jenn," the light fully dawning on Mina, "you can sense Casey."

She nodded. Looked at her mother, then added, "always."

"Turn it off."

"Rosie?" Dad glanced at me briefly from the front seat. "You're back."

"Turn it off. Please."

"But you love *High Society*."

"I never want to hear Louis Armstrong again."

Chloe clicked off the stereo.

The car kept going.

Jenn's revelation created enough distraction in Mina's world that I was able to sneak to the kitchen and copy down the cell phone number from the emergency contacts note by the phone. I mentally whacked myself upside the head several times for being so dim, but cut myself a tiny bit of slack, given the circumstances of our week.

Going anonymous, I slid upstairs and pulled my cell phone from its exile at the bottom of my backpack, blessing it for its superior battery life.

"Stupid small buttons," I muttered, but I knew my shaking fingers were the problem.

"Hello?" I heard Bill, far away and tired.

"Uncle Bill?"

"Rosie?" Surprised at first, then angry, whispering, "Rosie, what are you doing calling me on this—"

"Uncle Bill, tell me what's going on."

"What's going on?" he sounded confused.

"Yes, where are you. What's going on with Casey."

I heard him sigh. "We're in Stockbridge, Rosie. I had to bring him somewhere far away from people."

"Right," I nodded, "and?"

"And what? And he's in bad shape."

"And can he talk?"

"Talk? To you? On the phone?" Bill's voice echoed incredulity.

My small voice squeaked back, "Yes, please?"

"No. No, Rosie. He can't talk to you. *He can't talk at all.*"

I swallowed hard, not accepting, "But I can help—"

"Rose," Bill wasn't whispering any longer, "You can't—just . . . just give it time and let him heal."

"But he can't heal without me. He needs me."

"I'm sure your little crush is telling you that—"

"It's not a 'little crush' Uncle Bill, I'm not twelve!"

"No, you're not. But you are old enough to know that sometimes things take time, and—"

"Then let me be there to help. You can't do this all on your own. I need to. I need to help him, Bill." I felt tears burning behind my eyes again.

"No, Rosie. You've done enough. Just let us do the work we have to do to get him better."

"I've done enough? What the h— what does that mean?"

"What I said. Enough. If . . . if he hadn't known that you and Jasmine were down there, he would never have run off alone. I know Casey. He would have grabbed me or Mina and we all would have gone together. Instead he ran off —"

"He ran off for Jasmine."

"And you."

"Maybe, but he kept saying 'Jasmine' to me."

"When."

"When I found him."

"Regardless, Rose, he needs time to recover and he needs solitude. And that's it."

"I'll take a bus up."

"There's no bus."

"I'll take the train."

"There isn't a train to here from there."

"I'll—" I didn't know what I'd do.

"You'll stay there with Mina and learn things and practice. And when Casey's better you'll get to see him. Not before," the phone clicked off.

I tried to draw in my journal but all the pictures looked like birds and towers.

I tried to write about what happened, but the words always wound up being about Casey.

I heard Chloe and Dad talking in the front of the car, whispering about me.

They didn't know what to do to help.

I didn't either.

Justin stood in my doorway. "Jenn's going to show us Casey."

"Casey now?" I was hopeful.

"Casey then."

"I already know," I said.

"No, you don't. You know what Bill told you and you know what you found." I didn't bother asking how he knew I'd talked to Bill. "You are not Casey and Bill is not Casey. You need to see through his eyes."

"I can't."

"You have to," he walked over and took my hand. "You have to, and we're going to do it together. Right? We can't help him and we can't help you if we don't know what we're dealing with."

It took a minute but I nodded, and he helped me get up and prepare myself for the inevitable. Izzy was napping, and we let her stay that way. Jenn was going to transfer what she saw from Casey into the rest of us. She'd been able to connect to him for days but had blocked his memories to protect herself.

Jenn, Justin, and I sat in a tight circle, holding hands, breathing together like we do.

Slowly the images of Casey's day filled me, rolling from Jenn, over, and into my head.

Beautiful morning sunlight. Wave goodbye to me. Window seat, coffee, paper, then NO! Then Damnit where are the keys Where are the keys gotta get Jazz Can't breathe Jazz can't breathe Got to get to her before Got to go Got to run Where's the van? There's the van Get down Get to the bridge Get Out of My Way.

His breath is ragged and too fast as he leaves the van and he runs and we run with Casey. Recoiling from flashes of light, too many people too close, breaking shields. Faster. Faster, get-to-Jasmine pulls us forward even though we're tired. Too tired. The people pull at us, breaking through, grabbing at our sleeves, shirt, arms. Scared, scared people and terrified, horrified us as we run and dodge and try to keep away from all of them and still get to Jasmine. Hands sweat, faces sweat, panting we get there with Casey and we look up. The towers are there above us and the wreckage we have to run through is ahead of us and—

We can't move.

We can't breathe and we can't move and the people are more now and all coming at us. Fast, too fast. The people and the light and the terror rips through our hearts and pulls at our souls but we can't move. We can't get away and we can't block any more and we're exhausted and can't go further and we can't go back and we try to send to Jasmine or Rosie and we can't get—

And the sky falls.

The dark grey pounds the ground in front of me, buildings crashing, people crashing, crashing, clawing into me and everyone runs, run into me, drags at me, clawing at me, at my shields, more slam through me and scream and hold onto me like a baby with night terrors and don't let go and more and more hit and slam and pile on and in, trying to get in, begging, and they shriek and cry and beg and I can't move and I can't run and —

We all gasped and dropped hands, breathing hard, tears streaming.

No one spoke.

After a long while, Justin squeezed my arm.

You saved his life, Justin said in me, *don't you see that? He would have died if he'd gone in.*

I shook my head. *I killed him—as good as. And Jazz.*

We all thought, but no one said aloud: *no one could take that and not break. Not even Casey.*

Especially not Casey.

"Lunch, Rose." Dad had my door open and his hand was out to help me get up. I didn't need the help, but I took his hand anyway. It was warm.

I knew food was in front of me, but Mina didn't cook it. I want Mina food. Where's Mina? The bread was dry and the lettuce soggy and the tuna tasteless and I miss Mina and her tea.

"Drink this," Mina held a mug out to me. "Drink this before you go."

The tea felt good going down, and it did help some. Now I felt like walking down to the memorial at PS 321 would be a good idea after all.

"It's time," a little blue ball whispered next to me. I washed out my mug and left it on the rack. Justin had managed to rally Izzy, and we planned that if we could form a protective barrier around her, to reinforce her exhausted shield, that she would be able to go out for at least a little tonight. Mina thought it was important, so we went.

I'm sure it was a lovely night. It was dark. So many people were out. So many standing together on the sidewalk. In the street.

As we neared the elementary school that was the nexus of the neighborhood, I could hear music drift over us. Without knowing all the words

—some of us barely knew the tune—we sang, "... and guide her ... God bless ... my home sweet home ... " The sound of voices grew and rolled around us.

It was lovely.

Jenn, Justin, Izzy and I held onto each other, faces streaming, but we kept singing. We *all* kept singing. "... for thee I sing ... "

On and on, song after song we rambled through tunes my parents know, but I vaguely recognize. We sang of home and country and God and all of us, Jews, Muslims, Christians, kids, ancients, and adepts, we all sang with one voice and it was a prayer and it was beautiful, and if we could all see this and *be* this every day of our lives, I just knew that we would never ever see anything like this horror again—never. Anywhere. There is so much love. There is so much good that we, all of us, carry.

Tears hit the pavement with the candle wax, and then we started the long walk.

We walked from 1st Street to Union Street, blocking traffic that didn't mind. We walked on and on to the Squad 1 house that lost 11 out of their 20 firemen. Our men. Good men who let the kids sit on the truck—who let me sit on the truck—who sat out and spoke to the neighbors when they weren't saving lives. The men who were gone now, leaving wives and children and mothers and fathers without their smiles, or their arms like Casey's arms around me, and the wax fell on the ground, protecting the firehouse from more pain, and we sang as we walked and we wept.

And we wept.

"Rose?" It was Chloe. I think. She was wiping my cheeks softly with a tissue.

"Rose, you're going to have to snap out of it. You're freaking Dad out!"

I looked up.

My sister's pretty face came into focus.

"Why . . . " I had to clear my throat, "Why are you here?"

"I wasn't going to let Dad drive all the way alone. We took shifts driving and sleeping."

"That's why you got here fast?"

Chloe clarified, "Got to Brooklyn? Yeah. Mom completely freaked. She had no idea this was coming. Nobody did."

I just looked at her.

"I mean, none of *us* . . . " she shrugged. "Anyway. You can come back to earth, now. You're safe."

I shook my head and felt the hot, angry tears struggle to get out. I *wasn't* safe. And anyway, it didn't matter if I *was* safe when Casey was . . . how far away was he now?

Was he still screaming?

"Where—" I picked up the tissue from where it fell on the floor of the backseat, "Where are we?"

"Uh . . . something, Ohio, no, Indiana . . . hang on," Chloe pulled the map from the space between her seat and the hand brake. "No, we're closing in on Indianapolis. We're making fantastic time. You'll be home soon. Then Mom'll be there and you can unwind. Why don't you knit for a while? That always makes you feel better."

The tears pushed up through me. I tried to keep them inside. Chloe always found a way to get to me, even when she was trying to be nice.

I had to race to roll down the window in time.

The morning after the vigil I notice that Casey moved in the night, but he's sleeping soundly, now, facing me. I watch him sleep, his face is peaceful and his breathing is regular. I am holding his left hand with my left like we are arm wrestling. I move my hand to his cheek. He needs a shave and his scruffy cuteness makes me smile. If I just can hold us here in time it will be like nothing had happened. He opens an eye, looks at me sleepily and says:

"Why . . . " his voice is out of practice, "why are you in my bed? Not complaining . . . "

"Jenn's been here too," I said. He looks surprised. "So we had a chaperone—get that look off your face, boy."

He laughs, then I say, "But really, we've been grounding and centering you, helping you heal. And . . . I guess it worked."

"I guess so too. It's good having you here."

I hear feet on the stairs coming up to our floor—all the way up. I look at Casey and he shrugs. "I'm blind," he said.

I sit up, "Should I boost your shields? What will help?"

"My glasses."

I laugh and lean over to pull them off the nightstand. He kisses me before he puts them on and there is no zap. Then he kisses me again.

Then.

I really did hear feet on the stairs. Dream Casey evaporated, replaced by my damp pillows.

I heard Mina, far away, "David, I'll get . . . really . . . needs quiet . . . in no shape for . . .

"Hannah Rose? HR? Pack your bags. It's time to go!"

Dad?

It took me as long to recognize my father's voice as it did for him to reach the doorway of my room.

"Rosie, we're going home."

"Dad?"

"The car is running. Let's get going."

"Car . . . ?" I sat up rubbing my eyes and noticed Jenn, groggy, doing the same, "You drove?"

"There were no planes to take. Chloe and I are here. Let's get your things and go."

"I can't go, Dad," I shook my head, "I have to stay to help Casey."

Dad turned behind him, "What's she talking about, Mina?"

"Casey is . . . another student here. The two of them have a connection and—"

"He's here?" my dad broke in.

"Well, no," Mina tried to explain, "Bill has him—"

Daddy turned back to me, "Rosie if he's not here, then obviously you don't have to stay here to help him. I have a cell phone in the car. You can talk to him all you want."

"No, it's not like that, Dad . . . " but he was already opening the armoire and pulling things out, stacking them on the foot of my bed.

"We can put everything in the trunk. Chloe and I traveled light."

And it snapped.

Jenn had the connection to Casey, not me. She was the one who could find him.

I hadn't learned enough.

I couldn't help.

In fact, I'd all but killed him.

Dad was right.

It was time for me to go.

I felt everyone's eyes on me while we loaded the car.

It's not your fault, Rosie! I heard Justin say as I watched my dad put the final bag in the trunk. *You did the right thing.*

It just made me cry harder.

My forehead rested on the cool window glass. I watched the white broken line skim past, a solid blur of white blips below the car.

I watched.

And I planned.

No more playing. I'll be ready.

Next time.

All the way home, I planned my next move as I watched the ground.

End of Book One

Acknowledgements

Nothing of this nature happens in a vacuum.

This particular book all began with NaNoWriMo. Ever since I finished the first draft of this book I've donated to their cause. Theirs is a labor of love, one that deserves to keep going, and in our world nothing good and free (and often connected to the Humanities) can keep going without patrons.

Please be one for the things you love.

Many, many friends—and particularly knitting friends—read and responded to this book in very early drafts. I would specifically like to thank Meg, Dawn, Dianne, Julie, and Rose, and Jonathan for their thoughtful reactions and their willingness to read. I send a very big thank you to Hunter and Tara—who Know All The Things. Katie, my editor, was also invaluable for her insight and her guidance. I felt rich and spoiled every time she wrote to me.

I send enormous thanks to Sam Stone for her advice, her extraordinarily broad knowledge base, and for being my friend.

I have to thank my family who read various iterations of various drafts and claimed to enjoy them. I also especially have to thank my mother, Barbara Hutchinson, and my father-in-law, Abe Ordover, for having the courage and love to tell me what worked but also what didn't work for them. Their comments came at an important time and made the book a better one, I think.

I wish to share a special thank you and a huge hug with my students who evacuated with me on September 11th, 2001. I needed to put this book and its sequels in a time when cell phones weren't everywhere and when they certainly didn't have cameras. Eventually this is where I wound up.

Everyone around the world has different memories of that particular day and my plan was not to co-opt yours but to share a few of ours. As soon as the first plane hit on that blue-skied morning, I had my students write down their memories. I knew they would fade and morph with time. Six months later, when we were finally back in that same classroom (having the air tested every 45 minutes), I had them type their passages into my classroom computers and I posted their memories—as typed, with no outside editing—along with my blog. You can read their entries still (http://crafting-a-life.com/911.php and http:// crafting-a-life.com/911_student.php). You may be surprised by the similarities, but I'm constantly struck by the differences. We were all there together. All there in the same room. All seeing the same thing. Nothing else has made it more clear to me that humans are individuals and our experiences are absolutely our own than reading those passages—and watching how differently each and every one of us healed from that day.

While the planes-hitting-the-building moment, as presented in this book, is, in fact, pretty darn close to my memories, once our magnificent 6/7ths are out of the building the narrative is then loosely based on other eyewitness accounts from survivors I spoke to. Any inaccuracies are the fault of my memory or my imagination and not theirs.

The fire station in Park Slope, Brooklyn is real and the men we all lost, eleven of them, are missed. They were, as I tried to show here, lovely, helpful, funny guys who kept us safe and let little kids look at and love their beautiful engines. Gone but not forgotten.

You can still ride the carousel in Prospect Park. Let me know if you see any strangely glowing guys, though. I'm curious. Coney Island is still there (as is Nathan's). You can also find the Joan of Arc painting at the Met. She's still there —or was the last time I visited—and is still looking out of the frame with that same, amazing face. The armor and the wooden room are there, too. You should go when you have a chance.

And, finally, I need to thank the family I live with every day.

My husband is the best writer I know. His plays made me laugh and weep (all at the right times in the right places) over the last twenty-five years. He told me there is something inherently selfish in writing because of the time it takes and the amount of brain that is always working on solving the problems you've set up for your characters. He's right. And yet, we manage to both scrape out time to write and still stay in love after many years—17 of them married.

Then there are our boys.

When I began writing this book my my younger son was four and the older was eight. Thing 1 is 13 now and has grown into a pretty decent writer of his own, when he puts his mind to it. He also read an earlier draft of this book when he was 12 and gave it a Tween Seal of Approval—which mattered enormously to me. They've both shown themselves to be powerful storytelling allies when critical comments came in or weaknesses in the narrative became clear. A number of scenes you read were their idea.

I look forward to seeing what they will write for you in the future.

And finally, thank *you*. It takes time and effort to read books these days, and the fact that you made it to this page and are reading this now means the world to me. I can't wait to share more of Rosie and Casey's adventures with you. I hope you're looking forward to that, too.

Thank you,

Heather

ABOUT THE AUTHOR

Heather Ordover is a writer of stories, teacher of things, knitter of socks, and mother of boys.

She can be found on her weekly podcast *CraftLit*®, at her knitting blog, *Mama O Knits too Much,* and on the road speaking about *Cognitive Anchoring.*

Ms. Ordover can be booked for signings, readings & talks, and knitting classes from her website http://crafting-a-life.com/shop/ and you can find sock patterns for our Magnificent Seven along with an invitation to write shawl patterns for Rosie at http://groundedseries.com/updates.

Everything else Ordover's up to can be found via her hub http://crafting-a-life.com.

The sequel to *Grounded,*
Shattered—The Seven, book 2,
is underway!
Check GroundedSeries.com
for news and sneak peeks.

If you enjoyed *Grounded,* please share!
You can *Like* the *Grounded* Series on Facebook, or Tweet about the series to your followers, or pin the cover on Pinterest, or just drop Heather an email to tell her what you thought!

Thank you for supporting independent publishing!

www.ingramcontent.com/pod-product-compliance
Lightning Source LLC
Chambersburg PA
CBHW051429260626
47162CB00001B/16